PRAISE FOR TO

"Lily Wong is one of the gre... century."

CrimeReads

"Loyalty, family and martial arts take center stage in *The Ninja's Oath*, a smashing thriller that climaxes with a death-filled battle royale that would make Quentin Tarantino blush. Tori Eldridge kills it with this tale, interchanging tender family moments with explosive, slashing fisticuffs... The dichotomy of family and violence makes for an exceedingly absorbing read... This might have been my first Tori Eldridge book but it won't be my last!

Best Thriller Books

"Tori Eldridge had me at ninja warrior, but this wonderful series offers so much more than propulsive action. Eldridge's Lily Wong avenger is pure hustle and all heart, a character you'll not soon forget. Love this series. It offers all the feels."

Tracy Clark, two-time Sue Grafton Memorial Award-winning author of Hide

"One word: Badass. Lily Wong is as tough as she is smart and will go to the ends of the earth to put bad guys in their place. I love this heroine, I love Eldridge's stories, and I love *The Ninja's Oath*. Tense, evocative, with beautifully-choreographed fight scenes that only a trained dancer and martial artist like Eldridge could write, *The Ninja's Oath* is as action-packed as it is thrilling."

Tosca Lee, NYT bestselling author

Tori Eldridge

THE NINJA'S OATH

DATURA

DATURA BOOKS
An imprint of Watkins Media Ltd

Unit 11, Shepperton House
89 Shepperton Road
London N1 3DF
UK

daturabooks.com
twitter.com/daturabooks
I do solemnly swear to do good

A Datura Books paperback original, 2025

Cover by 2Faced Design and Sarah O'Flaherty
Set in Meridien

ISBN 978 1 91552 374 7
Ebook ISBN 978 1 91552 376 1

Printed and bound in the United Kingdom by CPI Group (UK) Ltd, Croydon CR0 4YY.

9 8 7 6 5 4 3 2 1

For Moana, my precious granddaughter born in Shanghai.

Chapter One

Soggy leaves squished silently beneath my boots as I picked through a tangle of branches and vines. After sprinting up the mountain, the need for stealth had slowed my pace. My lungs hurt – hot, wet air, like drowning to breathe. The sickening sweetness of flowers and decay. I swallowed hard and picked my way through the treacherous roots, following voices through the jungle to my quarry ahead.

A cigarette burned brightly beneath a canopy so dense it blotted out the sun. The man wore a patchwork of military castoffs, American, French, and Vietnamese. Baggy pants bunched over combat boots, clownishly big for his size. Even so, he had a half foot of height and a sandbag's weight more than me. I approached from behind and melded with the trees.

He sucked in the smoke and tipped his head back to exhale. Bored and careless. He didn't even flinch until I leaped into the air and chopped the blades of my hands into the sides of his neck. Nerves deadened, the guard crumpled to the ground.

I crushed his cigarette with my toe, relieved him of the pistol, and stuffed it behind me in the waistband of my pants. I took his hunting knife and lighter as well. Since my stunning attack wouldn't keep him out for long, I slammed the knife hilt against his head, gagged his mouth, and tied his wrists and his ankles behind his back. Trussed like a turkey, I left him in the mud.

Men shouted up ahead. Although I feared what they might be preparing to do, I circled the perimeter to search for other threats.

Muddy leaves sucked at my boots. A second sentry snapped his head toward me. I froze, hands to my chest so my arms wouldn't create a human silhouette, and held the hunting knife poised vertically to throw. After three measured breaths, the man looked the other way.

I could silence him for good if I let the knife fly.

Was I willing to take a life?

Perhaps, but not yet.

I followed the voices toward a clearing with structures on one side and a training area on the other. Sunbeams spotlighted a horrible scene. As a handful of men chanted and jeered, boys fired rifles too powerful for their adolescent shoulders to brace. The younger boys strained to fire pistols. A few breadfruit targets exploded off stumps. Most remained untouched.

Closer to me, dried-grass dummies suffered a more violent fate as child soldiers with machetes hacked off chunks of faces, shoulders, and legs. As the children shrieked battle cries warped by their fear, their trainers heckled and laughed.

Bullies like these needed killing.

Easy, Lily. All in good time.

I scanned the clearing for a familiar face. When I didn't spot him, I darted past Jeeps and motorbikes to the first structure in the camp, a barrack with hammocks and cots. I followed the stench of feces and sweat out of the main room into cells with cement floors, piss pots, and rotted threshes for beds. A rat glared at me from a food-crusted tin plate.

The next barrack was homier than the first, with assorted comforts and belongings clipped to hammocks or stacked on the ground. The sight of books surprised me, although I didn't know why. What else did these men have to do in their downtime between raining terror and training children to kill?

Gunshots.

Focus, Lily.

My friend needed help. I was running out of time.

I hurried into another room where a woman rose behind a kitchen counter with a bag of rice in her hands. I held out my palm to forestall her scream and slid the hunting knife in my cargo pants pocket so she wouldn't be afraid. Bruises marred her face and arms, but her slumped posture and dead eyes told me more.

"Do you want my help?" I repeated the question in French, then pantomimed taking her with me as I left.

She shook her head and returned to her work. Either she doubted a lone woman like me could protect her from an army of men, or she had accepted her fate and simply wanted to survive. I couldn't bring myself to believe that she truly wanted to stay.

I stepped forward to ask again, but froze when an engine rumbled outside. The woman jerked her head for me to leave and knelt to clean up the rice she had spilled. I pulled the knife from my pocket and headed for the door.

A new crop of children had arrived in an open-bed truck. The driver stopped. Men jumped to the ground. One of them opened the tailgate and motioned with his rifle for the boys to get out. Most were teens. A couple might have been seven or eight.

They regrouped into a huddle except for one lone boy, skinny as bamboo yet rooted to the ground. Spine straight.

Shoulders squared. He lifted his pre-adolescent chin. Not in fear. In defiance.

A boss man unstrapped his rifle and shouted commands at the boy. When he didn't move, the man jabbed the barrel into his narrow chest. The boy stumbled back a few steps, then recovered his balance with a skipping ninja-like step. Sensei had trained me to do the same. The movement came naturally to the boy, as if ingrained.

When the boss man yelled again, the boy faced his new peers. The child soldiers lowered their weapons, puffed-out chests and taunts hiding their relief. Fresh meat had arrived. Their masters would have someone else to abuse.

The boy, on the other hand, gave nothing away, except for a slight lift of one peaked brow. His steely calm sent a chill up my spine. Although half the size and age of the youngest adult, he had the jaded composure of a man.

The guerrilla warriors laughed and congratulated their boss on the tough new recruit. When one of them grabbed the boy's arm, he sidestepped him easily. Not to resist. To move of his own accord. Was it pride? Or did this boy not want to be touched?

The men and child soldiers parted to reveal a prisoner kneeling in the dirt, face lowered, wrists tied behind his back. Another prisoner lay dead beside him, limbs disjointed on the blood-soaked earth. Organs had escaped through the machete gashes across his belly, the head partially detached by unskilled hacks.

A soldier strode behind the kneeling prisoner and toe-kicked his spine.

As the man arched, I saw the person I had come to save. A man I had known all my life. The friend who had called me for help.

Uncle was more than my father's crotchety old cook. Lee Chang had been the chief enforcer of the Shanghai Scorpion Black Society. A few days earlier, we had fought together in a Hong Kong alley where he bested tough young gangsters without breaking a sweat. How could Red Pole Chang have allowed a ragtag army of bullies to do this to him?

I darted past Jeeps, barrels, and bales of dried grass, some bound into human-shaped dummies, just in time to see a gun slapped into the boy's hand. The weight of it made his arm dip and flex. Other than that, the boy didn't move. He stood perfectly still in front of the prisoner I had come to save.

Soldiers shouted commands. Their trainees took up the chant, whipping into a frenzy as if volume alone could prove their worth and keep the violence pointed away from them.

I grabbed a metal rod and pried open a barrel. Black and oily. It smelled flammable to me. I stuffed the legs of a dummy inside, lit the dried grass with the sentry's lighter, and ran into the fray, pistol drawn to gun down as many soldiers as the magazine would allow.

The erupting fireball made the boy stumble and illuminated his face.

His cold eyes narrowed. The corners of his mouth raised into what would become a hauntingly familiar smirk. He didn't run or hide. He didn't slip into the chaos and hope to be forgotten. He aimed the gun at Uncle's chest and fired.

The wheels hit the tarmac, drowning the gunshot with a roar, as I stared out the double-pane glass at my first glimpse of Shanghai.

Where had I been? And why had I dreamt of a young J Tran?

Chapter Two

The man I had known as Uncle waited for me on the other side of Pudong International Airport's customs gate looking more tense than when we had waltzed into the Scorpion den the previous week in Hong Kong. I checked the terminal and saw no sign of the pro-democracy protesters I had grown accustomed to seeing nor the Scorpion thugs who had damaged my grandfather's business and tried to kidnap and murder Ma. And why would I? Neither was responsible for my presence in Shanghai.

If Lee hadn't called while Ma checked us in for our flight home to Los Angeles, I would have been reclined in a luxurious business-class traveling pod, sipping chrysanthemum tea, and rewatching a new action release. Instead, I was trudging my battle-torn body into yet another unknown war. This time, trouble had most definitely come looking for me.

Lee glanced at my backpack and marched toward the doors.

"Wait. I have luggage."

"I didn't invite you here for a vacation, Lily."

I dug in my heels. "You didn't *invite* me at all. Look, if I'd known in advance you were going to hijack me to mainland China, I would have repacked and sent my luggage home with Ma."

"Aiya. I called you as soon as I heard."

As annoyed as I felt, I was glad to see him ornery and alive. My dream on the plane had rattled my nerves. If the wheels hadn't hit the tarmac, would young J Tran have shot Lee Chang? Or would my own bullet have torn through the boy's head?

I shook off the horrid thought.

J Tran had grown up in a Vietnamese orphanage after the war, named J for his unknown G.I. Joe father and given the placeholder surname they used in Vietnam. He had killed an older boy when he was seven and a man soon after that. Although he hadn't shared why, the implication was clear. Regardless of what he had suffered to drive him to such violence, the nuns threw him out and the guerilla warriors took him in.

Had I imaged Tran's transition from an abused Vietnamese orphan to guerrilla child soldier? What would I dream of next? His mentor in Cambodia with an "eye for talent" who had shaped him into what he was now? I didn't want to think of J Tran at all. Yet he had shown up in Hong Kong to, what...watch my back? How had he even known I was there?

"Eh, lazy girl. Stop daydreaming and find your bag."

Lee's scorpion tattoo peeked from beneath his shirt as he crossed his sinewy arms. It's tail aimed at me, poised to sting. Although older than my father and almost as slightly built as me, my father's cook had fought with ruthless efficiency against my enemies in Hong Kong. I hadn't known he was triad before this trip, and I still hadn't decided whether I should alert Baba of this fact. Nor could I bring myself to call a gang enforcer "Uncle" as I had done all my life.

I heaved my suitcase onto the shuttle and squeezed

beside Lee. Had I come to Shanghai out of friendship or debt? Either way, I had made my decision. Time to put aside these distractions and help.

"When was she taken?"

"Last night."

"Why didn't you call me then?"

"I didn't find out until morning. My grandniece lives with her family on my brother's farm in Chongming. He and I don't get along."

"Then why call you at all?"

"As always, he lays the blame at my feet."

Lee hurried off the shuttle bus and onto a train before I could ask why his brother would blame him. He sat in a lone seat and made it impossible to talk. I aimed the full force of my ninja intention at him and willed his eyes to raise. His cheek twitched. His fingers curled into fists on his knees. The stubborn ox just stared at the floor. I increased my efforts until the veins in Lee's neck bulged and turned blue.

Reactions to targeted energy were personal. Some claimed to feel burning ice or heat. Some leaned toward the danger. Others rocked away. Some described the sensation as insects crawling on their skin, a sense of dread or an urgency they couldn't ignore. When directed at me, focused intent stung my skin with electric shocks. Although every person radiated and sensed energy on an unconscious level, it required dedicated practice to hone it into an intentionally directed and quantifiable skill. Through a thousand hours of exercises and drills, my ninjutsu teacher had taught me to control, confuse, and calm my opponents with projected intent. He had also attuned my ability to sense and locate the source of energy directed at me.

When the train slowed at the station, Lee rose abruptly and jammed his shoulder into mine. "If you're done playing games, ninja girl, this is our stop."

Chapter Three

"Will you *please* slow down?" I said, yanking my roller suitcase up yet another curb. I would have enjoyed the paved sidewalks and tree-lined avenues if he'd only given me a chance.

Lee picked up his pace, still annoyed with my prank on the train.

"Hey," I yelled. "You're the one who called me."

The tension in his shoulders eased a notch as he slowed just enough to let me catch up.

"Thank you." I took in the brick and stone façades around me. I recognized this iconic neighborhood from photos in the flight magazine. "Where are we going?"

"To my apartment."

"You have an apartment in the French Concession?"

"*Former* French Concession."

I gaped in surprise. Back in Los Angeles, Lee caught the bus to my father's restaurant, wore inexpensive clothes, and only took time off every few years to go home to Shanghai. I had assumed most of what he earned at Wong's Hong Kong Inn went to squeaking out an existence for him and his wife.

"I didn't mean to sound incredulous. I just thought you'd be staying with family is all. I suppose it's cheaper to rent an apartment than stay in a hotel."

"Rent? Ha. Expats lease it from me." He chuckled at my surprise. "They moved out last month. We can stay until my new renters move in."

Triad, linguist, and duo-property landlord? What else didn't I know about Baba's irascible cook?

The sweet scent of pork wafted in on the breeze, making my stomach growl loudly enough for Lee to stop and stare.

I shrugged. "They didn't serve much on the plane."

He sighed impatiently then detoured up a one-way road. Steam rose from a corner dim sum stand where giant metal steamer baskets were stacked taller than me.

"What do you want?"

"A couple bao?"

He grumbled. "As if that would ever be enough for you."

He greeted the merchant in Shanghainese and rattled off an order I couldn't understand. The woman unstacked the top two steamers, pulled four bao from the next level, and stuffed them in a bag. Lee pointed to the bottom steamer and said something that made her look at me and laugh.

"What did you say?" I asked.

"That she better add a sesame ball or you would cry all the way home."

She bagged the sticky treat separately and handed it to me. The greasy-sweet smell made my stomach grumble and her and Lee howl. I nodded my thanks and backed my suitcase into a customer by mistake. The man scolded me in Mandarin and shooed me out of the way.

"Stop wasting time," Lee said. "You can eat while you walk."

I stuffed a pork bun in my mouth and swallowed my annoyance. I was carting an over-stuffed backpack, a full-size suitcase, and a bouncing bag of steaming bao. Would it have killed him to slow down?

We walked past a cement lane of narrow three-story structures. Some hid behind stucco walls while others showed tiny gardens and elaborate stone designs.

"Are those single-family homes or apartments for rent?"

"Aiya. I almost forgot. Keep up. It won't take long."

He turned a corner and darted down the street to another dead-end lane, same security camera system at the entrance, same recycling and garbage receptacles built into a wall. Parked cars lined up on the side, leaving only enough room for another car to enter and back out.

I followed Lee through a garden gate to a tree bursting with yellow blossoms and racks of drying laundry over meager grass. Tools, possessions, and a small washing machine overflowed from a tiny ground-level apartment. I shoved down the handle of my suitcase, lugged it around the motor scooters parked on the path, then lifted it over a puddle of sewage water leaking around the stones.

"Lee," I yelled, grunting from the effort. "Where are we going?"

He waved from the sliver between buildings and vanished through a door.

I followed and dropped my bag over the threshold beside towers of boxes, bins, and crates. The open door on my left led to a cluttered kitchen and the hanging laundry in the front garden beyond. A bed was crammed against a table set with a meal. The spicy scent of cooking mingled with the sewage odor from outside.

I peered up the dank wooden stairs. "Lee?"

"Leave your bag and come up. No one will steal it."

After a moment's deliberation, I opted for trust over effort and wedged my suitcase against the wall. The first flight of steps led to a tiny bathroom and a studio apartment on the right. Both doors were open with excess belongings, cigarette ash cans, and kitty litter stacked on the landing. A calico cat leapt off a perch and charged down the stairs.

Please don't spray my luggage.

I continued around the bend where the decrepit steps changed abruptly to polished hard wood and found Lee in a refurbished penthouse apartment with peaked ceilings and open French doors. Autumn colors rioted beyond the balcony amidst picturesque slanted roofs.

Lee spoke rapidly in English to a twenty-something man in a Stanford t-shirt and shorts. "The sewage leak is fixed. Don't worry about it. The water will dry up later today."

The guy nodded nervously. "Um...all right."

"You like the apartment?"

"Yeah. It's great."

"Good."

Lee twirled his hand for me to turn around and go down the stairs. I waved at the tenant on my way out.

"What the hell, Lee? I could have waited at the gate."

He shrugged. "You asked about the lane houses. I thought you'd like to see one inside."

I hauled my suitcase down the gap between buildings, over the sewage puddle on the path, and around the scooters to the lane. He was right, of course. But I wished there had been an easier way. I yanked out the handle of my suitcase and caught up with my muttering friend.

"Most of these houses were divided into separate apartments before you were born. My tenants on the first two floors came with the building. The ground-level apartment has the kitchen. Second level uses a hot plate. They share the bathroom off the stairs. I'm sure you find it shocking, but these conditions are acceptable to them."

I stuffed my American privilege and tried to listen with an open mind. My upbringing in Arcadia's affluent Chinese community had not prepared me for the lane-house living I had seen. Interpreting conditions based on my values and perceptions would only perpetuate my beliefs. I needed to ask, listen, and observe how the locals – collectively and as individuals – perceived their own world. How else could I find Lee's grandniece in the third most populated city on Earth?

If I had observed this keenly back in my father's restaurant, I might have noticed more about Lee Chang.

His fluency with the English language surprised me the most. Although Lee discussed restaurant business in complete sentences when speaking with my North Dakota-born father, he spoke in broken phrases to me and our staff. Mostly, he grumbled in Shanghainese or snapped in Mandarin when he wanted me or our dumpling chef from China to appreciate his rebuke. I had studied Mandarin from middle school through college and attended Cantonese class on Saturdays since I was a child. Although out of daily practice, I had always assumed my language skills were superior to Lee's, until he joined me in Hong Kong. My father's cook continued to reveal skills I didn't know he possessed.

Chapter Four

If I lived in the Former French Concession and had the money Lee apparently had, I would have chosen a refurbished garden villa with old-world charm. Lee had chosen a doorman and polished granite floors. We rode the elevator to a tenth-floor apartment with a narrow entry corridor. Taking care not to bang my suitcase on the sterile white walls, we emerged into a generically furnished apartment, brightly lit by the window at the end.

"Your bedroom is around this corner. Store your luggage, then come out to eat."

The tiny room had a bed wedged in the corner and a shallow closet stuffed with blankets, towels, and only a foot of hanger space and two empty shelves. Since I had no idea how long we'd be here or where else we might go, I dropped my backpack on the bed and left my belongings in the case. I made a mental note not to trip over it if I woke in the night.

"You found everything you need?" Lee called as I emerged with my bag of no-longer-steaming buns.

"Yep. It's all pretty clear."

He beckoned me into the eat-in kitchen and stepped aside so I could see. "Go ahead," he said, and slid open the glass doors.

I walked onto the wraparound terrace and gaped at the unobstructed view.

Lee chuckled. "Not bad, eh? Most buildings look up the asses of others. But the low houses in this area give me room to see."

The russet-colored rooftops and lush green and golden leaves gave way to endless miles of vertical urban life. I walked to the railing and looked over the edge. What most people would consider to be a dizzying drop presented an abundance of ledges and crevices for a skillful kunoichi to climb.

Lee slapped my arm. "Don't get any ideas."

He knew I scaled the walls of my father's restaurant to clean the signboard that hid the entire second story – and my apartment – from the street, climbed cliffs in the Santa Monica Mountains, and honed my freerunning acrobatic abilities on the structures in downtown Los Angeles. After our adventures in Hong Kong, he knew exactly how I put these skills to use.

I stepped up onto the corner bench and then the ledge. A few miles out, buildings shot to the sky.

"How long have you had this apartment?"

Lee shrugged. "Twenty years? I bought it on my first trip home. I rent it and the top floor of the FFC lane house to executive expatriates. Smart, right? Makes a good profit."

I'd bet my meager savings that Lee's profit was a smidge better than *good*.

"Enough gawking," Lee said. "Finish your snack so we can go."

He led me to the kitchen and disappeared down the hall. I gobbled up the fried sesame ball, then took my time with the bao as I checked my messages. Since the great firewall of China blocked most of the foreign internet websites and tools, the only app I could access without installing a virtual private network was WeChat.

I tapped my father's profile square and brought up a message he'd left four hours earlier.

Why are you in Shanghai?

An hour later.

Are you on a plane? Call me when you land.

Two hours after that.

Dumpling, please answer. It's getting late.

The endearment emphasized his concern.

I calculated the time difference between Shanghai and Los Angeles: 3:30 p.m. for me was 12:30 a.m. for him. He'd be fast asleep if I answered him now, but he'd see my message when he woke.

Lee needed help with a family matter. Nothing dangerous. I'm fine.

Five seconds later, my phone chimed with a call.

I accepted the video chat and offered a reassuring smile. "Hey, Baba. You're still up."

He stifled a yawn and sat up straighter in bed. "I couldn't sleep. Not with you gallivanting across the globe."

"I'm not *gallivanting*. I'll explain everything in the morning."

"Nonsense. I want to hear about this now."

His tousled blond hair and bloodshot eyes told me he wouldn't be able to sleep until I put his mind at rest.

"Lee's grandniece is missing. He asked me to come to Shanghai and help him find her."

"What do you mean by missing? And how did he know you could help?"

It was a fair question. Aside from Sensei and – as of two

months ago – my father, I had managed to keep my ninja exploits a secret from everyone in my life except Aleisha and Stan, who ran the women's shelter I worked for back home. After Hong Kong, Ma knew as well. None of this explained why Baba's head cook would call me for help.

I stalled for time. "Um...Lee's more observant than we thought?"

"Balderdash. Your story has more holes in it than a rusted milk bucket."

I couldn't argue with that. But how could I explain why Lee had called without revealing his criminal history or how I owed him a favor after he had reconnected with the Scorpion Black Society in Shanghai to help me with the Scorpion triad in Hong Kong? Lee's history was his to tell. If his secrets didn't endanger the people I loved, I preferred to skirt the whole truth and parcel out crumbs.

"He heard about the rescue protection work I do for Aleisha's Refuge. Since I've found kids back home, he figured I could help him find his niece in Shanghai."

Baba raised his brows. "Uh-huh. Because you're so familiar with the city."

I ignored the sarcasm. "No. Because kids are kids."

"Then she's a runaway?"

"I don't know, Baba. I only landed a couple hours ago. Look, I've gotta run. I'll message you when I know more. Go to sleep. There's nothing to worry about."

I ended the call and hoped I hadn't lied.

Chapter Five

"Are you ready yet?" Lee called from the living room. I put on my stretch jacket and stuffed the pockets with my wallet and phone. When I came out of my bedroom, I found Lee standing in the main room beside two retro bicycles with step-through frames and baskets on the front – a far cry from my racing bike back home.

"We have time for a picnic? I thought we had to find your grandniece."

"We do. But I have something unavoidable I have to do first."

He shoved the extra bike toward me and stuffed a fabric bag into his basket. He looked like a harmless old man. If the Scorpions had seen him like this, we never would have made it out of Hong Kong alive.

I followed him into the elevator and nodded at the bag. "Are we going shopping?"

He punched the lobby button. "You aren't on vacation. We have work to do."

"I know, but..."

He rolled out of the elevator and onto the noisy street. After the quiet of Lee's insulated apartment building, the city buzzed like an electrical plant on the brink.

I hopped on my granny bike and headed after him, joining

the flow of traffic. Shanghai was a bike-friendly city where the majority of cyclists sat erect with handlebar baskets like ours. Despite the sedate conveyances, Lee managed a crisp pace. He wove between slower bikes to keep up with the cars and sped forward to catch the lights. No one blared their horns as they might have in Los Angeles, but I did hear scooter beeps amid the urban buzz.

Although insanely crowded, the varied heights of the buildings and sizes of the roads in Shanghai gave the city – or at least this portion of it – a more spacious feel, not like Hong Kong, where high-rise apartment blocks had pressed so close I needed to crane my neck for a sliver of sky. I breathed in the exhaust and caught a whiff of tar, sewage, and spice. I hadn't had time to upload an air quality app onto my phone, but I suspected the smell came from a more tangible sources than smog.

"Are we heading toward a river?" I asked when we slowed for a light.

It changed and Lee sped on his way.

Resigned to an unknown destination, I focused my attention on the lay of the land. This part of Shanghai mixed Chinese culture with European and American flair, thus earning its nickname as *Paris of the East*. But it also seemed at war – or in competition? – with its past, present, and future. Modern high-rises encroached on historic cottage communities while new construction grazed the colonial-past with promises of China's new vision. A massive elevated highway cut through it all. Then we passed an unseen border into an older, more bedraggled, even noisier Shanghai.

Lee coasted past the dusty construction sites, buildings, and paint-flaked cement. No London planes or osmanthus bushes here, just taller structures to replace the old and the head-pounding racket of jackhammers.

We turned away from a crumbling highway onto a road beneath a canopy of chaotic wires. Undergarments and sheets dried overhead from rods. Scooters lined the curbs, several with quilted wind guards hanging across the handlebars. Many had storage trunks or sidecars attached. Small delivery vans parked in front of markets to unload their produce while painted French shutters stood open from second- and third-story windows of drab houses from days gone by.

Lee slowed his pace so I could ride abreast.

"This is the Old City, where I grew up. My great-grandparents moved here from Nanjing and built a lane house in the South Gate community of Qiaojia Road. The government has relocated most of the residents. Until recently, my family has refused to leave."

"What changed their minds?"

"The government and I gave them no choice."

"You?"

He shrugged. "I own the building."

We hopped off our bikes and walked them along the sidewalk. Although surrounded by highways and high-rises, this tiny neighborhood had taken us back in time.

"What was this area like when your great-grandparents arrived?"

"How should I know?"

"Didn't anyone tell you stories?"

"Only my grandmother, but she didn't move here until the Japanese bombed her parents' home in Pudong. After they were killed, she fled to the Puxi side of Huangpu River and landed here. My grandfather's family took her in. My grandfather married her a year after that."

"It must have been terrifying."

"Things grew worse. Refugees and citizens packed their belongings on their backs or stuffed them into man-pulled carts, rushing for the International Settlement and French Concession where the Japanese wouldn't bomb. The streets were thick with fleeing people. Wai Po told me she couldn't see the ground. The same was true for Suzhou Creek where the river was so crowded people could walk across the water from boat to boat."

"Did your family go west to the French or to the north to the Americans, Italians, Germans, and Brits?"

"You've been studying."

"I always do when I travel to an unfamiliar place."

His jaw tensed. "Well, my family didn't go anywhere. They survived on what had been left behind. They scrounged for food, breathed in the rubble, and dumped their sewage in the street. They lived like rats too stubborn to leave."

I imagined Lee's family watching through their windows as their neighbors packed the road – a mass of humanity churning between storefronts, shoving against one another to squeeze through and escape.

As I stared at nothing, I conjured the terror.

Babies cried.

Mothers shrieked.

Men hollered at each other to move out of the way.

An explosion jolted the ground.

A barefoot rickshaw driver stumbled to his knees, trampled by his own cart as desperate families pushed it from behind.

Cannons fired in the distance from Huangpu River and beyond. Smoke billowed into the sky from fires too far away to see while planes roared overhead, bombs whistling as they dropped.

The Japanese soldiers had landed.

Everyone had to leave.

I breathed in the stinging smoke and coughed the grit from my lungs. How would everyone survive? Where would they live? What would they eat?

"Lily," Lee shouted. "Are you deaf? What's the matter with you?"

I coughed the imagined ash from my lungs as Lee rolled his bike away from mine. He stuffed a new parcel into his basket. I focused on the details to anchor me in the present.

"What's in the bag?"

"Supplies for my mother." He pointed behind him at a dry goods shop. "I was only gone for a moment. Did you fall asleep?"

"Of course not. I was watching your bike."

He glanced at a surveillance camera. "Someone was watching my bike, but it definitely wasn't you."

Lee had a point. China was the most surveilled country in the world, with a million cameras in Shanghai alone. Even if I had fallen asleep, a thief would have been foolish to steal a bike off the street.

"Can we leave?" he asked. "Or do you have more daydreaming to do?"

I looked at the street with its run-down shops and modern cars and tried to picture the Old City when it had still been the lively center of Shanghai. Instead, my imagination returned to the exodus of terrified families swarming down the road. Was I still in a dark mood after my jungle dream on the plane? Or was this a harbinger of bad things to come?

Chapter Six

Lee paused in front of a stone arch and an open metal gate that led to a courtyard wedged between three-story dwellings, several with wares and produce for sale stacked along the walls. "This is the south gate for the Qiaojia Road community. It's different from the shikumen you saw near my apartment. Those were fixed up for Western tastes. Only local Shanghainese live here."

Faded brick and dilapidated concrete pressed in from the sides as we rode, single file, through the tight corridor of houses. Colorful rows of laundry dangled between the buildings like banner flags in a race. Electricity cables crisscrossed above and jumbled in coils on the sides.

Unlike the offshoot lanes in the Former French Concession, these cement alleys were not intended for cars. Residents parked their bikes and scooters beside crates of excess belongings, potted greenery, and outdoor sinks. A cluster of stools sat around an overturned bucket. It must have been a friendly place back in the day. Now, more than half of the houses had bricks plastered across their windows and doors.

As we rode from one semi-deserted lane to another, I glimpsed the tops of high-rise buildings that would soon replace Lee's ancestral home.

"Where will your family go?"

"My mother will live in my sister's fancy home with her husband. My relatives will move to a government-subsidized apartment across the river in Pudong."

We cut through a claustrophobic passage between bricked-up buildings onto a slightly roomier alley where an old woman washed her hair with a hose over a freestanding laundry tub. She had rolled up her sleeves and took care not to slosh water onto her quilted jacket. Although the weather felt warm to me, I imagined someone her age would feel a nip in the air.

When Lee questioned her in Shanghainese, she looked up with a smile and answered in kind. He shook his head and leaned his bike against the wall.

I did the same. "What did you say?"

"I asked her why she's washing her hair outside when we've had indoor plumbing for years."

"You mean..."

He nodded. "This is my mother." He addressed her in Mandarin so I would understand. "Uma, this is Lily Wong."

Lee's mother patted her wet hair with a towel, then held the corners together under her chin. She said something in Shanghainese that I assumed to be hello.

I responded in Mandarin and called her grandma to be polite.

She rolled her hand and beckoned us inside.

Three impressions hit me at once: the squalor, the smell, and fury at Lee.

How could he allow his mother to live under these slum-lord conditions when he had a pristine apartment in the FFC? I glared in accusation, but he clenched his jaw and refused to meet my gaze.

As his mother shuffled over the cracked cement floor in her floppy rubber slippers, I tried to make sense of the room. Crude wooden counters, a stained sink, a basic refrigerator, and an antiquated burner and oven were haphazardly arranged between stacked containers of non-perishable foods. Fishing nets of fresh produce and dried chilies, mushrooms, fungus, and fish hung from the flaking walls beside an alcove spilling over with supplies. A chopping block counter was positioned in front of a pane-less window with wooden shutters open toward the lane with two metal stools tucked underneath. Flies lighted on food left behind.

We stepped over a doorframe into a communal space with two long tables and numerous mismatched chairs. Lee pushed aside the clutter. His mother commented in Shanghainese, glanced at me, then switched to the national language. I nodded in acknowledgment, but her accent was so thick I couldn't decipher a word. If she stayed within the boundaries of the Old City, I doubted she would need to speak Mandarin at all.

Lee pulled out the heavy-duty garbage bags he had bought at the store and told her to fill them with clothes, toiletries, and shoes. She headed for the kitchen in a huff.

"Listen to me, Uma. Meimei and her husband have pans and dishes of their own. They will also provide towels and bedding, so only take the ones that are special to you."

She switched excitedly to Shanghainese and beckoned us up the steep wooden stairs.

"Watch your step," Lee said in English. "Some of the planks have rot."

When we reached the second floor, we followed his mother past the open door of a bedroom stuffed with belongings and a twin-size bed.

Lee rolled his eyes. "She keeps this room for my sister in case she leaves her rich husband and comes home."

"Why would she leave him?'

"Uma says he's old and mean."

"Is he?"

Lee shrugged. "Meimei married her widowed boss and raised his daughter as her own. We aren't in contact. I don't know much."

He nodded toward the bathroom with hooks of towels, wash cloths, and robes. Baskets of toiletries covered the remaining wall space in and out of the shower. "As you can see, my mother could wash her hair indoors with hot water if she chose."

His mother's room was larger and homier than his sister's, with room for a table and chair. The quilted comforter and pillows looked hand-stitched with skill. The plastic bins with her belongings were neatly stacked along the walls. She had a shallow closet and a window overlooking the hanging laundry and cables draped between her house and the one eight feet across the lane.

Lee opened the closet and raised his hands to stop an avalanche of clothes. Once secured, he questioned and lectured his mother in Shanghainese, pointed to the garbage bags, and lectured her again. She shrugged and muttered as though he was making a big deal out of nothing, which exasperated Lee even more.

He whispered to me in English. "The government will evict her in three days, and she has not even begun to pack."

"Maybe she needs help."

"Ha. She's stronger than she looks and stubborner than you and me put together."

A man in a tank top and shorts appeared in the doorway.

He must have heard us whispering because he interrupted us in English. "Who's this?"

Lee wrinkled his nose as if the man exuded a smell, which, in all fairness, could have come from the house. "This is my employer's daughter from Los Angeles. Lily, meet my cousin Chester Wu."

The man grinned. "Are you a tour guide now? Or does your boss pay you to babysit as well as cook?"

Lee sneered. "How about you, Chester? Are you and your parents ready to move to Pudong after living in my house for decades rent free?"

Chester held out his hands. "Are you kidding? We'll have a modern apartment all to ourselves."

"In the middle of nothing."

Chester bristled at the dig, clearly not as enthused about the move as he claimed. "Pay your respects to my parents before you leave. It's the least you could do after this trouble you have caused."

When he was out of sight, I whispered to Lee. "I thought the government was relocating them."

"They are. I waited until last the moment to accept their offer because my mother didn't want to leave her community and the house my father's ancestors had built."

"Your cousin feels the same?"

He nodded. "He and his parents resent me for having the money to buy back this house after Mao Zedong abolished property rights in the fifties and turned our home into a multi-family apartment."

I watched as his mother pulled belongings from the overstuffed closet and divided them into piles on her tiny bed.

"How could they rent this room as an apartment? It's barely big enough for her to sleep."

"Times were different then. When my brother and I were young, seventeen people lived in this house. My great-grandmother, first grandaunt, and Chester's twenty-year-old father lived together in this room. A family with two kids lived in that cubby hole Uma saves for my sister. Since we had no indoor plumbing, everyone shared the matong in the second-floor bathroom and took turns emptying and scrubbing the bucket in the public toilet several blocks away. We washed ourselves, our clothing, and our dishes in the trough outside. Before the government provided hoses to our buildings, we carried in the water from a public faucet."

His mother held up a thread-bare blanket and pleaded with Lee. When he nodded, she stuffed it into a garbage bag and continued through her closet.

"My sister has plenty of room, but I don't want Uma to take advantage of that. She should use this opportunity to adjust to new and better things."

He motioned me out the door, but stopped at the stairs.

"Is something wrong?" I asked.

"I haven't gone up there since I moved to Los Angeles – the year before you were born. So many ghosts. Maybe they'll leave when the government knocks this place down." He started up the stairs with a snort. "Or maybe I will return as a hungry ghost to pay for my sins."

When he reached the top, he paused with concern. "Don't be surprised by how much nicer it is up here, okay? I renovated the apartment where Chester lives for my mother and sister. I was only your age, but I made more money with the Scorpion Black Society than everyone in my family combined."

"Why did your mother move downstairs?"

"She took over the cooking after my grandmother died

and wanted to be closer to the kitchen. My sister moved with her. Chester and his parents moved to the third floor. My elderly cousins live in the apartment I had updated for myself before I met your father."

"Is that Chang Lee?" an old woman called in Mandarin.

"Yes, Auntie. It's me."

The woman sat on a cushioned armchair in a Western-style studio apartment with built-in cabinets, entertainment console, and its own private bath. A man dozed on the bed beside her. She looked younger than she sounded, still in her seventies, maybe fifteen years older than Lee. The man might have been close to her age. It was hard to tell with his skinny arm draped across his face.

She looked me over and frowned. "Chester said your girlfriend was foreign. He didn't say she was so young."

Lee stilled my objection with a glance.

The woman's irritation grated on my nerves.

"The government is forcing us to leave. Did you hear?"

"Yes, Auntie. I heard."

"They're sending us to a village."

"Yes. To live in a modern high-rise apartment."

She hissed through her teeth. "It's so far from the city. We will never see our friends. Our grandson will never bring our great-granddaughter to visit us."

She held out a photograph of an adorable three-year-old girl. I looked at Lee with concern. He shook his head. This was not his kidnapped niece.

"There's nothing I can do, Auntie. You must go where the government tells you to go. Unless Chester's son will take you in."

"Psiu. He and his wife make robots in Putuo. Their company apartment has no room for us."

Lee feigned sweetness and nodded toward her son's room. "You have Chester to look out for you."

She laughed as if what he said was absurd. "Go away, Chang Lee. You show no respect for me, the wife of the son of your grandfather's eldest sister. You never have."

Lee backed out of his old apartment, marched down the steps, said a curt goodbye to his mother, and stormed out of the lane house with a sigh of relief.

"The wife of the son of your what?" I asked teasingly, trying to lighten the mood.

Lee coughed out a laugh. "Her mother-in-law was my grandfather's eldest sister. She believes this gives her seniority over my mother."

"Does it?"

"Who knows? All my life, she and my other relatives made my parents and grandmother feel inferior because they ran away from the Communists and followed a gangster hero to Hong Kong. I was a baby when they returned like refugees after my grandfather was killed. They treated my grandmother as a servant and my father like a coward – which he was – but I made up for that. Now they resent me."

"Huh. And I thought my family was complicated."

"They are. But in a nicer way." He shook off his mood. "We have time before our next appointment. We can ride home past the Bund."

"What about your grandniece? The chances of finding her decrease every hour she's gone."

"You think I don't know? But in case you haven't noticed, this city is huge. My connections aren't as solid as they were when I was Red Pole Chang. There's only one person I can ask for help. And for him, we have to wait."

"What about the police?"

"That's up to my brother and his son. I don't know who they have called. Besides, the Bund is to Shanghai like the Great Wall is to Beijing. You can't come all this way and not see such an iconic site."

I grinned with excitement. The lights along the river's bend were purported to be more spectacular than Hong Kong. "Thanks, Lee."

He waved it away. "I owe you a little fun while you're here."

"And food?" I asked hopefully.

"Hah. Your body eats calories like a fire eats wood. I knew four bao would not be enough to fill your bottomless gut."

He hopped on his bike and pedaled up the lane, shouting the familiar idiom in Mandarin: *Don't hurry, be quick.*

Chapter Seven

Despite the promised food, we pedaled straight for the Bund, or as straight as the winding bike path would allow. When I spotted a man emerging from a doorway with a takeout bag, I guilted Lee to stop for xiao long bao. When my sister was still alive, Ma would treat us to soup dumplings at Din Tai Fung. After Rose's death, Lee made them in Baba's kitchen especially for me.

"Will these be as good as yours?"

"It's a Shanghainese specialty. What kind do you want – steamed, pan fried, shrimp, pork, spicy?"

"Yes."

He rolled his eyes. "We don't have time for a meal. This is only a snack."

I tried not to feel disappointed. "Whatever's quickest will be fine."

Once we had nibbled the corners of the pan-fried cubes he had chosen and sucked out the heavenly hot soup, we gobbled the dumplings and rode away from the Old City grime to the ritzy strip along the river with historic European buildings, modern high-rises, and luxury hotels. When the promenade began along the waterfront, we dismounted and walked our bikes with the ambling locals and enjoyed the magical transition into dusk.

"I'm glad we came here," I said.

He nodded. "We need a moment to breathe."

Lee had left on his trip a week before I had left with Ma. He hadn't bargained for the additional stress I would cause.

"I didn't mean to drag you to Hong Kong."

"Well..." He laughed. "I meant to drag you to Shanghai. This business with my brother's granddaughter couldn't have come at a worse time. I have to help, of course, but I also need to relocate my mother and make sure the government pays me what I'm owed. If I don't do things properly, I could be chasing money for years." He looked back the way we had come. "As horrible as it probably seemed to you, that lane house was my home."

"It wasn't so horrible."

"Liar."

We shared a moment, him with his memories, me praying I could help. Then I swept my hand at the splendor around me. "This isn't a hardship."

"Yeah? Enjoy it while you can."

As if commanded by his words, the custom house, banks, and hotels on our side of the river lit up in twenty-four karat gold with a giant emerald pyramid capping the building at the north end. Although not fully dark, crowds of tourists and locals had already begun to swarm across the boulevard and down the upper-promenade steps, hoping for prime viewing spots near the railing above the docks.

Lee pointed to the Pudong side of the river at a pink tower with two enormous spheres near the bottom and the top. The needle pointing to the sky made it look like a giant syringe. "That's the Oriental Pearl TV Tower. The color will change all night. It has observation decks and a hotel.

I would take you to the revolving restaurant at the top, but it's too expensive to eat."

"This is more than enough."

"Good. Because it's all you get."

He backed his bike out of the crowd and rolled it up the steps to the upper promenade.

"Hold up." I whipped out my phone. "We have to take at least one selfie for Ma."

Lee groaned as I angled the camera to include both of us plus the fanciful ferries and tour boats in the shot. One had a projection of dragons slithering across its flat-sided hull.

"One more," I said, turning around to catch the golden buildings lined across the street. But no matter how I angled the selfie, I couldn't get them in.

Lee scowled with impatience and gestured for the phone. "Let me take it. We don't have all night." He motioned me to the left. "Back up. Now more to the right."

"I thought we were in a hurry."

"We are. But you'll whine like a baby if I don't get this right. Hold still and smile."

He returned my phone. Then he bolted across the avenue without giving me time to check the shot.

Chapter Eight

We made it back to Lee's apartment in time to drop off the bikes, change for the evening, and whisk out the door.

"Where to now?"

"To meet that friend."

"What kind of friend is he?"

"The kind you don't ask questions about."

"Ugh. You're more annoying here than you are back at home."

"And you are equally nosy wherever you are."

He led me to the rideshare car, confirmed it was ours, and hopped in the back.

"What about your family? Can I ask questions about them?"

He grunted his impatience. "What do you want to know?"

"Why didn't your mother or cousins ask about your missing niece?"

"They don't know."

"You haven't told them?

"It's not my news to share."

He glanced at the driver and back to me.

I took the hint and focused on the trip, something I should have been doing in case I needed to find my way back alone. We were headed due north past mid-size buildings and upscale shikumen neighborhoods toward an elevated highway lit up in neon blue – not just a channel of neon around the edges or pillars of light at the base; the entire underside of the highway and everything below it was lit up in Disneyland Space Mountain blue.

As we wove through lanes upon lanes of streaming cars, the magnitude of this city struck home. Shanghai was five times the size and seven times the population of Los Angeles. What I had seen so far represented a minuscule fragment of the whole. How would we ever find one missing girl?

I turned away from the lights and studied Lee's face. From the grit of his teeth, I didn't expect a warm greeting from his not-to-be-discussed friend.

The driver dropped us off in front of a dazzling building with a street-level club. A neon outline of a purple face sang into a microphone beneath Chinese characters and the words Happy Lounge KTV.

Lee threaded through the river of pedestrians and paused at the door. "Mouth shut. Ears open."

"Does that mean I won't have to sing?"

"I'm serious, Lily."

"So am I."

"Stop joking. Who do you think I called when you stuck your nose in the Scorpion's nest? Old friends, that's who. Friends who wished I had stayed dead."

I wiped the humor from my voice and hopefully my face. Lee had resurrected his criminal relationships in Shanghai to help me with the triads in Hong Kong. The least I could do was show him respect.

Chastened and mute, I followed him into the karaoke bar, braced for tone-deaf singers and cheesy pop tunes. Instead, the chic lounge piped in soothing instrumental jazz.

An attractive young hostess greeted us in Mandarin. "Welcome to the Happy Lounge. May I book you a room?"

"We are guests of Big Tooth Fong."

She blinked in surprise, then smiled. "Of course. Please come with me."

She led us down a corridor with rooms on either side. The cheesy music and bad singing I had expected seeped through the walls. Bass beats vibrated the floor. A sexy women emerged from the last room, pulled the hem of her dress, and vanished into a restroom across the hall. As she entered, another scantily-clad woman emerged.

The hostess opened a door into a lounge with red leather couches, red patterned carpet, and indigo velvet walls. "Help yourself to the bar. I'll let Mr. Fong know you have arrived."

A Chinese pop-music video played on a wall-mounted television, framed in the same pink neon that outlined the recessed ceiling above. Two cordless microphones waited on stands beside a display menu of songs.

I sealed my lips against a flood of snappy comments and kept my expression as neutral as Lee's. When he motioned to the far couch, I sat. A moment later, a smartly-dressed man entered with a toothy smile and unfriendly eyes.

He held out his arms in mock welcome and addressed us in English. "This is an unexpected visit."

Lee nodded. "Yet you do not seem surprised."

The man's smile grew wider and colder. "Who else would have the nerve to call me Big Tooth Fong in my own establishment?" He headed for the bar. "You want a drink?"

"No, thanks."

"How about your girl?" He leered at me. "It's important to hydrate before a busy night."

Lee ignored the insinuation and sat on the center couch.

Fong poured his scotch and took a seat across from me.

"So, *American* Lee, what do you want this time?"

"Information."

"Hmm." He raised his glass to indicate me. "I gave you lots of information last week. Why are you bothering me again?"

"I'm looking for my twelve-year-old grandniece."

Fong laughed. "I don't hire them that young."

"What about the girls you don't *hire?*"

Fong sneered. "Be careful, Lee. You are not Red Pole Chang anymore."

"True. But there might be some old timers who wish I would return. Or a new hierarchy who wish I would leave. Maybe enough to provide *encouragement?*"

"You think she was taken?"

"I don't know. Do you?"

Fong sipped his scotch, then set it carefully on the lacquered table top. "If I help you in this matter, will you go back to your adopted country and leave me alone?"

Lee nodded. "As soon as I find my grandniece and relocate my mother."

"Ha. Old people are stubborn. It took years to move my grandparents out of the Old City." Fong stood and brushed the creases from his slacks. "Attend to your family. If I learn anything, I will call."

Chapter Nine

I held my temper until we had escaped the dubious karaoke bar, then turned my wrath on Lee. "Your gang prostitutes women?"

He grabbed my arm and yanked me down the sidewalk. "They are not my gang anymore. And from what I've heard, the Happy Lounge is a legitimate business."

"Yeah, right. A legit biz with sex workers on the side. What did you mean about the girls Fong *didn't hire*? Do the Scorpions traffic children as well?"

"Aiya, Lily. They dip their fingers into many pots. I stay out of their business. They stay out of mine. Or they did before I stirred up trouble helping you."

I stopped on the sidewalk, eliciting angry looks as I disrupted the flow. I knew better, but I just didn't care.

"Enough with the guilt, Lee. You helped, I thanked. You called, I'm here."

Pedestrians veered out of our way, leaving an unobstructed line between my fury and Lee's. Then he turned abruptly and marched up the road. Several blocks past commercial centers, hotels, and shops, he finally slowed his pace. When I joined him, he glanced at me and shrugged.

"I'm glad you came, but I don't know what's going on. Until I do, we must think fast and act slow. We'll learn more tomorrow when we question my brother. For now, dinner and sleep is the best we can do."

As if on cue, my belly rumbled and I stifled a yawn. Since I had planned to sleep on the long flight to Los Angeles, I had purposely stayed up late in Hong Kong. Without my anger to sustain me, my energy drained. If not for the shocks of electricity on the back of my neck, I could have dozed off as we walked.

"What's the matter?"

I turned my head toward the buildings and checked the reflections in the glass. As I did this, the electrical sensation moved from the back of my neck to the side.

"Why are you walking so slowly? Don't you want to be fed?"

"Pause at the next window and look at the display."

"Why should I do that?"

"Because someone is following us, and I want to see who it is."

I continued for a few yards, then turned back toward Lee, scanning the area for anyone out of step with the crowd before joining him at the display.

"So?"

"Nothing unusual. But I know what I felt."

Instead of arguing, he accepted my ninja sense with a nod. "Do you feel it now?"

"No."

"Maybe your slow walking irritated a pedestrian."

"That's possible."

He nodded to a surveillance camera. "No one will try anything here. Keep moving and monitor what you feel."

As we approached the multi-level intersection, I flinched.

"You feel it again?"

I flashed my eyes upward without raising my face. Lee did the same. Elevated walkways crisscrossed between us and the highway. The wash of blue over the street blended with taillights and neon to create an eerie purple glow. Pedestrians on the walkway above were silhouetted in black. Once out of their sight, I darted to the left.

Lee yelled at me to stop.

I motioned for him to continue and sprinted up the stairs. Although in great shape for a man in his sixties, Lee couldn't match me. In Los Angeles, I ran and biked across the city and hiked in the Santa Monica Mountains, in addition to the hours I spent training or tangled in a fight. Even in his prime, Lee would have been challenged to keep up with me.

At the first landing, I spotted a man leaning over the railing. When I reached the walkway, he was gone. I sprinted to where he had been and looked down to see Lee pretending to chat with someone hidden beneath the walkway, presumably me. I waved for his attention and pointed to my right, then I dashed across the ramp to an intersecting walkway. I checked every direction for a sprinting man but, aside from me, no one even rushed.

I descended the stairs and met Lee on the street. "Did you see anyone running?"

He shook his head. "Only you."

"A man was watching you from the railing as you pretended to talk to me."

Lee grinned. "Smart, right?"

"Very. Except he left before I made it up the stairs."

"Just one man?"

"Yep. Taller than us, broad shoulders, long hair pulled back at the neck."

"Do you still feel watched?"

I tuned into my senses and shook my head. "Nothing. Although he could be masking his intent."

Lee frowned. "If he has the skill to do that, I don't want him following us to my apartment."

We crossed the bright-blue avenue into a warren of less-populated streets. The neighborhood shops had closed for the night, giving this area a more tranquil feel. Even so, Lee turned at random and checked behind us for a tail. After passing the entrances of numerous shikumen lanes, he stepped inside the nook of a building and paused.

"Feel anything now?"

"Nope."

"Good. Let's go inside and eat."

The tiny place was crowded with diners hunched over rustic wooden tables set with small bowls of intriguing food. A chalkboard menu ran the length of one wall from the hostess podium to the open-view kitchen, with cartoon drawings and choices written in yellow Romanized pinyin and pink Chinese characters. English words written in green chalk read, "Five Star Haiwanese Chicken Rice." Below that, a slogan in blue read, "Die Die Must Try." Every word, character, and cartoon on the board exuded color and fun.

We took an open table and pulled out the nested square stools.

"Did you choose this place for me?"

Lee shrugged. "You always like Hainan chicken rice when I fix it at home."

When I was a toddler, Lee had fed me broth-soaked rice and chicken fat bits in a highchair in Baba's kitchen. When I grew older, he served the poached chicken with an array of sauces at the prep counter and questioned me about my day.

Home.

With that one simple word, Lee became *Uncle,* and Red Pole Chang faded away.

Chapter Ten

At seven the next morning, Uncle shooed me out the door with promises of tea and breakfast on the go. I added an extra energy bar in my runner's backpack and filled the water pouch just in case. The minimalist pack sat between my shoulder blades and secured under my breasts for a snug yet comfortable fit. In hindsight, I should have put the bar somewhere I could reach.

"What about that breakfast?" I asked as he swiped his transit card and hurried through the gate.

"Metro doesn't allow food or drinks on the trains."

"You didn't know that before?"

"Of course I did. But we don't have the time."

We squeezed through the station and onto a train. It was Sunday morning and the platform was packed.

"Where are we headed?"

"To see my brother on Chongming Dao."

He brought up the island on Baidu Maps. Chongming was the largest of three in the estuary where the Yangtze River widened into the East China Sea. We would need to travel north, cross the winding Huangpu River, and catch a ferry to one of Chongming's ports.

"What does your brother do?"

"He farms." Uncle waved away my puzzlement. "I know.

Most people move from farms to cities, not cities to farms.
But Qiang is a stubborn man and claims it was all anyone
ever taught him to do."

I pictured the decrepit lane house where the brothers had
grown up. The only crops I had seen in the Old City was one
spindly tomato plant struggling for life in a clay pot.

"Did you have a home in the country?"

"What, like Hollywood celebrities?" He choked out
a laugh. "No. Qiang received his agricultural education
in Anhui Province during the Down to the Countryside
movement. You know about this?"

I shrugged. "It sounds familiar. Maybe from Asian history
class?"

Uncle frowned. "It was personal history for us. Qiang
was born during the Great Famine. When he was nine and
I was eleven, Chairman Mao Zedong shut down schools
and universities for three years. By the time we went
back, I cared more about the skills I could learn from the
Scorpions than from school. Qiang was different. When
I joined the gang, he studied harder and excelled. Then
the government ordered every urban household to send
one of their 'intellectual' teenagers to rural districts to be
re-educated by farmers. Qiang was the eldest of us still in
school. If my family had tried to send me, I wouldn't have
gone."

"Is this why he resents you?"

Uncle sighed. "Qiang has many reasons to resent me. This
is only one."

"But you said he received an education in agriculture.
Wasn't he appreciative of that?"

"I was joking, Lily. The government sent those kids to
the poorest rural areas in the country to stamp out their

intellectual ways and teach them Communist values. The farmers in charge of Qiang nearly worked him to death. When he finally returned to the city, he had aged so much our mother didn't recognize him."

The story was tragic, but it still didn't make sense.

"It wasn't your fault the government sent him away."

"Oh, no? Then why do you blame yourself for your younger sister's murder?"

I gaped at Uncle, shocked to hear him bring up Rose. If I had commuted to UCLA instead of living on campus, I would have known my fifteen-year-old sister was going to clubs with a fake ID. I would have answered her text and rescued her from that monster instead of losing my virginity to Pete. I could have protected my sister in so many ways if only I had cared more about her life than my own. Rose was murdered seven years ago. No matter how many lives I save or how many joys I deprive myself from experiencing, my mission to help others would never make up for my failure as an elder sister. Although furious with Uncle for dredging up these feelings, I understood the comparison between him and his sibling and me with mine.

"You wanted your own life more than you cared about Qiang."

He shrugged. "We can't change the past."

A simple truth, but so hard to accept.

We rode the train in silence as a new puzzle nibbled at my brain.

"On the ride from the airport, you said Qiang blames you for his missing granddaughter. When we spoke with Big Tooth Fong last night, you implied that she might have been kidnapped as leverage against you. Why would anyone use her as leverage if you and your brother aren't close? Wouldn't it be smarter to take your mother, whom you obviously love?"

"This has also occurred to me. Which is why I need to speak with Qiang, face to face."

When we reached the ferry station, we grabbed a breakfast of fried dough sticks wrapped in sesame pancake – carb on carb, the Shanghai way. To wash it down, Uncle bought cups of freshly pressed hot soy milk. It tasted so good, I hardly missed my morning tea. Once done, we squeezed onto the ferry and took interior seats on the cheaper lower level away from the windows. I craned my neck to catch the shoreline view.

"What are you doing? There's nothing to see except buildings and smog."

"Buildings and smog in *Shanghai.*"

He slumped in his seat and pretended to nap. I struggled to see over the passengers, then gave up on the shoreline and islands and checked WeChat instead.

Ma: *Smooth flight. Heading home now. Everything okay with you?*

Her message had come in during the night, which would have been early morning in Los Angeles. Now it would be late afternoon.

Me: *On a ferry to meet Uncle's brother. Shanghai's great. We went to the Bund!*

I uploaded the selfie of Uncle and me in front of the colorful skyline and riverboat lights. The early evening glow and the golden lights from the boulevard lit my cheery face and Uncle's impatient scowl.

Me: *See how much fun he's having showing me the sights?* 😂

Then I saw the other photos in my gallery and paused. Uncle had taken a series of them as he moved me back and forth, changing the framing and catching my animated expressions and positions. I hadn't seen myself look this happy in photos since the ones taken of me at UCLA. I added three of them, ending with the smiling shot of me in front of the golden buildings and the emerald-topped hotel.

I thought about messaging Baba before his dinner prep began, but I didn't want to get cornered into telling a lie. Unlike my mother, he asked pointed questions that were hard to avoid. Better to wait for him to reach out to me.

The ferry docked, and Uncle leapt to his feet, suspiciously awake after avoiding me with his nap. "Let's go, lazy girl. Time to rent bikes and ride."

Chapter Eleven

We rented mountain bikes despite the flat terrain of fields, marshes, levees, and mud, not because Uncle anticipated off-road biking, but for the multiple gears that would help him match my pace. As it turned out, the thicker tires came in handy once we turned off the thoroughfares onto ruggedly paved roads. I breathed in the earthy scent of fertilized soil and irrigation channels. It was hard to believe we were still within the municipality of Shanghai.

Uncle paused to check Baidu Maps, then took a dirt road into an orchard. Once through the trees, he followed the levee to a stone-walled property with acres of fields. Leafy crops grew on mounds while others, like rice, grew in watery rows. I inhaled the spicy scent of turnips, onions, and bok choy. When Uncle waved to a farm worker and yelled for directions, the man pointed to a skinny three-story house at the back of the property and continued to hoe.

"Does your brother own this land?"

"No one owns land in China. Farms are run by rural collectives and regulated by the government. When I was young, Shanghai farmers produced one hundred percent of the vegetables we ate. Then came urbanization, and the government relocated farmers to the cities. When they no longer had enough local farms to grow food, they reversed the trend. Now they're maximizing all of the arable land around Shanghai, which means, once again, they're relocating farmers away from their homes. This time, they're doing it to make room for more crops."

"What happens to the farmers?"

"They move and have to commute."

"Did that happen to your brother?"

"Not yet. Qiang has managed to keep his home, but he's not allowed to build new structures or expand the footprint of his house."

We rode between the fields past a handful of farmers taking a break beneath a tree. From the coolers and supplies stacked around the trunk, they appeared to have packed enough food and comforts for the day.

"How far do they travel?"

Uncle pointed to a line of row houses in the distance. "Maybe from there. Maybe from the urban area we passed on our ride from the dock. Maybe the other side of Chongming."

A man and two boys walked in a field, stooping occasionally to check the plants. When the youngest child pointed at us, the man shielded his eyes from the sun, then continued his task.

As we rode closer to the farmhouse, the fields changed from mounds of soil to marshy paddies where tall green rice plants emerged from the water. A man close to Uncle's age but shorter and skinnier than him waded through the gaps in the rice. He carried a wire fishing basket. When he saw us approach, he climbed out of the water. The fish inside the basket flopped as they struggled to breathe.

Uncle dismounted and walked his bike toward the man. They greeted each other in Shanghainese without any physical contact or fondness in the tone. After this initial exchange, Uncle introduced me in English.

"This is Lily Wong, my friend from America who specializes in finding missing girls." He pointed at the man. "This is my brother, Qiang."

Qiang dismissed me with a glance, but replied in English all the same. "My granddaughter isn't missing. She was taken by your criminal friends."

"You don't know that."

"Of course I do. Who else would bring such misery to my home?"

He shook the fishing basket in anger and dislodged the crayfish climbing up the wire. They scrambled over the dying fish with as much disregard as Qiang had for his brother.

How could someone so attuned to symbiotic relationships in sustainable farming and ecosystems have alienated himself so completely from his family? Neither his mother nor his cousins had asked about him or known about the situation with his granddaughter. And although Qiang demanded Uncle's help, he was pushing him away. I needed to ease the tension before Uncle gave up on his brother and left.

"Where was your granddaughter abducted?" I framed the question to align myself with Qiang.

He relaxed his arm and let the fishing basket hang. "From the kitchen on the first floor. She falls asleep reading by the oven. My son forgets to take her upstairs."

I pointed to the tiny house at the end of the field. "Do you and your son's family live together?"

"We do. Jun and I live on the third floor. Tao and his wife live on the second floor with their two sons and Chyou."

"Chyou is your granddaughter?"

"Yes. She is twelve years old."

I thought about the man and younger boys examining plants in the fields. "She's the eldest."

"How did you know?"

Uncle grunted his impatience. "In Los Angeles, people pay Lily to notice such things."

"Pay?"

"Don't be alarmed," I said. "I'm here as a friend."

"Huh. Lee always has friends to clean up his mess."

The comment sparked a flurry of angry Shanghainese.

So much for my temporary peace.

If I had any hope of finding Chyou, these brothers needed to put aside their resentments and work together. Or, at the very least, communicate without destroying their fragile relationship.

"May I see the kitchen?"

Qiang stopped arguing and glared. "What?"

"Will you take us to your house? I'd like to search for clues. So we can find your granddaughter?"

"Oh. Of course. Follow me."

I shot Uncle a cautionary look. He rolled his eyes but kept his mouth shut.

The house was even smaller than I thought, with a footprint about half the length of my narrow apartment back home. Since China's government wouldn't allow farmers to expand their homes over arable land, Qiang had expanded in the only possible direction – up.

We parked our bikes beside a smelly outhouse and shed where I noticed boot and slipper prints in the dirt. Deeper impressions molded into the hard ground from people having tread through mud.

"Do other farmers use this outhouse and shed?"

Qiang nodded. "And our kitchen when it rains."

"Did it rain the day Chyou went missing?"

"No."

A dirt road cut through the center of the property. Beds of assorted vegetable plants surrounded the house. Dirt paths led into the fields and the rice paddy fisheries. The nearest house was a mile away.

"It must be very quiet here at night. Did anyone hear a car or a struggle?"

"No."

I crossed the threshold and paused to take in the space. Mats and cushions defined the living area on the right, with a narrow staircase that ran against the side wall. The eat-in kitchen on the left occupied most of the space. A long dining table with a bench on the kitchen side and chairs on the other divided the rooms. I saw a wood-burning stove behind the bench where I imagined a twelve-year-old bookworm might enjoy lying on her stomach to read.

"Was anything disturbed in the kitchen?"

"No."

"What about the book?"

"What book?"

"You said Chyou likes to read beside the oven. Did you find her book in the kitchen?"

"No. Why does this matter? Why are you here instead of questioning Lee's friends?"

Uncle threw up his hands. "Stop calling them my friends. I left the Scorpion Society twenty-four years ago. I have nothing to do with them. I've been home several times. They don't bother me. Why are you so certain they would cause trouble for you?"

"History." Qiang spat the word with such vehemence

that both Uncle and I recoiled. "While you ran with those criminals, they persecuted me."

"We were young."

"You were cruel."

Uncle shook his head, but I saw doubt in his eyes. Qiang saw the same and moved in for the kill.

"Did you stop them from calling me a famine-born runt? Did you tell them I was lucky to have survived? Did you tell them how proud you were of your smart younger brother? Of course not. You were too afraid they would see my weakness in you."

"No," Uncle said, more forceful than before. "It wasn't *your* weakness. It was Lau Tia's. I had to be twice as tough as any Scorpion to make up for our father's cowardice."

"Lau Tia did the best he could."

"And I didn't?"

"He was an accountant. You were a thug."

Uncle glared at his brother. "You never understood. The Scorpion Society kept us alive. When we returned to Shanghai, the local tong that helped our father get a job was affiliated with them. But that was not enough to save us. Our grandfather had supported the Kuomintang. Everyone in the neighborhood knew this was why they had fled. Our mother's family fled as well and ended up staying in Hong Kong."

"I know all of this."

"And still you do not understand. The local Communists branded Lau Tia as an intellectual and a KMT supporter. He lost his job. He had no money to pay rent in the government-owned house our ancestors built or to buy the scraps of food available during the famine. Our great-grandfather starved to death. You almost died. Our whole family suffered. The

Scorpion Society saved our lives. But when they needed help, our father stood on the sidelines and watched his boss die."

"The gunman killed Lau Tia too, Lee. What more did you want?"

"I wanted him to pay back his debt and fight."

"Fight? Our father was a gentle man, not a killer like you."

"Well, your killer brother kept our family alive, paid our rent, bought back our house, put food on the table for everyone–"

Qiang slapped his chest. "Everyone except for me!"

The pain in his cry tore at my heart. What horrors had this man suffered as a child to keep his emotions this raw as an adult?

Qiang slumped into a chair.

Uncle sat beside him with a sigh. "I shouldn't have let them send you away."

Qiang shrugged. "You made your choice."

Uncle frowned. "I don't regret saving myself. But I could have asked the gang to save you."

"Why didn't you?"

"Lau Tia was still alive. I was seventeen, with only two years as a Scorpion. He had been a member for twelve years. You were his son. It was *his* duty to ask."

"Then why didn't he?"

"I told you. He was afraid."

Chapter Twelve

I left the brothers in the kitchen to sit with their past and – I hoped – reconcile their perceptions of what had transpired. Qiang's grandsons found me by the rice paddy watching the fish.

"Who are you?" the older boy asked, addressing me in Mandarin.

"My name is Lily. I'm a friend of your grandfather's brother."

The younger boy tugged at the older boy's arm. "Yeye has a brother?"

The older boy ignored him and turned back to me. "What are you doing here?"

"I'm trying to find your sister. Do you know where she is?"

When the older boy shrugged, the younger did the same.

"She could be in trouble. Don't you want to help?"

The older boy picked up a clump of dirt and threw it into the water to scatter the fish. "Why should we?"

The younger boy copied him. "Yeah. Why should we?"

I nodded somberly. "Sisters can be boring."

The older boy grunted in agreement. The younger boy did the same.

"Has anyone new come to the farm?"

"You mean like you?" the older brother said.

"Yeah. Anyone other than farmers or family."

The boys looked at each other in silent communication, then spoke in unison. "The hungry men."

"What hungry men?"

"The hungry men who bother Yeye," the older boy said.

"What do you mean by bother?"

"You talk funny," the younger boy said.

"I'm from America."

The older boy switched languages. "Yong and me speak English."

Yong grinned and did the same. "Yeah. Good like Yeye."

"Don't exaggerate." The older boy turned to me. "Our grandfather is very smart. We will be too."

"I'm sure you will. But what's *your* name?"

"Zhi."

"I'm happy to meet you, Zhi and Yong. Can you tell me more about the hungry men?"

Zhi continued in English, but reverted to Mandarin whenever his vocabulary failed. "What do you want to know?"

"How they look. What they do."

Zhi shrugged. "They come each month. Drive too fast. Make dust. Talk to Yeye. Sometimes yell. Baba keeps us away. He calls them Hungry Men."

"Does your grandfather pay them money?"

"Of course not. He gives them a bag of food."

"What kind of food?"

"How should I know? He puts it in a bag."

"That's right," Yong said in English, as if to prove that he could. He switched back to Mandarin. "One man is big like a giant. But the smaller man scares me more."

I knelt in the dirt. "Why is that, Yong?"

"The scar on his cheek makes his mouth go like this." Yong stuck his finger in the corner of his mouth and pulled.

"Is this the big man or the scary man?"

"The scary man. The giant follows him and drives the car."

I glanced back at the house. Why hadn't Qiang told us about these men?

"Do they ever talk to your sister?"

"Why would they do that?" Zhi interrupted.

I shrugged. "Maybe she was around your grandfather? Or in the road when they arrived?"

Zhi scuffed the dirt with annoyance. "We don't pay attention to her. Do we, Yong?"

The younger boy crossed his arms with a decisive nod. "We do not."

"She acts so important. But she's only one year older than me."

Did Zhi mistake importance for maturity? If so, could Chyou have caught a sex trafficker's eye?

I gazed across the fields, far from the decadent lifestyle of urban Shanghai. If Big Tooth Fong forced girls to work the back rooms of his karaoke bar, why would he abduct them from here? And if the Scorpions were angry with Uncle, why wouldn't they deal directly with him? It seemed more likely to me that the Hungry Men had issues with Qiang.

"When did you last see your sister, Zhi?"

"Two nights ago. In the kitchen before we went to bed."

The boys waded into the water, picked up crayfish, and pretended to fight.

"One more question. What do you think happened to her?"

Zhi paused, holding the creature by its back so its legs wiggled at me. "She probably ran away with friends."

"What friends?"

Zhi tossed his crayfish into the water. "How should I know? Come on, Yong. Let's catch up with Dad."

Qiang's sibling troubles seemed to have trickled down to his grandchildren. Was Chyou as snobbish as Zhi made her seem? Would she have run away to the city for a grand adventure with friends?

I returned to the house and found Uncle alone in the kitchen.

"Where have you been?" he asked.

"Practicing my language skills with your grandnephews. Where's Qiang?"

"Upstairs talking to his wife. Our fight upset her. He will come down soon."

"Good. Because we have questions to ask."

"Like what?"

I related my conversation to Uncle, ending with the Hungry Men and how they arrived every month and left with a bag the boys assumed to be food.

Uncle glanced at the stairs. "That would explain how my brother still has a house on this land."

"You think he's paying an official?"

"I think he's paying protection money. And not only that. Have you noticed how nice his fields are compared to his neighbors? His farming methods are more sophisticated. It would have cost him money to adapt."

"The Scorpions?"

"No. He would never go to them."

"I would never go to who?" Qiang asked as he came down the stairs.

"A restaurant," I said. "For fish. Because you have so many here."

Qiang nodded. "I would offer you lunch, but it is time for me to work."

"Of course," said Uncle. "We'll stop by another time, when we have information about Chyou."

We collected our bikes and rode to the other side of Qiang's farming collective. When we reached the stone border, we stopped. Uncle was right. The neighboring fields were not as sophisticated as Qiang's.

"Who do you think lent him the money?"

Uncle took out his phone. "On Chongming Island? I have no idea. But I know who to ask."

Chapter Thirteen

After Uncle made the call, we rode up the straightaway to meet the local crime boss who provided loans, support, and protection to vulnerable residents, struggling immigrants, and ambitious farmers like Qiang.

I hugged the side of the road as a bus passed inches from my leg. The two-lane highway cut through an expanse of flat farmland with green, tan, and brown crops sectioned into a grid. Every five miles or so, we crossed cement lanes leading to gray tract house apartments or cookie-cutter red-roofed homes. Small gardens lined the front of the structures with a channel of water between the pavement and the soil. None of the fields had a house on the property like Qiang's.

When the crops transitioned into orchards and walled us in with trees, the automated voice from Uncle's Baidu Map directed us off the main road, where a network of lanes led us to a secluded estate.

I scanned the area for trouble. No one in sight meant no one would hear us scream.

"Should we be concerned?"

Uncle shrugged and pedaled toward the house.

No contacts. No weapons. No idea where we were or who we might face. I was completely dependent upon Uncle, who I wasn't entirely sure I could trust. I had only learned about his violent past and criminal connections the previous week. Since then, I had observed as many reckless decisions as smart. Which one was this?

Sensei's voice whispered in my ear.

Embrace the uncertainty, and become one with the void.

My ninja teacher's wisdom reminded me not to cling to my preconceptions and desires. Attempting to control the uncontrollable would bind my thoughts and actions to the outcome I wanted to achieve and blind me to other possibilities and routes to success.

As we neared the house, a man built like a tank rose from a bench. His frame was so short and wide I had mistaken him for part of the porch. A leaner man advanced from the side, as pretty as a singer in a K-pop band.

Uncle and I dismounted from our bikes.

Tank questioned us in a dialect I didn't recognize. When Uncle didn't respond, he switched to strongly accented Mandarin. "This is private property. Go back the way you came."

Uncle didn't move. "We're here to see the Chongming King."

Tank chuckled, as if Uncle had told a marvelous joke. "A king? Why not an emperor? Turn around and get off our land."

Uncle stepped forward. "Your boss, Edward Fu, would prefer that we stay. Tell him Red Pole Chang is waiting."

Tank's eyes narrowed with suspicion. He nodded to K-Pop. "Watch them." Then he marched into the house. A few minutes later, he beckoned us inside.

Unlike Qiang's spindly farmhouse, Edward Fu's sprawling home radiated sophistication and wealth. Glass, laminate, and polished wood gleamed against walls painted crimson and cream.

Tank nodded toward a bench. "Leave your shoes at the door."

He, on the other hand, kept his shoes on his feet.

As we walked through the house, I made note of the throw rugs and furniture I should avoid if we needed to flee and the statues and lamps I could wield if we were forced into a fight. A downward strike to the base of the neck with Edward Fu's silver goddess, for example, would drop most men to the floor.

Most.

Probably not the linebacker guarding the doorway at the end of the hall.

Although too small for the NFL, he could have tucked Qiang's granddaughter under one arm like a football and carried her for miles. The man would have seemed like a giant to little Yong.

Uncle marched forward and stopped inches from the man's chest. The giant's bulk looked flabby compared to Uncle's sinewy physique.

A gravelly voice called from inside. "Let them pass."

Edward Fu – sixties, with graying hair and oily skin – remained behind his desk. He focused on Uncle, but did not look at me. "Come in, Mr. Chang. Have a seat."

As Uncle sat in the cushioned chair, I stood off his shoulder as I had done when we met with the Scorpion Triad's leader in Hong Kong. Fu acknowledged this arrangement with a nod.

A man stepped out of the corner. A scar pulled the side of his mouth as Yong had described. The knife sheathed at his waist made me long for the karambit I had left in Los Angeles.

The crime boss leaned back in his chair. "What brings you to my home unannounced?"

"My brother, Chang Qiang."

Fu examined Uncle's face. "Not much family resemblance."

"He's led a harder life than me."

"Ha. Don't be humble. I remember you, Chang Lee. But harder is not the same as rougher. Is it?"

Uncle inclined his head.

Fu switched to English. "Are you here to pay your brother's debt?"

The Scorpion triad leader had also conducted their meeting in English. Had Fu, like him, chosen a language his men wouldn't understand? Or was he treating Uncle like a foreigner because he had moved away from Shanghai?

"That depends," Uncle said. "How much does he owe?"

"Two hundred thousand yuan."

"Hmm. That's a lot of money."

Fu shrugged. "About thirty-one thousand US. Not much in America, but two year's profit for your brother in Chongming. He should have relocated to a non-rural apartment like his neighbors. Instead, he leased more land and followed the trends. Organic farming is costly. So is living on crop-growing land."

Uncle nodded. "Qiang has always walked his own path. But his decisions affect more people than him. It would bother me greatly if his granddaughter was harmed."

The crime boss tensed at the undefined threat. "Be careful, Chang Lee. You are not the Scorpion's enforcer anymore."

Uncle smiled. "And yet I found you."

The guard with the scarred mouth shifted his stance.

I did the same.

Fu held out his hands to calm us both.

"Do I look like I'm hiding? Everyone knows where I live. But no one is stupid enough to threaten me in my home."

He leaned forward. "Unless you brought money, you and your girl should get on your bicycles and pedal back to Shanghai."

Uncle scraped his chair on the floor as he stood. "Remember what I said."

Fu fluttered his fingers across his face. "Already forgotten like a passing flock of birds."

Chapter Fourteen

"What the hell was that?" I said as we road down the lane.

"A shot across the bow." Uncle chuckled. "Isn't that what they say in the movies?"

"You've become too American for your own good."

He inclined his head. "I believe Edward Fu would agree."

"What now?"

"Another talk with my brother. This time, for the truth."

"Will you pay his debt?"

"It's more complicated than that. If Fu kidnapped Chyou and I pay to get her back, what will he do the next time Qiang is late on a payment? It might be smarter to rescue her on our own."

We turned onto a dirt road and cut through an orchard. Although the peach trees were bare, the enveloping green bathed me in peace. A welcome break in a tense and hectic day. As the stress eased from Uncle's shoulders, he slowed his pace to a leisurely ride, giving me the opportunity to voice a question I'd wanted to ask since Hong Kong.

"Does my father know you speak English this well?"

He snorted with amusement. "It's not that complicated to talk about food."

"You talk about more than that. You've been friends my whole life."

"I work in his kitchen."

"As his second in command."

"In charge of noodles and duck." He waved his hand in the air. "Okay, fine. I'm his head cook. Big deal. He has never fought at my side like you."

I pedaled in silence as I considered the magnitude of his words.

Three weeks ago in Los Angeles, Uncle had treated me like an ungrateful child and launched cooking chopsticks at my face to keep me alert. Everything changed when we fought together in Hong Kong. What would our relationship be like when we return to my father's kitchen in LA?

Uncle turned a corner into a new orchard, zigzagging our way back to his brother's farm.

I inhaled the sweet scent of ripe tangerines. "I understand why your brother farms out here. Close to the city. Beautiful country. Sustainable living. It makes a lot of sense."

"Ha. He moved to Chongming to preserve his hukuo benefits."

"What are those?"

"Healthcare, housing, higher education. Government assistance is tied to residency. Urban hukuo is more valuable than rural. Shanghai has the best. If he had returned to the Anhui countryside where he had slaved as a teenager, married his sweetheart, and leased his own farm, he would have sacrificed the most valuable hukuo in China for a peasant's status."

I gestured to the trees. "It's rural here."

"But Qiang's residency is connected to our childhood home. As long as he pays into the system, he benefits from an urban hukuo."

"So, he married Jun in Anhui Province and brought her here to live?"

"No. He sent his sweetheart a farewell postcard and started a new life."

"Ouch."

Uncle shrugged. "Another brick of bitterness to add to the wall."

We turned onto another dirt road, stepping our way through the orchards to the main road that would return us to Qiang. Lost in our thoughts and the tranquility of the country, we didn't register the rumble of tires on earth until the electric motor scooters broke through the trees.

They cut us off from the front and the back, then circled around so we couldn't escape. Scar Mouth and Giant remained on their bikes. Tank and K-Pop plus another two men advanced. Six against two, all of them armed with knives or batons. In different circumstances, we might have held the center and fought our ambushers back-to-back. Or we might have forced them into a line and taken them one by one. Instead, we leapt from our bicycles, rolled them into the men, and attacked.

As K-Pop floundered with my mountain bike, the new man with dead gray eyes swiped at me with a metal baton.

I rotated inside the arc, blocked his forearm, and chopped the side of his neck with an upturned Ura Shuto strike. Sliding my blocking arm to the outside of his, I snagged his elbow in a Musha Dori lock and dragged Dead Eyes backward with his baton arm bent by his ear. Brought lower than me with his body at a slant, I hammered his sternum with the full force of my weight. Air whooshed from his lungs, first from my fist and again when the ground struck his back.

One guy down. Another five to go.

Having freed himself from my bike, K-Pop attacked with a round kick to my head. I ducked his foot and snatched the fallen man's baton. As I rose, K-Pop continued his motion with a spinning heel kick to my face. With no time to think and only a second before impact, my body did what Sensei had trained me to do – I moved to a position of safety and struck his hamstring with the baton. The trigger point stunned his entire leg and stole the power from his kick. As the leg floundered, I swept the baton downward and broke his supporting knee. The young man crumpled to the ground like a string-less marionette.

Two down. Four to go.

As Uncle fought Tank and a guy with snakes inked up his arms, the Chongming King's personal guards advanced toward me.

Giant had the muscle. Scar Mouth had a knife. I had a metal baton christened on K-Pop's knee. Although two to one, I felt okay about the odds.

Until Giant unsheathed the freaking machete strapped to his back.

Scar Mouth laughed, his grin more hideous than before.

I fueled my resolve with Sensei's words.

A weapon is only a tool, Lily-chan. It's the person who wins the fight.

No way in *hell* would I let a machete-wielding thug or this nasty excuse of a human end my time on this Earth.

I jumped to the side as the machete breezed past my head and placed the smaller man between us as a shield – which would have worked nicely if Scar Mouth hadn't slashed my arm with his knife along the way.

I ignored the cut and snapped the baton against his wrist as he came at me again. He retracted so fast it slid off his arm.

Then he lunged and stabbed at my gut. The blade missed by a hair as I threw back my foot. I slammed the metal down on his arm, but the guy kept coming, shoving me backwards with every murderous attempt. It was only a matter of time before his blade struck home.

I needed to stop defending and attack.

The next time he thrust, I captured his wrist, slipped the baton under his elbow, and yanked his locked arm and knife hand against my chest and hip.

A knee to his inner thigh knocked back his legs.

A second knee to his groin stunned him with pain.

A forehead smash to his face rushed blood from his nose and blinded him with tears.

I had assaulted his base, mind, and sight with three quick strikes. Then I jolted his locked elbow and felt his knife slide down my leg. When I cracked the baton against the side of his head, Scar Mouth lost consciousness and collapsed on the ground.

My sigh of relief was cut short as the machete-wielding giant attacked. If I hadn't inverted the baton and shifted slightly off line, he would have cleaved through my clavicle as easily as Uncle chopped duck.

Strength mattered. This man had considerably more of it than me.

I leaped back to disengage from the fight as another butchering strike sailed toward my neck. Without time to maneuver, I dropped to the ground, delivering a crippling shot to his knee with my baton as I rolled out of the way.

Yards down the road, Uncle fought unarmed against Snake's knife and Tank's metal pipe. Although the gangsters looked bloody and bruised, Uncle's energy was fading. He'd last another minute at best.

With Giant temporarily disabled, I flew to Uncle's aid with a double side kick aimed at Snake's chest. As Snake stumbled off the road, I battered Tank's wrists and knees with my baton, then tripped him backward into a ditch.

I hurried to Uncle and handed him the baton so he'd have a weapon in the fight. "You okay?"

"Yes." He eyed the knife gash on my arm. "And you?"

"Hundred percent."

The lies would have been easier to swallow if all six ambushers hadn't regrouped to attack.

Chapter Fifteen

Faced with seemingly insurmountable odds, I called upon Kuji energy to rekindle my fire and help even the score. Considered folk magic by some and superstition by others, the esoteric practice had deep spiritual and historical roots.

Sensei had introduced me to all nine mudra and mantra over the years. The ritualistic hand positions and phrases, which he had taught in Japanese, had accompanied lessons, meditations, and philosophical talks. I had learned to heal myself with Sha, raise my awareness with Jin, and direct my internal and external energy with Pyo. At this moment, I folded my fingers into the Kongorin seal of the thunderbolt mudra and recited the corresponding Rin mantra to channel my power and intent. Then I followed the mantra with a prayer of my own.

Fuel my humble heart. Strengthen my resolve.

I unfolded my mudra, sliced the air with two fingers in nine decisive Kuji-kiri cuts, and recited the nine syllables that would call the warrior deities to assemble with me and fight.

Meanwhile, the Chongming gang fanned in front of us and to the sides. All had sustained injuries. Each was more cautious than before.

I lowered my hands and stepped away from Uncle, giving

us room to maneuver and defend. Regardless of the odds, we had to succeed. Too many people depended on us in Shanghai and Los Angeles for us to fail.

"*This* is friendship," Uncle said, then braced himself to fight.

Before the Chongming gang could launch a unified attack, a sleek electric motorcycle raced through the trees. Silent as a ninja, the rider jumped his bike onto the road and plowed into the biggest target of the group.

Giant buckled.

The machete flew from his hand.

Men scattered.

The rider swerved as the blade flipped, end over end, then snatched the handle as it fell.

"Who's that?" I yelled.

"Who cares?" Uncle answered, and ran into the fray.

The dark angel had bought us another chance to win.

As our unknown friend scattered the gang, the man with snake tattoos ran toward me. I had knocked him away from Uncle with a rib-breaking kick. Now, I stopped him with a perfectly-structured forearm to his chest. He rammed into the obstacle like a train into a piling, doubling the impact, and slamming himself to the ground. Before I could finish him off, our dark angel drove onto his chest.

As Snake struggled to breathe beneath the front tire of the bike, the rider flipped up his visor and focused his cruel, dark eyes on me. Only a moment passed before he snapped it back down. Long enough to send a chill down my spine.

Our dark angel was the assassin J Tran.

He rode over Snake, skidded in the dirt, and charged at the gang. Instead of attacking or disarming their weapons, he veered toward their motorcycles parked along the road.

He circled the machete like a polo player and slashed open their tires.

Taking advantage of the distraction, I descended on K-Pop, who, despite his broken knee, was still determined to fight. With a hobbled gait, he swiped at me with a knife. On his second attempt, I intercepted his hand with a trapping crescent kick and drove it and the knife into the ground. I picked up the blade, crushed his metacarpal bones with my heel, then kicked him into Tank.

I yelled in Mandarin for them to go and nodded at Snake, moaning in the dirt, Tran's tire mark over his chest. "Take him with you. And don't bother us again."

Dead Eyes and Tank grabbed K-Pop under the arms. Giant yanked Snake off the ground. Scar Mouth waited on the road as his gang left their slashed motor scooters and limped into the trees. "Mr. Fu will hear about this. You have made a great enemy this day."

"You came after us," Uncle said. "This aggression, I will not forgive."

The man's scarred mouth pulled into an ugly grin. "Until we meet again, Red Pole Chang."

My battle tension eased as the gang hobbled out of sight. "That went well."

Uncle scoffed. "Only thanks to our new friend."

Tran took off his helmet and released waves of dark hair. His half Vietnamese and half whatever dark ethnicity he had gained from his G.I. Joe father had synergized into a stunningly exotic man with chiseled features, intense black eyes, and peaked brows that made him appear both sinister and amused. A black muscle tee, pants, jacket, and boots completed the look as he straddled the ninja-style motor scooter. I choked out a laugh. Even in farm country, J Tran exuded the coolest of cools.

He smirked at me and winked. "Hello, K."

"What are you doing here, J?"

"You know him?" Uncle asked.

"Yep."

"You trust him?"

"Nope."

Tran laughed as he planted his helmet on the tank of his bike, kicked a leg over the back, and glided toward us with panther-like grace. He stopped a sword's distance away and, as always, stood perfectly still.

"Why are you here, Tran?"

He glanced at my bleeding arm. "Joining the fun."

"I don't mean in this orchard. Why are you in Shanghai? And for that matter, why were you in Hong Kong? Have you been following me? Did you even leave Los Angeles when you said you would?"

"Why would I lie?"

"Because you're a very bad man."

His chuckle rumbled places in my body I did not want to feel.

"I don't lie, Lily."

"Right. You only kill."

He shrugged as if to say he wasn't alone in that. Together we had left a hefty body count back home. *My* home. I had no idea where Tran actually lived. Was he a Chinese national? Could foreigners rent motorcycles without a permit in Shanghai?

He followed my gaze. "I borrowed it from a friend."

"Really."

He clicked his tongue in disappointment. "You don't believe me."

"No."

"Which part? Borrowing or friends?"

"Either. *Both.*"

He laughed again. "I have friends all over the world who are happy to repay their debt to me."

I didn't want to know the favors – or jobs – he had done in Shanghai or anywhere else in the world. It was bad enough knowing the death he had delivered in Los Angeles while helping me.

Uncle stepped forward, baton gripped in his fist. "I pay my debts."

Tran nodded and raised an inquiring brow at me. "How about you, Lily Wong?"

I sneered. "Put it on my tab."

He burst into deep, throaty laughter, the kind you'd hear in a bar.

I checked the trees for signs of the gang.

Uncle headed for our bikes.

I lingered with Tran, too filled with conflicting emotions to speak yet incapable of simply walking away.

"Let me help you, Lily."

I knew he could. But at what cost?

My heart raced as I remembered the acrid bite of gunfire in the air, the horrified expression on the innocent gang groupie's face, the blood seeping through her towel after Tran shot her in the chest. If I had shot him first, she would still be alive. But how many others, my family included, would be dead? Tran had saved my life. In return, I had spared his. Deed for deed. Another indebted friend.

Chapter Sixteen

We stopped at a grocery shack with a picnic table by the side of a canal where I brought out the first aid kit I carried in my pack. After washing off the blood with the water from my pouch, I disinfected and glued the slash on my arm. I did the same for the cuts on Uncle's shoulder and cheek. Feeling more presentable, we left Tran to watch his motorcycle and our rideshare bikes while Uncle and I bought tea eggs, sweet potatoes, and bottled water for lunch.

I unwrapped my egg and admired the tea-stained designs that had seeped through the cracks. The shop owners had partially boiled the eggs, cracked the shells, and soaked these beauties in a spiced brew of black tea. The Shaoxing rice wine and soy gave it a gorgeous color and an inviting scent. I bit into the egg and showed it to Uncle.

"They made the yolk soft like yours."

He nodded with approval. "The trick is to soak the eggs overnight instead of boiling them a second time."

Tran peeled open his sweet potato and revealed the purple flesh. "You cook for her father's restaurant?"

Uncle frowned my way. "How much does he know about you?"

"More than I'd like."

He eyed the assassin and stuffed the entire egg into his mouth.

Tran shrugged. "I asked out of courtesy. I know all about Red Pole Chang."

"Then tell me about you," Uncle said, his mouth full of egg. "Lily called you a killer. Out of fun or for hire?"

"Hire. Mostly. Never for fun."

"American?"

"Depends."

"On what?"

"Convenience."

Uncle wiped his mouth. "Why are you here? And what do you want?"

"To help."

"Help is the means. What do you want from *Lily?*"

Tran stared into my eyes with the same uncomfortable fascination he had shown in Los Angeles. Then he looked back at Uncle and stuffed the entire sweet potato into his mouth.

"Enough with the micro aggressions," I said. "Do you know anything about Lee's missing grandniece?"

Tran shrugged and continued to chew.

"What? Too busy following me to check it out? I saw you on the overpass last night. You know what...never mind. I'll just spell out the facts so you can catch up on what's actually important." I gestured toward Uncle. "His twelve-year-old grandniece was allegedly abducted from her family home, a three-story farmhouse shared by Lee's brother, sister-in-law, nephew, nephew's wife, and two young boys."

Tran swallowed the potato. "Allegedly?"

"The boys think she might have run off with friends."

Tran looked at Uncle. "What do you think?"

"She was taken."

"By whom?"

"I don't know."

"No one has claimed credit," I said. "But the family is in turmoil. Qiang resents Lee for things done in the past and believes his granddaughter was kidnapped by the Scorpion Black Society because of trouble Lee caused while helping me in Hong Kong. Lee believes the Chongming gang has abducted the girl as collateral against Qiang's outstanding debt from a loan he took out for his farm."

I leaned across the table toward Tran. "Can you help with any of this?"

He finished his water and rose from the bench.

"You're leaving?"

He placed his egg in front of me. "I'll be in touch."

"You said you wanted to help."

He put on his helmet and straddled the bike. "Eat your egg, Lily. You're looking a bit thin." Then he flipped down the visor and left.

Unbelievable.

"You see how he is, Uncle? Infuriating."

I picked up the egg and shook it. "And I am not looking *a bit thin*. He's needling me about my taste in food to remind me about our *sushi date*."

I bit the egg in two, wanting to bite off Tran's head. "Rides in through a freaking orchard like a knight on a steed. Who does that?"

Uncle leaned back as I spewed egg from my mouth. "Acting all noble and shit. He's not a hero. He's a cold-blooded assassin."

I stuffed the last of the egg in my mouth and masticated it to death.

Uncle just watched.

"What?"

He shrugged.

"Are you comparing him to Daniel Kwok? Well, don't. Tran is not another example of my poor taste in men. In fact, I don't think of Tran as a man at all. He's a monster. An arrogant psychopath who manipulates everyone for his own gain. We are not alike. There's nothing between us, no matter what he thinks."

Uncle chewed his potato and swallowed.

"You have something to say? Say it."

He folded up his trash, as closed mouthed as a North Dakota farmer on a frigid January day.

"Ugh. You're worse than Baba." I cleaned up my mess, dumped it in the garbage, and returned to the business at hand. "We have a girl to find. Where's the nearest school?"

Uncle frowned. "It's Sunday."

"I know what day it is. I want to ride her route home. If Chyou's brothers are right about her running off with friends, we might find a clue on the way."

"Or find Chyou lying in a ditch?"

"I didn't say that."

"You didn't need to. It's written on your face."

He searched the app on his phone and pointed to the map. "There are three middle schools the same distance from Qiang's home. All in different directions. Two urban areas. One rural."

I sighed. Each school had multiple routes from the farmhouse. Each were too far for a twelve-year-old girl to bike. If she *had* run away, she could have left the island by now and vanished among the twenty-six million people in Shanghai.

"What do you suggest?" I said.

"We go back to Qiang." Which might have been a good idea if Uncle's phone hadn't chimed.

He answered in Mandarin, then promptly switched to Shanghainese, face tense with impatience, annoyance, and – eventually – resignation. With a final comment, he ended the call.

"Is everything okay?"

He rolled his eyes, too angry to speak.

"Your brother?"

"My sister."

"The one who's taking in your mom?"

"The one who is *supposed* to take in my mother."

"What happened?"

"Her husband is grumbling. Meimei is worried that if we don't move Uma into her house soon, he'll change his mind. I must attend to this immediately. Qiang will have to wait."

Chapter Seventeen

Hydrated and recovered from our fight with the gang, Uncle and I pedaled back to the dock twice as fast as before, turned in the bikes, and hopped onto the first ferry back to Pudong. He called for a ride, and we headed across the Huangpu River back to Puxi, the cultural, residential, and commercial center of Shanghai.

The massive scope of this city hit me again as we sped across elevated highways past endless apartment blocks, skyscrapers, and overlapping roads. So many bodies to house and to move. So many people struggling to survive.

My phone's vibration interrupted my thoughts.

Since I hadn't paid for an international phone plan or set up a VPN to access Google, Facebook, and other non-Chinese apps, the vibration had to be signaling a WeChat message from Baba or Ma. At eleven thirty at night in Los Angeles, my money was on Ma, whose sleep schedule would still be disrupted by her time in Hong Kong.

Ma: *Your father's in the hospital. Please call.*

"Oh my God."

"Everything okay?" Uncle asked.

I hit the video icon. "Something's happened to Baba."

Ma answered my call, bundled in her robe on the couch

in the dark. Her voice sounded quiet and small, like a mouse afraid to be heard. "Hello, Lily."

I quieted my voice to match hers. "Hey, Ma. You okay?"

"Mmm..."

"Wanna turn on a light?"

"Not really. I look like hell."

"Okay... What happened to Baba?"

"He collapsed in the kitchen again."

"At the restaurant?"

"Where else? Slaving over those damn woks."

First *hell*, now *damn*? It was never a good sign when my proper mother swore.

"Did he hit his head?" When he'd fallen last week, it had taken twelve stitches to seal up the wound.

"No, thank God. He's blaming it on dehydration – again."

"They kept him overnight?"

"Yes. The doctors wanted to run some tests before they let him go. He argued, of course."

"Let me guess. He regaled them with stories about growing up on a farm, healthy as an ox, trudging through the snow, never sick a day in his life."

Ma chuckled. "Something like that." She snuggled deeper into her robe. "He closed the restaurant."

I nodded. With his head cook sitting next to me in a car in Shanghai, Baba didn't have anyone capable enough to manage the kitchen and prepare the main dishes. But Ma didn't care about that. Wong's Hong Kong Inn was my father's passion, not hers. What bothered my mother was why. Baba had only shut down the restaurant two times before: once last week when he split open his head and seven years ago when my younger sister was murdered.

"I'm sorry, Ma."

"For what?"

I paused, full of regret. "For not being there."

For you or for Rose.

She shook her head. "I'm fine, Lily. I just wanted you to know." She attempted a smile. "The photos you sent were beautiful. It's good to see you having fun."

I forced a smile and ignored the throbbing knife wound on my arm. "Get some sleep, Ma."

"I will."

"I love you."

"I love you too."

I ended the call and stared at my phone.

"Is Vern all right?" Uncle asked.

I shrugged. "Did he seem different to you before you left?"

"Different how?"

"I don't know. Weaker. Sick?"

"Ha. He'd never show it. Your father is too proud."

"Don't I know it. Remember when he sliced his wrist with the box cutter?"

"How could I forget? Blood spurted from him like water from a hose. Hit me all the way across the kitchen. Took me an hour to clean up that mess. Stubborn man. Wouldn't go to the hospital until the dinner rush ended. Good thing we had Brett to tie up his wound."

Brett had fought in the First Gulf War. He said washing dishes calmed his mind. He also said he hadn't seen that much blood since fighting in Iraq.

"Your father will be fine, Lily. Besides, there's nothing you can do."

I nodded in agreement and pocketed my phone. Not only would worrying about Baba not help him or Ma, it would distract me from helping Uncle and his family. I needed to choose. Either I wasted my energy over things I could not change. Or I applied my efforts to the things that I could.

Chapter Eighteen

After an hour spent arguing with Lee's relatives and cajoling his mother to pack, we gave up and took care of it ourselves. We bagged and boxed her favorite possessions – or so we hoped – and carted them in a wheelbarrow to a rideshare van parked on a larger lane. As we walked Lee's mother away from her home for the final time, she pointed to the bricked-up houses we passed and told stories about each. I didn't need to understand the language to appreciate her sorrow. The picked-over carcass of her neighborhood said it all.

I clapped the dust from my hands. Uma had made us clear the left-behind artifacts in our path: former treasures deemed too bulky, broken, or pointless for her neighbors to keep.

"Were the lanes this messed up yesterday when we rode through on our bikes?"

"Not this bad. But things change fast in China. Especially in Shanghai."

"Funny. I think of China as traditional and slow."

"That's because you didn't live through the Cultural Revolution. The Red Army's favorite slogan was 'Destroy the old and establish the new.' In two weeks, the government will plow this neighborhood to the ground. A month after that, no one other than locals will ever guess it was here."

"I'm sorry."

He shrugged. "Life is change." He repeated the statement in Mandarin and again in Shanghainese.

Life is change.

One of Sensei's bits of wisdom as well.

Uncle's mother didn't agree. She scolded him vehemently as tears rolled down her face.

"What is she saying?"

"How bad of a son I am to drag her from her home. How my sister's husband will torture her in their house. How I will forget about her when I return to America."

He helped Uma into her seat and closed the door on her old way of life. We loaded her possessions in the back and left the wheelbarrow in the lane.

"There is nothing else I can do. She won't leave Shanghai. Meimei is the only one who can care for her in a quality home."

The old woman wailed as we drove her away from the river toward an unfamiliar future.

Had Uncle's mother ever left this district? Had she ever ridden the Yan'an Elevated Road or visited the Former French Concession where her son owned property? From her frantic energy as she searched through the rear window for landmarks she knew, I feared she had never traveled farther than she could walk.

When we finally exited the elevated road and took an expressway back to surface streets, Uncle's poor mother had cried herself mute. The gated offices and apartment complexes didn't look inviting to me. I could only imagine how unfriendly they seemed to her.

"Does you sister live near here?"

"Very close. Trust me. The area is nicer than it looks."

A few blocks later, we turned onto a smaller road with townhouse complexes and a cluster of colonial-era villas. White pillars and balcony balustrades peeked through the trees. As the driver pulled into the central courtyard, Uncle called his sister on the phone to let her know we had arrived. We unpacked the van while his mother sulked in her seat.

A woman in her late fifties hurried out of a metal garden gate. She yelled a greeting in Mandarin and waved her soft arms, her bland face flushed by the excitement of our arrival. She had her mother's gentle features – not the angular bone structure that made her brothers look severe – and childlike exuberance that overwhelmed Uncle before he could retreat.

"Okay, okay," he said. "We've said hello, Meimei. Now please get Uma out of the car."

Meimei waved through the open door. "Hi, Uma." Then she glanced at me.

"I'm Lily," I said in Mandarin. "Lee's friend from Los Angeles."

"Oh. My brother didn't mention a *friend*."

Uncle rolled his eyes. "Lily's younger than your step-daughter."

"So? Men are always interested in younger women. Look at my husband and me."

"Speaking of your husband, what's this about him changing his mind. Is our mother welcome here or not?"

"Sure, sure. We just need to move her in before he comes home."

She leaned into the car and pulled her mother's arm. "Come on, Uma. I can't wait to show you your beautiful room."

I grabbed several garbage bags of clothing and towels and

followed the women up the path to a quaint New Orleans-style home. Instead of the bayou, the rounded balcony and pillared porch overlooked a small yard closed in by a wooden fence, shrubs, and trees. Neighboring villas pressed in on all sides.

Meimei led her mother into the entryway. "See how bright and new it is?" She pointed to the marble floors. "No more rotted wood to catch your feet." She gestured through the windows. "You can look at the garden whenever you want." She pointed to the open kitchen and dining area, designated from the living room by white tile lines on the floor. "You can eat your morning porridge and watch the birds. Won't that be nice?"

"Where do I hang my pots?"

"Don't be silly, Uma. We have everything you need stored in the cupboards. Come upstairs and see your room."

Uncle carried in the remainder of his mother's belonging and stacked the ratty boxes on the polished floor beside me. "What do you think?"

I took in the showroom furniture and design. "Have you been here before?"

"Not inside."

"Will she be safe on the marble steps?"

He shrugged and picked up a box. "Let's move this to her room before Meimei's husband comes home."

Although grand in style, the villa had a minimal footprint, with only two tiny bedrooms and a main suite at the end of the hall. We found Meimei and her mother in the first room, decorated with the keepsakes of a teenage girl.

"This was our daughter's room. She graduated from University of Science and Technology in Hefei. She has an important position at a chemical company near there. Isn't that impressive, Uma?"

Her mother opened a crowded closet and frowned.

Meimei closed the door. "Don't worry, Uma. I will pack up her things and make room for yours. Come and see the rest of my house."

I set the garbage bags full of the old woman's clothing on the bed and whispered to Uncle as he set down the box. "Are you sure this is going to work?"

"We have no other choice."

We followed Meimei past her husband's cozy den into a bedroom suite with French doors opened onto the rounded balcony with a table and chairs. Trees and rooftops blocked the city view except for the high-rises jutting behind.

Meimei patted her mother's arm. "See how well I live? You should have come sooner. When I asked before." Sadness dampened the cheeriness of her tone.

Her mother responded in Shanghainese and slumped back to her cluttered room.

Uncle watched her go, then snapped at his sister in English. "Why didn't you make room for her?"

"No time."

"Don't lie to me."

She started to argue in Shanghainese but Lee stopped her and glanced toward me.

His sister sulked. "My English is not good like you or Qiang."

"Then lower your voice and speak in Mandarin so Lily can understand. Why didn't you make space for Uma?"

"Our daughter moved out of her apartment in Hefei last week."

"So what?"

"Her roommates thought she might come home."

"And where would you put our mother? In your

daughter's closet?"

"Of course not. They could sleep together like she used to do with me."

"Don't be silly. Uma doesn't know Suyin. Why would you make them share a bed?"

Meimei sniffed. "Because I want my daughter and my mother to know each other. I miss them both. My daughter is so busy. We used to video chat every night. We haven't talked in a week."

A man called in Mandarin from downstairs. "Qizi. Why are these dirty boxes on our floor?"

Meimei shoved us out of her bedroom and hurried down the hall.

Uncle grabbed her arm. "Stay with Uma. I'll bring the boxes upstairs."

"What will you say to my husband?"

"Nothing."

"Nothing?"

"Go."

As Uncle dealt with the husband, Meimei and I stashed her daughter's old belongings under the bed and stuffed the garbage bags of Uma's possessions into the closet. The old woman remained on the bed and pretended to sleep. Stern voices carried up the stairs. A moment later, Uncle brought in the boxes and stacked them in the corner.

"Did he ask who you were?" Meimei whispered.

"He assumed. What did you tell him about me?"

"Nothing. Why do you ask?"

"The mixture of distaste and fear in his eyes."

She waved it away. "That's just his face. Come downstairs. I'll fix tea."

She kissed her mother's cheek and whispered soothing

words in Shanghainese. I heard longing and loneliness in Meimei's voice. When I saw her husband, decades older without a spark of joy on his face, I understood why.

Meimei brightened her disposition and called out to her husband as we came down the stairs. "How was your visit with friends?"

"Like always."

"Did you meet my brother Lee?"

He nodded and averted his gaze.

Although not quite as old as my grandfather in Hong Kong, Meimei's husband and former boss had a similar condescending air. Retired banker, perhaps? Whatever he was, he still treated his wife like an employee.

"This is his friend from Los Angeles. Lily, this is my husband, Feng Honghui."

He nodded curtly to me and responded to her. "It takes both of them to move your mother into my house?"

"I'm just here to help, Mr. Feng."

He ignored me and kept looking at her. "So, *Qizi*." He punctuated her name to silence me. "Is your mother settled in my house?"

"Yeah, yeah. She's napping like a child."

He sighed in resignation and walked across the room.

As Meimei followed him to the stairs, I leaned toward Uncle. "What's your sister's name?"

"Huh?"

"Her name. You call her Younger Sister. He calls her Wife. What is her actual name?"

Uncle looked genuinely confused.

"You don't know?"

"I haven't heard it spoken since she was a child in school, and that was only for one year."

"One year?"

"I graduated from middle school and joined the Scorpions the year after Mao Zedong restarted China's education. Don't worry. It doesn't matter. Everyone in the family calls her Meimei. You should too."

But it did matter.

Uncle's sister only existed in relationship to others. She had no identity of her own. No wonder she hungered to have her mother and daughter living under her roof. Without them, she was only her former boss' wife.

Chapter Nineteen

Constellations of light whizzed past my window as we sped across Yan'an Elevated Road back to Uncle's apartment in the Former French Concession. Red, yellow, white, and green mixed with the Space Mountain blue illuminating the underside of the highway and cast the FFC in the familiar purplish hue. When we descended onto the streets and drove away from the retail zone, the brilliance grew more intimate with smaller shop signs and twinkling trees. That said, even the darkest alleys and shikumen lanes were illuminated by Shanghai's urban glow. The apartment complexes on Uncle's boulevard shone most brightly of all.

As I stepped out of the rideshare car, WeChat pinged with a message from someone asking to connect. The profile photo showed Will Smith in his *Men in Black* suit, smirking behind impenetrable shades.

J: *Meet me at The Center.*

Me: *When?*

J: *Now.*

I looked at Uncle. "Is there a place called The Center near here?"

He pointed across the avenue at a plaza with a tall building, benches, and trees. "Why do you ask?"

"Tran wants to meet."

"Now?"

"He must have been waiting for us to return."

As we crossed the boulevard to the plaza, Tran emerged from behind a pillar. Unlike us, he was dressed for the night in a custom-fit leather jacket the same dark hickory color as his hair. I crossed my bare arms against the evening chill. Although Shanghai had a similar latitude to Los Angeles, the high air pressure from Siberia made the September night feel cooler than home.

Tran's eyes glinted in the lamplight. "You look chilly, K. Would you like my jacket to keep you warm?"

"Hard pass, J. But thanks for asking."

And thanks for planting the thought in my mind, you sly bastard.

He smiled mischievously as if he knew I was imagining his body-warmed leather against my skin. As if I could smell the intoxicating scent of *him*.

Uncle huffed at me and glared at Tran. "Enough about the weather. What did you learn about Chyou?"

Tran strolled across the lighted glass tiles in the pavement, speaking in a chatty tone as if out with friends. "You have an interesting family, Chang Lee. Such a full history. So many skeletons. Even more enemies."

"Are you suggesting that my grandniece was taken because of me?"

Tran shrugged. "People don't like your brother much either."

"What people?"

"Neighbors. Farmers. The Chongming King." Tran held out his hands to forestall Uncle's remarks. "I know. You knew all of this before. But you and your brother aren't the only ones making enemies. The Chang family has been pissing off the wrong people since your grandfather started idolizing Chiang Kai-shek."

Tran turned to me. "The general enlisted the notorious Green Gang to purge the Communists from Shanghai. They massacred thousands in what became known as the White Terror purge. Apparently, some of the officials still hold a grudge."

Uncle snorted. "That was a long time ago. My grandfather never joined the Green Gang."

"Only because your *great*-grandfather forbade it. If your grandfather *had* joined, he could have paved your way into Shanghai's criminal history. Lucky for you, his sister's marriage paved your way instead."

"What does my grandaunt have to do with this?"

"Maybe nothing. Maybe a lot." Tran turned to me. "When Chiang Kai-shek fled to Taiwan, he encouraged the three leaders of the Green Gang not to do business with the Japanese or to facilitate their invasion. Huang and Big-Ear Du, who would later become grandmaster, complied. Zhang did not. The traitorous thug collaborated with the Japanese during the invasion."

Tran stopped strolling and looked at Uncle. "Was your family scandalized when your grandaunt married a member of Zhang's traitorous new gang? Or did they benefit from his Japanese connections?"

Uncle clenched his teeth.

"Your grandaunt must have gained a few perks when her husband was martyred trying to prevent Zhang's assassination. What a shame your cousin Chester didn't inherit his grandfather's entrepreneurial spunk. He and his parents could have been living the high life in Japan instead of freeloading on your couch."

"How did you learn all of this?"

Tran grinned. "Your elderly cousin is a chatty woman with an appetite for sweets."

I grabbed Uncle's arm before he could swing. Although a skilled fighter with dozens of kills under his belt, the former Scorpion enforcer was no match for a trained assassin in his prime.

Uncle shook his arm from my grip and glared at Tran. "Did you learn anything useful that will help us find Chyou? Or did you spend the afternoon eating cake?"

Tran chuckled. "I did more than that, old man. Apparently, your grandaunt wasn't the only member of your family who made questionable choices and alliances. Her brother – your grandfather – was quite vocal against the Communist Party. As I mentioned, certain government officials hold grudges against Kuomintang sympathizers. Guess whose family is on their list?"

"Ha. You found the name Chang on a list? *Chang*. How could you possibly know that was us?"

"Because it listed your family address on Qiaojia Road. Not only did your grandfather idolize Chiang Kai-shek, I think he also had puppy-dog eyes for Big-Ear Du. Why else would he have followed the Green Gang leader all the way to Hong Kong?"

Uncle spat. "Over a million people fled from the mainland during the Civil War. Why would anyone still care about him?"

"I wondered the same thing." Tran resumed his stroll. "Did you know your grandfather caused trouble for your relatives in Shanghai when he moved his wife and son to Hong Kong? He made the move with his Kuomintang-sympathizer friend, his wife, and their young daughter. Do you think he and his friend pledged their children to marry each other in advance? Or did they let your parents fall in love on their own? Either way, the families doubled down on their political beliefs. Another bad alliance for the Changs."

"That's enough," I said. "Make your point and stop bullying my friend."

"Bullying?" Tran laughed. "Do you feel *bullied*, Red Pole Chang?"

Uncle froze in the lamplight glow, eyes full of hatred, body tensed to fight. "This is my city, not yours. Make your point or get on a plane."

I looked from triad to assassin, gaging who would strike first and whether I should risk my life to intervene. Never had I encountered two more deadly opponents. I needed to reset this conversation without drawing fire onto me.

"Hey...we've all had a long and illuminating day. Maybe we should call it quits for the night and regroup in the morning."

"No." Uncle glared. "I want to hear what else this *bastard* has to say."

Tran flinched at the word.

I shook my head, letting him know I had not shared his anything about his past.

Satisfied, he turned back to Uncle. "You say this is your city, but you haven't lived here in twenty-four years. There could be alliances, debts, and grudges of which you are unaware. You and your father were Scorpions. Your grandfather was KMT. Your grandaunt married a former Green Gang leader who sold out his people and collaborated with the Japanese. Your family name is on a city government watch list. I learned all of this in one afternoon. What will I discover about you and your family tomorrow?"

Uncle's phone chimed. He swiped to ignore. A moment later, it chimed again.

"Family?" I asked.

"Meimei. I need to take this. It could be my mother."

Uncle stepped aside for a private conversation.

I smacked Tran's arm. "What the hell?"

"You asked for my help. I reported what I found."

"You intentionally antagonized him. Why?"

"Come on, K–"

"And stop calling me K. I gave you that name as a joke, before you knew who I was, before you investigated everyone in my family, before you waited for me in the back alley of my home."

"Relax, Lily. Your friend and I are getting acquainted."

As I prepared to *acquaint* Tran with a kick to the gut, Uncle returned looking very concerned.

"Is your mother okay?" I asked.

"It's not about her. Meimei's worried about Suyin. She wants me to find her and drag the woman home."

Tran stepped closer. "Who is Suyin?"

"My sister's stepdaughter."

"How old is she?"

"Thirty. I think. But Meimei treats her like a child."

"Did you tell Meimei about Chyou?" I asked.

"I did. But she barely knows the girl. My sister's life revolves around her husband. Neither of them has visited Qiang in Chongming, nor has Qiang visited her. Our family hasn't been together under one roof since my grandmother died."

"When was that?"

"Before you were born."

Uncle's family dynamic was definitely more intricate than my own.

"We saw your sister an hour ago," I said. "Why this sudden alarm?"

"All that talk about Uma sharing a bed with Suyin made Meimei feel lonely. She called her daughter's roommates. Not only did Suyin move out last week, she quit her job several months before. During all those nightly video conversations my sister bragged about, her daughter never consulted her about this important decision."

"Where did Suyin work?" Tran asked.

"I don't know. Some biotech company in Hefei. It doesn't matter, Meimei is only thinking about herself."

As I commiserated with Uncle about family and stress, Tran vanished into the night.

Chapter Twenty

Thoughts of Tran permeated my dreams, not as a child soldier in Vietnam or as a tantalizing enigma as he frequently appeared. This time, he asked a single question and vanished into the night.

Where did Suyin work?

As Uncle prepared breakfast in the kitchen, I lingered in the cramped guest room and searched for information about Feng Suyin.

With the bits of history Meimei had shared, I learned that her daughter had graduated with honors in chemistry. Soon after, she landed a job at a biotechnology company in Hefei that specialized in research and development for pharmaceutical intermediates as well as chemical ingredients for cosmetics, pesticides, and customized products. An additional internet search defined *pharmaceutical intermediates* as chemical compounds that form the building blocks of active pharmaceutical ingredients. These compounds were used in the production of bulk prescription drugs for biopharma companies around the world.

Before I could hunt down more information, Uncle called me to breakfast. I switched my sleep clothes for cargo shorts and an army-green tee, summer clothing for September's ninety-degree heat. The short sleeves kept fabric from rubbing against the glued knife slash on my arm. It was sore if I pressed on it, but otherwise fine.

Uncle yelled from the kitchen. "Come on, lazy girl. We don't have all day."

I emerged from my windowless bedroom to see clear blue skies through the window beyond the couch. No air quality alerts would be issued today.

"Stop gawking and eat your jook."

Uncle scooped a ladle full of rice porridge and shoved the bowl along the kitchen counter toward me. His sleeveless shirt showed taunt muscles and a red gash beneath the glue. I had done a serviceable first aid job for us both.

The scent of sautéed garlic, ginger, scallions, and shrimp made my stomach growl. "How did you fix it this time?"

"With dried seafood and mushrooms. I keep them in the pantry. I went out to the market for fresh scallions and yau ja gwai."

Oil fried ghosts.

"Why do you call the dough sticks by their Cantonese name? And why do you call the porridge jook instead of zhou or congee?"

Uncle ladled jook for himself and dropped a handful of sliced yau ja gai into his bowl. "Your father named his restaurant Wong's Hong Kong Inn because he wanted to serve authentic Hongkonger food. So I learned the Cantonese names for everything we fix."

"Do you speak the language?"

"No. It's completely different from Mandarin and Shanghainese. Once my parents and grandmother returned from Hong Kong, they forgot the little bit they had learned."

He shoved the plate of sliced oil fried ghosts toward me.

"Eat quick. The driver arrives at seven thirty to take us to Qiang."

"Driver?"

Uncle gobbled down his jook and nodded for me to do the same. With Chyou still missing, he itched for a fight.

I wolfed down my breakfast, wishing we had time for another bowl, and grabbed two dough sticks to eat on the way. Who knew when Uncle would feed me again?

When we settled into the backseat of the car, I finished my snack and waited for him to tell me what he had planned for the day. He had paid extra for a rideshare all the way to Chongming Island. I figured he would want to use the time well. After ten minutes of silence, I forged ahead.

"I researched Meimei's stepdaughter online. The company she worked for manufactures chemical compounds to make pharmaceutical drugs."

Uncle stared out the window. "My mind has no room for Meimei's drama. Not until we find Chyou and bring her safely back to Qiang."

"What if Suyin is in trouble?"

"Suyin is thirty years old. Meimei cannot treat her like a child. Sooner or later, a mother must let go."

I thought about Ma and how often we communicated. Even during our most difficult times, I rarely ignored her messages for more than three days. Suyin was only five years older than me – four, once I turned twenty-six in November. Did Ma need to let go of me as well? Or, more importantly, did I need to let go of her?

I checked the time. It was four in the afternoon in Los Angeles, and I hadn't heard a peep.

Me: *Any updates on Baba?*

When I didn't get an immediate response, I reminded

myself not to worry. Hospitals had sketchy internet and strict cellphone policies. The moment she had news, she would relay it to me. Uncle was right: we needed to focus on finding and rescuing Chyou.

Uncle nodded at my phone. "Send a message to Tran. Have him meet us at Qiang's."

"What's the address?"

"I'm sure he knows. If not, he can find it himself." His tone was still bitter from the previous night.

"Anything else I should add?"

"Yes. Tell him to come prepared for a war."

I sent the message. "Did *we* come prepared?"

He kicked the bag between his feet.

Weapons or money?

Although Uncle could afford to pay off his brother's debt, he knew the ways of gangs. If they extorted what they wanted without injury or repercussion, they would likely do it again. Qiang would be theirs for life. This would kill his brother's spirit and turn him into what he never wanted to become.

My money was on guns.

I tapped the bag with my foot and hit metal. "Still don't want to pay?"

Uncle shrugged. "I will if I have to. But first, they'll pay me in blood."

We rode the rest of the way in silence with only brief exchanges between Uncle and the driver to help him locate Qiang's farm. I spotted workers tilling the fields and wading through the fish-pond paddies. I didn't see anyone small enough to be Zhi or Yong.

The car stopped in front of Qiang's farmhouse in a cloud of dust. By the time it had settled, Uncle's angry brother and his worried son were waiting on the stoop.

"Where have you been?" Qiang said in Mandarin.

Uncle glanced at me. "We speak in English or we don't speak at all."

Qiang sneered. "Fine. Where have you been?"

"Moving our mother to Meimei's house. Which you would know if you kept in touch."

"Me? We're the ones in trouble. Why haven't they called us?"

"Do they know?"

"Didn't you tell them?"

"This is your news to share. If you want family support, you must ask for it yourself."

Qiang stomped off to the vegetable garden, muttering loud enough to hear. "As if that would do any good."

His son stepped forward, a decade older than me but with sun-aged skin. "Good morning, Uncle Lee."

"Good morning, Wei. This is Lily Wong from Los Angeles. She came to help us find your daughter."

Wei bowed in greeting and turned back to Uncle. "Is my father right? Would your mother, cousins, and sister care about Chyou?"

"Have you introduced them to her?"

"When she was little. We visit my *wife's* family during Spring Festival." He looked at me. "I believe you Americans call it Chinese New Year."

You Americans? Guess I wasn't Chinese enough to satisfy Wei.

The fact that he didn't visit his paternal relatives during a two-week national celebration devoted to family reunions did not reflect well on him. When I told him I celebrated *Spring Festival* with my family back home, he felt the intended rebuke.

"I know it's not right. But Chang gatherings are difficult for my wife and children when my father won't attend."

Uncle nodded toward Qiang, still muttering at his plants. "If you follow your father's example, you will have no family at all. You must honor your elders and teach your children this respect. The Changs are their relatives too. It is your duty to foster these relationships."

"Yes, Uncle. You are right, of course. And I am very thankful for your help. But have you learned anything about my daughter?"

Uncle delayed his response long enough to embarrass Wei. "Do you know about your father's outstanding debt to Edward Fu?"

"The Chongming King? Father would never borrow money from him."

"And yet..."

Wei yelled across the garden. "You borrowed money from a gangster?"

Qiang spat in the dirt and stomped back to us. "Who do you think comes by every month? Did they look like my friends to you?"

"No, but–"

"How else could I afford to upgrade this farm? Or keep this house? Or support your children?"

"I work hard–"

"For ME." He gestured around him. "I did all of this myself, long before you entered this world."

Wei turned his back on his father. "Did Edward Fu take my daughter to get back at him?"

Uncle glanced at Qiang. "We think so."

"What can we do to get her back?"

"Pay him two hundred thousand yuan."

"We don't have that."

Uncle shrugged. "Then you will have to fight."

Qiang scoffed. "We aren't killers like you, Lee. Besides, I still think this trouble comes from your criminal activity with that Scorpion gang."

Uncle glared at his brother and ignored Wei's shock. "I thought time would have helped you grow up. But you still look in your neighbor's yard for what you misplace."

"And how have you changed, Lee? A driver brings you to my house. You own property in Shanghai. You are richer than before. And still, you are unwilling to give even a hair."

"Unwilling? I support our mother and cousins. You expect me to pay for you?"

"I expect you to help."

"Why do you think Lily and I are here?"

"To embarrass me in front of my son."

Anger rushed in and out of Uncle until only the sorry remnants of sadness remained. Beside him, Wei hung his head in shame.

"Oh, little brother. You do that all by yourself."

The rumble of an approaching vehicle cut through the silence between Uncle and Qiang.

"Where are the boys?" I asked. When no one answered, I turned to Wei. "Where are your sons?"

His father's exploits with the Chongming King had shaken him badly. "My wife took them to school."

"And your mother?'

"At the market, I think."

Uncle reached into his bag and brought out a folding knife and tossed it to me. I opened the talon-shaped blade and smiled. The karambit was the same model as the trusty blade I had left in my apartment back home.

He pulled out a pistol, checked the chamber for brass, then relaxed his arm to let the gun hide behind his thigh.

"What are you doing?" Qiang said. "You can't have weapons here."

Uncle slid his bag behind us with his foot. "Are you ready, Lily?"

"Yep." I rested my fists on my hips, hiding the open blade behind my waist.

"There could be five," he said.

I nodded. Two in the front and three in the back.

Qiang watched us with alarm. "You can't attack people on my farm."

Uncle stayed focused on the road. "You misunderstand, brother. It is them who may attack us."

The black SUV stopped in a cloud of dust, shielding the driver as he opened the door. Uncle and I tensed.

Tran strode into view, wearing his standard charcoal ensemble of jacket, muscle tee, pants, and boots. He looked at our weapon hands hugging our sides. "Expecting someone else?"

Uncle nodded toward the SUV. "Where did you get that?"

"Lily's message said to come prepared for war. I brought a tank. Or as close as I could find on such short notice."

Uncle stowed the pistol in the bag while I folded my karambit and slid it into my pocket. Although knives were illegal to carry, I felt more confident armed.

Qiang fired a question in Shanghainese.

Uncle replied in English. "This is Lily's friend from..." When Tran didn't offer, he threw out his hands. "I don't know much about him. But he fought with us during the ambush in Edward Fu's orchard."

"What ambush?" Wei said.

"Six of Fu's men attacked us after I asked about your father's debt and Chyou."

"Go home," Qiang said. "You are causing more trouble. I will speak with this man myself."

"Do you have the money to pay him back?"

"Not yet. But I will assure him that I will."

Tran chuckled. "Is your brother always this naive?"

Uncle nodded. "Unfortunately, yes."

Wei stepped forward. "Give me a weapon."

Qiang grabbed his arm. "Don't be ridiculous."

Uncle considered Wei. "Have you ever fired a gun?"

"No."

"Trained to fight with a knife?"

"No."

"Stay here with your father. If we're going to rescue your daughter, we cannot worry about you."

"But you said we should fight."

"I was wrong. Stay your wife and sons. Leave the Chongming gang to us."

"About them," Tran said. "Fu's men hole up in a warehouse on the east bank of the Buzhen Gang River."

Uncle nodded. "The Buzhen spills into the Yangtze between the Baozhen and Xinhe ports. It's a good location to smuggle contraband in and out of Chongming."

Qiang sneered. "What violence do you plan this time? Invade a triad hideout with your tank? Shoot gangsters with illegal guns? You could endanger Chyou and get us all arrested."

"Chyou is already in danger," Wei said. "If Uncle Lee and his friends are willing to risk their lives to save her, I want them to try."

Qiang stared at his son in surprise and confusion, as if

Wei had never voiced an opinion so strongly before. When Wei held his ground, he sighed.

"Your daughter. Your choice. But you should know that all of my brother's endeavors end in blood."

Chapter Twenty-One

Uncle brooded in the backseat as Tran drove us to the Chongming gang's base. Every interaction with the Chang family had been worse than the last. No wonder Uncle rarely came home to Shanghai.

"Have you eaten?" Tran asked.

"Huh?" I said.

"Breakfast."

"Why?"

"Just trying to be polite."

The ordinary banter was freaking me out. "I had jook. You?"

"Hot sauce noodles."

"In this heat?"

He grinned and let the implication hang in the air: nothing was too hot for a man like Tran.

"I brought you a tea egg in case you needed a snack."

I struggled to decipher his meaning as he drove.

"It's just an egg, Lily. Relax."

Tran was right. The Chang family had me on edge. He was only trying to ease the tension in our car.

He grinned. "Although, I could round up a sex tonic boba if you would prefer."

Son of a bitch.

"I knew you were there."

He laughed. "No, you didn't. You were too wrapped up in your dream date with Daniel Kwok."

A week ago, Daniel and I had strolled along Victoria Harbour while waiting for Hong Kong's famous Symphony of Lights. I had glimpsed a man who had reminded me of Tran, but when I looked back, he had left. Apparently, my gut reaction had been correct. "Keep your snacks, and focus on Chyou."

"Whatever you say, *Miss Wong*."

"Oh, good lord." Tran was imitating my grandfather's driver so I'd know how carefully he had spied.

Uncle tapped the back of my seat. "We must be close. A cargo ship passed under the bridge."

Tran crossed the river and turned onto a tree-lined road with buildings on the left and the muddy Buzhen Gang on the right. A cement dock began after that and ran along the street with cargo vessels moored, side by side, from four docking stations spaced along the cement. The first three barges lashed together were empty. Each had a three-story conning tower on one side and a long-arm crane on the other. The next docking station had two similar barges lashed together, each loaded with tarp-covered containers. The types of freighters varied farther down the road. The east bank of the Buzhen Gang looked like a parking lot for river-sized ships.

I examined the warehouses as we passed. "Which one is theirs?"

"According to my contact," Tran said, "it's a gray building across from the dock."

"They're all gray."

"That's all I was told."

Uncle leaned forward between our seats. "The one with the blue roof has motor scooters parked in front."

Two instead of six, but they resembled the bikes our ambushers had ridden. The warehouse doors were rolled down and locked, hiding any other conveyances they might have used. A metal security gate protected the front door. A walkway ran down the side.

Tran drove past the warehouse and parked between the next two buildings out of sight.

Uncle opened his weapons bag in the backseat and removed his pistol and knife. "Did your contacts verify that Chyou was here?"

"No." Tran watched him in the rearview mirror. "I'm surprised you brought a gun."

"You didn't?"

He smiled at me. "I have what I need."

I glanced at his torso for signs of the stiletto he had used to assassinate two punks in a Koreatown garage. The deadly efficiency with which he had killed still haunted my dreams.

Tran noticed my hand drift to the right pocket of my shorts. "You traveled with your karambit?"

"Uncle bought one for me here."

He nodded. "It's good to begin a fight with a familiar tool. After that, we can pick up what we need."

Uncle opened his door. "Enough talk. Let's find my grandniece and leave." He pointed to the security camera mounted on the front corner of the building. "Pay attention. Less surveillance on Chongming Island does not equal none."

I angled my face down as I followed Uncle out of the alley to the street. If the Chinese police caught us in a crime, I could kiss my American privilege goodbye.

A handful of mariners strolled across from us in front of a tarp-protected barge. Ship cranes unloaded cargo from a massive vessel at the end of the road. I saw no action around the container ship to our immediate left.

Uncle bypassed the front entrance of what we assumed to be the gang's hideout and led us down the side walkway instead. After testing the lock, he brought out a set of picks. In less than a minute, we walked through the rear door.

Tran and I separated from Uncle as we entered. The lights were on. Men spoke Chongming-accented Mandarin I couldn't understand. Stacked crates and boxes shielded me from view.

Chinese characters marked most of the goods I passed. Many had company logos in Russia's Cyrillic alphabet or Korea's hangul. There were also US brand names like Kellogg's, General Mills, and Revlon. Cereals and American cosmetics were overpriced and hard to acquire. Edward Fu would make a tidy profit selling them to locals or smuggling them elsewhere in China.

I peeked between stuffed burlap sacks that smelled of citrus, rice, and wheat and saw a sleeping mat littered with food containers, empty water bottles, soda cans, and snacks. A package of cookies had been neatly rolled closed beside a shackle chained to a grimy bathroom sink.

Was this where they had kept Chyou and the family members of other farmers who couldn't pay their debt?

The men laughed. A chair scraped on the cement. I adjusted my position in time to watch two men walk out the door and switch off the lights.

I raced back the way I had come and found Uncle and Tran doing the same. "Chyou's gone."

"I know," Uncle said. "They put her on a ship."

"Which one?"

"They didn't say the name."

We reached the street in time to see Scar Mouth and Giant drive their scooters up toward the bridge. The strolling mariners had left. I detected no movement in the conning tower of the nearest tarp-covered barge. Nor did I see anyone on the cement dock in front of the container ship moored to its left. The crates and cargo on both barges were stacked and piled too high to see anything beyond.

Uncle checked both directions as frantically as me. "We need to split up."

"And look where?" Tran said. "These ships are two football fields long."

The face of the warehouse had promising grooves above the front door.

"Give me a boost."

Tran created a step, then hoisted me into the air.

I dug my fingers into the grout and clung. Once secure, I climbed up the wall and onto the roof. With the added height, I could see the other vessels lashed side by side away from the dock.

"There."

I pointed beyond the container ship, climbed off the roof, and jumped to the ground. Before my partners could ask, I sprinted down the road in a three-hundred-yard dash. Tran might keep up with me. Uncle never would. But it didn't matter because the movement I had seen was on a barge with a clear route to leave.

Although low for a ship, the hull of the container barge loomed ten feet above me, making it impossible to see if anyone was on board. I raced up the retractable gangway that ran alongside and ended up in the center of a walkway that circumvented the deck. Since the movement I had seen from the warehouse roof came from two vessels away, I climbed onto the platform and bolted between the double-stacked containers like a mouse in a maze.

When I reached the other side, I paused.

The gangways to the next ship were located near the bow and the stern. Since I was in the middle, each was a football field away. Mooring lines and giant fenders kept the two vessels in place, about two yards apart. The bulk cargo barge sat lower in the water with coal heaped into mounds like a serpent with shiny black scales. If I undershot my leap, I'd have a long way to swim – provided I didn't crack my head and get sucked under a hull.

I was so close. I couldn't lose Chyou.

Hoping for the best, I climbed onto the railing and leaped, stretching my legs as a surge of tide separated the hulls. Even sailing in a full Wushu split, I missed the deck's ledge and crashed against the side.

My backup plan saved me as I landed on a fender and clung to the rope. Dangling between hulls, these monsters felt closer than they had seemed. With the container barge knocking against the fender dangerously close to my back, I climbed up the rope and onto the next barge. Rather than sprint to the stern where I could cross beneath the tower, once again, I chose the more expedient route.

As I climbed over the massive serpent's back, loose coal shifted beneath my feet and hands, sinking me to my calves and slowing me down. A man yelled when I reached the top. Bad enough to be spotted, the next ship was unmoored and pulling slowly away.

I sprinted along the side of the deck to gain speed, leapt up to the railing, and launched myself over the edge. Paddling the air with my legs and arms, I made it to a mooring line and smacked against the hull.

A gasp of pain cut short my curse.

I clung to the mooring line and looked back the way I had come as the ship's hydraulics reeled me toward the deck. Beyond the coal barge, Uncle looked tiny in front of the stacked containers and two stout red cranes. On the road beyond that, Tran's black SUV sped out of sight behind a larger vessel unloading its cargo at the end of the dock. Cranes swung and tilted from the deck, as if trying to pluck an annoyance off of the ground.

Way to go, Lily. You've done it again.

My phone sat useless in my cargo shorts pocket. No Wi-Fi for WeChat. No international plan for a call. No way to organize a rescue with Uncle and Tran. I had set myself adrift in more ways than one.

Chapter Twenty-Two

As the mooring line raised me up the side of the freighter, I berated myself for the hasty decision that had separated me from my team. If I had taken the time to explain what I had seen from the roof of the warehouse, we could have plotted a more sensible plan to intercept this ship and rescue Chyou. Instead, I had allowed my impulsive actions to negate years of grueling ninja training and introspective work. Rose's murder had destroyed my trust in humanity and in myself. Sensei's insightful teachings rebuilt both. He had given so much of himself to make me strong enough to collaborate with others. How disappointed he would be if he knew his efforts were for naught.

Voices chatted in Mandarin above me on the deck. I needed to get off the mooring line before it reached the slot in the railing on the way to the winch.

I grabbed onto a hot metal ledge and walked my hands to the side. When the ledge ended, I swung my legs sideways until I had enough momentum to release my grip and grab a new hold three feet away. The ship moved at a crawl, no doubt pulled by tugboats until it could navigate on its own. If I could find Chyou quickly, I had a chance to rescue her before we powered into the Yangtze River for destinations within China or other counties beyond the East China Sea.

Instead of coal or containers or tarp-covered freight, this barge had flat cargo holds that formed a platform taller than me. From the warehouse roof, I had seen giant metal hatches covering the holds with markings for a helipad in the center. Four cranes stood between each hatch with a conning tower at the stern. If Chyou was on this ship, it had to be in a storage room or cabin.

I hugged the platform to stay out of sight and ran.

The mariners manning the winch had left – hopefully to work on the tugboat side of the ship – which gave me a straight shot to the window-plastered tower. Stairways up the sides led to the viewing and command decks above. I needed an internal staircase that would lead me below – beneath all those vantage points where someone could easily spot me.

Just as I made it to cover, two familiar gang members walked out the door. The first man I had fought in the orchard ambush focused his dead-eye glare at me. His partner with the snake tattoos dropped his jaw in surprise. I coiled to attack, then stopped. Behind them, two mariners approached. Before they could see me, I bolted around the wall and ran under a viewing deck toward the stern of the ship.

I needed to eliminate this threat and find Chyou before the ship went to sea, preferably without raising an alarm or leaving two corpses behind. Above me, a message stenciled in red letters encouraged the same.

Work Safely. Avoid Accidents.

I raced up the steep metal stairs through the hatch and ducked beneath the portholes as I ran along the deck. Another set of stairs led me around the back of the tower where the giant red funnel shot up to the sky.

No portholes back here. And many opportunities for two criminal landlubbers to *accidentally* fall.

I headed for the last staircase to a landing overlooking the stern. Dead Eyes closed in quick. I stalled him with a mule kick to the chest, then hurried up the steps of a launching deck where a free-fall lifeboat hung at a steep angle, ready to plunge into the water and bob to the surface away from a sinking ship.

Promising hazards at every turn.

A fall from the narrow platform would land my pursuers on the funnel deck one flight below. If I shoved them off the steel launching racks, they'd fall another flight to the stern. Lure them onto the lifeboat's smooth steel hull or onto the ends of the racks, and I could kick Dead Eyes and Snake into the Buzhen Gang River for an unpleasant swim.

Provided they didn't dispose of me first.

This time, I allowed Dead Eyes to make it up stairs and made room for him and Snake to follow me onto the landing. The back hatch of the nose-down orange boat was sealed shut, creating a forty-degree surface on which I could lean and launch kicks. Above me on either side, white steel beams angled up from the point of the launching racks like a clip for a giant bag of chips.

I grabbed one of the four yellow chains that hung from a cross bar hooked to cables attached to the boat. I stood on the slanted door and kicked Snake in the face. He fell back against the guard rail and spit blood over the edge. Dead Eyes shoved his partner aside and charged.

I kicked him in the temple as I swung off the door and landed on a steeply sloped white metal grate. The maintenance ramp ran down the side of the lifeboat's launching rack. A fall from here would smash me onto the main deck two stories below.

I had traversed more precarious footing while scaling Los Angeles buildings, stairwells, and roofs. I was accustomed to heights and could scamper across ledges with squirrel-like ease. Whether running from danger or flipping over obstacles just for fun, I relied on my ninja and parkour training to keep me safe.

Dead Eyes pursued more recklessly.

He lost his footing and crashed me into the hydraulic arm of the lifeboat's rack. My legs shot back with his, and we both landed hard on the grate, chest to chest, with our feet dangling through the protective bars at the end.

He stank of tobacco and sweat.

I slammed my forehead into his nose, releasing a gust of hot breath and a splatter of blood. Then I ground my forearm into his throat and dug my knee into groin as I crawled out of his sticky embrace.

He shifted and tucked his foot against my hip. As he tried to shove me off of the ramp, I grabbed the guide rope attached to the lifeboat's shell. My legs flew up, but my torso stayed down. This time, we landed farther down the ramp, face-to-face on our sides.

With out feet braced against the guard rails to keep us from sliding through the gap, we kicked at one another's feet in a frantic attempt to knock them off the rails. A fall from here might clear the ship. More likely, we would hit the deck and break our backs before we bounced off the stern.

I tired of the contest and double stomp-kicked him in the gut.

His narrow hips slipped through the side railing. My next

kick shoved him through the hole and sent him swinging off the railing post by his knees. The momentum of the arc cleared him from the stern in a flip and plunged him into the water with a back-smacking splash.

The freighter's engine rumbled as it separated from the tugboats and made its own way.

Dead Eyes bobbed to the surface and grew small.

We had already reached the final moored ship unloading at the end of the dock. When we reached the Yangtze River, I'd lose my opportunity to extract Chyou from this ship.

As I rolled onto my knees, Snake advanced down the ramp. His mouth bled from my kick, and he moved stiffly, as if Tran's motorcycle tire during the ambush had broken his ribs. To improve his odds, he flicked open a telescoping baton

Remaining on my knees, I snapped open my karambit and lunged at his calf.

I was fighting from the low side of a steeply sloped grate. Snake had the advantage of gravity and height. Fortunately, Sensei had taught me to draw swords and knives from seated and kneeling kamae. I applied the concepts of these traditional fighting scenarios to my current state of affairs. Even so, I had a hard time evading Snake's boots and baton.

The knife flew out of my hand.

His baton struck my neck.

I scrambled beneath the hydraulic arm that connected the steel beam and the boat's launching rack. They joined in a point a few inches behind my heel. Both were angled steeply to launch the free-fall lifeboat away from the ship. But without the sliding momentum, I would suffer a harder fate.

Snake whacked my fingers with the baton.

I re-gripped farther down the steel beam.

There was no way to win from this untenable position. The smooth nose of the lifeboat offered nothing to grab. Snake blocked my route back to the maintenance ramp. Nothing below would catch me or slow my descent. I had no choice. All I could do was retreat with my life.

Gripping the sloping steel beam, I jumped onto the end.

Snake grinned and swung his baton at my face.

As it approached, I shoved backward off the beam in a Hail Mary dive.

Chapter Twenty-Three

White clouds drifted in the sky as I sailed, chest open, back arched, away from the ship. I had gaged my trajectory based on an estimated forty-foot dive. As I brought my hands together, I saw a small motorboat racing across the river. If it didn't slow or swerve, it would surely crash into me.

I focused on the water, intending to cut through like a dagger and swim beneath the boat. There was nothing I could do if it hit me on the way.

Ma, Baba, Sensei...I didn't have time to send goodbyes to anyone after that.

Eyes shut, I pierced the surface and exhaled as the water rushed along my body. When my speed slowed, I paused underneath and listened for sounds of a motor overhead. The river was too muddy and polluted to risk opening my eyes, so when my chest grew tight, I swam up to see.

I gasped in air and wiped whatever contaminants might have clung to my face. Only then did I look down the river at the departing cargo ship. No mariners swarmed the stern in alarm. Nor could I see Snake gloating from the lifeboat launch above. I had back-dived off the ship with the same anonymity as I had arrived.

"Want a lift?" a man asked.

I snapped my head to the left and found Tran smirking from the helm of a small fishing boat. "Where did you get this?"

"Borrowed it from a local."

"Borrowed?"

"Close enough."

I swam to the side. "You could have hit me."

"Could have. But didn't."

He pulled me onto the boat and handed me a grimy fishing rag in place of a towel.

I crinkled my nose. "I'll air dry."

"Good choice. But shower as soon as you can. Did you open your eyes in the water?"

"Nope."

"Smart."

"Thanks."

"But not smart enough not to avoid getting thrown off a ship."

"I dove."

"Small difference."

"Not from where I was fighting."

"Point taken."

He started the engine.

I looked upriver toward the coal and container barges I had crossed. "Where's Uncle?"

Tran shrugged. "He ran after you. I sped for a boat."

"Yeah. I saw your SUV driving down the road."

"Really? When did you have time?"

"During my ride up the mooring line."

"Slacker."

"Hey. I'd like to see you sprint a mile down a dock and climb across three different ships."

"Wouldn't happen."

"Too old?"

"Too smart."

We powered downriver alongside the final cargo ship moored at the dock. Its hull was so high off the water I couldn't see the cranes. At the mouth of the river, the ship with Uncle's grandniece eased into the Yangtze.

"We've lost her," I said.

"Not for long." When I continued to sulk, he added, "I saw the ship's name."

I studied Tran as he steered the fishing boat past the end of the cement dock toward a short wooden pier jutting out from a dirt bank. Time and again, he showed up when I needed him most.

"Why do you help me?"

"I already told you."

"When?"

"K..." He pretended to pout. "You hurt my feelings."

I snorted out a laugh. "As if."

"I'm interested to see what you will do."

Much as I wished to forget, I remembered the conversation we had in Los Angeles when I was still worried he might put a bullet in my head. "That's not all you said."

"No. I said violence recognizes its own."

Although I had replayed those words a hundred times in my mind, it hurt to hear them spoken out loud. "Maybe so. But that doesn't explain why you care."

The rumble started in his belly and worked its way up his throat before turning into mirth that lit up his eyes. "Why I care? I hadn't realized we had reached this stage in our relationship."

"Not funny, Tran. Not funny at all."

"Oh, come..." He looked at my furious expression and laughed.

I slapped the wetness off my shirt and shorts, wishing I could slap the smug off his face. Instead, my fingertips whacked against something hard. When I cried, "Ow," Tran lost it again. He laughed even louder when I pulled out my soggy phone.

I tried to dry it with the fishing rag, but I knew it was a hopeless cause. Although tech companies promised to have a phone the following year that could survive a twenty-foot plunge, the best water depth mine could handle was three.

"Don't worry," Tran said. "We'll get you another phone."

"When? During all our free time?"

How many messages from Ma would I miss?

An irate fisherman yelled from the shore, several car lengths beyond the end of the road. Tran waved amiably and pulled up to the pier. "I'll find you a phone, Lily. I promise." Then he pulled out his wallet and handed the fisherman 300 yuan, thanked him for the use of his boat, and led me up the pier to the dead-end road.

He pulled a tarp from the trunk and laid it over my seat.

"Do I want to know why you have a tarp in your car?"

He grinned. "Probably not."

I checked for blood stains, then sat.

While he walked to the driver's side, I swallowed my annoyance and braced myself for what I needed to say. The last time I had spoken these words to Tran, I had mistakenly thought I was buying my family's life. Since then, my gratitude tab had grown long overdue.

He stuck the key into the ignition and paused. "What's wrong?"

"Nothing."

Why was this so hard?

"Thank you for picking me up in the boat." I took a breath. "And for fighting with us in the orchard." *In for a penny...* "And for showing up at the riot in Hong Kong."

His brow raised in surprise.

I braced myself for a snarky comeback.

"My pleasure," he said, and started the car.

Chapter Twenty-Four

Fury emanated from Qiang as Uncle explained what had happened to Chyou.

"How could you let her get away?"

"She was already on the ship."

"But why?" Qiang yelled. "If Edward Fu took her as you claim, he would have kept her on Chongming Island."

"Not if there's a better way to get back what he has lost."

Wei gasped. "By selling Chyou?"

"I don't know. But this doesn't look good."

Wei turned on his father and pounded on his scrawny chest. "What have you done?"

Qiang shoved him away. "Nothing. This is all because of him. Where are they taking her, Lee?"

Uncle turned to Tran. "Anything?"

Tran looked up from his phone. "The freighter is headed up the Yangtze River for Wuhan. But there are several ports along the way."

"Wuhan?" Wei threw out his hands. "Why would anyone take her there?"

Before Tran or Uncle could venture a guess, a car drove up the road. When the dust settled, Scar Mouth and Giant emerged. They stood near their open doors and glared at Uncle, Tran, and me.

Qiang marched forward, yelling at them in Mandarin, too fast for me to follow. Giant shoved him back.

Uncle grabbed Wei's arm so he wouldn't interfere.

Scar Mouth stepped forward, eyes watching Tran.

When everyone had settled down, Scar Mouth focused his attention on Qiang. "Our comrade is taking your granddaughter to Hefei," he said in Mandarin.

"*Hefei?*"

Scar Mouth ignored Qiang's outburst and glared at me. "Our other comrade returned to us wet but unharmed."

I wrung a few drops of river water from my shirt and smiled.

He snorted and turned back to Qiang. "If you want your granddaughter back, find your sister's stepdaughter, Feng Suyin."

Wei grabbed Qiang and yelled at him in English. "Who is Feng Suyin?" When his father didn't answer, his voice rose to a shriek. "This is your fault, Father. If you hadn't borrowed money from criminals, they wouldn't have kidnapped Chyou."

Qiang pointed at his brother. "Your uncle is the gangster. You want to blame someone, blame him." Then he switched back to Mandarin and challenged Scar Mouth and Giant. "Why are you targeting my family? If you want Suyin, go bother hers."

Tran interjected in English. "Because your family has triad connections that these bozos don't."

"See?" Qiang said to his son. "I told you this mess was all because of Lee."

Tran shook his head at Qiang. "Not just your brother. Your father and his uncle."

"They're dead," Qiang said.

"Yet their connections remain."

Qiang turned on his brother. "What is this man talking about, Lee?"

"Our elderly cousins."

"Uncle has dementia. The last time I saw him at the Qiaojia house he didn't even recognize his own son."

"Not him. His wife. Auntie's mind is still sharp as a pin."

"What connections could she have? All she did was marry a gangster-traitor's son."

Uncle shook his head. "She married a *martyred* gangster-traitor's son."

Scar Mouth yelled, "Zhùkǒu." And everyone shut up. He berated them in Mandarin and laid out the situation. When he was done, he and Giant returned to the car and left.

"Did you catch any of that?" I asked Tran.

He nodded. "A gang in Hefei paid the Chongming gang to kidnap Chyou and send her to them. Lee's family has three days to find Suyin and deliver her to Hefei. If they don't, the Hefei gang will sell Chyou into prostitution."

I slumped.

"Oh," Tran added. "And the pretty one told Qiang not to worry about Chyou paying for his debt. He and the big one would return next week to carve every fen Qiang owes from his body until the loan and interest is paid in full."

Qiang sank into a squat and clutched the sides of his head.

Wei stared at the departing car, eyes glazed in shock and despair.

Uncle sighed and walked back to us. "What were you telling me this morning about Suyin? Something about the company she worked for?"

I nodded. "They manufacture precursor chemical

compounds that are used to make cosmetics, pesticides, and pharmaceutical intermediates."

"What are those?"

"Chemical compounds to make synthetic drugs like oxycodone, methadone, and fentanyl."

"What did Suyin do for them?"

"She worked as a chemist."

"Making?"

"I don't know. But if I had to guess? I'd say fentanyl. Before May 2019, it was perfectly legal for companies like the one Suyin worked for to sell fentanyl and its precursor compounds to anyone in the world."

"What changed?" Uncle asked.

"Pressure from the US forced China to ban its production and sale. Fentanyl and several of its analogues are now categorized as controlled substances."

"What are analogues?"

"Any variation in the molecular construction of fentanyl that still produces a similar effect is called an analogue. Some of these fentanyl analogues are stronger and more dangerous than the original drug."

Uncle shook his head. "Chinese companies will still find a way to evade the government and sell. But criminal organizations will benefit the most. If Suyin created one of these analogues, a drug-trafficking gang would want her working in their underground lab."

"Uncle Lee?" Wei said. "I'm sorry to interrupt, but I don't know what to do." He glanced at his father still squatting in the dirt. "We don't know Suyin, and my father is scared for himself. I only care about Chyou. Will you help me get her back?"

Uncle looked at his nephew with a mixture of pity and

disgust. "Criminals have just told your father they will carve pieces out of his body. A gang in Hefei wants to enslave the stepdaughter of your aunt. And all you care about is Chyou?"

"She's my daughter. She is your grandniece."

"And your father is my brother, and your cousin is my niece. We are family, Wei. No matter how hard you and your father pretend we are not."

Uncle looked at Tran and me expectantly. When we nodded, he turned back to Wei. "We will find Chyou *and* Suyin. You will do your filial duty and help your father stand on his feet."

Chapter Twenty-Five

We stopped at Uncle's apartment so I could shower off the river water and disinfect the glued gash in my arm. Although the seal over the knife wound had held, I doused it with rubbing alcohol just in case. God only knew what bacteria I had encountered during my impromptu swim.

I checked in the mirror for any new cuts that needed tending and grimaced at the purple-green bruises ripening on my skin. This was not an empowering look for a ninja protector.

Since displaying evidence of my previous ass kicking would not inspire confidence from Suyin's parents or fear in the gang members we would likely encounter next, I covered my torso and limbs in a t-shirt, black jacket, and pants, and dabbed concealer on my cheek to soften the blue. I could hide it completely with full makeup, but it wasn't worth the work.

Feeling suitably intimidating, I joined Uncle and Tran in the kitchen and grabbed an icy bottle of water from the fridge.

"Won't you be hot?" Uncle asked, still in his shorts.

I nodded toward Tran. "Girl's gotta suffer to look as cool as him."

Tran grinned and brushed his finger along his cheek to indicate a spot my concealer had missed.

Could this man be any more annoying?

I turned to Uncle. "What's the plan?"

He slid a paper plate down the counter with two rou jia mo sandwiches for me. The chewy rounds of fried bread had been split and filled with fragrant minced spicy pork.

"When did you have time to braise the meat?"

"The morning before you arrived. I know how you are about wanting to be fed."

"What? You guys don't eat?"

"Not like you," they said in unison, like a couple of childhood pals.

I ignored them, took a huge bite, and moaned. At least one of these annoying men could actually cook. Then again, I didn't know what all J Tran could and couldn't do.

Uncle wiped the counter and tossed the sponge in the sink. "Bring your food. You can eat on the way."

"Way to where?"

"My sister and Honghui's place. One of them has to know something about Suyin."

Tran checked an incoming text. "Perfect timing."

"For what?" I asked.

"To leave."

He went ahead and waited for us at the front door. When we arrived, he had a package in his hand.

"What's that?" I asked.

"Supplies."

Uncle pushed me from behind. "Stop wasting time. We have places to go."

With the men acting like best buddies, I was surprised when Uncle hopped in the backseat. I understood better when he began making calls. As Uncle chattered in Shanghainese and Mandarin, I ate my rou jia mo and studied an old scar I had never noticed running through the downward angle of Tran's brow.

Had the boy he had killed as a child cut him with a knife? Or had it come from the man he had killed after that? Tran had endured more violence in his childhood than most killers see in their lives. How much of his personality had been forged by those fires? Or had Tran come into this world as detached from human emotions as he appeared?

"Do you ever get scared?" I asked between bites.

"Of what?"

"Anything."

He shook his head.

"How about love?"

He smirked. "If you're flirting, you need more finesse."

"I didn't mean me. Have you ever felt love, any kind of love, for anyone?"

He drove up a ramp and merged with traffic. "Why are you asking me about love?"

"Curious, I guess. I've seen you fascinated and intrigued, cold and enraged. You seem continually amused, usually at my expense. But I've never seen you act as if you're—"

"Human?"

"I was going to say happy."

He raised his scarred brow. "What makes you think I'm not happy?"

"Are you?"

"By your definition or mine?"

"That's a revealing question. How do you define happiness?"

"You first."

I opened my mouth to respond, then closed it on the sandwich to buy myself time. The word felt too cheery for what had become my natural state. Caring and satisfaction? Sure. Moments of joy wedged between concern, fury, and relief? Check. Then I remembered Daniel, and my face flushed with heat. But even that euphoria had come with complexities too conflicting to define.

Tran chuckled. "Your question was not as easy as you thought."

The challenge in his voice sharpened my mind. "I'm happy when I'm with my family and friends. I'm happy when I help others and protect them from harm. I'm happy when I stop a bad person from doing evil things." I held up the last bite of Uncle's rou jia mo. "And I'm happy when I eat truly delicious food."

Tran laughed as I stuffed it in my mouth. "And don't forget...you're happy when you are sparring with me."

Damn this man.

The delicious sandwich turned to paste in my throat.

Uncle kicked the back of my seat. "We're here."

I swallowed my thoughts with the food. We had more important issues to address than my convoluted feelings about Tran.

Once again, I followed Uncle up the path to his sister's front gate. Instead of running out to greet us, Meimei waited until we reached the front door. Stress and worry about her stepdaughter had replaced the effusive exuberance I had seen. How would she handle the truth about Suyin?

She greeted Uncle in Shanghainese and motioned us into her house.

"You remember Lily Wong," Uncle said in English. "This is her friend J Tran. We need to speak to you and Honghui. Is he here?"

"Have you found our daughter?"

"Not yet. But there are things you need to know."

Honghui strode down the stairs like a king. "Why are you here, Lee? Your mother is fine. Unless you want her back? If so, please take her. Return the peace to my home."

"No, no, husband. They are here about Suyin." Meimei turned to her brother. "What have you learned? Please tell me she is safe."

I gestured to the couches and chair. "Maybe we could sit?" A soft couch with a wide coffee table in between would create a safer, more cordial environment.

Honghui exhaled at the inconvenience and claimed the massive armchair closest to the stairs. Meimei settled near him on the couch. Uncle and I chose the chairs on the side. Tran strolled to the garden window, seemingly entranced by the view.

"Are you comfortable now?" Honghui said to me.

I ignored his snide tone. "I am. Thank you."

He grunted under his breath and turned his attention to Uncle. "Well?"

I entwined my fingers into a Kuji mudra and rested them casually in my lap, radiating a calming energy I hoped Uncle and his relatives would feel.

After an uncomfortable silence, Uncle turned to me, at a loss. "I don't know where to begin."

None of the crisis management he had done for his family, or as a triad enforcer, or as my father's lead cook had prepared him for the emotional task of breaking bad news to parents. It required a level of empathy and tact he and I both knew he didn't possess. My work with Aleisha's Refuge, on the other hand, had put me in this unfortunate position more times than I would have wished.

I nodded to Uncle and smiled compassionately at the Fengs.

"My job back home is to find and rescue women in trouble. When you told Lee that Suyin quit her job three months ago, I checked into her former company. They manufacture chemical compounds that are used to make a variety of products, including a dangerous prescription drug called fentanyl. Several months ago, your government made this drug illegal. Shortly after that, Suyin quit her job. Your daughter is a chemist. We believe that a criminal organization in Hefei recruited her to make a type of fentanyl in their illegal laboratories. We think Suyin ran away, and they want her back."

Meimei whimpered in distress.

Her husband remained silent.

Uncle motioned me to continue.

Tran offered an encouraging nod from the window and continued to watch for threats.

I glanced at Honghui, then focused on his wife. This story was tied to her family, not his.

"Your brother Qiang has a granddaughter named Chyou. She's twelve years old. Three days ago, she was kidnapped by a gang in Chongming. This morning, they put her on a ship to Hefei. The criminal organization in Hefei has threatened to sell her into prostitution until we return Suyin to them."

"What?" She fired off questions at Uncle in Mandarin, then begged her husband to tell me I was wrong. When he didn't respond, she returned to speaking English and me. "Do you know where she is?"

"No." I turned to Mr. Feng. "Do you?"

He shook his head.

"But you knew she was in trouble, didn't you, Mr. Feng?"

"What?" Meimei said. "Don't be ridiculous. Of course he didn't know."

I ignored the wife and focused on the husband. "Did you know your daughter was manufacturing illegal drugs?" When he didn't answer, I pressed. "Did you know she was working for a criminal gang?"

He grunted. "My daughter does many foolish things. Things that cost me much money and threaten my reputation."

"Did she reach out for help?"

"She did not. I learned about her actions from criminals."

Meimei grabbed her husband's arm. "They called you? When? What did they say?"

"Suyin's employers called me last week. They threatened my life. They even threatened to hurt you. But I refused to cower. I also refused to help Suyin out of her mess."

Uncle bolted to his feet. "*Her mess* has endangered my twelve-year-old grandniece."

Honghui rose in challenge. "Or maybe they kidnapped the girl because they know you are one of their kind."

"Their kind? They kidnapped Chyou because they know I have the courage to do what you are too cowardly and selfish to do."

"Which is what?"

"Protect your family. These men force your daughter to work for them, and you do nothing. They threatened your wife, and you do nothing. They kidnap your wife's grandniece, and you do nothing."

"Your grandniece is not my blood."

"And Suyin is not mine. Yet here I am, with my friends, willing to do what needs to be done."

Honghui scoffed. "That's the difference between us,

Chang Lee. Pigs are always eager to dirty themselves in the mud."

Meimei leaped to her feet as Uncle lunged across the table. She yelled at him in Shanghainese and created such a racket that her mother joined in from the top of the stairs.

Honghui yelled in Mandarin for the women to shut up.

Uncle shook off his sister and punched her husband in the face.

Meimei screamed.

I rushed forward to yank Uncle back, but Tran reached him before me, walked Uncle toward the window, and said something to deescalate his rage.

Meimei sobbed. Instead of checking on her husband, she ran to her mother for a hug.

As the women whimpered and cooed, Honghui wiped the blood from his mouth, caught me watching him, and sneered. "Get out of my house," he said in English. "Or I will call the police."

I held out my hands. "What will you tell them, Mr. Feng? That your daughter manufactures illegal drugs? Because that is the story we will tell."

He looked from Tran and Uncle by the window to his mother-in-law consoling his wife. Then he settled his fury on me. "What do you want?"

"To find Suyin."

"She was in Hefei the last time she called."

"When was that?"

"Three weeks ago, I think. She wanted money. I told her to go back to the biotech company and beg for her job. She said she couldn't. I told her..." He sighed with regret and then steeled himself with belligerence. "I told her...too bad."

Chapter Twenty-Six

It took all of the anger management and de-escalation skills Sensei had taught me to whisk Uncle out of that house before he murdered Honghui Feng. Even now, on a train to Hefei, I couldn't be sure he wouldn't kill him after the fact. All I could do was focus on rescuing Chyou and Suyin.

Tran returned from the bathroom and took the aisle seat across from Uncle. "How do you want to play this, Lee?"

"I don't know. All of the options are bad. If we find and try to rescue Chyou, we will probably be outgunned. Even if we succeed, Suyin will still be missing. The gang will come after my sister. Which her husband will do nothing to stop. They might even come to Shanghai and pressure my family directly or to seek their revenge on us. We could find ourselves fighting a gang war on Qiang's farm. Or...we could hunt down Suyin and turn her over to the gang. They're drug dealers, not traffickers. If we return their chemist, they would probably hand over Chyou."

Tran nodded in agreement.

The choice was simple for him. I knew from experience that Tran would kill or betray anyone to protect a child. As a child abuse survivor himself, this was the chink in his otherwise sociopathic armor.

The choice was more complicated for me. "We can't sacrifice Suyin."

Tran's expression hardened. "The child is innocent. The adult made her choice."

I thought of all the women I had met while working with Aleisha and Stan whose apparent *choices* had landed them in violent relationships or prostitution. The trail of responsibility was not as clear as Tran made it seem.

"Suyin could have been tricked or coerced," I said. "She could have been desperate to get out of financial trouble. She might have thought there was no moral difference in making the same drug for a gang that she had made for a major biotech company for years. Even if she was originally motivated by greed, she might have changed her mind and wanted to stop. We don't know enough about Suyin's life and situation to pass judgment."

I looked away from Tran's unyielding face and focused on Uncle. He had left the Scorpion Black Society for a reason. He had never told me why, but I could venture a guess.

"If we return your stepniece to the gang, how many people will suffer or die from the fentanyl analogues she makes?" The tension in his jaw told me my guess was correct.

"Drugs are bad news," he said, then sunk into thought.

After a while, he nodded to me and looked across at Tran. "My sister loves her stepdaughter as if she were her own. I cannot sacrifice Suyin without trying to save her. But Chyou must come first. I say we hunt for them both and let chance guide our path."

"Okay," Tran said. "But if they hurt the child..."

Uncle nodded. "We exterminate them all."

They looked at me to see if I was on board with the plan. I had killed two men before Tran entered my life. The first was my sister's rapist-murderer who had drugged and attacked me. The second was a mobster from an LA Ukrainian gang. Both times had I killed in defense of my life. In the two months I had known Tran, my death tally had tripled, with a dozen more victims hospitalized from the injuries I had inflicted. Although Tran wasn't to blame, I couldn't help wondering if he had changed me in some fundamental way.

An assassin, a triad enforcer, and a ninja walk into a bar...

What did my choice of friends say about me?

"Well, Lily?" Uncle asked.

This is friendship, he had said in the orchard as we fought side by side. Now, he waited for a definition of friendship from me.

Although I loved Uncle dearly and probably owed him my – and Ma's – life, I would not commit murder for him. That said, I had saved and lost children from and to unspeakable horrors. If the gang we encountered were similar monsters, they all deserved to die.

Tran watched me deliberate, then nodded, as if he had heard every thought in my head. As if he always knew what troubled me the most.

What you really want to know, Lily, is whether you are like me.

I fired the question back at him with my mind. He countered with a slight rise of his brow. Only I could answer this question. Only I could end our debate.

I turned to Uncle and nodded my consent.

"Good." He took out his phone and glanced at Tran. "Do you have connections in Hefei?"

Tran smirked. "I have connections all over the world."

As Uncle searched through his contacts, Tran took a small box out of his travel bag and handed it to me.

I looked at the logo in surprise. "When did you have time to buy me a phone?"

"At the dock, while we were waiting for Lee."

"Is this what arrived at the apartment before we left?"

He shrugged. "Anything can be delivered in Shanghai."

He nodded to the charging outlet between the seats, then began texting before I could thank him or offer to pay.

Had he done this out of friendship or had he added to my debt?

Either way, I was anxious to set up WeChat and see what messages I had missed. Late afternoon in China would be the wee hours of the morning for Ma. What had happened with my father during their afternoon and night?

Once I had logged into the app, I scrolled past Ma's recent messages to the last one I had left.

Any updates on Baba?

I had sent it from Uncle's apartment that morning before we left for Qiang's farm. She had responded while Uncle and I had driven to Chongming.

The doctors are running blood tests to rule out vitamin deficiencies, to which your father listed all the vegetables in his diet. Every last one!

She sent another message two hours later when Uncle, Tran, and I would have arrived at the dock.

No deficiencies. Now they're checking for a possible infection he might have contracted during his last trip to the ER. This makes no sense to me since his head wound has healed and the stitches have dissolved. Apparently, infections can hide in the body and cause muscle aches, dizziness, and fatigue. All of which he has.

Ninety minutes later.

No infection. They will run more tests tomorrow, but they won't tell me what for. My mind is filled with horrible possibilities.

Don't they understand the stress caused by the information they withhold?

Thirty minutes later.

Now he's having trouble with his vision. He thought I was a nurse! They've added an ophthalmologist to his team. They're sending me home for the night. I'm at my wits end. Please call when you can.

This last message had come in as I had sailed off the cargo ship in my Hail Mary dive.

"Is your father okay?" Uncle asked.

Tran looked up. "What's wrong with him?"

"He's in the hospital. The doctors are running tests. My mother is dealing with it alone." I narrowed my eyes. "I'm surprised you didn't know."

"Why would I? You're here in this train with me."

Tran returned to texting.

Had he just admitted to stalking?

I shook my head and returned to Ma's messages. She hadn't sent another before she had gone to bed, probably too worried and heartsick by my lack of response. Thanks to Tran, I could remedy that now.

Hi, Ma. I'm so sorry I didn't answer. My phone fell into a river and I had to get it replaced. 😳I know... sounds like a dog-ate-my-homework excuse, right? 😄

I added a paragraph space and considered what to write. The possibility of an infection scared me, but I didn't want to pass my fear onto her.

Infections can be dangerous, I typed and deleted.

You know what Baba would say... Don't borrow trouble. I deleted that too.

Glad they're testing for infections. Let me know what they find.

I stared at that for a moment and moved on.

The vision trouble is weird. Hope he didn't give you a hard time thinking you were his nurse! I'm sure he's grumpy with everyone and wants to go home.

I added another paragraph space. If she had the phone near her bed, I didn't want it to chime more than one time.

I love you, Ma. I hope you're sleeping soundly and don't hear this message come through. You need to be rested and stay healthy. I'll check in during your morning. ♥♥♥

I reviewed what I had written and hit send.

Chapter Twenty-Seven

The South Hefei Train Station resembled a sleek international airport more than the retro train stations in Los Angeles or New York. It made sense. Millions of passengers traveled by high-speed and bullet trains from Hefei to Shanghai, Wuhan, and Beijing every day. Even so, I was duly impressed.

We bypassed mass transit and opted for taxis. Tran took one to arrange our accommodations and supplies while Uncle and I shared a ride to the apartment address Meimei had provided. Although rude to arrive after dinnertime unannounced, we hoped to catch Suyin's former roommates at home.

A young woman with short blue dyed hair and a comfy sleep t-shirt and pajama pants answered the door. The security chain dangled unused. As she questioned us in Mandarin, I bit back a home-security lecture and smiled.

"We apologize for interrupting your evening," I said in Mandarin. "We came to visit Suyin."

She smiled with surprise. "You are American."

"How could you tell?"

"Your accent," she said in English. "You don't sound Chinese."

I smiled politely. "Well, your English is very good."

She beamed. "I hope you did not come all the way from America to see Suyin. She doesn't live here anymore."

"Oh. Well, this is her uncle Lee. Do you know where she went?"

"Sorry. She left without telling. She took very few belongings. She didn't call or pay her rent, so we gave her things to charity and rented her room." She looked worriedly at Uncle and switched to Mandarin. "We would have called her parents, but we didn't have their phone number. I hope you understand. We needed a paying roommate to afford our expensive apartment."

Uncle didn't look understanding at all.

"May we come in?" I asked, hitching up my backpack and nodding toward Uncle's small travel bag. "We just arrived by train."

"Of course. I didn't mean to be rude."

She opened the door wider and called to her roommates in Mandarin to alert them of our presence. Another young woman of a similar college age peeked out of her room and asked the blue-haired woman who we were and why we were there.

"This is Suyin's uncle. Her friend is from America. Come practice your English."

"America?"

The long-haired woman chattered to someone behind her, then she and a matronly woman with glasses came out of the room. Through the open door, I saw a cramped and messy space. The door to a second bedroom showed the same. Sounds of a shower could be heard from behind door number three.

Our hostess motioned us to the couch and opened the folding chairs stacked against the wall beside the front door for her roommates to sit.

"Do you want water or tea?" she asked in English.

"No, thank you. We don't want to intrude. But we do need to find Suyin. Do any of you know why she left?"

The long-haired woman leaned forward in concentration. "You want Suyin?" When I nodded, she sat back. "I no see her. She no call."

The matronly woman picked up the slack. Her British-accented English suggested an education abroad. "Suyin video chatted more frequently with her gentleman friend before she left. Perhaps she went to live with him?"

"Do you know who he is?"

"This is a small apartment. We respect each other's privacy as much as we can."

"What about the woman in the shower? Would she know?"

"I'm afraid not. Min joined us after Suyin's hasty departure."

I turned to our blue-haired hostess. "You shared a bedroom with Suyin, right? Did she mention this man?"

"No. But he had a sexy voice."

"Did you see what he looked like?"

She chuckled. "Suyin always hid the screen."

The long-haired woman interrupted with excitement. "They speak English."

"Really?" I said. "Like me or like your roommate?"

She sat back. "Sorry. I not understand."

The British-sounding woman came to her rescue. "His English was good, but not fluent. Definitely not British. Maybe European or Asian? Americans have too many accents to tell."

"Did you overhear any of their conversations?"

"I tried not to listen."

"I did," our hostess said. "He talked like her boyfriend.

You know...flirting, asking how she is doing. Always in a very sexy voice."

"Why didn't you tell Suyin's mother about him last night when she called?"

Our hostess laughed and put a finger to her lips. "Friends don't tell mothers about boyfriends."

I didn't point out that friends also didn't give away their friends' possessions after only one month.

The older woman frowned, as if hesitant to chime in. "I don't know if he was her boyfriend, but he definitely wanted her to visit him."

"How do you know?"

"He promised to send her a ticket."

"To where?"

"I went into my room before I could hear more. As I said–"

"You didn't want to invade her privacy?"

"Exactly."

"What about her mood? Did Suyin seem stressed before she left?"

Our hostess laughed. "She stressed about everything – work, money, food."

"What did she say about work?"

"Her bosses were so mean. She cried at night when she thought I was asleep. Then she'd take her computer into the kitchen and call her boyfriend from there."

"The man on the video chat?"

"Mm-hmm. I heard his sexy voice."

"You've mentioned the quality of his voice three times. What about it sounded sexy to you?"

She glanced at Uncle and blushed. "I don't know how to explain. Like bedroom talk. Or when a man wants to take you home."

"Seductive?"

"Yes. And..." She searched for a word.

"Intimate?"

"Mmm... Yes, but..."

The older woman sighed, as if we were pulling her in a direction she did not want to go. "The word you're looking for is persuasive. The man was seducing Suyin into something. I don't know what. It wasn't my place to interfere. Young women rarely listen to spinsters like me. But he had that tone disreputable men use."

"You said they video chatted more frequently before she left. Did Suyin seem excited or in love?"

"Quite the opposite," the older woman said. "She seemed worried and upset."

"With him?"

"No. Oddly enough, he calmed her down."

I looked at our hostess. "Did Suyin ever share her troubles with you?"

"Never."

When I repeated the question in Mandarin for the long-haired woman, she shook her head no.

I had run into this scenario many times in Los Angeles while working for Aleisha's Refuge, most recently with the prostituted teenagers I had encountered while searching for Emma Hughes. I had witnessed a smooth operator entice a sweet, lonely girl into his car. I had watched a master manipulator prey on an ostracized teen, give her a makeover, and convince her to have sex with strangers out of love and gratitude for him. Had Suyin's video chat friend preyed on her distress and lured her into a different kind of hell?

The women exchanged concerned looks when the shower turned off.

I rose from the couch. "We should go. Thanks for your time."

Uncle nodded and hurried to the front door. Neither of us wanted to surprise a potentially naked roommate in her own apartment.

"You handled that well," Uncle said when we reached the street.

"I've had practice."

"It shows. But we are still no closer to finding Suyin."

"No," I agreed. "And if she ran away with a foreigner, she might never be found."

Chapter Twenty-Eight

The address Tran texted us sent Uncle and me out of the inner city and into dense residential districts packed with mid-rise buildings and high-rise apartment blocks. Even with all this land, China stacked its population in tight quarters so everyone would fit.

As we followed the river east, patches of farmland appeared. These rough plots of land had older dwellings only a few stories high – holdouts from the urbanization that pressed in from all sides. Our rideshare driver passed a massive complex with two dozen buildings beside an equally massive school surrounding a pristine athletic track and field. Soon after, he turned into a warren of modest five-story buildings, built so tightly they might have shared a common wall.

Tran waited in one of the doorways and led us to the back apartment on the first floor. He opened the door with a flourish. "Welcome to basecamp."

The tiny space that greeted us had a playpen jammed between shelves and a coffee table in front of a quilt-covered couch. Toys and baby paraphernalia had been shoved to the sides along with towers of shoe boxes and possessions of all kinds.

I was stunned. "We're staying with a family?"

"Not with. They moved out for us."

"No offense, but...this doesn't seem like your style."

"Too domestic?"

I tried to picture tiny Trans toddling about the apartment. "Little bit."

He chuckled. "We won't be here long. This building has a rear exit that might come in handy. It's also located within a mile of the gang's address."

"You found them?"

"It wasn't that hard. Once I mentioned fentanyl, my contact pointed me to them."

"The contact who lives in this apartment?"

"No. The contact who convinced this family to leave. There's food in the kitchen and a bedroom with a large futon we can share."

"We who?"

"That's up to you." He winked. "But the futon looks quite comfortable." He peeked into the child's room and grinned. "The boy has a race car bed. I'm too big, but your diminutive frame might fit."

"Flirt on your own time," Uncle said. "We have business to do." He tossed his bag into the parents' bedroom and headed for the kitchen to make us something to eat.

I set my backpack on the hood of the boy's race car bed. The compartment bulged from the clothes squished inside. When I emerged, I found Tran unpacking a box of weapons perched on a chair. He aligned the mini-arsenal on the table – two Sig Sauers, one Glock, three knives. This would replace the weapons we had stowed in Tran's SUV before we caught the train to Hefei.

"I don't want a gun," I said.

"I didn't expect you would. The Sigs are for me. Take your pick of the knives, Lee and I will divvy up the rest."

I chose an auto-release blade that fit nicely in my palm while Tran unpacked speckled coveralls, cans of spray paint, and assorted painting supplies.

"What's all this."

"Cover," he said. "Or insurance, depending how things play out."

"You know what? This has been a really long day. Tell me in the morning. Uncle can fill you in on what we learned at Suyin's old apartment."

"You don't want to eat?"

I glanced at the kitchen. "Actually, no."

Ignoring his dumbfounded expression, I returned to the boy's room, shut the door, and sat on his bed. Nine thirty at night meant six thirty in the morning for Ma. I took out my phone and typed.

Are you awake?

I counted the seconds before she replied.

Yes. Can we talk?

She answered in the kitchen while pouring a cup of tea.

"Hey, Ma. Sorry I didn't get back to you sooner."

She dismissed my apology with a twitch of her unpenciled brows. "I'm sure you had more pressing things to do."

I flinched from the barb, but what could I say? That her daughter had been risking her life fighting gangsters and chasing drug traffickers across China? I couldn't add to Ma's stress with worry about me.

"How are you holding up?"

She set down the teapot and sighed. "Not well."

Worry tracked across her lovely skin like spider cracks on a windshield. I hadn't seen her without makeup since I moved out of her house and into the apartment Baba had

built for me over his restaurant. Even so, I was certain the
age on her face hadn't been there before.

"Were you able to sleep?" I asked.

"Fitfully. I saw your message when I woke up. Sorry
about your phone. How on Earth did you land it in a river?"

"Fluke accident."

"Uh-huh. Never mind. I don't want to know."

Ma and I walked a thin line between open communication
and strategic ignorance.

"How's Baba's mood?"

"Cranky."

She brushed the hair from her eyes. "Who can blame him?
His legs cramp and spasm. His vision blurs then clears. He
falls asleep while we're talking then wakes up disoriented.
He's frustrated. And though he won't admit it, I think he's
afraid."

That admission alarmed me most of all.

"After my tea, I'll put myself together and drive back to
the hospital. They took him to Cedars when he collapsed
in the restaurant, so it's a bit of a haul. Once I'm there, I'll
camp out for the day."

"Do you know what they have planned?"

"More tests. And a neurologist, I think. Oh, and an
ophthalmologist to check on his eyes. Although poor vision
might work in my favor considering how horrid I must look."

I smiled. "Tired, maybe. Never horrid."

"If you say so."

"What about his legs?"

She shook her head in frustration. "Who knows? I'm not
even sure they believe he's in pain."

My father was stoic beyond belief. If anything, he was
downplaying any discomfort he felt.

Ma read my expression. "I know. I told them to add two frowny faces to his pain chart for whatever claimed."

"Frowny faces?"

She grimaced. "It's the hospital's method of measuring pain. They treat the patients like children and show them little faces from happy to sad. As if your father would ever label himself with anything less than a neutral expression. When his legs cramped up like arthritic fingers, they started listening to me. They gave him muscle relaxers to unclamp his muscles and ease the pain he insisted he did not feel. He was resting peacefully when I left last night. Thank God."

She stopped fidgeting and gazed through her phone straight into my heart. "Have you found Lee's grandniece? Because it would really help to have you home." The crack in her voice nearly brought me to tears.

She looked so fragile without her armor of makeup and couture. Although she was only fifty, I glimpsed a future when I would care for her in old age as she had cared for me as a child. I yearned to fold her in my arms and protect her from what lay ahead.

"I love you, Ma."

"Hmm. I guess that means you're not coming home."

My parents needed me, but Uncle and his family needed me more. Even if I raced home to Los Angeles, there wasn't much I could do besides comfort my mother and help her advocate on Baba's behalf. In China, my efforts could potentially keep Chyou and Suyin alive, not to mention Uncle and Tran. With only three warriors in the fight, the outcome hung on a silken thread. Each of us needed the others to survive.

"I'll come home as soon as I can."

She forced a brave expression and busied herself with something on the counter. "Well, I better hurry if I want to greet your father when he wakes up."

"Do they allow you to bring in food?"

"Not while they're running tests."

"Ooh, he's gonna be cranky."

"He certainly is. You know how he is about breakfast."

I smiled. "Most important meal of the day."

Baba had grown up on a North Dakota farm where my Norwegian grandmother had fixed massive morning meals for him and his father once they had completed their chores. On one of my visits, Bestefar had bragged about their breakfasts in great detail while bemoaning the strict diet Farmor and his doctors made him follow once he retired. Pancakes, eggs, biscuits, gravy, bacon *and* sausage, berries in thick clotted cream, hot coffee, and tall glasses of fresh cold milk would be served at one sitting after they had milked the cows, mucked the stalls, fed the chickens, and completed the other chores that needed to be done before Baba went off to school. Although my father had trimmed down his morning meals considerably, hospital cream of wheat and powdered eggs wouldn't satisfy him at all.

"Too bad you can't sneak in some jook," I said.

"Who would fix it?"

"Bayani or Ling."

"The restaurant is closed, remember? And your father thinks my jook is bland."

Baba had a point: my mother's talent for financial affairs did not extend to her kitchen.

"Give him a hug for me?"

"I will."

I blew her a kiss, which she caught and placed on her cheek. Tears welled in her eyes. She brought her fingers to her lips and blew me a kiss before they fell.

Chapter Twenty-Nine

I rolled onto my side and knocked my wrist against the car-bed's frame. Hours had passed and I still couldn't sleep. I shifted onto my back and stared at the ceiling. Even without a window, the room wasn't entirely dark. I could see where the wallpaper had begun to peel at the edge. *What colors were hiding behind the checkered flag motif?*

I shifted again and conked my head against the spoiler and my toes against the hood. Not only was the bed too small, the mattress had sunken into the contours of a body tinier than mine.

I checked the time on my phone. Three in the morning. The most I could hope for was a few hours of sleep. What difference would it make if I didn't sleep at all?

My belly growled.

I should have taken the time to eat, but I was so annoyed with Tran's teasing that I had fled into this room like a kid.

Tran.

Once again, he invaded my thoughts with that smirking, all-knowing grin.

The futon looks quite comfortable.

Yeah? Well, I hope it had lumps.

I swung my legs over the side and struggled to stand as the mattress sank under my weight. How was a kid supposed to get out of this thing? Crawl over the hood? Or was the point of the design to keep the wee ones in bed? Either way, I just wanted to be rid of the dang thing and get something to eat. What I didn't expect was to find Tran sleeping on the couch.

The moonlight shone through the window and illuminated his face, which looked younger in repose. No animated expressions creased his forehead and mouth. No hard eyes that had seen more bloodshed and trauma than any person should bear. I could almost see the child he might have been if not for the uncomfortably masculine ridges of his cheekbones and jaw.

I crept forward a few feet and stared at the curling black hair on his chin. If he let it grow, it would be as thick and dark as his peaked brows and his long, wavy hair. What ethnic genes had mingled with his Vietnamese mother's to create his undefinable looks?

Although an enticing puzzle, I couldn't restrain my gaze to his face.

When I had first seen him in the courthouse in his tailor-fitted suit, he had reminded me of a celebrity quarterback or welterweight boxer. Since then, I had seen his muscularity accentuated by tightly fitted shirts. None of this prepared me to see him naked to the drawstring of his cropped kimono pants.

Although embarrassed by my voyeurism, I couldn't look away.

The cuts in his pecs were so clearly defined they divided his chest into separate plateaus. The swells and chasms of his shoulders and arms were equally acute, which, combined with his low body fat, sculpted a breathtaking physique.

Tran's ribs expanded as he breathed, followed by an exhale so deep it sank his stomach into a shallow bowl beneath his pants. My hands opened as I imagined how that smooth slope might feel as I followed the enticing trail of hair.

Walk away, Lily.

My feet wouldn't move.

I noticed the stiletto resting on the coffee table within his easy reach and reminded myself of the horror I'd seen him inflict with a similar blade. Spell broken, I crept into the kitchen. As I opened a cupboard for something to eat, a familiar sensation electrified my back.

Since I had assumed the men were asleep, I hadn't bothered donning a sports bra underneath my loose racerback tank or changing into a less revealing top. My sleep tank offered as much protection as a pair of transparent scarves.

Tran's breath heated my neck while the energy from his hands ran up the sides of my arms.

No touch.

No skin.

Only the electrical heat of his intention and my willing, open nerves.

God help me, I wanted this man.

"No," he whispered as I tried to turn around. "Close your eyes and feel."

A shudder passed through me as Tran's energy played upon my skin, raising goose bumps to intercept his touch. When he moved his hands over my shoulders and down the front of my breasts, I leaned toward his touch. But he maintained his distance and exhaled another quiet yet commanding, "No."

The heat on my cheek dove down the side of my throat while he circled his hands around my arms to my back. The trail of energy ignited my nerves.

His name burst from my lips in a rush of strangled air.

"Feel, Lily."

He exhaled down my shoulder blade and into the racerback opening of my tank while the energy from his palms slid between my thighs. Never had I ever received waves of intention as powerful or as intimate as these. My cotton briefs offered not the slightest defense.

Without a single touch exchanged, I gasped, over and over, from the sweet anguish he caused. When I couldn't bear it any longer, his energy rose up my belly and grabbed my hips in a vice.

I stifled a cry.

It shouldn't have been possible. But I would have sworn on my life that he thrust up and into me.

His panting groan equaled my own. Although he denied me physical touch, my body didn't care. It responded to every projected intent in a battle of passion I had never fought harder to win.

Then he broke away, and I collapsed against the counter, shuddering and spent.

When I finally turned around, Tran was back on the couch, hand on his belly, eyes closed, as still as the dead.

Chapter Thirty

Tran drove the beat-up sedan out of our residential block and into a meager farmland in various stages of growth. Dense clusters of mid-rise communities like the one we had just left and towering apartment blocks pressed against this patchwork of old rural China.

I stared out the backseat window. Even the slightest glance at Tran flushed my face and neck. A ninja zukin and fukumen would have come in handy today.

Tran, on the other hand, seemed perfectly at ease.

He pointed to an eroded gray structure on the barren lot up ahead. "The gang converted that barn into their lab."

"Strange location." I kept my voice steady and my eyes on the barn. "Do they even have water or power?"

"The farms have wells. They wouldn't need electricity. Kerosene or propane would do. Isolation matters more for this kind of work."

"What about security? The property isn't even fenced."

Tran pointed toward the rundown community beyond the next field. "The gang operates from a house over there. According to my contact, they are well armed, respected, and feared. Since they sit at the top of Hefei's criminal food chain, even law enforcement and other black societies leave them alone."

"Did your contact say where they were keeping Chyou?" The normal conversation dissolved my discomfort and focused me on our mission.

"No. They hadn't heard anything about a kidnapped girl."

"They would keep her in the house," Uncle said.

"Agreed." Tran caught my gaze in the rearview mirror. "Which is why we're dropping you off to find her while Lee and I draw them to the lab."

"By doing what? Paint their ugly barn pink?"

Both Tran and Uncle wore paint-speckled coveralls and caps. Neither had bothered to explain why.

"Don't worry about how," Tran said. "When you see the gang rush out of the house, go in and find Chyou. We'll keep them busy. Take her to the commercial zone two blocks to the west and hide out in a shop. We'll pick you up when we're done."

I thought of the Sig Sauers and Glock, then leaned forward between their seats. "No collateral damage."

Tran nodded. "That's the plan."

I tapped Uncle's arm. "And no bloodbath. We don't know that they've hurt Chyou."

Before I could demand assurances, Tran turned onto a road with dilapidated houses that made Shanghai's Old City look pristine. The largest property hid behind stone pillars and a padlocked wrought-iron gate through which I glimpsed a courtyard with an old two-story house directly behind. The roofs of smaller structures peeked above the pillars on both sides.

Tran drove past the gang's compound and parked two houses down. "When they rush out the gate, find the girl, and text me where you land."

"Will do." I squeezed Uncle's shoulder. "I'll get her out safely. I promise."

He patted my hand. "I know."

I hid behind a farm truck while they left and watched the woman across the road pick a few weeds before she carried a basket of eggs into her house.

What would Uncle and Tran do to make the gang leave?

When my patience had almost run out, a percussive boom shook the ground. Two more explosions followed. Neighbors ran into the road, spinning in all directions searching for the cause. Men shouted from inside the gang's compound and engines roared to life. The gate flung open toward the street. Dust kicked up as a four-door compact and a white minivan whipped out of the compound and sped down the road. As the neighbors turned toward the departing vehicles, I slipped through the open gate.

Two stubby buildings ran along the sides of the gang's courtyard, a utility shed on the far side, a bunk house closest to me. A plume of black smoke appeared beyond the roof of the main house.

I hurried past sleep quarters, stinking of unwashed clothes, to the side walkway of the two-story house. When I reached a screen door, I broke the flimsy latch and squeezed between racks of drying laundry on my way to the kitchen. Nine plates of unfinished breakfast sat on the table and counters. Several more sat in the sink. The plates would have served more people than could fit in a minivan and a compact car.

I looked through the window as I crossed the living area and saw black smoke rising in the field beyond the wall. On the other side of the communal space, a corridor led to more bunk-bed rooms like the ones I had seen before. The door at the end opened, and a man armed with a bolo machete emerged.

I spotted him seconds before he spotted me.

Knuckles to his throat shut down his voice.

A chop from my bladed hand loosened his grip.

A strike to his neck knocked him into the wall.

When the man grabbed for my hair, I slid my arm between us like a wedge, guided him into a headlock, and kneed him in the groin. Before he could recover from my multiple assaults, I relieved him of the deadly agricultural tool and put him out of commission with a machete slice up his armpit and a handle butt to the head. He slid, bleeding to the floor, severely disabled but with a decent chance to survive.

I listened for sounds of alarm and heard none.

How many guards remained in the house?

I raced to the stairs, machete dangling from my hand. It was a death trap, but with sirens in the distance, I was running out of time. When I had almost reached the top, a gunman appeared. With no time or space to wield the machete, I powered up the final steps and lunged into his knees.

The gun fired beside my ear.

Deaf and unbalanced, I spiraled onto my back as he aimed his next shot between my eyes. I kicked my foot into his face as he fired, grabbed his gun wrist, and brought up my other leg to scissor his arm. When he leaned forward to attack, I rocked my body forward and launched him down the stairs.

The man cartwheeled into the walls and broke his neck on a step.

I picked up the fallen machete. Two shots had been fired. Despite the noisy aftermath of the explosion, someone must have heard and recognized the sound. I had to find and rescue Chyou before the Hefei gang returned.

This time, I held the machete ready to swing.

A door opened at the end of the hall. When an armed man rushed out of the room, I took aim and let the heavy blade fly. The gunman teetered backward with the machete cleaved between his brows.

I jumped over the body and found Chyou strapped to the bed, mouth opened in screams I still couldn't hear. I held out my weaponless hands and told her in Mandarin that I was a friend. The tones must have sounded correct because she asked me something in return.

I gestured to my left ear and shook my hands so she would understand. But when I removed the folding knife from my pocket, she cowered anew. I pointed to the strap and brought my finger to my lips, praying an army wasn't storming up the stairs.

"Your grandfather sent me. My name is Lily. Do you understand?"

She nodded.

I cut through the straps. "Do you hear people or cars?"

She shook her head.

"Good. Let's go."

Through the window, I saw the gang's laboratory barn burning in the field. Men watched from beside the white minivan. The first responders still hadn't arrived. Neither Tran's Toyota nor the gang's compact sedan could be seen.

I pulled her toward the hallway, but the grisly sight of the guard made her scream.

The sound cut through my deafness. Either I was regaining my hearing or Chyou had screamed loud enough to alert the neighbors in the street.

I led her down the stairway, past the body sprawled at the base. When I picked up the dead man's gun, she broke free and ran for the front door. I shoved her away from the handle as a car skidded into the compound and screeched to a stop.

"This way." I dragged her into the kitchen toward the screen door I had entered. "Stay behind me, okay?"

When she nodded, I stepped into another death-trap corridor, except this time, I had a gun.

Car doors slammed. Men shouted orders as boots stomped over cement and into the house.

I moved quickly up the walkway, listening for footsteps other than ours. The gang had entered through the front door. Some of them or all?

When a shoe crunched gravel, I took aim and nearly shot Uncle in the head.

He ducked and lowered his Glock.

I lowered my pistol and sighed with relief. Guns were too easy and deadly to shoot. This was precisely why I preferred knives.

He beckoned us to follow, positioned himself with a clear shot of the front door, and motioned me to take his grandniece and run.

Tran's Toyota waited just behind the pillar with the rear and front passenger doors opened. I shoved Chyou in the backseat. Then I turned and aimed the gun to cover Uncle as he ran. Once he joined Chyou, I hopped in the front, and Tran sped up the road.

Chapter Thirty-One

I turned in my seat toward Tran. "You blew up the lab?"

He exited the rural neighborhood, zipped up a main thoroughfare, and onto a highway. "It worked, didn't it?"

"Yeah, but–"

He took the next exit and blended with the flow of traffic in the general direction of our base. "We have the girl. They don't. Mission complete."

I turned to face Uncle, who had finished introducing himself to Chyou. They had only met once when she was too young to remember.

"I thought we were going to avoid a bloodbath," I whispered.

"We didn't kill anyone. How about you?"

His smug expression told me it was useless to lie.

"They left men in the house to guard her. I killed two, possibly three."

"Possibly?"

"If the gang gets him medical help, he should be okay."

Uncle hugged his niece at his side. "She told me about the dead man with the machete in his face and the twisted body at the bottom of the stairs. These are not sights a twelve-year-old will forget."

I thought of the cases back home where the children had

witnessed or suffered through life-altering violence. It broke my heart. "I'm sorry, Uncle. It couldn't be helped."

"Of course not. Which is why you should not be questioning us."

I watched as he stroked Chyou's messy hair. Each of us would do whatever was necessary to keep her safe.

When we passed a familiar landmark, Tran turned onto our street and drove the ubiquitous sedan into the garage of our generic mid-rise building. "Let's be quick. I want to be on the road within the hour."

So did I.

"Will we drive this time?

"Part way. I don't want to leave from a train station in Hefei, but the owners of the car are unwilling to retrieve it from Shanghai. We'll split the difference and drop it in Changzhou."

Chyou clung to Uncle as we exited the car, then glanced back at me nervously as we walked up the stairs. Halfway down the corridor, she offered a tentative smile.

"Thank you for rescuing me."

Her English was perfect. I would need to speak more carefully in her presence. To Uncle's grandniece, I must be the scariest person of us all.

"You're welcome, Chyou. We'll get you home soon."

Inside the apartment, Uncle held out his hand to Tran. "Give me your phone. I need to text the gang."

"You have their number?" I asked Uncle.

"Not me. Him."

Tran smirked.

Why was I surprised?

When Uncle finished, he showed us the text.

You have no lab, no product, no chemist. Come after my family, and we will eliminate you as well. Signed, Red Pole Chang.

Tran sent the message.

I wasn't so sure.

"You think that will work?"

Uncle held up a finger. Once Chyou had closed the bathroom door, he whispered to us. "Once they connect Red Pole Chang to the Shanghai Scorpion Society, my reputation will speak for itself. But just to be sure..."

He made a call on his own phone to someone who understood Shanghainese. After what sounded like a heated negotiation, he ended the call. His expression looked both satisfied and resigned.

"What did you do?"

"I arranged for protection."

Uncle had called in favors to help me in Hong Kong. Did he have more favors to claim, or had he used the last one on me?

"You'll owe them now, won't you?"

He shrugged. "My family will be safe."

"What will they ask you to do?"

"Whatever they want." He brought out his pistol, disconnected the magazine, and ejected the final round. "I was foolish to think I could leave this life behind."

"You wouldn't be in this position if you hadn't called in favors for me."

"And I wouldn't have rescued Chyou if you and your friend had not come to Shanghai. This is not the time for blame or regret. People like us do what needs to be done."

I glanced at Tran, who was packing our weapons to return to his contact and wiping down the apartment before the family returned. At what point had I become *people* like them?

Uncle smiled at his grandniece as she emerged from the bathroom. "Do you feel better?"

"Yes, Uncle Lee."

"Sit down, please. Before I prepare food for our journey home, I need to ask you a few questions."

She responded in a flurry of Mandarin as though bursting to explain the full horror of her ordeal, beginning with the scary men who pulled her out of the kitchen in the middle of the night.

Uncle stopped her and spoke slowly in English. "You can tell us about that during the ride home. Right now, we need to know about a woman named Feng Suyin. Did you hear the men speak about her?"

She shook her head. "Who is Suyin?"

"She is your cousin, the stepdaughter of your father's aunt."

"Stepdaughter?"

He explained in Mandarin, then switched back to English. "Did the men in the house speak or complain about anything?"

She bounced her head up and down, then alternated between languages to tell the tale.

Apparently, the gang argued about everything – food, belongings, television. Mostly, they complained about business. They were especially angry about an employee who had recently quit, but they talked about her as if she had run away from home. They were also angry with associates in Japan who had stopped communicating with them. The gang called them many names Chyou refused to repeat.

"Good girl," Uncle said. "But did they ever call them Yakuza?"

She nodded but kept her lips sealed as though this mysterious word might be particularly profane.

"It's okay," he said. "There is fruit in the kitchen. Eat a snack before we leave."

She obeyed, looking greatly relieved.

Uncle turned to Tran. "What do you think?"

"Possible. The Yakuza has fragmented into independently run gangs, loosely connected to the main organizations but not necessarily under their jurisdiction. The crime bosses did this to insulate their parent organizations from their unruly children, especially those who sold, made, or trafficked illegal drugs. So when the police bust a drug-dealing gang, they can't connect it to a prominent Yakuza boss."

Uncle hummed in thought. "Okay. Let's say one of these *unruly children* had a connection in Hefei. Why take Suyin? Wouldn't it be better if she stayed in China and made product for them to sell?"

"Not if the Hefei gang was undependable or too highly priced, or unable to keep up with their demand. If Suyin had created a new and potent fentanyl analogue, they might want her to manufacture it directly for them." Tran frowned. "Then again, Japan cracks down hard on illegal drug use and production. It might be safer and more lucrative to sell a talented chemist to a foreign manufacturer for a lot of money or a better distribution deal."

The more I heard, the worse this became.

If poor Suyin was enslaved for life in another gang's country, she'd never make it back to China, let alone to her family in Shanghai. All those teenage belongings lovingly preserved by Meimei in Suyin's childhood room would remain like a shrine to symbolize a mother's never-ending loss. We had rescued Chyou. I wanted to save them both.

"What are you suggesting?" I said. "That we sacrifice Suyin?"

Tran shrugged. "It's not a sacrifice if there's nothing we can do."

Uncle closed his eyes and groaned. "I know someone who can help."

"Who?" I asked.

"Not on an empty stomach." He headed for the kitchen. "I'll explain after we pack and get out of this town."

Tran returned to his weapons and motioned for me to work.

"In a minute," I said. "I need to check in with my mother while we still have dependable Wi-Fi."

"Okay. But don't take too long."

I went into the bedroom for privacy and sent a message to Ma.

Are you still awake?

She responded quickly.

Yes. I can't sleep.

I called and her haggard face appeared on my screen. Mascara and eyeliner had smudged into dark hollows beneath her eyes, lipstick and rouge long since worn away.

"Have you eaten?" Although a common salutation, I was honestly concerned. Deep pockets had formed in my mother's slender neck.

"Yogurt and leftover rice. I don't have the energy to cook."

"Edamame in the freezer?"

"Maybe."

"I think you should check. Seriously, Ma. You're not looking well."

She huffed in annoyance.

"I'm not trying to be mean."

"I know you aren't. And you're right. I need to stay healthy to care for your father."

"Exactly. Now, carry me into the kitchen while you find something to eat."

"Ha. You're bossy even when you're not here."

"Whose fault is that?"

She gave me a dubious look and opened the refrigerator door. She angled the screen so I could see inside. "Well? What do you recommend?"

The shelves were uncommonly bare.

"A kimchee omelet with sautéed greens."

"I told you I didn't want to cook."

"It takes less than two minutes. If I can make it, so can you."

She took out the family-size jar, the egg carton, and the bag of wilting greens. "What now?"

"Pour sesame oil in a pan and toss in the kimchee and greens. Then add three eggs–"

"*Three?*"

"You need the protein. And be generous with oil. No skimping because of calories."

Ma rolled her eyes. "Shouldn't I beat the eggs first?"

"You want to do this right or quick?"

"Quick."

"Then crack the eggs and mix them while they cook."

Ma did as instructed and slid her egg pancake onto a plate in two minutes flat.

"Now pour yourself a tall glass of milk."

"I'm not a child, Lily."

"Baba drinks milk."

"And he's in the hospital with God knows what."

"Humor me. And tell me about the tests while you eat."

She poured the milk and tasted the eggs, nodded with approval, and devoured several more bites. "Did your father teach you this?"

"Uncle."

"How's he doing?"

"We found his grandniece."

"Safe?"

"She is now."

Ma put down her fork. "And you?"

"I'm fine."

She peered into the phone. Although I had angled my face to hide the cut and bruise on my cheek, I could tell she was remembering what had happened in Hong Kong. Before then, she had assumed all of my injuries had come from training, climbing, or sports. I hadn't told her about my rescue and protection work. She hadn't asked. Now that she knew the truth, she would never look at me the same. Satisfied with the state of my face, she ate the rest of her eggs.

Tran appeared in the doorway and motioned me off the bed.

I backed away and kept the camera focused on me as Ma spoke.

"Use my credit card number when you pay for your flight."

"Sorry, what?"

"Your flight, Lily. Book whatever is quickest. Don't worry about the cost."

As I exchanged places with Tran, his energy brushed against my skin.

Ma studied my flushing face and set down her milk. "You *are* coming home now, aren't you, Lily?"

Tran leaned over the tiny bed where I had tried futilely to sleep. Could he smell my scent on the sheet? What might we have done in the privacy of this room?

"Lily?"

"Soon, Ma." I walked into the corridor and leaned against the wall.

"Soon?"

I lowered my voice so Chyou wouldn't hear me from the kitchen. "Another member of Uncle's family has been taken."

"Taken by whom?"

"We're not sure. But Uncle may have a lead."

She shook her head. "I don't like it. Bad enough you put yourself in danger. Now you're letting...whatever this is... take you away from us."

"I'm here, Ma."

"No, you're not. You're six thousand miles away fighting gangsters and risking your life." She scoffed at my surprise. "What? You think I don't know what you're doing? I'm your mother, Lily. I can feel it in my bones."

Angry tears rolled down her cheeks. "Your father needs you. *I* need you."

Her words hit me harder than a club to the head.

Chyou saw me from the kitchen and came to my side. My vulnerability seemed to have made her feel more at ease. "Are you okay, Lily?" she asked in English.

I nodded through my tears.

She peered into my phone and waved. Ma waved back, and Chyou slipped away.

"How old is she?" Ma asked.

"Twelve."

"And the other?"

"Around thirty. She's Uncle's niece."

Ma drank her milk.

I wiped my tears.

She took a breath. "They did more tests today."

"Yeah? What kind?"

"An MRI in the morning and a lumbar puncture in the afternoon."

"Aiya. Was it painful?"

"Not according to your father, but his back was aching when I left. They gave him pain killers that put him to sleep."

"What were they testing for?"

"Inflammation, infection, bleeding..." She shook her head. "Diseases too horrible to contemplate."

"Didn't they say?"

"They glossed over it so fast, then they left us with nurses who didn't say anything at all. Maybe it's better not to know."

I didn't agree. I opened another window on my phone and looked up what a lumbar puncture might diagnose. I didn't like what I found.

"Are you listening to me, Lily? Because you look like you're scrolling through something on your phone."

I closed the window. "Nope. Just considering what you said. I'm sure the doctors will know more by tomorrow."

"Let's hope." She looked at her empty plate and smiled. "You know, that kimchee pancake wasn't half bad. Tell, Lee I said so, okay?"

"I will."

"And tell him I hope you find his niece soon."

This was her way of saying she understood why I needed to stay. But after what I found on my web search, I really wanted to come home. In addition to inflammation, infection, and bleeding, Doctors ordered lumbar punctures to test for scary diseases and disorders like meningitis, Guillain-Barre syndrome, and multiple sclerosis.

We ended the call and I slumped against the wall.

They also ordered lumbar punctures to test for cancers of the spinal cord and brain.

Chapter Thirty-Two

Chyou leaped out of the backseat as the rideshare car rocked to a stop. We had called her parents from the train station before dinnertime and told them we were on our way. With the crates and buckets arranged on the dirt, it appeared as if they had waited outside ever since. Even Chyou's brothers, Zhi and Yong, lent their arms to the family hug.

Qiang stood in the doorway as a stout woman, whom I assumed to be Qiang's wife, waited between him and their son, as if unsure which way she should go.

Uncle stepped away from the car. "Hello, Qiang."

"Hello, Lee."

"Chyou is unharmed."

"I see that."

Uncle switched to Mandarin. "Hello, Xin Yi. A long time has passed. You look well."

The woman smiled and answered too softly for me to hear, making her a perfect fit for the *happy quiet* meaning of her name. She nodded at me, then retreated into the house.

Qiang's son broke free of his daughter's embrace and hurried to us. "Thank you, Uncle Lee. Thank you, Lily. Thank you for returning our sweet Chyou safely to us." He looked at the driver in puzzlement. "Where is your friend? I wish to thank him as well."

"He had things to take care of," Uncle said. "But he sends his regards."

Wei noticed my battered appearance. "Are you okay? Do you have injuries we need to treat?"

"I'm fine." I had taken more beatings in the last thirty-six hours than either Uncle or Tran, who – if he had come with us from the train station – would have looked as pristine and chic as he had when Wei had met him the previous day.

Wei shook his head in wonder. "You risked your life to help strangers. I don't understand, but I cannot thank you enough."

"Your uncle is my friend. I would do anything to help him or the people he loves."

Wei bowed his head. "I am ashamed to say I do not know my family as well as you know your friend." He glanced at his father, rooted like a tree in a fast-moving flood. The reason Wei and his family did not know the Changs was chiefly because of him.

Xin Yi appeared in the doorway and beckoned everyone toward the house.

Qiang stared at the dirt.

Uncle sighed. "We don't have to stay for dinner. The driver will take us home."

Wei took his arm. "Of course you do. Please join us. My mother made extra for you."

Qiang inclined his head in agreement and walked toward the door.

Uncle paused.

"You go ahead," I said. "I'll tell the driver he can go."

"Thank you. I don't think we'll stay long."

I retrieved our bags from the car and followed the men into the house, made tinier with nine of us in the room, and waited for the family to settle into their spots. Chyou had squeezed on the bench with her mother and brothers, leaving a few inches on the end near the sink, presumably for Xin Yi. Qiang sat against the back wall facing the door and gestured for his brother to sit across from him at the opposite end. Wei sat near his father and left the chair closest to Uncle for me.

It felt uncomfortable to have extra room for my chair and Wei's while two women and three children crammed on a bench, but I didn't want to embarrass anyone by offering to make space.

Xin Yi placed a platter of steamed fish with fresh ginger and scallions on the table beside bowls of steamed bok choy, steamed rice, and steamed watercress with noodles served cold. Each of us had a large cup of hot dumpling soup in spite of the kitchen's sweltering heat. I thanked her in Mandarin as she sat, perched on one cheek on the edge of the bench.

Wei served me noodles and watercress before serving himself while Xin Yi placed the best parts of the steamed fish onto Uncle's plate and mine. Then everyone helped themselves and passed the platters and rice.

Baba would have loved the fresh simplicity of this meal. Everything on the table had come straight from their farm.

"What's wrong?" Uncle whispered as he passed the bowl of rice.

"Worrying about Baba."

"Stop that and eat. Your worry can wait."

I rolled my eyes. "Yes, Uncle."

Chyou giggled at our exchange and stuffed her mouth with leafy bok choy. It pleased me to watch her eat a healthy dinner after the junk food wrappers and soda cans I had seen beside the shackle on her sleeping mat in the Chongming gang's lair. Neither she nor her family had spoken about her ordeal.

"Uncle Lee," Wei said. "Please tell us about our family."

Qiang slurped the dumplings from his soup as the older children leaned forward. Yong stood beside his grandfather so he could see as well as hear.

Uncle put down his spoon and addressed the children in Mandarin. "Have you studied our city's history in school?"

The children nodded.

"Then you have learned a version of the truth."

Qiang snorted in agreement.

"Our story is the story of Shanghai, full of adventure, heartache, danger, poverty, and reward. I don't have time to share it all tonight. But I will tell you about the house on Qiaojia Road."

Uncle's expressions filled in the words I didn't understand as he told the children how their great-great-great-grandparents had immigrated to Shanghai from Nanjing and built the shikumen house where their grandfather Qiang was born.

"Where were *you* born, granduncle?" Yong asked.

"In Hong Kong. But you are jumping ahead of my story. Keep eating. This will take a long time to tell."

He glossed over the hardships of the civil war and dramatized the Japanese invasion with explosive sounds that made the children gasp between bites.

"Your great-great-grandmother fled to the Old City after the Japanese attacked her village in Pudong. When she married your great-great-grandfather and had a son, eleven people lived in the tiny Qiaojia Road house."

Uncle opened his eyes wide at the children. "Can you imagine so many people living here?"

The boys shook their heads and stuffed their mouths with more food.

"And don't forget the bombs and the fighting. Shanghai was a dangerous place with the Japanese on our soil. When they took over the city, many of our neighbors fled to the International Settlement to be safe." Uncle dropped his voice to increase the suspense. "Imagine a sea of people with their belongings strapped to their backs and furniture stacked onto rickshaws and carts. The roads were so crowded they could hardly move."

Yong giggled nervously, but Zhi looked concerned. "Did our family flee?"

Uncle shook his head. "They wouldn't abandon the house they had built."

"But the bombs..."

"Destroyed many neighborhoods," Uncle agreed. "It was a hard time for everyone. Then the Americans dropped the bomb on Nagasaki, and the Japanese left. Our government took control of the settlements and concessions. World War II had ended, but China's civil turmoil continued between the ruling Kuomintang and the rising CCP."

Uncle gestured toward Qiang. "Our grandparents moved to Hong Kong, where our parents married and had me. After our grandfather died, our father brought us back to Shanghai. That's when your grandfather Qiang and Grandauntie Meimei were born. We grew up with twenty Changs squeezed into a house as small as yours."

As the children debated whether or not to believe their granduncle's outlandish claim, Qiang flashed his brother a worried look. The next part of their family's history was especially bitter for him. Uncle understood and bypassed it out of respect. When Qiang was ready, he could share his part of the story however he wished.

Uncle glared at the children, furrowing his brows like a demon in a play. "I am your granduncle. Of course I'm telling you the truth. We lived on top of one another like a bucket of crabs."

He ate a huge bite of noodles and slurped the tails into his mouth, then kept eating until they begged him for more.

He had done similar things with me, shaking a roasted duck leg at my nose, demanding my four-year-old respect. I had giggled then as these children giggled now.

When they finally quieted, he pointed his chopsticks at each of them in turn. "No matter what happened in China and in Shanghai, we had each other and the community around Qiaojia Road. I tell you this so you can appreciate how difficult it was for your grandmother and our relatives to move."

Wei leaned forward. "The family held on to the house for all those years?"

"Not exactly. The CCP took control for a while. I bought the building three years after our father died."

"Why did you sell it?"

"The government gave me no choice. I waited as long as I could, but they ordered everyone to leave. By then, only four people lived in the house – your grandmother and her late husband's brother, his wife, and their son. The government relocated our cousins to an apartment in Pudong. I took your grandmother to live with Meimei and her husband in an affluent part of Shanghai." He turned to Chyou and quieted his voice. "These are the parents of Suyin."

Wei gasped. "The woman the gangsters wanted to exchange for Chyou?"

"Yes."

"What happened to her?"

"We still don't know. But she might be in Japan."

"Japan?"

"It's a long story, nephew, better suited for another time."

Wei caught the hint and returned to his fish.

Zhi broke the silence, in awe of the single fact in their family history that seemed most remarkable to him. "You owned property in the *city*?"

Uncle spurt the soup into his bowl.

I came to his rescue, deciding his relatives should know what he was unwilling to say. "Your granduncle owns several properties in Shanghai and a house in Los Angeles."

"Really?" Zhi asked.

"Oh yes. He works in my father's restaurant as a cook, but he's a very successful man." I eyeballed Uncle. "He's just so modest that he keeps these things to himself."

Uncle snorted at my sarcasm and stabbed the fish with his chop sticks as he probably wanted to stab me.

I ignored him and smiled at the boys. "The truth is, your granduncle cares very deeply about people even when he hasn't seen them in years."

Wei and the women glanced at Qiang, then back at each other without saying a word. My description did not fit the man their patriarch had maligned over the years.

Qiang shoved his plate aside, gaze locked on his brother in the seat of honor opposite his own. How many decades had passed since they had shared the same meal? How many more would it take for the resentment to die?

Xin Yi broke the tension with a bowl of cold grass jelly cubes swimming in sweet condensed milk. She smiled at the children and asked who wanted cincau, to which they answered enthusiastically in Mandarin, "Me, me, me."

Chapter Thirty-Three

After a blessed night's sleep and a hearty breakfast of jook, eggs, and pork, we headed for the subway station to visit Uncle's elderly cousins in their new apartment in Pudong.

I took advantage of the free Wi-Fi to check the messages Ma had sent while I slept. Since it was 5 p.m. in Los Angeles, I had to scroll through several to find the start of the new thread.

Good morning, darling. Thanks for the call and cooking lesson last night. I'm not sure which helped more, but I was finally able to sleep. Thank God, because today is already off to a miserable start. Your father has been suffering from headaches all morning. We haven't seen the doctors yet, but his new nurse thinks it's a side effect from the lumbar puncture he had yesterday afternoon. She put in a request to give him something for the pain. I hope it's not another symptom of whatever brought us here.

An hour later.

He vomited his breakfast, which this nurse claims is another side effect from the lumbar test. She contacted the doctor and received permission to give him something for the nausea, which better work soon because, for some unfathomable reason, she won't give him headache medication until he can drink water and swallow a pill. Honestly, Lily...we're in a hospital. Why not give him a shot? None of this makes any sense to me.

Two hours later.

He can drink water. Hurray! But his nurse still won't give him anything for his headache until he can keep down his food because the pills might upset his stomach and make him vomit again. Why won't she give him pain medication through the IV? When I asked, she repeated what she had already said. 😩 *Your father is taking this better than me. He jokes that he'll be so slim from vomiting you'll mistake him for Ryan Reynolds when you return. LOL!*

Three hours later.

FINALLY! The doctors arrived. They said these side effects could last hours or even more than a week. Needless to say, your father was not pleased. But they did authorize pain medication for his headaches through...I'm sure you've guessed it...the IV!!! 😔 *Did his new nurse apologize for dismissing my suggestions? She did not!*

One minute later.

I was so angry, I forgot to tell you. The MRI results were inconclusive. Still no results from the LP test.

Two hours later.

Your father is resting. 😴 *I'm bored out of my mind but too distracted to work. Are you there? Can you talk?*

👋👋👋

I guess you're busy doing something exciting and important. Hopefully NOT dangerous. Seriously, Lily. I'm almost as worried about you as I am about Vern. I don't believe for a minute that your trip is as fun as those pictures made it seem. Please be careful and check in when you can.

Two hours later.

Nothing new to report. The commissary tea selection is atrocious.

No adorable stickers or GIFs.

"Is everything okay?" Uncle asked.

"Ma's losing it. Baba's suffering. The new nurse isn't helping. The doctors don't have a clue. But, hey...everything is peachy." I took breath. "I'm sorry. It's not your fault Baba's in the hospital. I just want them to figure it out and let him go home."

Uncle nodded as the subway doors closed. "Our stop is next. Send a message while you can."

I took a breath and stared at my phone. What could I write that would commiserate, encourage, and empower without instigating World War III? It might be safer to write nothing at all.

The train decelerated. Uncle stood. I typed faster than my mind could think.

What a nightmare! Keep advocating for Baba. Even doctors can make mistakes and miss obvious things. Never be embarrassed to ask your questions. The nurses are doing what they think is best, but they don't know Baba the way you do. Also, new nurses may lack information the old nurses had. Believe in yourself. And tomorrow, bring a book and good tea! 🍫☕❤️❤️❤️

I stepped off the train and hit send.

"You good?" Uncle asked.

"As good as I can be."

"Okay. Let's find a taxi."

"Can't we transfer to another train?" In Los Angeles, I opted for Metro whenever I could, and our mass transit didn't come close to the efficiency and convenience of Shanghai's.

Uncle kept walking. "Once the government has completed Line 18, people will be able to ride a train all the way to Hangtouzhen, which is close to where they have relocated my cousins. For now, this is as far as we can go. If we don't see a taxi, I'll call for a ride."

I stuck to his side as he cut a path through the crowd. "Tell me more about your cousin's connection to Japan.

Tran said something about a Green Gang, Chiang Kai-shek, and some gangster with big ears?"

"You mean Big-Ear Du. He took over the Green Gang in 1924 after Huang Jinrong stepped down. The two of them and the traitor-gangster Zhang Xiaolin were known as the Three Shanghai Tycoons."

He flagged down an aqua-colored Dazhong taxi.

"With Big-Ear Du at the helm, the Green Gang controlled gambling dens, prostitution and protection rackets, shipping corporations, and banks. They also ran the opium trade in the French Concession, which secretly funded Chiang Kai-shek's political rise in the Kuomintang."

Once we were on our way, Uncle lowered his voice so the driver couldn't hear.

"The year after my great-grandparents, my grandaunts, and my teenage grandfather built the shikumen house on Qiaojia Road, the Green Gang massacred thousands of Communist union workers in Shanghai. The gang provided muscle for the Kuomintang and fought against the Japanese invasion in 1932. When the Communists regained power, the Kuomintang retreated to Taiwan, and Big-Ear Du moved to Hong Kong."

Uncle whispered into my ear. "Since my grandfather was a known KMT sympathizer, he followed Big-Ear Du to Hong Kong with my grandmother and father. Zhang Xiaolin, the last of the three ruling gangsters, remained in Shanghai. Although Chiang Kai-shek had implored him and the others not to collaborate with the Japanese, Zhang formed his own gang and did exactly that. He betrayed his own countrymen for profit. The connections he established continue to this day.

"Is your cousin a descendant of Zhang Xiaolin?"

"No. He is the son of my grandaunt and her husband, who tried to prevent Zhang's assassination. You met him at the old house."

"*Chester?*" I couldn't imagine a more unlikely criminal hero's heir than the slovenly layabout living off of Uncle's dime.

"Not Chester. His father, the feeble man lying on the bed. He has dementia and can't remember the tales of his own father's heroics. His wife not only remembers the stories; she keeps the debt owed to her late father-in-law alive."

"That must have happened in the 1940s, right? I'm surprised the new gang members would care."

"They wouldn't. But my clever elder cousin has made them feel as if it is a matter of pride."

As Uncle had told the children last night, the Chang family's history truly did entwine with Shanghai. I hadn't experienced this growing up in Los Angeles because my parents had immigrated from North Dakota and Hong Kong. How hard had it been for Uncle to leave this city and come to LA?

Endless apartment blocks lined the broad avenue and every other broad avenue we had passed, broken up by patches of struggling urban farms. Even the homier midrise neighborhoods numbed my mind. Pudong's riverside skyscrapers topped the horizon like an enticing but distant mirage.

Uncle looked out my window at a strip of marshy land. "My grandmother grew up in a village near here before the government built this development over the swampy agricultural land."

The taxi turned off the thoroughfare onto a newly-paved avenue bordered by construction sites and empty lots. We followed it through abandoned agricultural land to a cluster of apartment buildings sprouting like weeds in parched dirt.

What a depressing place to live.

"The government relocated them here?"

Uncle shrugged. "It looks bad now, but in five years, the development will be complete."

"How old are your cousins?"

"Seventy-eight."

I thought of Baba's parents, still active on their North Dakota farm. Once they hit their mid-eighties, I imagined they would slow down. My mother's parents were older and already moving and thinking more slowly. The years before ninety were precious, indeed.

"I don't know, Uncle. Five years could be a quarter of their lives."

"Maybe for Auntie. I doubt Uncle will survive that long. But wait until you see inside. This complex will have its own markets, pharmacies, and parks on the ground level. Everything they need is only an elevator ride away."

Hong Kong had similar complexes, but nothing this remote.

At the end of the hall on the thirty-first floor, Chester answered Uncle's knock with a sneer. "What do you want?"

"We came to check on your parents and make sure they're okay."

"Who's at the door?" his mother yelled in Mandarin.

"Chang Lee."

"Why?"

"To see how you are?"

She laughed.

Chester led us into a stark but roomy space with white walls and wood veneer floors. Boxes and bags of unpacked belongings leaned against the familiar couch and chairs.

Uncle ran his hand along his former entertainment console. "Nice furniture."

Chester raised his chin. "You never said we couldn't take it."

"I never said you could." Uncle glanced at the modern appliances in the kitchen. "At least you'll finally learned how to cook."

"Why? So I can work in a kitchen like you?"

Chester's mother walked out of the bedroom wearing a flowered shift, rubber house slippers, and socks. "Are you trying to kill us, Chang Lee? Banish us to Pudong. Now encourage Chester to cook?"

Uncle walked to the window. "Impressive view."

"At what? No skyscrapers or people. Just empty, ugly land."

I had to admit, his cousin had a point.

Uncle gestured to me. "You remember my friend Lily Wong?"

"Why would I? All your child girlfriends look the same to me."

Uncle ignored the dig and sat on the couch. "Sit beside me, Auntie. I have news to tell you about our family."

She perked up with interest. "Oh? Is your mother sick?"

Just when I thought this horrid woman couldn't be any more offensive, the glee in her eyes said she could.

I turned my back as Uncle explained what had happened to Chyou and Suyin so I wouldn't have to watch the callous expressions cross her face. Since they spoke rapidly in Mandarin, it was easy to zone out. Even so, easy phrases broke through my fog: *Too long. Don't remember. Why should I care?*

Uncle's elder cousin wouldn't help him if she could.

I turned toward the couch in alarm as I recognized new phrases: *Buy me. Owe me. House in Putuo.* The woman gestured furiously about her apartment and out the window as she spoke.

Uncle held out placating hands. "I cannot afford to buy you a house, Auntie. What else can I do?"

"I guess nothing. Just like me."

Uncle slowed his speech, making him easier to understand. "Suyin is like a daughter to my sister. That makes her a cousin to you. All I want to know is who the Hefei gang is doing business with in Japan."

"This is no small favor, Red Pole Chang. If I ask this question for you, it will end their obligation to me."

"What else can I do?"

"Get me out of this hell hole and back to Shanghai."

Uncle didn't point out that the Pudong New Area was also part of Shanghai.

He stared at the floor and shook his head, as if arguing with himself. "Will the Former French Concession do?"

Her eyes lit up with greed as she pretended his offer was no big deal. "It's far from our daughter, but it's better than this. Where would we live?"

"In a shikumen house apartment."

"Top floor?"

"Yes."

"What about the kitchen? I don't want strangers eating our food."

"It has its own kitchen and a washing machine, all modern like this."

"When could we move in?"

"My renter leaves in two months."

"Hmm. That's a long time to wait at my age."

Uncle shrugged. "It will pass quickly. Like one morning and one evening, then you'll wake in the most coveted district in Shanghai."

She hid her excitement behind a devious grin. "I accept."

"Not so fast, Auntie. First, you must help me find our cousin."

"Sure, sure. I will ask."

"Not good enough. If you want to live in my expensive apartment, the information you give me must lead to Suyin."

Chapter Thirty-Four

"Welcome to Japan," the customs agent said, returned my passport, and flagged Uncle to come forward after me.

I joined Tran on the other side of the barrier. "Will they let him through?"

"They should."

"Should isn't yes."

He shrugged. "We'll know soon enough."

Japan permitted citizens from sixty-eight countries to visit for up to ninety days without a Visa. China was not on the list. Hong Kong was. Uncle had used nefarious means and his maternal grandparents' Junk Bay address to renew the Hong Kong-issued passport he had received when his parents moved him to Shanghai. He used the same means and address to acquire the new Hong Kong Special Administration Region passport that was created when the British transferred sovereignty to China. I had questioned him about this before we left Shanghai.

"Is that what you used to come to Hong Kong to help me?"

"No need," he had said. *"My Chinese credentials were good enough. This will be the first time I've put the false passport to the test."*

I couldn't believe it. *"You went to all that trouble on the off chance you might need it at some point in your life?"*

"HKSAR passports are valuable. I had an advantage to exploit, so I did."

So we booked our flights and hoped Japan would let him in.

Everything had gone smoothly with the airline. Uncle and I traveled by coach while Tran flew first class. He had offered to upgrade my seat, but I had declined. Even without focusing his intention, Tran's energy pricked my skin with electrical heat. Hours sitting beside him in the quasi-privacy of first class modules would have driven me mad.

I used the quiet flight, sandwiched between snoozing Uncle and the window, to raise my shields and shut down the energy receptors Sensei had trained me to hone. Tran's energy had vanished and left me blessedly detached. I couldn't even feel the urgency of travelers as they hurried through the terminal. The absence of sensation felt odd yet comforting to my over-stimulated nerves.

"There he is." I pointed across the terminal where Uncle rolled his carryon down the gleaming white tiles.

"Any trouble?" Tran asked him when he arrived.

"Just the normal delays. Get your luggage so we can go."

Although Tran and Uncle traveled light, I had brought the same luggage I had taken to Hong Kong. As soon as we rescued Suyin, I planned to fly straight home.

I yanked my suitcase off the conveyor belt and rolled it after Tran. "Don't we need passes for the train?"

He veered toward a parking lot. "My contact left us a car."

The vehicle turned out to be a gun-metal gray turbo-engine Subaru. Tran found the hidden key. Within minutes, we were on our way to the Naniwa Ward in Osaka where a former Yakuza group was rumored to buy fentanyl from the gang in Hefei. Uncle's horrid cousin had held up her end of the deal. If her information led us to Suyin, Uncle would have to pay her price.

"How much rent money will you lose?" I asked Uncle.

"With the shikumen penthouse?"

"Yeah."

"It's in the Former French Concession so...five thousand US dollars a month."

"That's a big hit."

He stared out his window. "What else could I do?"

I turned forward in my seat and considered my friend. I doubted anyone else in Uncle's family would have come to the same decision had the tables been reversed.

Tran sped through a light and then slowed into traffic.

"Wouldn't a train have been faster?" I asked.

"Faster and more convenient. But we may need privacy and flexibility to transport what we'll need, not to mention hiding Suyin."

I looked back at Uncle. "Speaking of privacy...now that we're alone, will you finally explain what your cousin meant by a former Yakuza group?"

Uncle shrugged. "She didn't go into detail. She just said they were no longer affiliated with the Yamaguchi-gumi and were trafficking drugs on their own."

"Who are the Yamaguchi-gumi?"

When Uncle shrugged, Tran cut in. "They're one of the three principal crime syndicates in Japan. The Yakuza operates with strict hierarchy and rules, which includes registering as a member. With Japan cracking down via law enforcement and social pressure, registered Yakuza members have been restricted from taking legitimate jobs, opening bank accounts, buying houses, renting apartments...all the things that people do in normal life."

"Wait," I said. "Criminals register as criminals and then go about their criminal activities in full view of the police? Why would they do that?"

"Without registration, the Yakuza leaders won't provide legal assistance."

That made no sense to me until I thought of the criminal watch lists compiled in the United States. Knowing a person was in a gang or even a known felon did not necessarily make them easier to bust. And with so many, they couldn't watch them all.

Tran continued. "The Yakuza syndicates have affiliated gangs working for them on various tiers. Since the money flows up, the low-level gangs have to scrounge to survive. As I explained in Hefei, this has led many of them to break off into the independent groups. Sometimes larger groups will break off in a quest for power, leading to urban Yakuza wars, like the Yama-Ichi feud in the late 1980s. Either way, the new group's affiliation to the Yakuza ends unless they continue to pay dues or are reinstated at a future date." Tran chuckled. "Or if they win the war."

"What kind of group are we looking for?" I asked. "An independent upstart or a crime boss vying for syndicate power?"

Uncle leaned forward between the seats. "They call themselves Kufuku-kai, which means Hungry Party. They've made a name for themselves all the way to China, but they are hungry for more. My cousin says they work independently but still pay Yakuza dues."

"Will their independent status make them easier or harder for us to find them and rescue Suyin?"

"Both," Tran said. "Easier to find. Possibly harder to take. Since Japan's gun laws are strict, some of the crime bosses have announced no-gun policies, thinking this proclamation will protect them from legal liability. This doesn't stop the use of firearms entirely, but it does make the Yakuza more judicious about their use. An independent gang like the Kufuku-kai can arm themselves however they choose. The more violent they are, the more notoriety they gain."

"Gee, aren't you full of good news?"

Tran grinned. "Happy to help."

Metal walls closed us in as we zipped across the elevated highway. All I had seen of Japan so far were blue skies, cars, and the occasional billboard in Japanese. The lack of skyscrapers was so unlike the photos I had seen of Tokyo, which appeared as crowded and vertical as Hong Kong.

I turned to Tran. "So, what's Osaka's drug culture like?"

He feigned offense. "What are you implying, K?"

"Nothing, J. You just seem to know an awful lot about this country's criminal underbelly."

He acquiesced with a nod. "I've been here once or twice."

"Killing drug dealers?"

He raised a brow. "Would that make you think better of me or worse?"

"Do you care?"

"Of course."

The seriousness of his reply cut me short. *What did caring mean for a person like Tran? Curiosity? Fascination? People cared for their pets. How, exactly, did Tran care for me?*

His mouth curled as he drove, as if he could hear every thought in my head. It wouldn't be enough to shield my nerves from his energy if I allowed my mind to obsess. Thoughts projected emotion and intent. I needed the mental discipline I had worked so hard with Sensei to achieve.

I focused on our mission and hardened my voice. "The drug culture, Tran. What is it like?"

"Complicated and unique."

"How so?"

"The government stigmatizes illegal drug use and encourages its society to shame addicts. Yet Japan is one of the highest per capita spenders of pharmaceuticals. Since Japanese physicians and hospitals are allowed to own pharmacies, it incentivizes them to prescribe. More drugs in circulation make them easier for addicts and dealers to acquire. Illegal drug use is lower compared to other countries, but it's higher than the government or law enforcement would like the citizens to believe."

"Do they cover it up?"

"It's subtler than that. Law enforcement perpetuates their low numbers by not performing autopsies or digging too deeply into suspected overdose deaths that would tarnish their crime-fighting efforts and force them into work they don't want to do. Meanwhile, the government collects their data through public means that can subject the survey participants to social and government rebuke. Neither can be trusted because the data reported only confirms what Japan wants their citizens and the world to believe."

"So, what's the bottom line? Is there a lucrative, illegal drug market here or not?"

"Definitely. It's just hidden beneath a deep cultural fog."

Chapter Thirty-Five

The bedrooms in our Osaka home base were even tinier than Hefei, with barely enough space to squeeze between a twin bed and shallow closet along the wall. Uncle claimed the first bedroom. Tran dropped his travel bag beside the futon folded in half on the common room floor. When he caught me watching, he grinned.

"Would you rather sleep out here? I know how you wander at night."

"Since when?" Uncle asked.

"Since never," I snapped.

Growling with agitation, I wedged my luggage into my room. When I returned, I found my partners perusing the assets Tran's contact had left. Each was focused on more important matters than me. Uncle snooped through weapons while Tran divided the cash.

He counted out 10,000 yen for each of us in 5,000 and 1,000 denominations. "This is for small items from local shops. Bigger establishments will accept your credit cards. When you're with me, I'll pay."

He picked up a white card with a thick aqua stripe and the acronym ICOCA and a duckbill platypus underneath. "These transit cards should be loaded with enough credit to travel locally and pick up what you need at convenience stores along the way."

I pocketed my card along with the bills. "Which mode of transportation will we use?"

"Whichever we need."

He smoothed a map of the area and placed his finger on the blue X. "This is us."

Locations were marked in Japanese kanji and Romanized script.

I tapped Uncle's arm. "Do you speak the language?"

"No. But their kanji and our hanzi have the same or similar meanings, so I can read a little of what I see. Has your sensei taught you to speak?"

"Only polite exchanges or what applies to my training."

Tran interjected in a flow of beautifully spoken Japanese.

I tried to feel grateful and failed.

He offered an uncharacteristically humble bow. "As I said, I've been here once or twice."

Uncle nodded at Tran, then frowned at my sour expression. "Why are you so grouchy? Didn't you sleep?"

Heat flushed up my neck as I thought about my erotic interlude with Tran in Hefei.

Uncle tested my forehead with his fingers. "You're burning up. Are you sick?"

"I'm fine," I said, swatting at his hand. "It's hot in here, that's all."

Uncle looked around as if he would be able to spot heat waves rising in the air. "It's not so hot. You have too much yang energy in your system. You need to cool down."

Tran snorted with amusement.

I clenched my teeth. If I broke a molar on this trip, I was sending him the bill.

Uncle glowered at us both. "What's wrong with you two?

Stop acting like children and focus." Once we appeared suitably chastened, he examined me with concern. "We'll look for a pharmacy when we go out. One might sell a tonic that can cool your heat."

Tran lost his shit while I shrank into the floor. *If only ninja magic could make me truly disappear.*

Uncle waved his hands with disgust. "I'm going to change my clothes. When I come out, I better catch the two of you behaving like adults."

We bit our lips until he had closed his bedroom door.

Imagine the adult behavior Uncle would have seen the previous night if he had come to the kitchen for a late-night snack.

We glanced at each other and snorted a laugh, inhaled deeply, then lost it again. What had happened between Tran and me seemed too absurd to be real. If he hadn't been laughing beside me, I would have convinced myself it was a dream.

Once recovered, Tran looked seriously at me. "Are we good?"

I thought about the killing and the teasing and the torturing remarks. I thought about the games he played and the way he manipulated not only me, but everyone around him for personal gain. I thought about his cold calculations and his unfathomable generosity. Time and again, Tran had watched over me. Now, he had flown across the East China Sea to rescue the stepniece of a man he hardly knew.

Are we good?

My skin tingled with remembered sensations I had never experienced with Daniel or Pete. Two nights of sexual exploration in my entire adult life had not prepared me to handle what had transpired between Tran and me in Hefei.

Was he toying with me again?

I searched his inscrutable eyes.

The only thing I could count on were the emotional walls I had erected and the energy receptors I had reversed. If I could padlock my bedroom door to keep myself inside, I would do that as well. Although a partner in battle, this man could cause me more damage than a bullet through my heart.

"Yeah, Tran, we're good."

What happened before would never happen again.

Chapter Thirty-Six

Uncle slurped ramen noodles out of the spicy red broth I topped with thin slices of pork and a bobbing poached egg. Tran and I opted for thick soba noodles and vegetables in rich chicken broth, mine with fried chicken katsu and his with tofu. All of our soups were garnished with curling scallions and sheets of crisp nori planted inside the rim like seaweed sails on a boat. This noodle shop had been circled in red on Tran's map as a frequent hangout for the Kufuku-kai.

Uncle nodded toward two men hunched over their bowls. Tran shook his head and plucked a tofu cube from his soup. So far, none of the customers had set off his alarms. Instead, he watched the people passing outside. When we had finished our early supper, we joined them on the street.

I tied my black stretch jacket around my waist and pointedly avoided looking at either of the men. Although I would appreciate the added warmth in the evening, the soup and lingering sun had me sweating in my tee.

"Where to now?" I asked Tran.

"I was thinking about a bath."

"Is that a hint?"

"No."

"Can't it wait?"

"It could. But this is the most popular time."

I looked to Uncle for help.

He nodded at Tran. "Which one?"

"Let's start with the closest, a small neighborhood joint."

"What are you guys talking about?"

"The red circles on my map," Tran said. "Two of them are bathhouses that admit customers with tattoos."

"What's the problem with tattoos?"

"They are associated with Yakuza and other criminally-inclined people."

"Profiling much?"

"Hey, until recently, tattooed customers weren't allowed in any."

"Okay. What am I supposed to do while the two of you are enjoying a bath?"

"Do the same on the women's side."

"I thought the Yakuza only admitted men into their ranks. Wouldn't it be more useful for me to wait outside and keep watch?"

"Yakuza blend in. You wouldn't recognize them on the street."

"Then what good will I do on the women's side of the bathhouse?"

"Look for their wives and girlfriends."

"How?"

"By the designs inked on their skin."

As we walked, Tran described what to expect in a sento and how I should behave. Then he stopped on a corner and nodded toward a small bathhouse with vending machines outside and a white curtain hanging from a warped pole across the entry. The cloth was split into three panels that stopped halfway to the cement floor.

"Phones aren't allowed," he said. "So we'll need a method

for finding each other after we're done. Return to your locker in thirty minutes to check for texts. If you don't see a message from one of us, go through the washing process again and re-enter the bath. After thirty more minutes, meet us out front. If you see any Japanese women with tattoos, follow them out and text us where you are. We'll do the same. If possible, one of us will follow and the other will wait outside the sento for you."

I chuckled. This would be the cleanest stakeout I had ever done.

Uncle pointed a warning finger. "Just don't fall asleep in the heat. If you start to get drowsy, get out and dump cold water on your head."

"I'm fine, Uncle."

"Ha. So you say."

Tran let the comments pass without so much as a smirk. "Come on. We can buy shower supplies from the vending machines before we go inside."

After removing our shoes, he and Uncle went through the blue fabric divider. I entered through the red. An elderly woman sat on a stool between the male and female areas inside where she accepted payment from Tran and handed each of us two towels, one small and one large.

Inside the women's section, I undressed and stowed my clothes and belongings in a locker.

The knife wound on my arm from the Chongming ambush was healing nicely and hidden by protective surgical glue. The ripening bruises from the cargo ship and Hefei fights looked bad. Without the time or opportunity to rest, elevate, and ice, the bruising had spread and darkened into deep purple splotches on my arms, ribs, and legs. The lack of injury to my face made me look as if someone had intentionally beaten me in places I could hide. I had seen strategic bruising like this with some of the women at Aleisha's Refuge back home. Although my appearance might alarm others, the hot soak would feel heavenly to me.

Naked with my hair tied in a messy bun, I walked into the bath area and hung my large towel on a hook.

The shower side of the room had six green plastic stools that came up to mid-calf with handheld showerheads mounted on a tile wall. I sat between two women and wet down my body. Neither of them glanced my way. Once I had scrubbed off the day's grime and rinsed all the suds, I placed my purchased toiletries neatly beneath my hanging towel and walked along the shower trough's edge to decide on a tub.

The first was too cool. The second too hot. The third fit my Goldilocks temperature just right. I stepped in carefully and sighed as the water enveloped me up to my throat.

The two women finished their showers and chose different tubs. Neither of them had any ink I could see. My eyelids grew heavy. This was my first relaxing moment since the ten minutes Uncle had allotted for us to enjoy the spectacle of lights at the Bund. Between the hot water and the comforting soup, Uncle had been wise to warn me not to fall asleep.

I shook my head to wake from a worried dream about Baba and Ma. I glanced at the wall clock. Four in the afternoon would be two in the morning for them. No sense borrowing trouble when we couldn't even chat.

I stretched my muscles in the water. The young women left. An old woman arrived. After thirty minutes, I toweled dry and found a message on my phone from Tran.

Too quiet here. Meet us outside. We'll check another place.

The next bathhouse was a super sento spa with a café in the lobby where rosy-clean patrons were sipping cold milk, coffee, and beer.

"This is fancy," I said. "Do they also have a gym?"

"You get enough exercise," Uncle said.

"How about a facial or massage?"

"Stop joking."

"I'm serious. It's stressful to date a gangster. I'm thinking that's where they'd be."

He rolled his eyes.

Tran cocked his head. "Actually, you make a good point."

"See? Our Yakuza expert agrees."

Tran chuckled. "As much as I would love to treat you to a full body massage, you'll spot the women faster if you wander *outside* the rooms." He leaned close to my ear when Uncle looked away. "Night will come. Patience brings surprising rewards."

My pulse remained steady. "Really? I can't say the same for you." Sensei's technique for dulling my nerve receptors had worked. Tran could shove his intent at me all day and I wouldn't feel a thing.

Uncle waved us toward registration. "Hurry up. We're losing the day."

I smiled sweetly at Tran. "After you, money bags."

"Ha. Okay, Lily. Have it your way."

Despite needling him, Tran registered me at a VIP level so I would be able to roam where I pleased. If we hadn't been here for Suyin, I would have happily indulged in every spa service they offered. Instead, I left my clothes and belongings in a locker and trod naked to the bathing area for my second wash within the hour.

The sit-down shower section in the spa was large enough

to accommodate the pre-dinner, post-work rush. Even undressed, I could tell by the hairstyles and manicures that this was a more contemporary crowd. Several were Caucasian. Only a few washed the makeup from their faces. The ladies with long hair fastened their tresses in lovely twists and clips. This time, I also noted several discreet tattoos, none of which seemed elaborate enough for a Yakuza girlfriend or wife.

No one else appeared battered or bruised. No one other than me.

After drawing sympathetic and discomfited glances, I wrapped my body in a towel and strolled past the many baths to another section of the spa. Although most women walked around nude, I drew less notice once I hid my bruises from sight.

In addition to massages and facials, the super sento sported three tanning beds that were already in use. I waited for the women to emerge, then moved on to the sauna and additional baths in the back. I chose a sunken rectangular tub lined in bright green tiles. With my back to the mountain mural, I watched the entire section through half-lidded eyes.

I planned to soak for thirty minutes, check my messages, then return to the main bath area by the showers. Or I had, until three towel-wrapped women strolled my way.

The first two were in their mid to late twenties. They had the quiet assurance of women with money yet lacked the assertive energy usually acquired in the corporate world. The one with the more impressive diamond wedding ring wore her sleek black hair in an elegant French twist anchored by a stunning cloisonné pin. The woman with the rounder face had braided her hair in a complicated bun that turned in on itself. Both seemed surprisingly conservative for their age.

The third woman was younger, closer to eighteen. Her hair was cut in a chic layered bob dyed to a soft ashy brown. She wore no jewelry except for a platinum cuff on the outer rim of one ear. Although her nails were as beautifully manicured as the other women, she sported blue nail polish instead of a neutral shade of pink.

Aside from me, they were the only women who hadn't arrived in the nude. Once they unveiled themselves, it became obvious why.

The towel dropped from the French twist woman's back to reveal a spectacular dragon that began at her shoulders, snaked around her trim belly, and descended down her buttocks and the back of her thighs. The cross-bun woman's fuller back and hips featured peonies and chrysanthemums with a Meiji Period maiden peeking from behind an intricate fan. Both designs were stunning works of art.

I closed my eyes to slits as they stepped into the steaming bath. Then I tipped back my head so I could watch the youngest woman fold her towel and lay it neatly on a bench. Every inch of skin that could be hidden by a high-neck, sleeveless, above-the-knee dress was covered in blue serpents, demons, and knives. The base of the intricate design had been shaded in blue-black ink up to her waist while her upper back and chest had yet to be filled in. This seemed particularly cruel to me since the tattoo artist had tackled the most sensitive regions first. Even unfinished, the effect was stunningly erotic yet oddly modest, as if forever covering her in conservative, formal attire. Out in public, the teenager would never be able to wear a tank top, midriff, or shorts. Not even a shorter-than-fingertip-length skirt. Her body had undoubtedly been claimed by a Yakuza man.

I closed my eyes fully and listened to the women speak

in Japanese long enough to establish from their tone that the French twist woman held the most power. The teenager didn't say anything at all. Rather than stay until they left, I rose out of the water and stepped out of the tub. With my back to the women, I wrapped myself in a towel and returned to my locker to text Uncle and Tran.

Chapter Thirty-Seven

The cold bottle of coffee milk cooled my heat as I sat in the lounge waiting for the men to arrive. Two hot soaks had relaxed my muscles and relieved the tension built up from travel, worry, and Tran. As if summoned, he strode out the men's side of the bathhouse like a model on a runway ramp, wavy mane tied behind his neck, his wild magnetism impossible to ignore.

"Lee's still primping," he said as he draped his jacket on the chair beside me with a view of the lobby. He bought a fruit milk and a plain milk from the vending machines and set the fruit milk bottle in the spot where Uncle could watch the blue and red noren spa curtains after he arrived.

"Milk?" I said.

"You know what they say." He twisted off his cap and guzzled half of his drink, somehow managing to flex every muscle from his hands to his chest, then he set it down with a satisfying "ahh."

"Give me a break."

"What?"

"You know what."

"Can't I enjoy a cold bottle of milk?"

"Do you have to make it such a spectacle? I thought we were on surveillance."

"Have you seen them yet?"

"No."

"Then the only one who's watching me is you."

I brought the coffee milk bottle to my forehead, then drank a bit more.

He glanced at my long sleeves. "Are you hiding your bruises?"

"They saw me step out of the bath."

"Must have been quite a sight." Although he hid his smile behind another sip of milk, the crinkle around his eyes gave him away.

"You know what I meant. They'll remember what they saw on my body and forget all about my face."

He inclined his head. "True for them. Never for me."

Uncle pulled out his chair and picked up the bottle as he sat. "What's this?"

Tran grinned. "Strawberry milk."

"Huh." He popped the top and drank it all down. "Tell us about the women."

"Good question," I said, my sarcasm aimed at Tran.

He leaned forward with exaggerated interest, which I pointedly ignored.

"They'll probably come out together, two in their mid to late twenties, one still in her teens. The woman who appeared to have the most status pinned her hair with a fancy cloisonné clip in the bath, so I imagine she'll wear it again when she comes out. She's tall for Japanese, angular face, no earrings, but her wedding ring has at least two karats worth of diamonds. Her contemporary had a rounder figure and face, soft rather than plump, with her hair braided in a bun. The youngest kept silent in the bath, I think in deference rather than indifference, but I couldn't be sure. Her hair is dyed light brown and cut short against the back of her neck. She didn't wear any jewelry except for a platinum cuff on her left ear."

"What about the tattoos?" Tran asked.

I described what I had seen.

He nodded in agreement. "The dragon woman with the pin sounds like the wife of a highly ranked boss, which doesn't track for an independent gang. The man smoking outside is probably her bodyguard. Important Yakuza wives are rarely left alone. I suppose the Kufuku-kai might do the same."

Uncle hummed thoughtfully. "Unless the older women are Yakuza and mentored the younger woman from before the Kufuku-kai split off on their own."

Tran nodded and turned to me. "You said her tattoo was still in progress?"

"Yep. She has another half to detail."

"Okay. You stay with her. She'll be less likely to notice another young woman than two older men. Lee and I will follow the others in case they're attached to our gang. Even if they're not, we might learn something that will help us locate members of the Kufuku-kai."

Uncle glanced from the curtained entrances to me. "Is that them?"

"Mm-hmm."

The two older women were dolled up for a night on the town. The teenager – I couldn't think of her as a woman, not after all the prostituted teens I had helped or failed over the summer – wore a blue tunic dress that showed as much unvarnished skin as her hidden tattoos would allow. Had this girl been coerced into Japan's darker life like the teenagers I had met on The Blade?

Tran collected our bottles and dropped them into the recycling bin. "Stay in touch with us, Lily. Keep your distance if she meets up with a man."

"Got it." After an hour of sitting, I looked forward to the walk.

The teen in the blue tunic plucked a phone from her purse and came alive for the first time as she made a call. She chatted animatedly as she crossed the street at a brisk yet happy pace, like a puppy unclipped from a leash. Wherever we were going, the prospect pleased her more than the bath.

She veered off the ugly main roads and chose a picturesque route past neighborhood markets, businesses, and homes. Although crowded compared to Los Angeles, the tightly packed structures were only a few stories high, nothing compared to Shanghai or Hong Kong. This made the Tsutenkaku Tower up ahead look taller than it was.

Whenever I travel, I read the tourist magazines on the flights, so I recognized Osaka's landmark straight away. How not? Even the reconstructed version had an Eiffel Tower vibe. The original had been built in the early 1900s as part of the New World neighborhood called Shinsekai, half inspired by Paris and the other half with a Coney Island flair. According to the flight magazine, Shinsekai was a tourist attraction not to be missed. From the wall-to-wall shops, eateries, and arcades, I guessed it was a fun place to hang out for locals as well. I couldn't wait to see the banners and murals lit up in neon tonight.

I was so busy gawking, I almost missed the squeal of delight as Blue Tunic and another young woman spotted each other and hurried in for a hug. The new arrival wore her hair long and her skirt short with sneakers and a puff-sleeve schoolgirl kind of top. I didn't believe the act. This schoolgirl had adult resignation and wariness in her eyes. They hugged again and held on extra tight.

I wouldn't have understood their words even if I had been close enough to hear, but their body language suggested a shared experience one had escaped that another still lived.

Had a member of the Kufuku-kai fallen in love with a lady of the night? Could that be why Blue Tunic's body was covered in ink, to keep other men from gazing at the property he had claimed?

Members of street gangs back home added to their tattoos over the years. It seemed logical to me that Yakuza girlfriends and wives would do the same.

When they settled on a restaurant, I texted Tran the address.

He called back right away. "She went to Shinsekai?"

"Yep. She met a girlfriend who looks about her age, dressing cutesy with a haunted look in her eyes. Think our gang's into prostitution?"

"Probably."

"Think any of them might fall for their employees?"

"Possible. It might explain the full coverage of your girl's design and the disregard from the other women you observed."

"How about your ladies?"

"On a subway heading north. I'll text you an address when they reach their destination."

I put away my phone and searched for an ideal spot to keep watch. The pedestrian street was narrow, crowded, and blanketed with color, art, and advertisements three stories high on both sides. The Tsutenkaku Tower stood in the distance at the end. Retro street lamps hung overhead. The most conspicuous people were the ones standing still.

Chapter Thirty-Eight

I entered a souvenir shop across the way and was instantly greeted with, "Irasshaimase!"

I returned the shop keeper's bow and smiled at the man leaning on his counter who was smiling at me. He wore a martial art's t-shirt with a logo in kanji and the sketch of a fist. With courtesies completed, they resumed their conversation and let me peruse the merchandise on my own.

I hadn't seen written English since leaving the airport. Instead, I had depended on Tran, pictures, and the translation app on my phone that used my camera to identify kanji and offer suggestions as to what it might mean. According to the menu pictures in front of the restaurant across the street, Blue Tunic and her friend would enjoy deep fried vegetables and meats.

I ignored the rumbling in my belly and read through the exciting amusements offered in Osaka and its neighboring prefectures. Osaka Castle was only six miles away and, according to one flyer, could be experienced in costume as an authentic *ninja experience*. I snorted out a laugh and picked up another brochure for the Samurai and Ninja Museum in nearby Kyoto.

"You don't like ninja?" the martial arts man said.

"I do. But I would rather meet actual practitioners of the art than play dress up in a castle with a bunch of tourists."

"Oh." He chuckled. "You think ninja are real."

"You don't?"

"It depends who you believe. Maybe you should take a trip to the Iga-Ryu Ninja Museum instead."

"I've read about that. Is it far?"

"An hour by car. Over two hours by train."

I picked up the brochure. I knew about the museum's collections of scrolls and weaponry, and the research they did on the more esoteric aspects of our art. I had also watched a video interview with Kawakami Jinichi, the museum's honorary director who proclaimed himself to be the last true ninja in existence. I had never asked Sensei how he felt about that claim.

I held up the Samurai and Ninja Museum brochure. "What about this one?"

"More for tourists. But maybe that's what you like."

"I'd like to train with actual ninjutsu practitioners. Do you know of any schools nearby?"

"No such thing."

"Sure there is. I train in it myself."

"Where? In America?" He laughed. "It must be a sham."

"How would you know?"

He thumped his fingers on the logo of his shirt. "Because I train in real martial arts."

This guy grated my nerves, but he also gave me an excuse to linger in a shop with a clear view of the restaurant's door. If I engaged him in conversation, it wouldn't seem odd if I stayed.

"What style?" I asked.

"Kyokushin. You know it?"

"Of course." Kyokushin was a hard, full-body contact style of karate known for vigorous stand-up kumite in the dojo and tournament fighting with knockdown karate rules. No doubt, this guy had a shelf full of trophies that proved he was better than me. "Do you train in anything else?"

"No need. Kyokushin is the best."

Spoken like a true narrow-minded devotee.

I had trained for seven years in Wushu before I met Sensei and begged him to teach me the ninja arts. I continued in both until my sister's death, when I stopped competing and focused only on what could help me rescue and protect girls or women like her. Even though ninjutsu was a truly comprehensive art that balanced hard and soft techniques, pressure points attacks, joint locks, throws, and a broad array of archaic and modern weaponry, I still augmented my training with American boxing and MMA to familiarize myself with common martial arts maneuvers. I also trained to defend against the uglier street attacks more popular with gangs. If I had the time, I would have loved to train with the Osaka ninja community.

"Do you know of any ninpo or ninjutsu schools in the area?"

"Why bother? They only teach made up techniques. Ninja were spies and assassins. They didn't have combat methods of their own." He gestured toward the ninja souvenirs and tees. "All of this comes from movies and cartoons to please Americans like you."

Faced with such astounding ignorance, I would normally walk away. But since Blue Tunic was still in the restaurant, a lengthy debate would eat up time. Besides, it might be fun to expand this Neanderthal's mind.

"Ninja were more than spies and assassins," I said. "They

evolved from Yamabushi priests in the mountains on the fringes of feudal society. To protect their communities, they made use of nature, magic, spiritual energy, and both Chinese and Japanese fighting techniques. Their rural lives influenced their style and the weapons they used, which included plants, weather, and their environment. Many were also samurai. But the ninja way of fighting was designed to protect self, family, community, and their lords. So, yeah... ninja were skillfully adept at infiltration and intelligence gathering. Some also worked as assassins. All were masters of stealth, illusion, defense, and escape."

He laughed. "You know so much. You should work at the Ninja Museum."

"My knowledge is more practical than historic."

His eyes squinted with mischievous delight. "Did your teacher train you to please men like the kunoichi of the past? If so, I would be happy to offer myself as a training partner during your stay."

If this were America, I would have offered a surreptitious knee to his groin. Neanderthals like him always assumed their art was the best and never showed any respect to the women in their schools. It didn't matter if they trained in boxing, karate, kung fu, or mixed martial arts, their chauvinistic arrogance ticked me off and gave a bad rap to the rest of the men.

I smiled pleasantly as I remembered the payback I had delivered on the mat over the years, most recently to a pedophile boxing instructor who had tried to take me down in the ring. I never complained or burst into tears. I simply taught him a "lesson" in return.

"Thanks for the offer, but I doubt you could handle the abuse."

He chortled, as if I had made a sexual joke. Then he flexed his arm and thumped on his abs. "My training makes me strong. I'm sure I would have the stamina for you."

"Oh my God. Are you always this obnoxious?"

"What?" he asked innocently. "I meant for fighting. Did you mean something else?"

I replaced the brochures and stared through the window at the restaurant doors, willing the teenager in the blue tunic to emerge. If I ignored the karate Neanderthal, would he get the hint and leave?

"Hey," he said. "You should visit my dojo and see what a real martial art can teach."

Oh, for Pete's sake. This guy would not let up.

"Hey. You came all the way to Japan. Don't you want to train in a traditional Japanese art?"

I gave him my best school teacher glare. "Ninjutsu has an ancient lineage from at least nine families, tested in combat and passed down through centuries of oral and written transmissions. That's traditional enough for me."

He crossed his arms, making sure to force flex the muscles in his chest. "You believe everything your teacher claims? You women are so naive."

Naive? Time to put this cretin in his place.

"I believe in skill, knowledge, and results. My teacher is more effective at seventy than fighters a third of his age. His teacher must have thought the same because he passed his family's densho scroll to him with a record of all the master instructors in his lineage."

The man narrowed his eyes. "What school? From where?"

"In Iga. I don't know the name."

"Why would he keep such a thing secret from you? Teachers always show off certificates."

"Maybe in a modern karate club like yours, but ninja originated in a time where they and their families could be boiled in oil if they were caught. Their art, practices, and identity had to be kept secret, which is why they passed down their knowledge via oral transmission for centuries before ever writing them down. The grandmasters only showed their scrolls and booklets to senior students. Even then, they reserved the innermost teachings for the heir they had chosen for their school."

"You aren't a senior student?"

I paused. "Actually, I may be his only student."

The man stopped flexing his arms and studied me more carefully. "If this is so, he would pass his martial arts system to you."

I sputtered a laugh. "I don't think so."

"Why not?"

"I'm not a typical student."

"Those are exactly the ones who inherit. That is...if he really is the soke of his family's school."

"I don't think it was his family. I think it was his teacher's family."

"Then how do you know this densho exits?"

"I saw it on his table before he put it away."

"He didn't want you to see it? Maybe it was a fake."

The scroll was the most beautiful artifact I had ever seen, written in calligraphic kanji with simple sketches and the occasional chop. Sensei had said it was precious but hadn't explained why. I felt honored that he would even allow me a glimpse. I wasn't about to deface the memory by sharing the slightest description of it with this arrogant, disrespectful man.

"Think what you want, but my training and my teacher are real."

"What's his name? I may have heard of him if he's such a big deal. After all, Iga is not too far away."

It would have felt so great to make this guy eat his words, but the truth was – Sensei had never told me his name. In fact, he hadn't shared much about his personal life at all. When I had prodded over the years, he had diverted my questions as skillfully as he diverted my training attacks. I finally gave up asking and assumed it was a matter of professional propriety he wished to maintain.

"Come on, ninja girl. Tell me more about your great teacher. You said he's seventy? Wow. When did he leave Japan?"

"Before you were born."

"Oh, yeah? Maybe he knows more than I thought. What jutsu does he know – kenjutsu, jujutstu?"

I struggled for patience. This guy's scrutiny annoyed me more than his previous disregard. "Yes...plus ninpo taijutsu, bojutsu, sojutsu, kusari-fundo–"

"He taught you how to fight with a weighted chain?"

"And knives and shuriken. Why are you asking? You already said you don't believe that ninjutsu is a legitimate martial art."

He shrugged. "If your teacher is a true ninja, maybe he stole the scroll and escaped."

I froze, insulted to my bones. "We're done."

I turned back to the window to check on the restaurant and conceal my fury. *Stole the scroll and escaped?* How dare this pompous Neanderthal impugn Sensei like that.

The sun had set into twilight, awakening storefront lights and neon outside with just enough darkness to reflect my expression back to the man – or it would have if he hadn't been texting on his phone. When I turned around, he held it up higher.

"Did you just snap a photo of me?"

"What? Of course not. I'm texting my friend."

"Let me see."

"No." He pocketed his phone and recrossed his arms.

I was fairly certain he had snapped a photo, but short of fighting him for it, there wasn't much I could do. I wasn't a thief, or the student of a thief as he had implied. He might have my image, but he didn't know my name.

"Eh," he said as I started to leave. "Where are you going? We were having a nice conversation."

I kept walking.

"Hey. I'm serious. Stay here and talk."

"No, thanks."

"We can go to that restaurant you keep staring at." He flashed a smarmy smile. "They serve good kushikatsu. My treat."

I turned so fast I could have knocked him senseless if I had let my knuckles fly. "You insulted my teacher and my art. If you keep harassing me, I will show you exactly what I learned from both."

I stormed out of the shop and walked up the road. When I had cooled off, I returned to the restaurant to make sure Blue Tunic was still inside. Before I entered, I saw the martial arts man watching me through the window of the souvenir store.

Chapter Thirty-Nine

The corner restaurant was larger and busier than it looked from outside, making it easier to blend in as I scanned the room for Blue Tunic and her friend. When the hostess guided new customers to their table, I followed as if I were part of their group, then veered in a new direction. I spotted the teenagers giggling over beers.

Were they older than they looked? Or had they provided false IDs?

Although I still didn't know if Blue Tunic was dating a member of the Kufuku-kai or some other independent or Yakuza gang, according to Tran, the tattoos I had described marked her as part of Japan's criminal world.

My belly growled.

The skewers of fried vegetables still on their plates told me I'd have time to grab a bite of my own. As delicious as it looked, I didn't want my stalker to follow me inside. Nor did I want him to see me exiting through the front door. Macho karate guys sometimes tested their ability by provoking fights. I had issued a challenge he might decide to accept. Although I wouldn't mind adjusting his ego, I needed to stay focused on my mission and avoid a scuffle that might attract the police.

I headed for the restrooms in the back. Not surprisingly,

an alarm sign hung over the rear door so customers wouldn't dine and dash. All I needed was a private place to tie my hair into a bun like the rest of the long-haired servers in black long-sleeve t-shirts and pants. Grabbing a tray off a bus station rack, I collected the dishes from an empty table and strode through the kitchen doors as if I belonged.

Having lived over my father's restaurant for the last seven years, I knew the layout and temperament of the cooking staff I would find. I also expected someone to question who I was. Rather than fabricate an answer in a language I didn't speak, I marched up the side aisle, dropped off my tray, and headed out the door.

The chilly evening greeted me with sounds of live jazz and voices nearby. I zipped my jacket to my throat, unwound my hair, and followed the alley walkway to another festive pedestrian road.

The sky had darkened during my short journey through the restaurant and made the Shinsekai spectacle even brighter than before. When I reached the corner, I glanced toward the left where I had been watching my target from the souvenir shop. I couldn't see the storefront because the entire road was lit in a solid mass of lighted artwork, giant chochin lanterns, and vertical kanji neon signs. The decorations and advertisements jutted and slanted over the ambling crowd as if fighting for attention with the Tsutenkaku Tower lit up in bright pink at the end. The kanji down the front, according to the flight magazine I had read, spelled out Toshiba in hot white light.

I crossed the road and searched for a new surveillance spot on the right where I could grab something to eat without going inside. My nose led me to a street-food stall partially hidden behind a golden statue of the Billiken god, which, oddly enough, wasn't a god or even Japanese at all.

The Osaka mascot had emerged in the early 1900s from the dreams of an American art teacher in Kansas and then grew in popularity as a good luck "God of the Way Things Ought to Be." Now, the tubby figure with the naughty smile sat all over the city with its bare feet extended for good-luck seekers to rub. Thinking of my parents and Suyin, I did the same. Rather than feel better, it reminded me how long it had been without a message from Ma.

I checked my phone. The time difference was killing me. Eight in the evening was 4 a.m. in LA. If she didn't send a message when she woke up, I'd call her at ten from a less noisy place.

Canned J-Pop and live jazz from opposites sides of the block made the pedestrians speak louder and the takoyaki cook shout, reminding me of where I was headed. I had discovered the fried octopus balls in Little Osaka back home. I couldn't wait to compare LA's version to Japan's.

"Irasshaimase," the takoyaki chef said as I stopped before his stand.

"Konbanwa. This looks delicious."

"Hai, so desu. Best in Osaka."

He stood over two sets of griddles, one filled with batter and the other empty so I could see the half-dome molds. He crisscrossed the points of wooden skewers to separate the overflow of batter into individual portions. Each had a yellow center that made it look like the yoke of an egg speckled with bits of octopus, spring onion, and red pickled ginger. As the batter cooked, he sprinkled tempura flakes over the top and then used the spears again to loosen and flip over the balls.

"How many you want – four, six, or eight?"

I stared at the tempura dusted golden brown orbs and paid him 400 yen. "Eight, please." My belly growled. "Definitely eight."

"Yoi!"

He squirted a dark sauce onto a shallow cardboard boat, skewered a takoyaki ball, and dropped it on top. When he filled the boat with eight, he squirted them all with ribbons of mayonnaise and bonito fish flakes. He handed it to me with a toothpick to eat. "Meshiagare."

I bowed. "Itadakimasu."

He smiled at my politeness and went back to work.

I carried my dinner to a bare stretch of wall where I could watch the restaurant's entrance over the Billiken's feet. Using my toothpick, I tore at the balls and released the steam. When sufficiently cooled, I popped a yummy morsel into my mouth.

Oh. My. God.

Hong Kong's fried curried fish balls were delicious, but Osaka's takoyaki were off the charts. Crunchy on the outside. Gooey on the inside. The perfect balance of savory and sweet. I might have to order another plate.

I had just sucked the last bit of sauce from my toothpick and tossed my trash into the takoyaki stand's bin when my phone chimed with a call from Tran.

"What's up?"

"We followed the women to a nightclub in Umeda. Lee couldn't get in, so I left him outside."

"Was Uncle too casually dressed?"

"No. His face was too old."

I laughed. "Don't be mean."

"I'm just stating the facts."

Music pounded in the background.

"Sounds like you're having fun. Did the women meet up with men?"

"They're dancing with each other under the bodyguard's formidable gaze."

I chuckled. "No hanky-panky for them."

"Not a chance. What's going on with yours?"

"She's eating and chatting it up with her friend."

"Where are you watching from?"

"Across the road at an awesome takoyaki stand."

"Why am I not surprised?"

"Hey, it beats the lecture I just received in the souvenir store."

"What did you do?"

"*Nothing.* I got into an argument with a karate Neanderthal. It wasn't my fault. He was a jerk."

"Why were you talking about martial arts?"

"The store sold brochures for the Ninja Museum. He struck up a conversation and proceeded to tell me all the reasons why my art and my teacher are fake. Then he hit on me."

Tran laughed.

"It's not funny. The jerk took my picture. I'm hiding behind a Billiken so he won't see where I've gone."

The music buried his response.

"You still there?"

"I have to go," he said. "The women are on the move. Stick with your girl for as long as you can, then meet us back at the apartment. If she connects with her boyfriend, make sure you're not seen."

"Check and check."

Blue Tunic exited ten minutes later, kissed her friend on the cheek, and strolled past me down the well-lit street.

Chapter Forty

I stuck to the darker side of the road where off-shoot alleys led to the remnants of what this area used to be before developers turned it into a shopping arcade. It felt good to finally be on the move. I hoped Blue Tunic had had her fill of this chaotic tourist trap and would head home to her gangster boyfriend, who may or may not be a member of the Kufuku-kai. Tran, Uncle, and I could easily be chasing the love interests from the wrong gang.

At least I had seen a few sights. During my seven hours in Osaka, I had bathed twice, soaked once, eaten eight octopus balls, and rubbed the toes of a goofy monkey god for luck. Who says Lily Wong doesn't know how to have fun? Ha! I should have snapped a selfie of me with the Billiken and sent it to DeAndre. But if he knew I had moved on to Japan, my father's delivery kid would have asked me for more souvenirs. I'd grab him a mini-statue in the airport on the way home.

Home.

No one would be awake at five in the morning except for Baba, unless the drugs they had given him for his muscle cramps and headaches had made him sleep late. My poor mother was in for another stressful day. As soon as Blue Tunic landed for the night, I would head back to the apartment and video chat with Ma. Maybe we could fix another breakfast together. Helping her cook kimchee eggs had been surprisingly fun.

Before I could enjoy the thought, someone yanked me to the side and bagged my head with a hood.

Everything went black.

Hands grabbed my arms.

Something wound around my throat.

When I felt the next yank, I accelerated the pull and struck my shoulder into a firm and masculine chest. Catching up with quick steps, I slipped a foot behind my would-be-abductor's leg and helped him to trip.

The strap around my throat pulled me back as another attacker enveloped me in a hug.

I sunk out of the embrace and rose with my arm against his to feel where he was, scooped his elbow with mine, and walked him backward onto the ground. Instead of finishing him off with a stomp to the face, I rotated out of the next likely path of attack.

Sensei had trained me to fight multiple attackers while blindfolded or in the dark, but I had never put it to the test until now.

I raised my hand and felt the next man brush against my arm as he attacked, giving me a sense of his larger body in relation to mine. With this spatial awareness, I shifted around him and caught his nostrils with my fingers. Even the strongest man's head followed his nose. Once his skull met the pavement, I shuffled away.

The hood over my head plus the exertion made it harder to breathe.

I grabbed the fabric around my throat and unwound it with one hand as I fanned the other in front of me as though searching for the next attack. When a hand grabbed the irresistible target I had offered, I used the point of contact to my advantage. Circling my supposedly-trapped hand outside his grip, I folded his wrist and followed the man's pull with a painful Taki-ori lock of my own.

He surprised me by reversing my technique.

With the smooth skill of an aikido or ninjutsu practitioner, my would-be-abductor had me falling backwards with my wrist, elbow, and shoulder hopelessly locked. Instead of fighting, I gave in.

Sensei had begun teaching me new concepts and strategies that, in many ways, went against what I had previously learned. Although he had trained me to fit inside an attack and flow with the energy until I could redirect its course, this new way of fighting was even ghostlier than that. Once I gave up my attachment to what I believed I already knew, a world of magical possibilities had appeared. I fully intended to hole up with Sensei and do nothing but train as soon as I put out the fires that kept igniting in my life.

I released all the tension in my limbs and melted my spine into the pavement, stealing the resistance my attacker hoped to control. The hood over my head blacked out the distractions of sight and intensified my perception of what I could feel. The more he tried to contain me, the easier it was to escape.

Once freed, I ripped off the hood.

Three men crowded me in the alley. One still on the ground. One blocked my exit. The third attacked from the side. I gave in to this as well and drove his face into the wall.

I sprinted between the buildings, dodging trash bins and chained bikes, but no off-shoot alleys or walkways appeared. My would-be-abductors had herded me into a dead end. Worse, there were no doors, windows, or ledges I could use to escape. My only chance was to turn and fight three skilled attackers in a confined space or to run up the building at the end and hope I could reach the rim around the roof.

I had launched myself up walls close to this height while free running in downtown LA. I hoped my dire circumstance would give me the extra foot of lift I would need.

I set my commitment and ran full speed at the wall.

As every dedicated free runner could attest, there was always a chance that my foot would slip and ram me into the building, dislocating or breaking my shoulder and jaw. Even so, I launched off one foot into an epic jump at the building, tucked my knee to my chest, and planted my foot, hip height, to bounce off the wall. Directing my motion straight up toward the roof, I pawed at the building with one hand and stretched my other arm to add a few precious inches to my reach. Eyes on target, I focused my intent and willed my hand to grab the metal rim.

Yes!

I curled my fingers over the edge, dug my other foot into the wall, and reached my other hand for the roof. I almost had it. Until my fingers slipped off the rim.

With my feet against the wall, my upper back fell away from the building. If I continued this way, I'd break my back or my neck. Before I lost all contact with the building, I shoved against the wall. Rather than arch as I had done with my back dive off the cargo barge in Shanghai, I contracted my stomach as if for an inward flip. The brief contact with the wall righted my body just enough to touch down with my feet and roll back onto ground.

Three sets of hands pinned me in place as a familiar man peered into my eyes.

The karate Neanderthal smiled. "Yes. This is the girl."

Then pain exploded in my head and everything went black.

Chapter Forty-One

George Ren Tanaka pulled his sumi brush through the black ink on his suzuri grinding stone until the brush hairs formed an elegant point. Pleased with the amount of ink, he poised his brush over the rice paper and contemplated his next stroke.

The first stalk of bamboo he had painted rose with the thickness and slant of age. Its branches were plentiful yet occasionally brittle where older leaves drooped toward the forest's floor. This bamboo cane would grow older for decades and flower a single time before its death.

The next plant he painted would have a different meaning to convey.

He poised his bamboo handle in a Tenchi no Kamae position with the stalk pointing to Heaven and Earth. When practicing bojutsu or kenjutsu, Ren would grip the wooden staff or sword handle with his pinky, ring finger, and palm, using a lighter touch with his other digits to produce dexterity and power in his techniques. With sumi-e, he held the tool in a gentler yet equally capable grip.

Synchronicity connected in all facets of Ren's life.

He took a breath and focused his intent. Then he pressed the brush on the washi and pulled the hairs – up and back, up and back, up and back – increasing the pressure of his brush at the beginning and end of each segment of the bamboo with darker ink to create a younger, more vital cane.

Once again, he dipped his brush and pulled it over the edge of the suzuri to sharpen its hairs. Instead of pressing the brush to the washi at the beginning of his stroke, he dragged the tip lightly – out and back, out and back, out and back – in three thinner segments to form a branch. He dipped again and used quick, fine strokes to add young, pointed leaves. When he had added just enough to convey his meaning, he wiped the excess paint from the brush and laid it on the porcelain holder to rest.

Ren picked up a tiny brass spoon and scooped a drop of water from an equally tiny bowl. He added it to the well of his stone suzuri and then used his brush to lighten the paint.

His subjects required perspective to establish their relationship with each other and their environment. To examine them alone without context was akin to shadow fighting on the mat, where all aspects of the martial interaction must be imagined. If he left his bamboo subjects as they were, his painting could be interpreted more vaguely than he wished.

He dipped his brush in the watery ink and painted three faint canes in the distance. Satisfied, he washed and wiped his brush clean and set it on the porcelain holder to dry.

During his thirty-three years in America, Ren had only taught four students the ninja arts. The first three men discovered the truth of the proverb: *Beginning is easy. Continuing is hard.* His fourth and final student grew stronger and more steadfast with each passing year.

He gazed at the jacaranda tree through his open bedroom door, whose lavender blossoms he and this special student had admired only six weeks ago.

As was often the case, her heart had ached with concern for someone she was trying to help. Other times, she would arrive on his doorstep seeking guidance to better understand herself. Regardless of purpose or location – on his home-dojo mat, his garden, or kneeling at his chabudai table to share a pot of tea – every moment presented an opportunity for enlightenment, learning, and growth.

Shiken haramitsu daikomyo!

It was more than a motto: it was the ninja way of life.

A life that Lily Wong had vowed to pursue.

He stamped his painting with his chop in red ink, then set it to the side of the table to dry. Once he had arranged his sumi-e supplies on his painting and carrying board, he folded the apron that protected his lap. Before he could rise, his phone pinged.

Ren eyed the inlaid-bamboo door of his closet, jutting from the wall on the far side of his futon bed. Although he possessed the necessary technology to function properly in Los Angeles, he rarely used the message applications on his phone. His carpentry business catered to the older first- and second-generation Japanese community who preferred to speak rather than type. And because he kept his spam settings high and his internet use low, he rarely received more than two emails per month, neither of which was due for another week. The only other entity who would ever send Ren an email or text was his student, which she almost never did, especially now when she was traveling in Hong Kong.

He rose from the cushion with a bad feeling in his gut that even the tranquil mountain scroll hanging above the olive-green pillows and comforter could not ease. Decades had passed since Ren had felt this level of alarm. Not since he had been known by a long-buried name.

As soon as he had arrived in Los Angeles, he had used his savings to procure a false passport under the name George Ren Tanaka – George for America's first president, Ren for the lotus flower that rises out of the muck, and Tanaka because it had topped the forger's list of most common Japanese surnames. With his new passport in hand, he moved to Arcadia, a predominantly Chinese neighborhood where no one searching for him would look. Nineteen years later, he met twelve-year-old Lily Wong.

He ran his hand along the bamboo inlay he had crafted and opened the closet door. Inside was as sparse and neat as the rest of his home. He didn't require much space because he wore out his wardrobe before replacing it with something new. As such, the phone sat directly on the shelf between a short stack of folded sweaters and pants.

He drew a protective kanji over the phone before unlocking the screen. An email had arrived from an unknown sender. When he saw the name in the subject line, he gasped.

Yoshito.

He hadn't seen, heard, or even thought of *this* name since dire circumstances had forced him out of Japan. If the message had come from his teacher, he would have rejoiced. But Tashigi Sensei had passed on to the next life many years ago. That left a handful of ninja Ren had tried very hard to forget.

Rather than open the message, he returned the phone to its spot and went to his kitchen desk where he could view the email on a larger laptop screen. He considered preparing tea. Then he forged ahead as courageously as he could.

His stomach clenched.

Even his best sencha could not have prepared his emotions to handle what he saw. How had they found her? Why was his dear Lily-chan in Japan?

He scrolled past her beaten, unconscious body to the message written below.

The time has come to return what you have stolen.

In lieu of a signature, the sender had left an Osaka address.

Chapter Forty-Two

Pain. Confusion. Thirst.

These were the sensations that hit me as I crawled my way out of the abyss.

I tried to open my eyes, but gave up as my left eyelid stuck. When I touched my face, I felt the swollen ridge of my brow and cheek and the crust of what I assumed to be dried blood. I brushed it away and tried again. Vinyl against my face told me I was indoors. Empty walls within reach suggested a cell or a closet of some kind. No windows or shelves, at least none that I could see while laying on my side.

I pushed up to my forearm and waited for the vertigo to pass. Then I sat up and leaned against a wall. My prison was as empty and featureless as I had expected, with minimal light seeping under the door. I glanced around for water. No cup. No bottle. Not even a pot, which I supposed didn't matter if I had nothing to drink.

God, my head hurt.

I squeezed my eyes against the throb and touched the welt on my bare arm. T-shirt. No jacket. They had stabbed me with a needle. But why? I sifted through the rubble of my memory.

Chair. Ropes. Questions. Fists.

As I pieced it together, the aches in my body flared. At least one rib was broken or badly bruised. The tops of my thighs and sides of my calves and arms burned where one or more batons had struck. My face felt swollen, and my mouth tasted of blood. Sons of bitches had had a field day beating me to a pulp, demanding answers I couldn't provide.

Not about Suyin.

About a man named Osamu Nakayama, who I didn't know.

After more punches and baton strikes, they offered the name Yoshito instead.

"I don't know who that is. You have the wrong woman. Please let me go."

They pumped me full of a disorienting drug that made me want to comply. If I had recognized the names, it would have been impossible to resist. I repeated the names so I wouldn't forget – and to block out the suspicions forming in my mind.

"I don't know anyone named Yoshito or Osamu Nakayama. I can't help you. Please let me go."

"Who taught you to fight?"

"Sensei."

"What is your teacher's name?"

"Sensei."

"Is your sensei Osamu Nakayama?"

"No."

"Is your sensei Yoshito?"

I repeated my mantra. "I don't know anyone named Yoshito or Osamu Nakayama. I can't help you. Please let me go."

"Where do you train?"

"In Los Angeles."

"Where is your dojo?"

"In my apartment."

"Where do you train with your teacher?"

"Everywhere."

The baton smacked against my jaw.

By the time they shoved my phone into my hands, my thoughts were too muddled to remember the code. Annoyed that I hadn't set up fingerprint security, they pulled the driver's license from my wallet.

"Is your name Lily Wong?"

"Yes."

"Is this your address?"

"The address on my license is correct."

"If you don't tell us the truth, we will track down your family. Is that what you want? For us to hurt your family the way we are hurting you?"

I had registered my license with a postal service address. I wasn't supposed to, but I didn't like anyone – especially government databases – to know where I lived. If only I had been smart enough to keep my mouth shut when the karate Neanderthal had grilled me about my training. I had no doubt he was the reason I was here. I must have said something about Sensei that had triggered an alert.

I knocked the back of my head on the wall, trying to remember what I had disclosed before the drugs had turned my mind into mush. His home address? His email? His phone number? I must have given them something useful, or why would they have stopped?

I patted my empty pants pockets. They had taken my jacket, shoes, wallet, and phone. Had they figured out the access code? Or had I remembered it and confessed?

A cry leapt from my throat.

I patted my pockets again, furiously searching for my only connection to Baba and Ma. Was he still vomiting? Had the headaches finally stopped? How many side effects from tests did my father have to suffer before the doctors diagnosed a disease they could treat? The potential maladies terrified me more than any torture my captors could inflict.

And what about poor Ma, shouldering this burden without any support from me? My captors had taken more than contact information and a means for escape. Without my phone, I couldn't even offer her a virtual hug.

I banged my head against the wall as a flood of fear and frustration rolled down my face.

Baba. Ma. Sensei. Suyin.

I was failing them all when they needed me the most.

Stop it, Lily.

Wallowing in guilt and fear was a luxury I couldn't afford.

I heaved back my sobs and brought my emotions under control. I needed to move forward and figure out how to escape.

Chapter Forty-Three

Ren flowed with the Osaka Station crowd as they hurried through the terminal to catch the next train. He monitored his speed to the low end of average to account for the elderly age he hoped to project. His tan polyester rain jacket, wrinkle-resistant high-waisted slacks, and floppy-rimmed bucket hat completed his look. His well-worn shoes, although deceptively supple, prioritized stability over style, as favored by older Japanese men. He hadn't brought much, just a nylon backpack with the bare essentials and a sling bag he wore beneath his jacket strapped close to his chest. With an occasional hitch in his step and the slump of age in his spine, he looked like a fit ninety-year-old man who exercised with other members of Japan's elderly community in the parks. In truth, he could have out-paced every commuter in the terminal.

Ren's usual way of walking was to lead with his hips and let his legs and feet keep up the pace. Although it looked no different to the untrained eye, the use of gravity in motion reduced his effort and increased his speed. At seventy, with a short and stocky build, he could sustain five miles per hour over a flat terrain. He could maintain four miles per hour in the hills. Although he couldn't keep up with Lily-chan, he easily surpassed the average unfit American and held his own with most athletic people half his age.

He boarded the escalator to the final leg in his twenty-hour commute from LAX, arriving via Kobe Airport instead of the more expected Kansai. He had used his American passport and his alias name since whoever had sent him the email with Lily's photo had not addressed it to George or to Ren. Nor had they mentioned his birth name from Japan. Instead, they had used the ninja name only those who had trained with Tashigi Sensei would know.

He waited on the platform and enjoyed a moment of space in front of him before the train arrived. After so many years living in America, he had forgotten the crowds and the efficiency of Japan's railway system. Twenty minutes later, it had whisked him to his final stop at Shinimamiya Station. Once outside, he breathed in the city night and noise. So different from the soothing chirp of crickets and the quieter urban drone around his woodsy Los Feliz home. Even the nicer apartment buildings crowding from the sides felt dingy and industrial to him. When he spotted Tsutenkaku Tower in the distance lit up in pink and white, he quickened his pace to escape the rumbling of the trains.

What was Lily-chan doing in Osaka?

How had she fallen into criminal ninja hands?

Despite all of his training and conditioning, George Ren Tanaka felt old. He had stayed awake during his flights so he would arrive ready to sleep, which made eleven p.m. feel uncommonly late.

He turned off the road that would have taken him to the emailed address and hurried the last few blocks toward his capsule hotel. He found it wedged between other buildings as narrow as it. The exposed stairwell looked almost as wide as the skinny seven-story tower it serviced. Osaka was the third most populated city in Japan, with too many people in a finite space.

Inside the lobby, he stored his shoes in a locker, donned the slippers he was expected to wear, and received a sensor that would light up his sleeping capsule when he drew near. Thanking the attendant, he walked past the vending machines in the common area and took the outside stairwell up to the fifth floor. He used the common facilities, changed into the sleep shirt and shorts provided for guests, stored his belongings in a coin locker, and walked down the hall.

The empty capsules had their privacy screens up to show a neatly made mattresses and pillows at the far end where the power outlets would be found. None of the capsules on this floor had the television upgrades offered for an additional three hundred yen. Nor did they house any women. The female guests stayed on the lower floors with separate access keys. Halfway down the corridor, an upper-level capsule lit up.

Ren climbed the steps, crawled into his pod, slid down his privacy shade, and fell immediately to sleep.

Chapter Forty-Four

I stared into darkness almost as black as if I had kept my eyes closed. My abductors had turned on an overhead light earlier so I could see the rice and tofu they had given me to eat. Since they had finally provided a chamber pot, I made use of it while I could see. An hour or so later, they collected the rice bowl and plastic spoon, left me the pot, and turned off the light.

I observed as much as I could on the two occasions when my guard – five foot eight, spiky gelled hair, no visible tattoos – opened the door. He came with a partner – stocky, shaved head, also no tattoos – who stood at the door with a baton in case I tried to escape. I couldn't tell if they had been part of the trio who attacked me in the alley, but I remembered Shaved Head from the basement where I had been strapped to a chair. He tapped his baton on his hand, as if to remind me of its feel.

The hallway behind them had the same cream-colored walls and speckled vinyl tiles as my cell. A television played in the distance but I couldn't tell what kind of show. No other voices or sounds. As I had discerned when I first woke up, I was locked in an empty closet with nothing I could use to escape. Best I could tell, that had been two or three hours ago.

I sat against the wall with straight legs, flexing and pointing my feet. Although I had stretched out my aches and tested for injuries after the meal with a surprisingly peaceful yoga flow in the dark, my body and mind had reverted to their previously locked-up, stressed-out state. If it were late evening as I suspected, an entire day and night had passed for my parents without any messages from me.

Had my hastily crafted words calmed and consoled my mother as I hoped? Or had I fueled Ma's temper to fight with Baba's nurse? If only I could reread the message I had sent from Pudong as Uncle had hustled me off of the train.

Then again, if I still had my phone, I'd already be out of this mess.

I folded over my legs, resting my face in my hands, and breathed through the protesting muscles that protected my ribs. The fact that I could still inhale deeply suggested only a crack or a bruise. It would be harder to fight with a fractured bone protruding from my chest. Even so, the pain was hard to ignore. When it subsided, my worries rolled into the void.

My father in the hospital.

My mother frightened and alone.

The horrible diseases the lumbar puncture could detect.

I clasped my hands and willed my father to hear. "I love you, Baba. Please, please, please be okay."

And what about poor Ma imploding from stress? What horrors would she imagine from my silence?

Nothing worse than the truth.

I had come to the conclusion that my skillful, tattoo-less captors were ninja and the karate Neanderthal was a stooge. For some reason I had yet to discern, they wanted Sensei, and they wanted him bad. Since they had stopped questioning me, I had likely given them enough information to locate my teacher via email or phone.

Please let me not have given them his Los Feliz address.

If they wanted something from Sensei, they would have offered me up in trade or threatened to kill me if he didn't comply. I didn't remember anyone snapping a photo, but it seemed likely they had. If Sensei had seen it, he would undoubtedly come to Japan.

All because of my ego and pride.

I thumped my forehead against my knees. What damage had my careless actions caused? If only I had known more about his life, I could have...

Could have what, Lily? Kept your damn mouth shut?

I knocked my head against the wall as I straightened my back. As if it would do any good – I was as hard-headed and stubborn as an ox. Clearly, I was born in the wrong astrological year or the impact would have broken through my fragile water rooster skull. Then again, roosters were notoriously boastful and vain. How ironic that my truest nature would be the source of my defeat.

All those years of training and exploration.

All the wisdom my teacher and family had tried to impart.

Wasted and ignored when I needed it the most.

Chapter Forty-Five

Ren greeted the morning with determined optimism. He meditated in his capsule, showered in the communal facilities, and changed into a long-sleeve shirt that he buttoned to the throat and tucked into the same high-waisted slacks and bucket hat he had worn the previous night. Aside from his wallet and phone, the only items he carried on his person was a key to a locker where he had hidden the scroll.

He walked down an alley, boxed in by narrow apartment buildings and wires overhead, then under the bridge of an elevated train before he reached a wider city street. Only nine in the morning and already the noise assaulted his ears.

He crossed the massive intersection and followed the map on his phone to a four-lane street that ran along the edge of Shinsekai. Instead of entering the shopping neighborhood from the pedestrian boardwalk on the corner, he continued down the street to the first neighborhood road. Fifty years had passed since Ren had entered Shinsekai. He wanted to refresh his memory and note the roads, alleys, and walkways that surrounded the address.

Ren had been twenty when he and his training buddies had come to Osaka for a day trip looking for cheap bars, women, and gambling. After striking out in the trendier tourist locations, Ichiro, the self-appointed leader of the expedition, had suggested they try Shinsekai. The original amusement area had lost its luster since World War II after the Luna Park rides and games had shut down and the original Tsutenkaku Tower had been replaced after the fire. What Ren and his buddies had seen was a shabby version of entertainment and a seedy warren of residential hovels, many of which were on alleys only wide enough for bikes. They had filled their bellies and gambled in a gaming hall, but they never found any young women interested in them. Then Ichiro had suggested the red-light district for what he called "sure things." He hadn't mentioned paying for sex. Ren had taken one look at the women kneeling on display in the "restaurant" windows while their madams waved men over for "tea," and took the train back to Iga on his own. He had never felt any need to visit Tobita Shinchi, Shinsekai, or any other part of Osaka again.

"So long ago," Ren muttered, playing into the elderly image he was trying to present.

This neighborhood was one of the oldest in Osaka, with two- and three-story structures built before the war. As he wandered through the warren of roads – some passable by car, others narrow enough to make a cyclist think twice – he greeted the middle-aged and elderly residents he passed. Since Shinsekai drew most of its business at night, most of the shops, bars, and eateries had their metal rolling doors down. When he spotted two women rolling their grocery baskets, he followed them to a covered shopping arcade and bought an egg musubi, which he nibbled as he strolled to the address where he had been instructed to come.

The building sat on a corner with a kushikatsu restaurant below and a second story above.

Offices? Apartments? Headquarters for Ichiro's ninja gang?

Whatever was up there had to be accessed from inside via the restaurant's main entrance or one of the two rear exits that fed into an alley walkway in back. The side road where he now stood was the closest egress, with another potential escape at the other end, a long distance away. Although both roads were open to vehicles in the daytime, they might be coned off for pedestrian use at night. Having identified all possible routes into and out of the building, he strolled to the corner to find an inconspicuous place to observe and to think.

The noodle shop across from the restaurant was ideal, if not for the two men seated at the window table Ren would have preferred. One was a Chinese man in his sixties. The age and ethnicity of the other man was not as easy to guess. Thirties or forties. Southeast Asian for sure. Possibly American Indian, East Indian, Latin, or African in the mix. Ren knew three things for sure: the man was handsome, athletic, and dangerous.

Ren lowered his eyes and continued to stroll. It would be just like Ichiro to post men on watch.

The Chinese man came outside and stepped into his path. "What are you doing here?"

Ren adjusted his position so he could surveil the road and check to make sure the younger, more dangerous-looking man was still in his seat.

The Chinese man scoffed. "Never mind. You can tell us inside."

"Excuse me?"

"I know who you are, George Ren Tanaka. I just don't know why you are here."

Ren brought his hands up in an apologetic bow while secretly preparing himself to attack. "You are mistaken."

"Aiya. You're Lily's teacher. We are her friends. Now stop the old-man act, get inside, and tell us what you're doing in Japan."

Ren relaxed as he recognized the man's ornery response. "And you are the cook who keeps Lily-chan on her toes."

The man shrugged as if this were a hopeless task and marched into the noodle shop. Curious beyond measure, Ren followed him inside. Although the dangerous partner remained seated, he inclined his head in greeting as if welcoming a friend.

Ren offered a slight bow but remained on his feet. "I fear you have me at a disadvantage. I am George Tanaka. You may call me Ren."

The man's dark eyes twinkled with delight – the kind of mischievousness that flashes the second before a bully kicks out a chair. Then his brows rose into devilish peaks that made him seem simultaneously seductive, sinister, and amused.

Ren nodded in recognition and sat. "You are the man who steals Lily-chan's center."

The man smiled. "Is that what she told you?"

"Was that not your intent?"

He nodded as if Ren had scored a point. "My name is J Tran. This is Lee Chang. You call yourself George Ren Tanaka but I don't believe that's your name."

Chang waved over a waiter. "Give us three beef noodle soups. And tea." He turned to Ren. "You want tea?"

Ren bowed to the server. "Dozo."

Once the server left, Chang scowled at Tran. "Who cares what he calls himself?" He turned to Ren. "Why are you here?"

"I received an email with a photograph of Lily-chan tied up in a room, unconscious with signs of a beating."

Chang cursed. Tran remained utterly still, like a snake poised to strike if Ren didn't tell the whole and exact truth.

"The subject line of the email used a name given to me by my former teacher in Japan." He nodded toward the restaurant on the corner. "The message told me to come to that address. How about you? Out of all the restaurants in Osaka, why have you chosen this noodle shop to eat?"

Tran glanced out the window. "It's the last address Lily gave us before she disappeared."

"Why was she there?"

"You first."

Ren could tell this man would not budge, so he brought up the email and handed him the phone.

As Tran examined the photograph and message, Chang crowded in for a look, then turned back to Ren. "It says you stole something. What did you take?"

Ren folded his hands. "My story cannot be told in one breath."

"Good," Chang said as the server brought three bowls of nikusui udon soup and three cups of green tea. He picked up a sliver of beef dusted with red shichimi spice with his chopsticks and pointed it at Ren. "You can entertain us while we eat."

Chapter Forty-Six

Ren sipped his tea as he pondered the best place to begin and how much of his history he wanted to disclose.

Steam curled around Tran's face as he leaned over his soup. "Lily is in danger because of something in your past. If we're going to help her, we need to know the whole truth."

"I understand. But that makes it no easier to tell."

Tran picked up a mouthful of noodles. "That restaurant won't open until eleven. Take all the time you need."

Ren nodded and opened the dam to a flood of unhappy memories. He closed his eyes and took a calming breath. When swept away by the tide of emotions, it was best to swim one stroke at a time.

"I grew up in the mountains of the Mie Prefecture, outside a city that is considered the birthplace of the ninja. You have probably heard of the Iga-Ryu Ninja Museum and the other touristy amusements and attractions that sprouted up after the ninja boom. When I was a child, tourists came to Iga to visit the forests and rivers and escape the bustle of city life. Ninja had become myths parents told to keep their children in line.

"My father was an artisan wood worker." Ren glanced at his soup and smiled. "My mother made udon for a noodle shop near our home. Both taught me to love and respect nature. Both were very surprised when I began training in an actual ninja martial art even though so much of it comes from and relies upon natural elements." Ren chuckled. "I find that amusing, don't you?

Although neither man answered, they both watched him keenly as they ate.

Ren shrugged. "My teacher came from a long line of ninja who passed their knowledge through their family since the sixteenth century, beginning with a Tendai Buddhist monk who studied Kung Fu in China and ninja arts with the Fujibayashi clan. He became what is known as Yamabushi or Shugenja, a mountain-wandering priest. He protected his family and community. But he kept his training secret and only passed it down to the descendants who showed the most skill. My teacher had no descendants. So he taught the art to me and a handful of enthusiastic boys."

"Only boys?" Tran asked.

"I know. It was sexist even then, especially in light of the skilled kunoichi of the past. If my teacher had accepted female students, their influence might have taken us down a different path."

"What happened?"

Ren chuckled. "What always happens between top students who are too close in skill. We veered in different directions so we wouldn't have to compete."

"We who?" Uncle asked, before slurping more soup.

"Ichiro Inoue and me."

"Is that who sent you the email?" Tran asked.

"I believe so. The name in the subject line of the email was Yoshito, the warrior name awarded to me by my teacher, Jiro Tashigi. It means—"

"Righteous person," Tran said.

"Ah. You understand Japanese very well. Then you will understand the meaning behind Zuruihito, the name Tashigi Sensei gave to my nemesis."

"Cunning person."

"Yes. Which, in the ninja arts, can be a valuable trait."

"But not with Zuruihito?"

Ren sighed. "Ichiro was more interested in the tricks of espionage and psychological manipulation. I wanted a deeper understanding of our physical training and the spiritual and esoteric teachings passed down from Tashigi Sensei's Yamabushi ancestor."

Chang sucked his noodles with excessive force. "This story of yours has taken a hundred breaths already. Will you please get to the point?"

"Soon, I promise. But there is an order to things if you hope to understand."

Ren sipped more tea. "I have always been a quiet and serious person. Ichiro had a magnetic personality." Ren looked at Tran. "He was seductive like you. He drew in the other students like flies to honey, offering sweetness, then sticking them to his agenda."

Tran raised a brow. "Which was?

"Making money. Ichiro had no other skills and no interest in school. He wanted to rise above his family's poor existence. He would trick people in Iga City into giving him products and services. Sometimes he would spy and extort. Other times, he would steal. He made everything he did seem like a ninja test or challenge. I told Tashigi Sensei about his actions and his sway over the other students. My teacher already knew, but he couldn't convince Ichiro to admit his wrongdoings or catch him in a lie. Ichiro was so good at what he did, even I couldn't supply any proof."

Chang snorted. "So your teacher kept teaching his criminal students?"

Tran gave him a look. "And you wouldn't have?"

"That's different," Chang said. "I was already a criminal. I never claimed to be anything else."

Ren hummed in thought. "I understand your perspective, Mr. Chang. But Tashigi Sensei believed he could direct his students onto the right path. As their teacher, it was his responsibility to try. I did not feel the same. By this time, I was thirty-three years old and had a ten-year-old son who had recently begun to train. I didn't want Haru to fall under Ichiro's spell. So I pulled him out of our dojo and taught him myself. But Haru had no interest in my old-fashion art. He thought he knew all he needed to know."

Ren closed his eyes, dreading what was to come.

"One night, I took my wife and son to a restaurant in the city to celebrate Haru's good grades. Kimiko left her sweater. I went back to get it. I returned in time to see Haru yank Kimiko's purse from a mugger. When the accomplice stabbed my son, Kimiko fell on them like a demon. I ran faster than I had ever run in my life. Thousands of miles running in the mountains, and still I was too slow."

He looked from Chang to Tran. "A little knowledge is like a loaded gun in the hands of a child. My family died because my son believed he knew all there was to know."

Chang put down his spoon and gazed at Ren with unexpected compassion. "You're hard on Lily, just like me."

Ren nodded. "I don't want her to make the same mistake as my son."

"What happened to the robbers?" Tran asked.

"I killed the murderer. The mugger escaped. When news reached my dojo, Ichiro rallied the other students. They found the killer and set up a plan for revenge. Before we ambushed him, I changed my mind. I tried to stop them, but Ichiro killed the mugger on my behalf."

Chang scoffed. "He didn't do it for you. He did it for leverage *against* you."

"Yes. After one brief telling, you see more of Ichiro's heart than I had discerned over twenty-five years of training."

Chang shrugged. "Only because I would have done the same." At Ren's surprise, Chang added, "I wasn't always a cook."

"I see. Then you can guess what happened next. Ichiro threatened to bare false witness to the police, who would naturally suspect me, unless I left our dojo and our town. He was tired of competing for our teacher's attention. He wanted me gone so Tashigi Sensei would pass on the Oku-hiden scroll to him.

"I went to my teacher's home dojo in the forest to tell him what Ichiro had done and to beg for his help. He was crushed, of course. But he also understood the truth of the situation.

"'*The police will believe Ichiro and the others over you.* You must do *what he says and go.*'

"'*What about our school?*' I had asked. '*How can you let your students corrupt our art in this way?*'

"My teacher had stared into the forest as if seeing the past, then turned his sadness onto me. '*Ichiro would have made a great spy back in the day. The espionage skills he wants to study are a valuable part of my family's ninja traditions. I will continue to teach what he and the others want to learn, but I will also try to teach them the integrity they need.*'

"I called him irresponsible and naive. He told me to hold my judgment until I had walked along his path. Then he gave me the secret Oku-hiden scroll."

Tran leaned forward. "So you didn't steal the scroll as your nemesis stated in the email."

Ren shrugged. "In Ichiro's mind, I did. As senior students, we had both seen and hand-copied the Shoden-, Chuden-, Okuden-, and Hiden-level scrolls. But our teacher had never shared the deeper secrets in the Oku-Hiden scroll, which he hinted might reverse everything we had ever been taught in order to achieve a truly magical level of mastery. There are other secrets that Ichiro may or may not suspect."

"What kind of secrets?" Tran asked.

"A different lineage than the one he has seen with the true masters of the Tashigi ninja clan's art. The first syllables of their names point to deeper secrets that can only be understood after deciphering the poem contained in the scroll."

Chang laughed and elbowed Tran's side. "They're digging in the wrong place!"

Ren furrowed his brows.

"It's a movie reference," Tran said.

"One of Lily's favorites," Chang agreed.

"I don't care about your movie. This scroll is important. Tashigi Sensei entrusted it to me so he would never be tempted to pass it on to Ichiro. I cannot tell you what it contains, but I can say that it would do considerable harm in his hands."

Chang shoved his empty bowl to the center of the table. "And I don't care about your super-secret scroll. Why would these criminal ninja know Lily is your student?"

Ren matched his contempt. "Why has a triad member and an assassin brought my student to Japan?"

"I'm not triad any longer. I can't answer for him."

"Not important," Tran said. "Ren has the scroll. Ichiro has

Lily. All that matters is getting her back safely so we can rescue Suyin."

Ren was lost. "Who is Suyin?"

"Aiya. We don't have time for this."

"Make time, Mr. Chang. The last I heard, Lily-chan had escorted her mother to Hong Kong."

"Fine. But keep up. I'll only say this once." Chang gulped down the last of his tea. "I asked Lily to come to Shanghai to help me find my missing grandniece, Chyou, who was kidnapped to force my family into using our connections to find my sister's stepdaughter, Suyin, a chemist who had been working for a drug-trafficking gang in Hefei. Suyin ran away. The gang wants her back."

"But why come to Japan?" Ren said.

"The gang in Hefei was selling a fentanyl analogue that Suyin created to a gang in Osaka. According to our information, they brought Suyin here."

"Brought or kidnapped?"

"No one knows. The Hefei gang thought Suyin ran away."

"And now?"

Chang's expression grew hard. "There aren't enough of them left to care."

Ren stared into his tea. How many more men had died from the lessons he had taught? This summer had been hard on Lily-chan and forced her to do things he himself had not done. When this crisis had passed, he would speak to her about this in depth.

"I have listened carefully, Mr. Chang. Your story explains why you all came to Japan. But why did Lily-chan go to the restaurant across the road?"

Tran took over. "She spotted three women with Yakuza-style tattoos in a bathhouse known to be visited by this

Osaka gang. Lily followed the youngest to that restaurant. She was watching from a souvenir shop a few doors down. When I called her later, she had moved to a takoyaki stand across the side road to get away from a karate jerk who was arguing with her about the Ninja Museum. She must have told him about her training because he lectured her on all the reasons why the ninja arts and her teacher were fake. Then he hit on her and took her picture. She said she was hiding behind a Billiken statue so he wouldn't see where she had gone."

Ren nodded. "I saw the Billiken on my way here."

Tran leaned forward. "Now answer Lee's question. What could Lily have said to this karate jerk that would connect her to you?"

Ren slumped in his seat, weighed down by the burden of his seventy years.

"If I had known she would come to this part of Japan, I would have warned her not to ask questions or mention her training. This is all my fault. I didn't tell her enough. No name. No history. No stories about my training or my teacher. Only that I lived and trained in Iga and came to America before she was born. Lily-chan is curious. She would want to know more. She is also proud. If this man doubted her training, she would have bragged and described what she knew about me." He took a breath. "She has also seen the scroll."

"That would do it," Tran said.

"Could the karate jerk be ninja?" Chang asked.

"Possibly." Ren shrugged. "Or he might have been manipulated or paid to spread misinformation to tourists. Whatever Ichiro is up to will not benefit from this ninja boom."

Tran sighed. "Lily is more trusting than she believes."

"This is true," Ren said. "Despite all that she has suffered and seen, Lily-chan searches for good in everyone she meets."

Chang snorted. "Of course she does. Why else would she be friends with criminals like us?"

Chapter Forty-Seven

I lowered my yoga plank to the floor, arched into cobra, and pushed into my heels for a downward dog stretch. With my hips to the ceiling, I extended one leg into three-legged dog and arched to the side to open my hips. As much as it hurt, this vinyasa came easier this time than my six preceding attempts.

I lowered to my knees and sat on my heels.

Another night on the floor had done nothing to help the ache of my injuries, all of which hurt more on the second day than the first. At least the long session of yoga had elongated my spine and loosened the cramps. Equally important, it had passed the hours since breakfast. I would do it again after lunch – provided they continued to feed me. Even a few spoonfuls of rice along with the water kept up my energy and helped to focus my mind.

If only I could stop worrying about Baba and Ma.

Two days without updates was driving me mad. I never should have let Ma deal with this alone. I should have returned to Los Angeles as soon as we rescued Chyou. I slumped against the wall. The *should nevers* and *should haves* overwhelmed me every time I sat still. My world had narrowed into a litany of regrets and shame.

And then there was Rose.

My ever-companion clung to me in death in ways I had not allowed her to cling to me when she still lived. I had moved onto campus to escape my mother's control and left my impressionable sister behind. I had freedom and autonomy. Rose fought for the same, lying to our parents and going to clubs with a fake ID. She would not have rebelled if I had still lived at home. And I would have answered her text if I had not been with Pete. My one night of freedom and love had cost my sister her life.

"Please forgive me," I whispered.

But my torment wouldn't end until I could forgive myself.

I bowed my head. "I have, from beginningless time, created negative karma through ignorance, greed, and anger manifested through my actions, words, and thoughts, misdirected and misused. For all of these, I here and now acknowledge and atone."

This translation of the San-ge Mon purifying affirmation had always held deep meaning for me. I strove to make reparations by helping other vulnerable women and girls like my sister. But in coming to Osaka to search for Suyin, I had abandoned my parents as I had abandoned them after Rose's death. Instead of bonding in our shared grief, I had detached from everything and everyone except for Sensei and the ninja arts. It wasn't until I had turned myself into a fighting machine and brought justice to my sister's killer that I reconnected with my parents and began working for Aleisha's Refuge. Although Ma might suspect, she still didn't know I had stalked Rose's killer and nearly become a victim myself.

I shook out my hands to dispel the negativity and clapped them in front of my forehead in Gassho. I closed my eyes and recited the first of several prayers that began my morning meditation.

"To receive human birth is difficult. Now I have received it. To hear the enlightenment teachings is difficult. Now and here I hear them. If I do not take the path of enlightenment in this lifetime, when again in the future will I ever have the chance to do so?"

I continued my affirmation to train hard and purify my thoughts, words, and actions, performing all manner of good works, and transferring all merit and virtue to help others find the peace of enlightenment and eternal unsurpassed joy I sought. I had just reaffirmed my commitment to the Three Treasures when I heard the bolts on my door slide.

I rose to my feet. This time, Shaved Head was armed with a gun.

"On the floor, face down, hands over your head."

Before I could plan my next move, Spiky Hair stabbed my arm with a needle. The effects hit me fast, dulling my senses and bathing me in calm. Although I struggled to fight it, I soon forgot why.

Spiky Hair helped me stand and turned me toward the open door. When I veered into the wall, he grabbed me by the arm.

I smiled as he set me back on course. "You're so sweet. But would your mama approve of what you've done with me?" I reached for the gelled spikes poking from his head. "Or your hair?"

He swatted my hand away.

I chuckled. "I get it. Look but don't touch."

He growled. "Keep quiet and walk."

I turned to Shaved Head. "Is he always this testy? Ooh, your scalp looks so smooth. Can I feel?"

He scolded Spiky Hair in Japanese and received a feisty retort in return.

I patted their arms. "Hey, hey, hey. Be nice, okay?"

They kept bickering in Japanese and led me past a room with computer monitors, surveillance grids, and a bunch of other cool electronics I was dying to touch. Did they stream movies in there? If I behaved, would they let me watch *Kill Bill*?

Spiky Hair shoved me from behind.

Around the corner, we came to a large room with martial arts mats and weapons mounted on racks. A Shinto temple sat on the spirit shelf in the center of the back wall with a shimenawa rope of rice straw hanging across the top from which paper lightning bolts dangled to purify the space. Offerings of plants, incense, and rice lined the shelf. The shrine even had a polished mirrored disk on a wooden stand for the kami to visit and rest.

I pulled away from Spiky Hair and hurried inside. "You have a kamidana and shintai mirror like mine. You *are* ninja. Can we train?"

When he reached for my arm, I slipped his grasp, circled around him, and checked out the artwork. The kanji on the calligraphy scrolls were similar to or possibly even the same as the characters I had seen on the fabric banners hanging on the front wall of Sensei's home dojo. There was even a colorful print of a familiar demon. But they didn't have the Taizokai and Kongokai Buddhist mandalas that hung on either side of Sensei's kamidana shelf.

Shaved Head yanked me out of the dojo before I could pick up a spear.

"Hey. I just wanted to look."

When we reached the next room, he shoved me inside where three more men waited around a table, buttoned-down business types with a slightly older man in the center.

"You remind me of Gung-Gung," I said, blurting the first thought in my head.

"Who?"

"My grandfather in Hong Kong. He has the same stern look. But you're too young to be as serious as him. Are these your business partners? Hi, I'm Lily."

I reached my hand across the table, lost my balance, and sprawled my arms and chest across the surface. I stared at the polished wood and ran my hand along the grain. "This is beautiful. What is it?" I giggled. "Wood, obviously."

I peeled my cheek off the surface and perched onto my arms as I blinked through the fog. The stern man looked very annoyed.

"How much did you give her?" he asked in English.

"Only one shot," Spiky Hair said. "But she's so small. Maybe too much?"

Mr. Stern waved him back and laced his fingers together on the desk, reminding me of my one and only trip to my high school principal's office. Except this time, it didn't bother me. Nothing bothered me.

I sank into a super comfy chair.

Mr. Stern leaned forward. "Why are you in Osaka, Miss Wong?"

"Miss Wong?" I snickered. "Just like HKIF."

"What is HKIF?"

"Gung-Gung's company in Hong Kong."

"I don't want to hear about you grandfather. Why did you come to Japan?"

"To find Suyin."

"Who is Suyin?"

"A friend. Not of mine. Uncle's."

"His friend?"

"His niece."

"She's your cousin?"

"Nope. Never met her."

"But your uncle–"

"Is my friend."

"And Suyin–"

"Is his niece. Stepniece, actually. Uncle's sister married her grumpy old boss and–"

"What does this have to do with Osamu Nakayama?" he yelled.

"Nothing."

"He didn't send you to Osaka?"

"Of course not. Why would someone I don't know send me to Japan?" Mr. Stern was confusing the heck out of me and disrupting my chill.

He lowered his voice. "Tell me about your teacher."

"Nope."

"Excuse me?"

I pressed on my temples and groaned.

"Miss Wong?"

My head throbbed as the room began to swirl. I didn't like this. I didn't like it at all.

"Miss Wong!"

Men bickered in Japanese. One of them pulled me to my feet. I fell against him and vomited on his chest.

Someone shoved me into the wall. Someone else caught me before I slid to the floor.

Everything slowed: The people. The sound. The beating of my heart.

Giant fish eyes peered into mine, its seaweed breath carrying silent words as I sank into a deep, dark sea.

Chapter Forty-Eight

Ren approached the kushikatsu restaurant at precisely eleven o'clock when it opened for lunch. Lily-chan's friends had left the noodle shop before him, going in opposite directions. Lee Chang would wander up and down the street, supposedly looking in shops. Tran would wait in the gray Subaru sedan he had parked on the side street. If Ren left the building through the front or rear exits, they would know, as long as he wasn't taken down the long walkway to the other side of Shinsekai or through the back entrance of another building. Tran hadn't liked the variables, but the narrow walkway behind the restaurant would have been too conspicuous for him to watch.

Ren wasn't concerned. If Ichiro had sent the email, he would want to meet with Ren on his own turf, which meant inside the building or in another location accessible by car – probably in the white Toyota Camry parked near the walkway on the street.

He entered the restaurant with confidence. Although still in the same washed-out blue shirt and wrinkle-resistant slacks, he wore the old-man clothing with a younger man's strength.

The hostess greeted him with a smile of recognition. "Yoshito-sandesu ka?"

"Hai."

She gestured with her hand. "Kochira e dozo."

Ren followed her through the dining area, past the stairs, toward the restrooms in the back. She paused at the rear exit and dismantled the alarm. Then she opened the door for him to pass and bowed. A burly young man rose from the steps while his leaner partner stamped out a cigarette and motioned Ren onto the walkway. Boxed between men and buildings, even a slender child could not have escaped.

Ren held out his arms and allowed his body to be frisked. He didn't bother with questions because he knew they wouldn't reply. Instead, he noted their postures, movements, and physiques for clues about how well and with what methods they might fight. Young men, in general, tended to hit harder than necessary and expel more energy than they should. The burly man would want to use the upper-body strength he so proudly displayed. The leaner man would rely on his agility and speed. Even forewarned, neither of them would expect Ren to take them out as easily as he could.

They led him to the Camry, where the leaner man joined him in the backseat. Lily-chan's friends would have no trouble following behind.

Ren tilted his head as if alone in his thoughts and glanced to the side for clues. The open collar and short sleeves of the man's shirt showed no sign of tattoos, no earbud for communication, no obvious bulge of a weapon. He wore chic pants, loose enough to fight, and expensive Nikes with exceedingly white trim. The floor mat was clean, with no mud or debris that would have tracked into the car if they had trained in the forest. His escorts had style, money, and enough confidence in their youth and capability not to worry about him.

They sped through expressways and elevated roads, then crossed the Kizu River via the Taisho Bridge. After turning to cross another bridge, they drove along the water. This part of Osaka felt open and clean, with bike paths, sidewalks, and benches for people to enjoy the day. Ren would have enjoyed a longer ride through the greenery, but the driver turned left toward the Kyocera Dome Stadium, a stunning architectural wonder made of shiny silver, blue glass and an abundance of white.

"We're going to watch baseball?" he said in Japanese, too surprised to keep his thoughts to himself. The spacecraft-like stadium had gone up after he had left. Reading about its progress in Los Angeles had made him homesick for Japan.

Once they entered the parking tunnel, Ren knew they would lose Chang and Tran. Not only was the place enormous, but his escorts had VIP passes for express parking and entrance. Ren wasn't the least surprised when they whisked him through the noisy stadium to a private viewing room.

The burly escort knocked four times and was admitted by an equally tough-looking character with strategically groomed stubble on his face. Ren supposed the guy thought himself cool since he wore his sunglasses inside. And maybe he was. What did a seventy-year-old man know about cool?

Two women and four kids sat on the couches and chairs snacking on American-style cold cuts, pickles, and chips while two men in their forties squirted mustard and ketchup on a platter of hotdogs. Two older men in casual business attire stood with their backs to the room, watching the game through floor-to-ceiling windows and a glass door. The heavier man turned to see who had entered. He informed the slimmer, silver-haired man, then he told the women and children to get their food and come outside to watch the game. The other men joined them until the only people left in the room were the guard by the door, the silver-haired man, and Ren.

Ichiro turned around, and for a long moment, neither of them moved.

Ren's nemesis had always been more handsome and charismatic than him. Tall and slender to Ren's short, stocky frame. Movie-star features to Ren's friendly, peasant face. The decades had intensified their differences, making them more of what they inherently were, increasing the distance between them like parting travelers after a fork in the road.

"Are you a crime lord now, Zuruihito?" *Sly, crafty, cheat – a meaning earned from devious ways.*

Ichiro smiled at his ninja name with pride. "I follow an older, more reputable path dealing in secrets, as our kind has always done." He gestured to the couch. "Please, have a seat. You must be tired after your travels."

Ichiro hitched up his tailored slacks as he sat in an armchair across the coffee table from Ren. He crossed his leg at the knee and gestured for the guard to bring them cold beers from the fridge. He studied Ren's appearance as he drank. "I would have thought living in Los Angeles would have improved your sense of style."

Ren held out his rough hands, scarred and stained from a lifetime of working with wood. "Why would I need fashion when I have art?"

"Oh, right. You picked up your father's trade. Do you make much money building cupboards and tables for Japanese immigrants?"

"I live well enough."

"Hmm. Words of aspiration. You never did have what it takes to succeed."

Ren contained his anger and waited. Ichiro had always been eager to fill silence with the sound of his voice.

"You travel light, Osamu, unless those old-man pockets are bigger than they look."

Ren glanced around the room. "And you are missing the person I had most wanted to see."

"Hmm. It seems neither of us has what we want in this room."

"Oh? I am quite content with what I have."

"If that were true, you wouldn't have come to Osaka to trade."

"What makes you think I am here to trade?"

Ichiro laughed. "You were always such a lousy liar. Remember that time we stole beers?"

"You stole the beers."

"But you drank one and then blabbed when we were caught."

"We were kids."

"We were seventeen."

"And now you have moved from stealing to kidnapping?"

"Your Lily Wong is not a kid."

"No. She's a woman who has nothing to do with you."

Ichiro smiled. "And everything to do with *you*."

Ren took a breath. His nemesis was as petty as he had always been.

"About your student," Ichiro said. "Why is she *really* here?"

"What do you mean by really?"

"She claims to be searching for a missing woman."

Ren shrugged. "That's what she does."

"So this has nothing to do with us or with me?"

"You think too much of yourself, Ichiro. I washed my hands of you a long time ago."

"If that were true, Osamu, you would not have stolen the scroll."

"I didn't steal it. Tashigi Sensei gave me the scroll to protect the knowledge and the reputation of our lineage."

"*Sensei's* lineage. Not yours. He passed his school on to me."

"So you say, but cannot prove."

Ichiro scoffed. "How would you know, hiding in America? Our teacher gave me all of the other scrolls before he died."

Ren smiled. "Then you shouldn't need the scroll I possess."

Ichiro brushed nonexistent lint off his slacks. "Need and want are not the same."

"And yet, you abducted my student to bring me and it back to Japan."

"Enough of this sparring, Osamu. Give me the scroll and I'll give you what you want."

Ren shot back his words. "Want and need are not the same. The scroll has more value than the person you wish to trade."

Ichiro laughed. "Let's say I believe you, which I do not. What more do you *need* for this trade?"

"Information about a Yakuza gang. One who works with a Chinese triad in Hefei."

"Huh. Is that why your student traveled here from Shanghai in the company of a Chinese citizen? Does she or her American companion work for the DEA?"

"What American?"

"James Tucker."

"I don't know who that is."

"Your student's other companion is Lee Chang."

Ren calmed his escalating pulse. What did Ichiro's men do to Lily to acquire these names?

Ichiro noticed his concern and smiled. "Your student is stronger than she appears. She would only tell us about the missing woman. Her passport and driver's license made it easy to find her flight. She booked it under the same name. Careless. The men traveling with her did the same."

Ren considered this information. Was J Tran's real name James Tucker? Which, if either, was the assassin's true name?

"You seem puzzled, Osamu. Or should I call you George?"

Ren's gut tightened as he struggled not to react.

"What? Did you believe flying into Kobe Airport could hide you from us? You have forgotten how much we know about you – your age, your height, your probable weight. Since you've been hiding in Lily's city, the American passport was a logical guess. Once we hacked into the surveillance cameras, we knew George Ren Tanaka was you. I have to admit, you still move with the same taijutsu grace even when you pretend to be decades older than you are."

Ren kept his breathing calm and his facial muscles relaxed. "You have established an impressively modern network."

"We have adapted and improved, the way ninja always have."

"Selling information to anyone willing to pay?"

Ichiro shrugged. "Your concept of good and bad has always been naive. Yoshito. *The Righteous One.*" He laughed. "Your lofty name holds you back."

Ren didn't care what Ichiro thought about his ninja name. He cared about his American alias and the trouble Ichiro could cause. There would be no running away from this. One way or another, he would need to settle this feud.

"What other exploits do you and your gang deal in besides information?"

Ichiro frowned. "Information is the most valuable commodity there is. Why would I bother with criminal pursuits when I can make money off of corporations, the government, and right-wing extremists?"

"And the Yakuza?"

Ichiro smiled. "They value information as much as the police. I am what you Americans call an equal opportunity provider. I sell to whomever pays me the most."

Ren nodded and made up his mind. There was no reason for Ichiro to roll in the muck with drug dealers when he could have everything he wanted selling information in a clean designer suit. Although Ren didn't trust the spy master, it might be advantageous to tell him the truth.

"As far as I know, Tucker does not work for the DEA. He and Lily came to Osaka to help Lee Chang find his missing grandniece, Suyin. She worked for a pharmaceutical company in Hefei before a local gang lured her into working for them. Chang thought she had run away. Now, he and the others believe an Osaka gang called Kufuku-kai may have brought her here."

"Why?"

"She is a chemist."

"We have chemists in Japan."

"She created a new type of fentanyl that is potent and hard to detect."

Ichiro nodded. "And cheap. Even here, where Japanese prefer methamphetamines so they can work harder and keep their jobs, fentanyl is on the rise. Users don't realize their stimulants are often cut with opiates. The cheaper ingredient increases the profit. The added euphoria it provides keeps clients happy and coming back for more."

"You know a lot about drugs for a spy."

"I know it's too risky for a gang to manufacture them here, especially a smaller, independent gang as you describe. They would be smarter to sell the chemist to a manufacturer in North Korea."

"Why North Korea?"

Ichiro picked an olive from the platter and popped it into his mouth. "You said this gang broke away from their manufacturer in Hefei. Maybe the Chinese government was coming down hard and slowing their production. Maybe they are looking for a manufacturer closer to Japan. North Korea has a long history of state-sponsored narcotic production and smuggling. Drugs like fentanyl combat hunger and make hard living conditions easier to tolerate. Synthetic drugs are so easy to produce. Many people make their own." The corner of Ichiro's mouth raised in a sly grin. "Or so I have heard."

Ren walked to the window where, outside, the kids waved their hotdogs and cheered for the game below. A Hanshin Tiger scooped up the ball and tagged the runner out to end the inning. The crowd erupted. The home-team advantage was real.

Although Ren had lived in America for thirty-three years, he had lived in Japan as Osamu Nakayama for longer than that. From another vantage point in this stadium, he would be able to see the Iga mountains where his family roots grew deep. Osaka might be Ichiro's city, but Osamu Nakayama had claims in this area as well.

Ren turned to Ichiro. "Will you help us find Suyin?"

Ichiro chuckled in surprise. "What makes you think I wouldn't sell your information to the Kufuku-kai gang."

"They won't pay what you *want* for information about us. But I am willing to give you what you *need* for Lily Wong's safe return and information about them."

Ichiro ate another olive and beckoned to Ren's escorts. "Return him to his friends." He rose with Ren. "You are in my city now, Osamu. There is no where you can hide that my web of spies and surveillance cannot find."

Chapter Forty-Nine

My tongue searched for moisture, then quit. Cracked dirt on a drought-stricken trail. Brittle cactus, fried from the sun. Dusty hooves chipping through wedges of hard-packed sand. None of this compared to the dryness in my mouth.

I cracked open my eyes and saw hardwood panels in place of vinyl tiles. A futon cushioned me from the floor with a slim pillow under my head and a light quilt draped over my curled body. I clutched the corner like a toddler's security blanket in my hands.

How did I get from my empty closet to here?

I tried to move but my head wouldn't budge.

A woman spoke, but I couldn't understand.

I should have learned more Japanese from Sensei while I could. Now, I might never have the chance. When the woman spoke again, I realized my mistake.

"Are you awake now?" It was a language I understood but didn't expect.

I craned my neck and saw a grimy woman in the corner of the room, knees up, heels tucked close, hugging her shins. She wore red-rimmed glasses framed by short black hair cropped just below her ears. Her round, terrified face was clearly Chinese.

"Suyin?"

"You know me?" she asked in Mandarin.

I rose onto my arms and squeezed my eyes as the vertigo kicked in. Had my jailers drugged my food? I had a foggy memory of sitting down to meditate when they entered my cell.

Not my food. They stabbed me with a needle. After that, I couldn't recall.

Suyin chattered in Mandarin too quickly for me to understand. She stopped when I sat up and leaned against the wall. We were in a bedroom barely large enough for a full-size futon and a low chabudai table between my pillow and the door. Aside from the quilt, the only other adornment in the room was a watercolor painting of mountains on a hanging fabric scroll.

"Do you speak English?"

"Fluently," she said. "My father paid for private English language institutes and tutors in Shanghai."

"That's good. Because my language skills haven't kicked in." I spotted a plastic cup on the floor beside her. "Is that water?"

She nodded and slid the cup toward the futon where I could reach.

I held a sip of water in my mouth and let it soak into my parched tongue and cheeks. Then I drank a little more and returned it to the floor.

"Thank you. How long have I been here?"

"They brought you with my lunch."

"How long ago was that?"

She shrugged. "Two hours? More?"

It sounded as though four or five hours had passed since my post-breakfast yoga. Hours for which I couldn't account.

Suyin studied me cautiously. "Who are you?"

"My name is Lily Wong. I'm a friend of your Uncle Lee."

"Who is Uncle Lee?"

"Your stepmother's brother."

"The one who lives in America?"

"Yes. We were in Shanghai when we learned you were taken."

"I was not taken. I was tricked."

"Tricked how?"

"It embarrasses me to tell you."

I smiled encouragingly. "I work for a women's shelter in Los Angeles. I know how devious these criminals can be. I also know you're a chemist and that you were working for a drug-trafficking gang in Hefei."

Suyin gasped. "I didn't mean to. I thought it was..." She shook her head in despair. "I worked for one of the biggest biotech companies in China. We manufactured compounds for drugs, cosmetics, and household products. We sold them all over the world. I was assigned to make compounds for fentanyl. When I created an analogue that was cheaper and stronger, my supervisor was very happy. Then China scheduled the drug and made it illegal to sell. Instead of giving me a bonus, my company moved me to another team with chemists more senior than me."

"Is that when the gang recruited you?"

"Yes. They offered me more money to do the same work I had done. I knew it was wrong. But how bad could it be if it was legal a few months before? They gave me my own laboratory. Can you imagine what that meant to a thirty-year-old chemist like me? No one to report to? Freedom to experiment? I wanted to make my new bosses happy so I wouldn't lose the job. After months of experimentation, I made my fentanyl analogue even more effective than it had been."

"Why did you stop?"

"I heard them arguing about the strength of my new drug. Dozens of users had overdosed in the United States. Other shipments led to other deaths. I looked it up on the internet. One article called it the deadliest fentanyl analogue yet. I felt so ashamed. How could a drug I had made legally before kill so many people now?"

"Is that why you ran away?"

"No. I was too scared to run. If my bosses did not care who died from my drugs, why would they care about me?"

When she stared at the floor, I took another sip of water and forced myself to wait patiently for Suyin's story to unfold. After a minute of silence, I offered a gentle prompt.

"I met your roommates."

"In Hefei?"

I nodded. "They told me about your video chats with a Japanese man. They thought you might have run away with him."

Suyin wiped her tears. "I met Kenji on WeChat. He commented on my posts and sent me messages. He was so nice and handsome. We started video chatting. Once a day at first, then morning and nights. He listened to my troubles. He said he loved me. He bought me a plane ticket to Osaka. He said we could start a new life together in Japan." She took a breath. "Kenji is a criminal. Just like my bosses in Hefei."

I slid the cup of water toward her.

She took a sip and wiped more tears from her face. "His gang sells my drug."

"Did they lure you here to make it for them?"

She shook her head. "He said they will sell me to a manufacturer in North Korea." Despite furious wiping, the tears flowed down her face. "Kenji says the North Koreans pay top dollar for chemists like me. They can also provide more product for Kenji's gang to distribute than the Hefei gang could."

Uncle was right: the Kufuku-kai were hungry for a bigger slice of the pie.

Suyin sniffed. "When I worked for the biotech company in Hefei, we competed with government-sponsored laboratories in North Korea. Some of these were legitimate companies, but many were not. Synthetic drugs are popular in that country because they suppress appetite and fight depression. They are also very easy to make once the molecular structure is known. Our company had to compete with state-sponsored production and smuggling through North Korean embassies. If Kenji's gang sells me to them, the government and police will not care. The drug lords will treat me like a slave and work me to death."

I opened the quilt and beckoned Suyin into my arms. Once she crawled onto the futon, I wrapped her in the quilt and hugged her while she cried. Her story reminded me of the prostituted girls I had met on The Blade. Like Suyin, many of them had been lured into the life by Romeo pimps who played on their insecurities and loneliness and convinced them they were loved. I had rescued and returned two of those teenagers to their parents. I hoped to do the same for Suyin.

"He doesn't love me," she said. "Nobody loves me."

"Shh. That's not true. Your mother loves you. She begged your uncle Lee to find you, and we have."

"But he's not here."

"Not yet. He and another friend are coming. In the meantime, you have me. I may not seem like much, Suyin, but I promise to protect you in every way I can."

Chapter Fifty

Three hours had passed since Ichiro's men escorted Ren to the main entrance where stadium security guards had delayed Lily's friends. Both were relieved to see he was okay. Both agreed with his gamble to tell Ichiro the truth. Neither trusted the ninja not to stab Ren in the back.

"Thank you for bargaining on behalf of my grandniece," Chang had said in the car.

"Lily-chan would expect me to do so no matter how much jeopardy she is in."

If Ren had to give up Tashigi Sensei's Oku-hiden scroll, they would at least have the location of the Kufuku-kai gang and Lily-chan with them to fight for Suyin's return.

But Ren had no intention of betraying his teacher's trust.

Not only would the Oku-hiden scroll legitimize Ichiro's claim to the Tashigi clan's lineage, it contained recipes for poisons, strategies for deception, and teachings that would elevate Ichiro's mastery of the ninja martial arts – provided he would recognize the key syllables in the list of names and could decipher the poem to break the code. Given enough time, his nemesis would succeed because, as much as Ren hated to admit it, Ichiro was cunning and smart.

Zuruihito.

Did Ichiro become the man he was by living up to his

warrior name? Or had Tashigi Sensei recognized the true nature of his soul?

"Stop daydreaming and help us," Chang said. He and Tran were sorting through a munitions bag and laying each item on the apartment's dining room table.

J Tran – or James Tucker – had resourceful connections in Japan. They had even coordinated a vehicle switch, en route, from the stadium so Ichiro's tech-savvy ninja would track their former gray Subaru up to Kyoto while Tran drove the newly acquired white Toyota to their Osaka home base.

Ren examined the guns and knives on the table.

"Which do you want?" Tran asked.

Although Ren knew how to fire a pistol, he preferred the deadly effectiveness of a blade. That said, he felt no attraction toward any of the military-grade folding and fixed combat knives he saw.

Tran offered a cane, balanced on two hands as one might offer a sword. "Perhaps you would feel more comfortable with this."

Ren noted Tran's smirk and smiled. "Perhaps I would."

Chang grunted in disgust. "You're only a decade older than me. How will we free Lily when you have one foot in the grave?"

"Never fear, my new friend. I can do considerable damage with an old-man's cane. Even so, there are other tools I need to prepare."

Ren opened his backpack and brought out a roll of tape and a six pack of small travel tubes one might use for toiletry products or pills. He filled these with a mixture of cayenne pepper he had purchased at the Shinsekai market and cigarette ash he had scooped from the sand bucket outside its door. He fastened the caps at the tops and used one of the knives to carve blowing holes at the bottoms. Then he covered each hole with a small strip of tape. This gave him the flexibility to either fling or blow the metsubushi powder at will.

Meanwhile, Chang outfitted his body with two folding combat knives, a Sig Sauer pistol, and several double-stacked fifteen-round magazines. Tran selected a similar pistol, an OTF automatic stiletto, and a set of bo-shuriken darts as long as Tran's hand and sharp on both ends. The main attraction lay in the padded compartments of the rectangular backpack Tran opened on the coffee table. Although Ren was well versed in the country bumpkin impression he had given to Chang, he had never seen a rifle as elegant as the one Tran assembled with ease.

Ren sat in the chair across from Tran. "You must have influential friends to acquire a sniper rifle in Japan."

"I do. Especially one as customized as this." He demonstrated the attributes of his rifle as he explained. "The manual bolt-action reduces the cycling sound. The suppressor eliminates ninety-nine percent of the muzzle blast. So the only noise you might hear will be the loud pop of the bullet breaking the sound barrier. Or you would if I didn't have these." He held out a box of lead solid-point bullets. "The subsonic ammunition will slow the speed and reduce the noise to a blast of compressed air barely louder than an unenthusiastic clap."

"Impressive."

"And effective." While seated on the edge of the couch, Tran opened a telescoping rod, perched the barrel of the rifle on the Y, and adjusted the scope for a target outside the window. "If we hit hard, fast, and silent, we can rescue Lily before anyone calls the police."

Ren's phone pinged with a message.

"Is that Ichiro?" Chang said. "None of this will matter if we don't have an address."

"It's from him. The Kufuku-kai have their headquarters in Tobita Shinchi."

Tran frowned. "The red-light district? What street?"

"Main."

He dismantled his rifle so he could pack it away. "Depending on the surrounding buildings, the tight quarters of the younger section might help."

"Younger, like new?" Chang asked.

"No," Tran said. "Younger by age. The *restaurants,* as they call the brothels, are grouped according to the ladies with the youngest *waitresses* on Seishun Street and older ladies available on Main. Customers may order from more mature women in their fifties and sixties in the Yokai section on the other side of the bridge."

"Order what?"

"Officially? Tea and snacks. Since prostitution is illegal, waitresses wave at potential customers from cushioned platforms behind open sliding or rising doors. Beside them, mama-sans take *food orders* from the men. When the waitresses enter the private rooms upstairs, they fall in love at first sight with their customers and have sex. Suffice it to say, they serve very expensive tea."

Uncle snorted. "To Japanese men only. Am I right?"

Tran inclined his head. "Some will accept foreigners at an elevated price since only Japanese men can be trusted to visit the bathhouses beforehand and treat the women with respect. I would guess the Kufuku-kai chose Tobita Shinchi for their headquarters because photography and videos are not allowed. The custom to protect women would also protect them."

"Tran is correct," Ren said. "Ichiro says they have taken over an entire building."

"How many stories?" Tran asked.

"Three."

"How many gang members?" Chang asked.

"Up to thirty men in the building at any given time."

Tran shook his head. "We'll need to take out a dozen in the first ten minutes to improve our odds."

"There's something else," Ren said. "Ichiro has given Lily-chan to the gang." Chang cursed, but Ren shook his head. "He says everything we want is now in one place."

Tran took out his phone and entered the address into Google Maps. Since photographing sex workers was not permitted, the street-view images were taken when the hentai were closed. The building they would target had two French sliding doors with wooden lattice and glass. The entry doors were made of solid wood.

Tran pointed to the image. "The gang would have knocked out the interior walls, but this building will still have two sets of stairs, two front doors, and two kitchens on the first floor that may or may not have been joined."

"They can surround us," Ren said.

"Yes. I can help. But assuming they've used tempered glass in the sliders, my first bullet will either shatter the glass into pieces or send a shockwave that will weaken it enough for true aim. Unless I am very lucky, the first shot will miss."

Chang scoffed. "Then what good is the rifle?"

"Subsonic ammunition has less of a kick. Using only three-times magnification that I'd need to cross a narrow street, I should be able to reorient quickly enough to fire one second apart. Unless my target reacts instantaneously, which they won't, I'll have a clean shot the second time around.

Same goes for the upstairs windows, although I won't take a shot unless I know for certain it isn't Lily or Suyin. If they haven't updated the building with air-conditioning, they might leave the windows and sliders open, and I can shoot through the screens.

"What about the doorway?" Chang asked. "That narrow opening won't offer much."

Tran pointed to the street-view map. "If I can get into this second-story bedroom across from that door, I can shoot from the middle of the room and add at least three yards of distance for my shot. That will improve my angle and give me more depth into the gang's entry. Just make sure neither of you are standing in the bullet's path."

"And the alley walkways?"

"If they try to surround you, I'll pick them off as they emerge."

Ren studied the hentai across the road. "The mama-san many not accept you as a customer."

Tran winked. "I'll pay a premium price."

"Even so," Ren said. "You won't have many opportunities to take out a dozen men."

"I never said the kills would all come from me."

Ren stared at the floor.

"Is that a problem?" Chang asked.

"No. It's just..."

"Can we count on you or not?"

"Of course."

Tran looked concerned. "You've only killed once."

Ren nodded. "During the attack on my family. What you are describing is similar to the ambush I refused to do for revenge, the very reason I was forced to leave Japan."

"And now?"

Lily Wong was more than a student. She had been a part of Ren's life longer than his own son. He had tried to remain impartial, especially when she was young, but she had wormed her way past his barriers and into his heart. Even then, he had kept her at a proper distance and only taught her in the park. Only after she had turned eighteen and moved away from home did he buy the cottage in Los Feliz and build a home dojo where they could train. He had taught her deadly techniques to protect others and herself. He would do no less to protect her.

"My past actions have put Lily-chan's life at risk. If I must kill to rescue her, I will."

"You may need to strike first," Tran said.

"I understand. My training includes preemptive attacks, dispensing of guards, and assassination techniques."

Tran offered his bo-shuriken with two hands.

Ren accepted with a bow. "You may count on me to act decisively and without regret."

Chapter Fifty-One

I tipped the chabudai table on its side, stood on one of its short legs, and pushed the underside away from me, attempting to snap the joint. When that didn't work, I struck it with my palms.

Suyin frowned. "If you break our table, we'll have to eat on the floor."

I sat on both of the end legs and tucked in my feet. "I'm hoping that won't be an issue."

I had a few inches to kick. Whether it worked or not, the impact on my sit bones wouldn't feel great.

"Come behind me and press down on the table legs."

When I felt Suyin's hands slide under my butt, I pulled my knees to my chest and stomped against the wood. The joint cracked. One more kick, and the top of the table broke away.

"Thanks, Suyin. I got it from here."

I returned the three-legged table to its spot near the entrance and perched the broken corner over my futon and rolled-up pillow. The table wasn't level, but the guard might not notice at a glance.

Next, I took down the fabric painting, used the end of the fabric to grip the nail, and began the arduous task of loosening it from the wood. "Jeez. Someone hammered this in well."

"Why do you want it?"

"You'll see." I doubled the fabric under my sore fingers and pulled out the nail as straight as I could. Using it to rip the fabric into three long strips, I knotted them together at one end and handed it to Suyin. "Hold this for me, okay?" Then I braided the fabric into a slender rope.

Armed with a foot-long club, a short length of braided rope, and a two-inch nail, I curled sideways on the futon with my back to the door.

I smiled encouragingly at Suyin. "Have you performed in any plays?"

"Never."

"Well, now's your chance."

I rushed through what I needed just as the bolt slid outside the door. The first guard entered and ordered us to the back of the room while the second guard brought in our food.

Suyin leapt to her feet, babbled in Mandarin, and pointed at me.

"Is she sick?" the first guard asked in English.

Suyin continued in Mandarin and raised her voice in distress.

As the first guard dealt with her, the second guard set the food tray on the broken table. When he stooped to catch it as it slid onto the floor, I rolled onto my knees and cracked my club against his skull.

The first guard yelled and swung his baton at my head. I rose to one foot and struck the inside of his arm. His baton flew out of his hand. He grabbed onto mine and tried to disarm my club. Rather than fixate on the weapon, I let it go and rose with a rising shin to his groin. Before he could recover and club my head, I grabbed the nail from my pocket, swiped it across the side of his neck, and sliced into his external jugular vein.

Blood spewed.

Suyin covered her mouth to stifle a scream.

I kicked the guard into the wall, picked up the quilt, and pressed it onto his neck. "Keep up the pressure. Don't move and you'll survive. Follow us, yell, or fight, and you'll die. Understand?"

He pressed the quilt against his neck and glared.

"I'll take that as a yes. The rest is on you."

Suyin whimpered.

I checked the unconscious guard who I had cracked in the head. A grapefruit-size lump was rising above his temple around a nasty, bleeding gash. The fluid leaking from his nose did not bode well for a full recovery. These gangsters should have copied my ninja abductors and locked me in an empty cell.

I tied his wrists and ankles behind his back with the braid. "He's alive, Suyin. Pull yourself together and pick up that baton. One way or another, we are getting out of this place."

Chapter Fifty-Two

Ren steadied himself with a cane as he ambled up Main Street, shoulders rolled forward, bony spine stooped as if from a lifetime of hard labor. His travel pouch dangled from the waist of his baggy blue-gray pants and faded blue shirt. The split-toes of his rubber-soled tabi shoes stabilized his feet.

Mama-sans in the doorways nodded but didn't beckon him toward their hentai as they did for the early-bird customers – Japanese men out of their teens and up to middle-age. A few foreigners ambled through the neighborhood, taking in the sights. The younger men and bolder tourists would come out in the evening when the tell-tale paper lamps would be lit and more of the ladies were on display. Aside from the occasional nod of a mama-san, no one looked twice at an old neighborhood man.

Tran, on the other hand, drew lots of attention as he sauntered down the road toward Ren in his black designer jacket and pants, flared in all the right places to conceal handguns and knives, and a fitted charcoal tee that displayed his well-muscled chest. With his glorious hair bound in a ponytail and his chiseled face neatly groomed, he could have stepped from the pages of a men's fashion magazine. Although not Japanese, the young ladies inside the storefronts waved enthusiastically from their cushioned platforms, adjusting their poses to best display their skimpy or cutesy attire, while their mama-sans beckoned Tran inside for delicious tea and cakes. The rectangular canvas pack he wore slung on his back didn't alarm them in the least.

Chang ambled on his own, dressed in a multi-pocketed travel jacket and pants, another tourist to be ignored.

Ren progressed slowly, giving Tran enough time to be admitted into the hentai, over-pay his waitress, and stage his sniper rifle in her room. When Ren saw Tran's signal from the second-story window, he began his approach toward the Kufuku-kai's lair.

He paused at the first closed establishment and pretended to knock on the door. He did the same at the next hentai. When he came to the Kufuku-kai's building, he knocked on the wood with the brass butt of his cord-wrapped handle. The French sliders on either side were shut. Through the glass, Ren could see flat hardwood where the display platforms had been. When no one answered, he rapped three more times on the door and moved back so he could be seen.

After a third set of knocks, an annoyed young man answered the door. "What do you want?" he said in Japanese.

Ren bowed and took a plastic tube from his belly pack. "I have special spices that strengthen the libido."

The young man crossed his muscular arms and displayed a tattooed jackal's head with its jaws ready to bite. "Do I look like I need help from an old man like you?"

Ren chuckled as he uncapped the tube and peeled off the tape on the bottom. "These spices are potent." He held it up, blocking the blow hole with his thumb. "Even one sniff will increase your strength, not only for romance but for fighting as well."

"Who's at the door?" another man yelled.

The young man looked over his shoulder. "An old peddler."

When he looked back, Ren blew the mixture of cayenne and cigarette ash into his eyes. The young man cursed. When the other man came to check, Ren flung a second tube of metsubushi powder at him and leaned against the door's frame. Both men fell with shots to center mass, wheezing as their lungs collapsed and their hearts failed. As promised, Ren didn't hear the shots.

He entered the building and dragged the younger man to the left of the doorway, out of sight. Chang followed inside and dragged the older man to the right. Neither gangster was armed. Neither would live.

A folding screen shielded the rest of the ground floor from street view, which explained why the gang hadn't replaced the glass in the French sliding doors. It also meant that Tran would only see people who came around the screen or down the stairs on either side of the six-foot-deep entryway.

Ren crossed the open doorway to the right. When a new man came around the screen, he thrust the handle of his cane into the pocket of the man's throat and stepped in with a lateral strike to his head. A pane in the French window crumbled as the man stumbled in front of the slider. A second later, the gangster fell with a shot to his chest.

When Ren saw that the wooden lattice had kept the other panes intact, he slid open the doors. Chang did the same with the other set of sliders, then spun as two gangsters rounded his side of the standing privacy screen. Before Ren could help, two gangsters rounded his side as well.

Three dead bodies, an old triad enforcer, an older ninja, and four young Kufuku-kai gangsters crammed into the six-foot-wide channel between three open doors and a folding screen. It could have been a dicey situation if not for Tran's deadly aim.

Ren widened his grip on the cane so he could strike and deflect more easily in the confined space. His loose grip allowed the cane to slide through his hands for a Tsuki to a throat and a Suso Haneage upward strike to a groin or chin. When he had immobilized his first attacker, he mule kicked him into Tran's line of sight and trusted that a subsonic bullet would put the man down.

When the next attacker swiped at Ren's belly with a knife, he shifted just out of reach, followed the man's arm with his cane, guiding it farther than he expected, then snapped the tip of the cane back with a powerful push-pull strike. The brass point struck into the fragile pterion, where the four cranial bones met. The impact was hard enough to rupture the meningeal artery and possibly cause brain damage or death.

Chang gutted another man in the stomach and kicked him to the floor.

Six bodies now clogged the entry channel behind the folding privacy screen.

The mama-san across the road shut her doors. No one passed on the street. If Ren and Chang didn't breach the building soon, the gang would attack in force and shove them outside.

"This way," Chang said, and bolted up the left-hand stairs.

Bodies fell behind Ren like shooting gallery targets as he ran across the open doors. From the steep, open staircase, he saw four more men racing around a long dining table out of the kitchen in the back.

He paused long enough to unsheathe one of the bo-shuriken, cupped the dart vertically in his palm, and secured it lightly with his thumb. He chambered it alongside his ear and let the iron slide through his grip as it launched, aiming for center mass as Tran had done with his rifle. The shuriken veered high and lodged in the gangster's throat.

A shot was fired at Ren from across the dining area where a man had squatted on the matching staircase to take aim. Before he could fire again, Chang knelt on the steps above Ren and shot the man in the head. With no railing or wall to stop him, the gunman fell off the steep staircase onto the hardwood floor.

The surprise attack had ended. Any Kufuku-kai they encountered would be armed and hungry to kill.

Chapter Fifty-Three

I led Suyin across the corridor to an empty room with a view. Narrow three-story buildings like ours pressed in from all sides. The utility wires draped over the single-lane road reminded me of Shanghai. Although I could have climbed down the building or up to the roof, Suyin would have needed a fire escape we didn't have.

A gun fired inside our building.

I clamped a hand over Suyin's mouth before she could scream.

We could hide in the bedroom until whatever was happening was done or use the commotion to escape. My choice was clear. Suyin didn't agree.

I gripped her arms as she tried to breakaway. "We need to get out of this building while they're distracted. Unless you can climb walls, we need to go down the stairs."

She looked from the window to the door with equal concern.

I folded her hands tighter around the baton. "If someone gets past me, aim for their bones – head, hands, elbows, or knees." When she nodded, I led her down the corridor to the left where a steep flight of steps shot down two levels to the ground floor.

Men raced into view.

I pushed her back and ran to the matching stairwell on the other side. Voices shouted in Japanese but, for the moment, our egress was clear.

"Leave a few steps between us so I can fight."

She raised the baton to indicate she understood.

The stairs were steep, shallow, and open on one side, which meant anyone on the second level would be able to see our legs before we saw them. I lay on the landing and peeked over the edge.

Tattooed men in tank tops and shorts scrambled on the floor below us to find weapons between the lounging area near the windows and the pool table in back. The quicker ones had already engaged the infiltrators with pool cues and knives. I wasn't surprised that Uncle had found me, but I was shocked to see Sensei fighting beside him instead of J Tran.

Armed only with a cane, my teacher struck vital points to shut down nerves, sight, and sound. He countered swinging pool cues with bone-cracking accuracy and returned knife attacks with organ-damaging thrusts. As one attacker fell, another took his place.

Sensei leapt back and drew a hidden sword from the cane-like sheath.

Although he and I had trained with live blades, I had never watched him in actual combat, nor had I seen him engage with anyone other than me. The poetry of it stole my breath.

He held off his attacker in Ichi no Kamae, then flipped his wrists with a quick slice to the man's hands. When his attacker pulled back his knife, Sensei flowed through Gedan no Kamae with an upward sweeping cut that pulled through tendons and muscles to bone. The man screamed as his blood spurted from the axillary artery that used to feed his limb.

Leaving this man to his fate, Sensei flipped his wrists again, flicking drops of blood into the air, and swept back to his right with a lateral cut across the next attacker's throat. It happened so quickly, as if he had felt rather than seen the danger and continued his motion to the blade's natural conclusion.

Uncle stabbed and slashed.

Sensei pierced and sliced.

Like the strokes of his watercolor brush, my teacher used his straight ninja-to blade to paint an exquisite scene of pain, death, and surprise. I was so captivated by the beauty, I almost missed the two men below me opening a cabinet hidden beneath the stairs.

Chapter Fifty-Four

Movement on the stairs caught Ren's eyes in time to see Lily-chan jump from the top of the ladder-like steps. She landed on the back of a bald-headed man like a cat. The fingers of one hand clawed over his head into his eyes and nostrils while her other hand reached around to dig her thumb and fingers into the pressure points of his throat. As her knees squeezed against his back, one leg snuck over the man's right arm to lower the gun that had been pointed at Ren.

All of this happened in a single leap – a leap Ren had not taught her or ever executed himself.

Lily-chan pulled her leg to torque the man's arm farther behind his back and leaned her weight to spiral him to the floor. The takedown pinned the man's gun-arm beneath his weight and hers. As a second man retrieved a gun from the stairway cabinet to shoot, Lily-chan grabbed the fallen pistol and shot him in the face.

His student's decisive precision froze Ren in his tracks. If not for Chang fighting by his side, a gangster would have stabbed him in the back.

"Stop gaping and fight," Chang said, shaking Ren from his daze.

More Kufuku-kai gangsters were running up the stairs.

Lily-chan fired another shot.

Ren yearned to watch her in action, but he had troubles of his own.

He whirled his sword over his head, tucked his foot behind the other, and spiraled with a sweeping 360-degree lateral cut. Men yelped and backed away, some bleeding, others not. Before the knifeman in front of him resumed his attack, Ren opened his belly with an upward diagonal slice.

Across the room, Lily-chan attempted to fire, then hurled her empty gun at the gangster rushing her from around the couch. Pain and blood slowed the gangster for a moment, but he quickly recovered and continued his charge. Ren wanted to help her, but he couldn't leave Chang, who was drowning in more adversaries than he could shoot.

Lily-chan can handle herself, but can we?

Ren focused his attention and summoned the knowledge from the Oku-hiden scroll. Instead of fighting, he gave way, becoming a ghost his opponents could see but not touch.

Although the *nin* in ninja meant stealth – drawing from the *nin-sha* Chinese pronunciation of the written characters or *shinobi-no-mono* in Japanese – the secrets Ren had learned from his teacher and through studying the Oku-hiden scroll elevated his stealth into a mastery of magic.

As men attacked, Ren didn't conceal, evade, counter, or attack. He didn't even fit into their space as he had taught Lily-chan to do. He offered no resistance at all. And yet the blood of his enemy flowed.

They tumbled into emptiness and slit their own throats. They eviscerated their bellies on his blade. They broke their bones from the weight of their own misalignment. Ren did nothing to steal their senses or restrict their mobility, yet they lost their ability to see, hear, or move. Ren exerted no will of his own. He simply – or not so simply – accepted their intention and allowed them to determine their own demise.

Chang expelled far more energy in his close-quarters fight, breaking cheeks and jaws with the pistol's butt as often as he shot. Once emptied, with no time to load a new magazine, he exchanged the pistol for a knife and slashed, swiped, and kicked. Despite the injured and dead surrounding him, more Kufuku-kai gangsters flooded up the stairs.

Across the room, Lily-chan fought three attackers of her own, two unarmed and one with a knife. Above her, a Chinese woman cowered on the ladder-like stairs. Using Ren's multiple-attacker fighting techniques, Lily-chan slipped in and out of the men. She caught a wrist, made use of a grab, positioned her feet, knees, and hips to tangle, off balance, and lock.

Ren could have watched her graceful efficiency for hours.

If only he had the time.

A bare-chested gangster retrieved pistols from the gun cabinet, tossed one to his comrade, and targeted Ren. As the man prepared to fire, Ren rolled out of the way, clearing the path for the bullet to hit the next man charging up the stairs.

The second gunman searched for a clear shot at Lily-chan, who had tangled her attackers into a Gordian knot of arm bars, spinal locks, and hyper-extended knees. Using the men as a shield, she peeled the knife from her captive's loosened grip, stabbed one of the tangled men in the kidney, and opened the carotid artery in another man's neck. As the men slumped to the floor, an opening appeared.

The gunman took aim.

Ren sent a bo-shuriken flying into his neck. Having provided a moment's distraction for Lily-chan to use, Ren spun back toward the stairs.

Chang had wrapped his jacket around one arm as he defended against knives. His fitted vest was covered in blood. Although some of it had to be his own, the wounded enemy and corpses around him attested to his skill. At some point, Chang had acquired a machete. The former triad enforcer might have been chopping ducks in the Wong family's restaurant for the last twenty-five years, but he had kept his killer instincts honed.

Chang dodged a knife thrust and swept the machete up through the knifeman's jacket. As he yanked the blade out of the man's arm, he shouted to Ren. "There are too many. We have to fall back. Have you spotted Suyin?"

Ren baited one attacker, leapt to the side, and severed the man's wrists. "She's hiding at the top of the other stairs."

"Aiya. We'll never get her out through this. Where the hell is Tran?"

Chapter Fifty-Five

As Ren and Chang retreated into the center of the room, a gangster rushing down the stairs from the third floor grabbed his chest, teetered a moment, and fell off the open flight onto the floor. A moment later, Tran appeared on the landing and slung his rifle to his back.

"About damn time," Chang yelled.

Tran smirked. "I had street cleaning to do."

Tran triggered his stiletto, grabbed the nearest gangster by his ponytail, and slid his blade into the hollow behind the man's ear and into his brain.

Now that Tran had joined the fight, Ren charged across the room to help Lily-chan rescue Suyin. But instead of facing her pursuer, his astounding student had vaulted up the side of the steep stairs, rebounded off the wall, and sailed back into the fight. As she dove over her pursuer, she clamped her legs around the man's ears, flipped him backwards, and broke his neck as she slammed his head onto the floor. She continued her shoulder roll into the knees of the gunman aiming at Ren. Instead of shooting Ren in the back of the head, the gunman shot the ceiling as he fell.

Lily-chan leaped back to Ren as a new batch of Kufuku-kai took his place. "What are you doing here, Sensei?"

He laughed at the irony. "I came to rescue you."

As Ren sliced the limbs of his nearest attacker, Lily-chan dodged and sliced at an attacker of her own. Her knife went flying as the man clubbed it from her grip. When he attacked again, she spun inside his swing, captured his arm, and accelerated his momentum to pull him off balance. Rather than spiraling him to the floor, she reversed the direction, locked his arm, and broke his elbow with an audible snap.

Ren returned to his own problems as a gangster rushed him from the stairs while the man he had sliced in the legs retrieved an abandoned gun. With simultaneous threats, Ren butted the charging man in the face with his hilt and skewered the other through the throat before he could fire. The would-be gunman dropped the weapon as he struggled to breathe.

Meanwhile, Lily-chan ducked under a haymaker punch and came up with a boxing uppercut to the gut, an elbow to the floating rib, and a stepping palm heel under the jaw that she delivered with perfect taijutsu alignment. Then she spun with some sort of jumping lateral kick at another attacker, landed on her knee to arch away from a third attacker's strike, and spiraled up with a spinning round kick and back fist combination. As the three men joined forces against her, she tumbled out of their reach with a springing front walk over.

Ren gaped.

In less than two minutes, Lily-chan had blended her ninjutsu with parkour, boxing, Wushu, and gymnastics in a spontaneous extension of herself. No rules. No identifiable art. She fought with complete freedom – creating, inventing, adapting on the fly. Although Ren had so much more to teach her, in this moment, *she* taught *him*.

"Behind you." She pointed to the far landing below where Suyin hid, where new men emerged from the floor below.

Ren had allowed his pride and fascination for Lily-chan to distract him from his task. A kohai mistake he would not repeat.

He rushed at the first man, circling his head with his ninja-to, and spiraled the blade into a lateral cut. Instead of slicing through flesh, the gangster deflected Ren's blade with a steel pipe and drove him back with a series of powerful and well-executed strikes.

Pain shot through Ren's arm.

The pipe deadened his nerves and loosened his grip on the sword. Deprived of the subtle dexterity of his right hand and fingers, he resorted to gross body movement to maneuver the blade. Generating momentum as one might swing a heavy sack, he shifted between his stances to adjust the direction and precision of his cuts. When his sword tip dropped, he raised it with his foot.

The gangster evaded the slicing blade, then charged with a head-bashing swing of his pipe.

Instead of attempting to deflect or evade, Ren sank into Ichimonji no Kamae. With his body angled, knees bent, spine and limbs aligned, Ren turned the blade sideways and braced the hilt against his hip.

The man's jaw dropped in surprise as the stabilized blade slid between his fourth and fifth ribs and into his heart.

Behind him, more members of the Kufuku-kai gang poured up the stairs.

For the first time since Ren had entered the building, he fought for his life.

Chapter Fifty-Six

As my friends and teacher fought valiantly, I stomped one attacker into another and caught my breath. As my adrenaline waned, I could feel the effects of my captivity, the beatings, and whatever drugs were still in my system.

My broken ribs screamed as I breathed.

Around me, tattooed men shouted, fought, bled, and died in a cacophony of violence I had never experienced before.

Uncle was cornered behind the pool table in the back, wielding a machete with one hand and trying to reload a pistol on the table with the other. A bullet pierced his shoulder and he dropped the magazine. He yelled in fury and resumed his butchering defense.

Tran fought at the front of the room near the couches and chairs. Seeing Uncle in jeopardy, he aimed through the battle and emptied his pistol into Uncle's biggest threat. Then he holstered his gun and used his newly-freed hand to check and counter as he slashed and stabbed. I recognized the quick footwork plus hand and blade integration from Filipino Kali martial arts. The last time I had watched Tran kill with a stiletto, he had assassinated two unsuspecting punks in a Koreatown garage. These opponents fought back.

Behind me on the landing, Sensei tried to stop more gang members from coming up the stairs.

Above him, still perched on the steeper flight of steps, Suyin played whack-a-mole with a man's head and fingers as he grabbed at her from the landing below. It was only a matter of time before someone realized they could race up the opposite stairs and grab her from above.

As thankful as I was to have Sensei, Uncle, and Tran fighting at my side, the Kufuku-kai continued to appear up the far stairs. How long could we last before they overpowered us? Where were the police? And now that I had stopped moving for a moment, would I even be able to restart?

I shoved the useless questions from my mind.

My parents were counting on me to return. Suyin was counting on me to escape. Sensei, Uncle, and Tran were counting on me to fight.

A bullet whizzed past my head. Guns and chaos. If I didn't keep moving, I'd catch a bullet for sure.

As Sensei fought the men rushing up the stairs, I dove into a cartwheel over a dead body and snatched a pool cue from the floor. I rose into Daijodan no Kamae with the staff above my head, high in the back and sloped down in the front, as my opponents fanned out between fallen bodies at my ten o'clock, twelve, and two. They were armed respectively with a pipe, bat, and dagger.

Every visible inch of these gangsters' arms and chests were inked with blue jackals hungry for blood.

As the men pressed me from the front and sides, I swung, twirled, and thrust the pool cue to kept them at bay. When the two o'clock man slipped through an opening, I clipped him in the knee and whacked him on the head. When the man on my ten charged from the side, I fell back with a snapping Suso Haneage strike to his groin. The center man was cautious. I enticed him with a weakly delivered strike, then clubbed him to the ground as I pretended to retreat.

I followed with more injurious blows, but what I really needed was a gun.

Or a dagger.

Like the one that had just swiped my ribs.

Blood wet my fingers as I clutched my side and redirected the knifeman's next attack with my cue.

Blinding pain shot down my left arm and seized my neck when my ten o'clock opponent slammed my collarbone with his pipe.

I clung to the staff, but the slice on the right side of my torso had made my good arm weak.

The men laughed and advanced.

Needing extra purchase, I grounded the base of the cue on the floor and used body movement and positioning to evade my opponents as I struck and parried their attacks with the tip. They circled me with freedom while I was rooted in place.

I kicked the base of the pool cue up under the pipe wielder's chin and fell back into a grounded stance so I could hug the staff close to my body as I struck down with the tip.

Wood cracked against my knee and buckled me to the floor as another swipe of the knife sliced through my cheek. The battle cries buried my howls. These jackals were picking me apart.

With my left knee and clavicle damaged or broken and blood dripping from my right cheek, ribs, and thigh, I clung to the pool cue as I struggled to stand on one leg.

Tran, Uncle, and Sensei fought for their lives.

I was failing with no one to help.

The jackals closed in for the kill.

As they drew back their weapons to bludgeon and cut, they cried out and arched in pain. They looked at me with hate as they fell, revealing the last saviors I had ever expected to see.

My previous interrogators pulled out their knives and finished the job with cold efficiency as more tattoo-less ninja slid into the battle and evened the score.

Shaved Head grinned at me, then stabbed a man in the kidney. Spiky Hair stomped a gangster's knee, pulled back his head, and thrust his blade into the man's neck. A kunoichi leapt onto an unsuspecting gangster and drove her knife into his spine

The female ninja was the first woman I had seen other than Suyin in days.

The Kufuku-kai attacked the new threat, but they were injured and exhausted from fighting with us. Even if they had been fresh, their thuggish methods would not have matched the ninja's skills, especially not after Tran, Uncle, Sensei, and I had decimated their ranks.

Six ninja cleaned up the rest.

Approaching sirens filled the sudden quiet in the room.

As we caught our breaths, a tall, silver-haired man in a tailored suit sauntered through the fallen bodies to my teacher and grinned.

"Time to go, Osamu, unless you'd rather ride with the police."

Chapter Fifty-Seven

I watched as Sensei followed the silver-haired man down the stairs and out a back door to a pedestrian alley. Suyin clung to Uncle as they walked. I hobbled after, supported by Tran. Our ninja saviors brought up the rear.

"You okay?" Tran asked.

"Define *okay*."

The last of my strength leaked from my body like blood.

Tran, on the other hand, appeared uninjured and in good spirits. Aside from slashes in his couture jacket at the waist, chest, and sleeves, only his wild hair, freed from his ponytail, seemed out of place. His black wardrobe hid all signs of blood.

I poked my fingers through the slashed fabric at his chest and felt the soft armor padding underneath. "And I thought you were just vain."

He smirked. "I am. But it pays to be cautious in my line of work."

Line of work? Had Tran switched from assassination to rescue-protection work like me?

When I slumped from exhaustion, he swept me up like a bride.

I woke on my back in a padded cargo van with Sensei's concerned face peering into mine. "Konichiwa, Lily-chan."

I cracked a smile and fluttered back to sleep.

When I woke again, I was perched in the corner, bolstered by moving blankets against vibrating walls. My upper arm was strapped to my chest. My pants had been cut into shorts. An elastic bandage wrapped my left leg from thigh to calf, swollen in the middle to three times my knee's normal size. Another bandage had been wrapped around my broken and slashed ribs with my black muscle shirt cut up the sides to create roomier flaps.

Sensei closed the gash in my right thigh with surgical tape. "How are you feeling, Lily-chan?"

I blinked away the fog my blood loss had caused. "Sore. Weak. Glad to see you."

He wrapped my thigh and smiled. "I wish it was under better circumstances."

"We're alive, right? What could be better than that?"

My attempted shrug seized my neck and shoulder. The pain was bad but manageable.

"Your collarbone is badly bruised. The most I could do was immobilize your arm. I gave you the prescription NSAIDs our rescuers provided. If it's not strong enough, there is fentanyl in the first aid kit."

"No way. That's what brought us to Japan."

He glanced at Uncle. "So I have heard."

Uncle jutted his chin in hello but otherwise saved his strength. For the first time, he looked older than his sixty-four years.

"Are you okay?" I asked.

Uncle shrugged his good shoulder and glanced at the other, bandaged with gauze over the bullet wound I had watched him receive. The gashes on his face and arms had been cleaned and taped, but dried blood still clung to his hands. His torn and crusted vest and jeans bore the evidence of battle – the triad enforcer's destiny Uncle had hoped to escape.

Suyin dozed beside him. Between the stress of dealing with the Hefei gang, the guilt of the deaths caused by her fentanyl analogue, and running away to a bogus lover in Japan whose gang had planned to sell her to North Korean drug dealers, the poor thing probably hadn't felt safe enough to truly sleep. As the window-less van transported us to God knew where, I wondered if we as safe as Suyin believed.

I touched the bandage beneath Sensei's torn sleeve.

"Not to worry, Lily-chan. It's only a graze." He nodded toward Uncle. "His bullet went through without hitting any bone. We were all very fortunate. Things could have gone much worse."

I stiffened. "You mean if our *saviors* hadn't come? They ambushed me in an alley and questioned me about you."

Sensei knelt his body in Seiza no Kamae and touched his forehead against the rumbling floor of the van. "Osoreirimashita. I am deeply sorry for the pain I have caused and the danger I have brought to your door."

His forehead was red when he rose.

Although I appreciated the formal apology, I wanted an explanation even more. "Who are these ninja? For that matter, who are *you*?"

He bowed again. "You are right to be angry. An apology is not enough. None of this would have happened if I had been as open with you as you have always been with me. I will share what I can. But most of our travel time has been taken up with first aid."

"Travel to where?"

"Into the mountains of Iga, I would guess."

"Where you trained as a youth."

"Hai."

After years of curiosity, I was about to learn the truth. But as my teacher prepared to disclose his secrets, panic gripped my chest. I had always held Sensei in the highest esteem, placing him on a pedestal as an example of enlightenment I never believed I could reach. If he told me something horrible, would I lose all respect? Or worse, would knowing the truth irrevocably destroy my trust?

Sensei paused, giving me an opportunity to change my mind.

Too late for that. Recent events had crumbled his pedestal into dust. It was time to know my teacher as a man.

I steeled my heart for what I might hear and forged ahead as dispassionately as I could. "Prior to my abduction, I had been looking at pamphlets for the Ninja Museum and asking about a dojo where I might train. A martial arts Neanderthal challenged my veracity. Soon after, the ninja attacked."

Sensei nodded. "Tran shared some of this with me. I believe your *Neanderthal* was paid by Ichiro to look out for anyone connected to me. I suspect he had been given keywords and a description that fit what he heard in his conversation with you."

"Why?"

"Because I fled Japan with something precious. The man with the silver hair trained alongside me as a boy and through our early adult years. We were our teacher's senior students. Ichiro was attracted by stealth and espionage while I dedicated my studies to taijutsu, weaponry, and the mystical and spiritual practices of the Yamabushi ninja. If Ichiro and I had lived in Feudal Japan, he would have made a great spy. I would have stayed in the mountains to worship and protect.

"What did you take?"

"A scroll."

"Then all of this is my fault."

"No, Lily-chan."

"Yeah, it is. When that Neanderthal challenged the authenticity of my training, I told him about your scroll. He texted someone soon after. He denied it, of course, but by then it was too late. After Ichiro's ninja took me down, the last face I saw was his."

Sensei shook his head. "None of this would have happened if I had told you more about my past and cautioned you into secrecy."

"You didn't know I was coming to Japan."

He bowed in apology. "Even so."

Anger, sadness, and shame warred inside my heart as I came to terms with my teacher's secrets and lack of trust in me. I didn't know why he had stolen the scroll, but I knew he was right to not share this information with me. I had bragged about my training, which Sensei had taught me not to do. What more damage would I have caused if he had entrusted me with the truth?

"The blame lies with me," I said. "I allowed others to manipulate my ego and play upon my fears. I would have given you up to protect my parents. I didn't only because I didn't recognize the names they called you."

"No, Lily-chan. You gave your torturers the perfect information that alerted me and satisfied them. Knowing my names would not have changed that. Understanding the reasons behind my secrets would have given you more tools and put you on guard."

The floor of the van jolted as we drove across rougher terrain.

"I don't have time to share everything," he said. "What else do you need to know now?"

"Your names."

"My US passport says I am George Ren Tanaka. I broke the law to have it forged. I was born in Iga Province as Osamu Nakayama. I trained under Jiro Tashigi of the Tashigi ninja clan. He awarded me the warrior name of Yoshito."

"What does it mean?"

"Righteous Person." Sensei grimaced, as though tasting something foul. "Tashigi Sensei showed more insight into Ichiro's cunning nature when he awarded him the name Zuruihito. Ichiro lived up to his name. I continue to fall short of mine." He clapped his hands to dispel his shame and continued without emotion. "As senior students, we were both allowed to copy the Shoden, Chuden, and Okuden scrolls. But there was another scroll Ichiro knew about but had never seen."

"The one in your bedroom?"

"Hai."

"Why is it special?"

"It reverses the first three to attain a higher level of mastery. It also contains the true Tashigi lineage. Our teacher entrusted the Oku-hiden scroll to me when Ichiro forced me to leave Japan."

The van hit rough terrain and jolted us against the walls.

"We don't have much time, Lily-chan. You know I was married, but I never told you my wife and ten-year-old son were mugged. I had run back to a restaurant to retrieve Kimiko's sweater. Haru tried to fight and was killed. I returned in time to watch my son's murderer stab my wife.

I killed him too late. The other man escaped. Ichiro located the accomplice and orchestrated my revenge – an ambush similar to how they trapped you. I couldn't do it. When I backed out, Ichiro killed the murderer's accomplice and threatened to tell the police it had been me."

Sorrow pooled in his eyes.

I wanted to assuage Sensei's guilt and tell him none of this was his fault, but I knew from my own demons that the best of my promises would fail.

He swallowed his regret. "I will share the entire story when we are safe at home. For now, all you need to know is that none of this is because of you. My bad karma has caught up with me. I must see it to the end.

Chapter Fifty-Eight

I stretched my reluctant limbs as the van lurched to a stop. Whatever waited for us outside would need me standing and ready to fight.

I grunted in pain.

Tran slid a hand around my waist and helped me to my feet. Uncle rose as well. Sensei stood sentry in front of us at the rear doors. A moment later, they opened to reveal a clearing in the woods.

The silver-haired man sauntered into view.

Sensei jumped to the ground, muttering in Japanese and then switching to English so we would understand. "You took over our teacher's property?"

Ichiro gestured at the majestic pines and the snow-crusted mountain top beyond. "I paid his wife a fair price when he died."

"Nothing you do is fair."

Standing toe to toe, the differences between the two men were pronounced. My teacher was barely taller than me, with a squat body and limbs. His nemesis was tall and lean like Tran. With his salon cut hair and classic features, Ichiro could have passed for a senior executive or a cinema star. Sensei looked like the carpenter I knew him to be.

Ichiro shrugged. "Fair? I could say the same of you, my old friend."

"We were never friends."

"We could have been."

"No. Your heart was poisoned from the start."

Ichiro pretended to be hurt. "Who found your family's killer after you let one of them escape? Who rallied the other students to help you ambush him in the alley. Who finished the job you were too cowardly to do?"

"You warp the truth like wood in a bog."

"At least I recognize the wood for what it is. You have too high of an opinion of yourself to see the harm you have caused."

"To whom?"

"Your wife and son. Our lineage." He nodded toward my battered condition. "Your student."

"Hey," I said. "You did this to me. Not him."

Ichiro shook his head. "And you are just as blind. The student follows where the teacher leads."

Sensei stepped forward, drawing Ichiro's attention to him. "We made an agreement at the stadium: the scroll for the Kufuku-kai's location and Lily-chan's safe release. Instead, you gave her to the gang."

Ichiro held out his hands. "Her value to you made her valuable to them, especially after I informed them of your hunt. Unlike you, Righteous One, I do not *give* things away."

"Then why help us?"

"The scroll. Although an alliance with an ambitious gang like the Kufuku-kai would have brought many lucrative opportunities, not only for espionage, but for all our ninja skills, I want – and need – the Oku-hiden densho even more. Tell me the location of the scroll, Osamu, and you may resume your pointless life in America as George Ren Tanaka."

Sensei relaxed into Shizen no Kamae, feet below his hips, weight balanced, arms hanging naturally at his side. My experience with him told me he was ready to fight. Ichiro must have known the same.

"You think teaching one girl has kept your skills as sharp as mine?"

Sensei smiled. "You don't know Lily-chan."

"Maybe not. But her injuries say she is not as good as you claim."

Ichiro turned his back on Sensei and strolled through the men gathered around him on the dirt. His turf, his advantage. The message was clear. Everything around us – including ourselves – now belonged to him.

He strode toward a large farmhouse with a gabled roof and eaves, wooden storm shutters pocketed on the sides of a veranda, slightly elevated for floods. I imagined eager, young ninja dangling their legs over the front. Would my quiet teacher have sat apart from them on the steps? Or had he been gregarious like me before tragedy stole his light? Either way, Ichiro would have commanded attention even then. Men like him burned for power right out of the womb.

Our escorts from the van, a twenty-something guy with red-tinted glasses and the one kunoichi I had seen with the bleached-white hair, motioned for us to follow.

"Think they will feed us a last meal?" Uncle said.

"You're hungry?" I asked incredulously.

"Saving you was hard work."

"Ha. Next time, do a better job."

"Next time? I'm going to lock you in the restaurant as soon as we get home."

I snorted. "Good. Then you can feed *me*."

The kunoichi barked an order in Japanese.

Tran responded and supported me as I hobbled after her. Joking aside, this situation didn't bode well. We were stranded in a forest on a mountain with a dozen skilled fighters – Uncle and I seriously impaired – entering a confined space with my teacher's enemy. I didn't expect tea.

I took more weight on my left leg as we stepped onto the veranda. The athletic wrap and pain killers helped. My damaged knee would support me as long as I didn't run, jump, or twist.

"Can you fight?" Tran whispered.

I met his uncompromising gaze with my own. "To my dying breath."

He nodded but continued to help me as if I couldn't walk. Any element of surprise on our part would help balance the scales.

The interior of the farmhouse greeted us with false coziness and promises of traditional hospitality. Although not as sophisticated as Sensei's woodworking artistry, the dark, rustic grains in the ceiling, beams, and structural posts blended beautifully with the translucent paper and dark lattice shoji doors. We removed our shoes in the entry and followed Sensei into the welcoming space.

The raised floor to our right had a square sunken hearth in the center with cooking grates and a kettle hanging from a decorative iron hook. Woven mats and cushions offered places to sit with quilted blankets folded and stacked nearby for warming laps and legs. The raised sections on our left led to interior verandas and shoji-hidden rooms.

Sensei slowed his pace to match mine. "This was my teacher's home before he passed away. He and his wife raised their daughters on this mountain before they moved to the city for higher education and jobs. I worry about Tashigi Sensei's widow now that Ichiro has taken over her home."

"Is this where you trained?"

"Yes. In the forest and through there."

We crossed a stone threshold into a large matted room.

Ichiro waited for us at the back wall below a kamidana similar to the god shelf in Sensei's home dojo and my own, but with two notable differences. Ichiro's Shinto temple had no offerings other than one water-starved plant and a burned-out stick of incense, and the lineage sketch on the wall began and ended with him.

Sensei walked forward to examine the sketch. "Have you begun your own martial art, Zuruihito?"

"No need. I am the rightful heir to the Tashigi ninja clan."

"You don't have the scroll to back up the claim."

"I didn't, but I will. Unless you have lost your honorable nature."

"You broke the terms of our agreement."

Ichiro smiled. "Then I will get it another way."

His crew closed us in, twelve strong, young ninja itching to prove themselves against their teacher's old nemesis and friends.

I moved away from Tran and stood on my own, finding a new balance point between my good knee and bad. I stuck my left thumb in the waistband of my cutoff pants to stabilize my bruised clavicle and remind myself not to fight against the bandage that taped my arm to my chest. The wraps around my ribs and my gashed right thigh provided additional support.

Uncle pushed Suyin behind him and moved forward between my teacher and Tran.

Sensei broke away from our unified wall and glared at his enemy. "You have grown soft, ordering minions to do your bidding. Perhaps you have not kept up your training as diligently as you believe."

Ichiro held up his hand to hold back his crew. "Perhaps you would like to find out."

Sensei bowed.

When he rose, Ichiro drove his extended knuckles into the pocket of Sensei's throat.

I gasped in warning a split second too late.

Sensei had already rippled his neck and spine backwards to diffuse the impact while turning like wind to collect Ichiro's arm in a leaf-like swirl of his hands. As Sensei shot a finger strike to the trachea, Ichiro vanished through a minuscule gap and countered with his own attack.

Ichiro's ninja stepped back, allowing room for their leader to fight while blocking us from the weapons mounted on the walls.

Uncle nodded toward the corner where we could better defend Suyin.

I hesitated.

"Do you believe in your teacher's skill or not?"

I nodded.

"Then leave him to his work and prepare yourself to do ours."

Uncle was right: We had come to Osaka on a mission that was only partially complete. Sensei was fighting an enemy who had changed the entire course of his life.

I backed up and positioned myself between my two closest friends to watch my teacher duel and prayed he had the skills I believed. Fighting criminal elements for survival and power had made Ichiro ruthless and clever, while Sensei's daily practice had been akin to Tai Chi, centering his mind and causing the least disturbance as he moved through his days. Which path had forged the deadlier warrior?

Ichiro unclipped a hidden folding knife and flicked open the blade. Then he stabbed it into Sensei's belly like a prison-style shank.

My stomach clenched as I imagined the pain. But Sensei evaded this attack as well, using moves I didn't know and techniques I could not see. Ichiro's alignment and reactions were the only indication of the effects. Even so, the espionage master did not yield.

The men fought differently at seventy than they must have in their prime, forsaking the speed and athleticism of youth for efficiency, precision, and results. Ichiro had the longer reach, Sensei the more stable base. Both fought with the caution that came from having lost in the past. Both benefited from maturity forged in the flames of failure and betrayal their younger selves would never have believed they could endure.

The beginnings of such hard-earned maturity had already left its mark on me, from the preventable death of my sister to the sex-trafficking horrors I had witnessed in Los Angeles and only been able to partially halt.

What demons pulled at Sensei and Ichiro as they fought?

What actions of the past ignited or dampened their will to live and dictated what they would or would not be willing to do?

Ichiro's blade flicked with alarming dexterity, barely missing Sensei's belly and throat before slashing through the faded blue sleeve of his shirt. The bright red stain proved he had cut through flesh.

As the leader of a criminal gang, Ichiro had honed his

skills with blood. Before today, Sensei had only killed once. I knew from experience how the lives he had ended would weigh on his soul. I only hoped the ghosts would leave him alone until he could turn the tide of Ichiro's assault.

The espionage master thrust again and followed up with a stomp to Sensei's knee. Once again, my teacher gave way, absorbed the impact, and vanished like a ghost. Before my eyes, he exemplified what it truly meant to become one with his adversary in the creation of a fight.

Blood from both men splattered the mats. Not even blade masters survived a knife fight unscathed.

While Ichiro strove to humiliate and conquer, Sensei embraced the man's fury and provided space for it to roam. Together they spun a maelstrom of slashes, reversals, and strikes as they stole and recovered balance, threw each other through the air, and rolled gracefully to their feet. As if sapping his energy, Sensei grew strong while Ichiro grew weak.

What was obvious to me as Sensei's student remained hidden to Ichiro as he fell for every ruse and attacked where – and how – my teacher wished. This would not have worked in their initial exchanges. But Sensei had taken control of Ichiro's emotions through the same empathy and acceptance he had patiently drilled into me.

"True empathy is the foundation for all meaningful relationships," he had said during one of our lessons.

"Even in combat?" I had asked.

"Especially in combat."

He was showing me in action what he had told me in words.

Ichiro emitted a roar of frustration and overextended his attack. Sensei captured his energy and turned the direction of his blade.

It happened so quickly. One moment, Ichiro held every advantage – the knife, the men, the dojo he had stolen from the teacher he supposedly revered. He should have won. He should have killed Sensei and all of us with ease. Instead, Ichiro's evil intent turned back on himself as Sensei stabbed the man's knife into his own throat.

Ichiro shuddered and froze, eyes wide in confusion and surprise. Never in all of his machinations had it occurred to him he might lose. As the realization sunk in, his fury returned. He grabbed Sensei's wrist and tried to push it and the knife, but Sensei turned the blade horizontally and ripped it through veins and arteries out the side.

Blood gushed onto the mat.

The men froze in a deadly embrace.

Supporting him by the arm, Sensei stared into the eyes of his former training partner and enemy. Although I couldn't see what passed between them as Zuruihito, the Cunning Man, crossed over into death, I knew this moment would haunt Yoshito, the Righteous Man, for the rest of his life.

I readied myself to fight as the body crumpled to the mat.

Tran and Uncle did the same.

Ichiro's ninja tensed, uncertain of what to do.

Then my chief inquisitor, the man I had named Mr. Stern, who reminded me of my Hong Kong grandfather, only younger and more chicly dressed, stepped forward to stake his claim. "You have what you came for, Osamu Nakayama. Now it is time for you to leave. Go back to your new country as George Ren Tanaka. This is no longer your home."

Sensei sized up the younger, stronger man. "I lived in Japan for more years than you've been alive. I will leave when I am ready to leave. But I have no more quarrel with you."

The new leader turned to Tran, Uncle, and me. "You're free to go." He motioned to our escorts. "Drive them into town and drop them wherever they want."

Chapter Fifty-Nine

The kunoichi tossed my jacket into the cargo van before closing the doors. I had woken without it during my captivity and didn't expect it to be returned. Nor did I expect to find my phone zipped into the pocket. Although low on battery, it still had some juice.

Uncle smiled at my discovery, understanding my relief, then returned his attention to his overwrought ward. The musical tones of her Mandarin filled the silence as Tran closed his eyes and Sensei stared at the floor. As each man dealt with the day's events in their own way, I opened my chat thread with Ma.

The first unread message had come while Ichiro's ninja had ambushed me in the alley two nights ago, when my mother was beginning the previous day. Seven in the morning would have been eleven at night for me, somewhere between the knuckles to my face and the kicks to my gut. Unlike me, my mother had enjoyed a peaceful night.

Good morning, my darling. Guess what. I finally managed to sleep! And I made another kimchee pancake this morning for breakfast. 😊 *Off to the hospital now. I'll keep you updated through the day.*

Ma's breakfast made me smile. Remembering the kidney

punches from my inquisitors wiped it off my face. Funny how the details of the beating became clearer now than before. Knuckles to my cheek. A baton cracked across my ribs. A band tied around my arm to pump up my veins. The next message from Ma would have come in after I had given up Sensei's email to protect my parents' lives.

Thursday 2 a.m. in Osaka would have been Wednesday 10 a.m. for Ma.

Your father's headaches and vomiting from the lumbar puncture have finally passed. He's supposed to be walking, but his legs are too weak. We're waiting for the doctors to report the results. Why does everything take so long?

Two hours later.

The doctors finally came. The lumbar puncture showed elevated proteins in the cerebrospinal fluid. (Fluid around the brain and spinal cord.) This could indicate an immune system dysfunction or possibly a stroke. They are looking more closely at the lesions the MRI spotted in your father's brain. LESIONS. Why didn't they tell us about those before? I'm so furious I could spit. Your father sent me to the commissary to get hot water for tea. He says it will calm me down. Calm ME down. I should be caring for HIM.

Ten minutes later.

I know dawn hasn't even broken in Shanghai but please respond when you wake. I love and miss you, Lily. I need my practical, loving daughter to calm my frazzled nerves. 🙏

Two hours later, she messaged me again. It would have been two o'clock for her and six the next morning for me, still knocked out from my drug-induced sleep.

Haven't you read my messages yet? It must be 7 a.m. in Shanghai. Please respond.

Then.

They've taken your father away for neurological tests, something to do with his vision and hearing. Once again, they explained it too fast for me to understand. Am I getting old? Or am I just too scared to listen properly? I wish you were here with a good set of ears.

Then.

I found a bench outside. The waiting is stressful. Can we talk?

Twenty minutes later.

I guess you're busy. Please be safe. I'm going back inside.

I pictured my mother on a bench with a phone wondering why her *practical, loving daughter* didn't care enough to call. How could I have done this to her again? First Rose. Now Baba. I was never with my mother when she needed me the most.

Two hours later.

Still nothing, Lily? Now I'm worried about you! I keep thinking about what you went through in Hong Kong. Falling from that roof. Fighting those gangsters. Getting thrown from that car. Please tell me you're okay. Every time I close my eyes, I see you covered in blood.

Sensei leaned closer in his seat. "Are you okay, Lily-chan?"

I shook my head. "Baba's in the hospital and my mother's alone."

"Is it serious?"

"She doesn't know. I'm catching up on all the messages I've missed. I'm afraid to scroll to the end."

Sensei squeezed my hand. "Take your time, Lily-chan. The messages will wait until you are ready to read them."

"What if I'm never ready?"

"Hmm. Were you ready to be ambushed and tortured?"

"Obviously not."

"And yet you escaped and saved Suyin."

"That's not the same."

"Then you fought a much more forceful enemy to come to my aid. You could not have prepared for what you did not expect, yet you responded as if you had. Your father's illness is the same. Whatever enemy your parents must face, you will do what you have always done and fight."

I considered the memories that haunted my mother from Hong Kong. As bad as they were, they didn't compare to other battles I had fought since or even before. I thought of Baba. How could I fight something I couldn't even see?

"With knowledge," I said, answering my own question.

"And fortitude," Sensei added.

"Agreed."

He smiled sadly, eyes shrouded by sorrow and regret, no doubt reliving all he had done. Killing someone he had known since childhood would especially eat at his soul.

"You had to end it," I said.

"I know."

"It doesn't make it any easier."

"No. It does not."

He leaned against the van's wall and left me to my phone. Perhaps one day, sitting in his garden, gazing at the jacaranda blossoms, sipping sencha tea, Sensei would share the feelings that overwhelmed him on this day. For now, he and I had to face our demons on our own.

Ma's messages continued during her evening about the time I would have woken up in the storage room, worried about rogue ninja coming after her and Baba.

I'm leaving the hospital. I'll text when I'm home.

Then, 2:00 p.m. Osaka (10:00 p.m. for Ma).

It's afternoon for you, Lily, and still no message. What's happening? My heart is filled with dread.

Thirty minutes later.

I washed my face and fixed some tea. I know you'll be angry, but I can't stomach any food. Not until I tell you everything that happened today.

The doctors shocked your father with electrodes in a series of neurological tests called evoked potentials. I listened more carefully this time and asked a lot of questions before the doctors had a chance to escape.

These tests measure how quickly and completely nerve signals reach the brain. They can also show problems too subtle for an MRI to catch. Combined with the brain lesions – I still can't believe they didn't tell us about those before! – any irregularities they find might indicate some sort of neurological disorder. They wouldn't tell us what they were looking for. They only said there were many possibilities they needed to rule out.

Your father was having none of that. "Do I have brain cancer? Yes or no?"

Can you hear his voice, Lily? I bet you can. But even his indignation did not compel them to answer beyond, "We'll know more tomorrow when we see the results."

What did Shakespeare say about tomorrows? A petty pace, indeed.

They also took more blood. Although I can't imagine what other tests he might need.

I'm going to leave my phone on beside the bed in case you call. Don't worry about waking me. I need to hear your voice. I love you, my darling. Please, please, please be safe.

I scrolled up a few paragraphs and reread my father's words.

"Do I have brain cancer? Yes or no?"

I bit my lips and stared at my phone until my mother's messages blurred. Although I understood the factors that had led me to Japan, they weren't enough to resolve my guilt. What kind of daughter abandoned her parents when they needed her the most?

A litany of disgusting attributes stabbed into my heart.

I was as selfish and self-absorbed at twenty-five as I had been as a child.

I hadn't looked out for my little sister as an elder sister should.

I didn't honor my parents and grandparents with the filial piety they deserved.

I dropped everything for dramatic missions to save strangers who might see me as the heroic person I was not.

Family was the foundation of my life, yet I crushed it with every decision I made.

The van jerked to a stop. A moment later, the kunoichi opened the rear doors. Despite my knee and ribs, I jumped out the back and scrambled to the apartment as a drowning person paddles up for air.

I needed my mother. I needed to atone.

The moment I connected to our apartment's Wi-Fi, I hit the video icon and called Ma. She answered on the second ring. She took one look at my battered face and burst into tears.

I held the phone to my forehead.

And cried.

Chapter Sixty

I rose from the floor of the tiny bedroom where I had tried and failed to sleep. My mind wouldn't stop and the aches had set in.

The doctor Tran had arranged to treat us in the apartment had confirmed Sensei's diagnosis of my bruised clavicle, my bruised and possibly cracked ribs, and my thankfully not broken knee. He had sterilized and stitched up my wounds, rewrapped my entire body, put my arm in a sling, and given me antibiotics and a high-potency non-steroid anti-inflammatory to take. I declined the fentanyl, morphine, and oxy he had brought. I hurt worse than I ever had in my life, but the pain caused by drug traffickers and opiates made me abstain.

Thinking another NSAID might help, I opened the door and left Suyin snoring in the twin bed – although Uncle had offered his room to her so I could sleep in comfort, he had snored so loudly, Tran sent him back to his room. With everything Suyin had endured, I insisted she take the bed. Even the softest mattress wouldn't have eased my battered body and heart.

I crept into the main room and found Sensei sleeping in perfect silence on a mat, hands folded over his lower abdomen. He had used ki energy on me to promote faster healing and reduce my pain. Was he stimulating his own life force energy while he slept? We would need more than Reiki to quiet the demons gnawing at our souls.

The silence helped.

The apartment was as still as when Tran, Uncle, and I had first entered it three days ago. So much had happened since we touched down in Osaka, more than I – or anyone – could have foreseen. My body suffered. My heart suffered more. Silence gave the illusion that I could reset time and choose a different course.

The illusion dissipated as quickly as smoke.

Despite my keen hindsight and renewed familial vows, I was still Lily Yong Shing Wong. Names influenced their bearers in unexpected ways. My floral first name reflected my belonging with my mother and sister, Violet and Rose. My father had sacrificed his Norwegian surname to smooth my mother's filial debt. Belonging and sacrifice bookended a powerful middle name, one my maternal grandfather had believed was too strong for a girl. *Courageous Victory.* Had my Yong Shing name driven me to the ninja heroics that separated me from home?

I welcomed the sting of a thousand bees as every nerve in my body fired. Not every nerve. Only the ones on my left.

I looked away from my teacher, lying on the floor, to find Tran watching me from the couch.

He reclined on a cushion with his hands folded on his navel above the waistline of his cropped kimono pants. The shadows cast from the urban glow accentuated the angles of his face, chest, and calves. No such aid was needed for his eyes. His piercing gaze would have found me in pitch darkness.

Had he heard my thoughts?

Did he understand my guilt?

He and I shared more than I cared to admit.

Tran rose like the mist – one moment reclined, the next, seeping into my pores and lungs. He breathed into every space, in and around me, as if he belonged. As if I had invited him inside.

In full knowledge of the danger, I raised my face to his.

Never had I experienced such a kiss. Not with Pete. Not with Daniel. Not during my most secret moments and unrestrained dreams. Tran savored my lips like his last meal on Earth, then devoured them as if he had waited all his life to taste the sweetness of my mouth. Pain leaked from my body as he infused me with passion and took his fill without permission or request.

I knew I should stop. He was not the man for me. This was not the time or the place. Yet, as Sensei had done in battle, I gave way.

I glanced at my teacher who appeared fast asleep. I didn't believe it. Neither did Tran.

He led me toward the kitchen, caught me when I stumbled, and scooped me into his arms. Safe behind the counter, he lowered me gently and kissed every wound: My cut and bruised face. My tender clavicle and shoulder. The knife gashes on my arms. The bandaged ribs clearly visible through the sheer fabric of my sleeping tank over shorts. My swollen but, thankfully, not broken knee. He met my gaze between each kiss, not with the sorry compassion one shows an injured child, but with respect and acknowledgment for the price I paid in battle. Wounds were inevitable. Suffering was a choice. Rather than wipe away my pain, Tran focused my attention entirely on him.

I slowed my breath as his hair caressed my thighs, afraid

to distract him from the next place he might seek. A needless concern. An earthquake would not have deterred Tran from his goal.

From villain to comrade, J Tran had charted his own course, tracked me across the world, protected me in secret, risked his life and resources for the sake of my friends. How foolish to believe he could ever be contained or controlled. Tran did as he pleased. Meanwhile, his disquieting fascination had evolved into something more. I shuddered in ecstasy. Not just for him, but for me.

Two months earlier, I had questioned if Tran's darkness reflected my own. Now, I saw us for who we truly were – warriors, survivors, two chambers of the same heart.

As he hoisted me onto the counter, I clasped his hair and sealed my answer with a kiss. Whoever he had been and whatever he had done, in this moment, J Tran and I were one.

Chapter Sixty-One

"You didn't have to come to the airport with us," I said.

Sensei bowed. "I was not here to welcome you to my country. I wish to properly send you home."

"You'll return to California?"

"Eventually. My parents are in their nineties. I have not seen them in forty-three years." He lowered his head. "I must care for them and atone."

"What about the scroll?"

"I will do what I can to reconnect with the ninja community and restore my teacher's reputation. This may require extensive travel throughout Japan. I do not know what damage Ichiro may have caused or what stories they will have heard."

"About you?"

"About all of us. I may need to train and teach here for a while."

"To prove yourself?"

"Myself and my teacher's lineage. The Tashigi clan were more than exceptional spies. They had strong spiritual roots in the Iga mountains. Although the deeper teachings and magic must remain secret, I can share enough to establish the empowering benefits, history, and honor of our clan. If I am successful in repairing our reputation, I will show the initial section of the Oku-hiden scroll to the soke of the most influential houses. This will authenticate my claim as Tashigi Sensei's heir."

Sadness weighed in my heart as I listened to his words. An heir had responsibilities to continue a lineage. Sensei might feel obligated to stay in Japan, help Tashigi's widow to recover her property, and re-open the school. The more I heard, the more I believed he would stay. After all, the only student he taught in America was me.

"Shall I water your orchids?"

He bowed. "Yes, please. If the travel becomes too much, take them to your apartment and care for them there."

I nodded stoically, then drew him into a hug. "Thank you. For everything."

His strong arms squeezed me back. "It is I who must thank you, Lily-chan. A teacher rarely has the honor of guiding such a special student." He pushed me gently away, clasped his palms, and bowed. "Arigatou gosaimashita. Thank you for enriching my life."

I bowed deeply and turned to Uncle before the tears came. I hated farewells, especially one I never expected to give.

Uncle held out his hands to forestall any emotional assaults. "I'll return to the restaurant as soon as I set things right in Shanghai with my mother, cousins, and Suyin."

"Take the time you need," I said. "Family comes first."

He scoffed. "You are more like family to me than any Chang. Even so, there is much to be done. It is possible my sister will not want to remain with her husband after he turned his back on Suyin. If so, I will need to find a new place for her and my mother to share."

"The FFC apartment?"

He shrugged. "I hate to lose another income property."

"Where else could you put them?"

"I could evict my longtime tenants in the Shikumen house and move my mother and sister into the rough apartments below. Uma might prefer it, but I fear Meimei would stay with her husband and the rich lifestyle he can provide. Regardless, that option is not acceptable to me. Even if I renovated those floors, I refuse to place my mother in a subservient position to her late husband's cousins. She's suffered that humiliation long enough. I want her to feel honored and comfortable for the rest of her days."

"Why not bring her to Los Angeles?"

"She would die from misery. I will have to put her, Meimei, and probably Suyin in the FFC apartment where you and I stayed. Or I might sell it and use the money, along with what the government pays me for the Qiaojia Road house, to find a decent place for them to live and another property for me to rent. It won't bring in the same income, but at least Uma and my sister would be safe."

I couldn't imagine what this sacrifice meant to Uncle or how it would change the future for him and his wife to have their revenue streams cut in one trip. As hard as that might be, the situation with the Scorpion Black Society would be worse. They had helped him in Hong Kong, on my behalf, to balance a debt. Now, he owed them new favors for their help in Shanghai. After moving across the world to escape a criminal life, my father's entrepreneurial cook might be forced to become Red Pole Chang once again.

"What about Qiang?"

Uncle scoffed. "My ungrateful brother will never appreciate what it cost me – what it cost all of us – to help him recover Chyou." He shook his head and sighed. "But, as you said, family comes first."

I placed my hand on his shoulder. Uncle exemplified the filial devotion I aspired to achieve. "You're a good brother, son, cousin, and friend."

He shook his head. "You and I are much more than friends. Thank you for coming to my aid. I know what it cost you to stay with me and not return home. I will light joss sticks for your father. Tell Vern I will come back as soon as I can."

I stepped back with a nod to avoid wrapping him in a hug. Then I said goodbye to Suyin in Mandarin and warded off her effusive thanks. I hoped she would find a reputable company to work for in Shanghai, far from the gang in Hefei.

And then there was Tran.

He stood apart from the others, waiting for me to say my goodbyes, raising his pointed brow in question when I finally met his gaze.

I flashed to my first impression of him at the courthouse. Even with his back to me, I had recognized him from the news photos by his relaxed fighter's stance, utterly still and confident, despite the scrutiny of his preliminary trial. He had worn a tailor-fitted suit as he did now, minus the armor padding that had protected him during the battle with the Kufuku-kai. His long, wavy hair and stunning good looks had struck me then as they did now.

What could I possibly say to him after last night?

"Don't wrack your brain, K. This isn't goodbye."

"It's not?"

He smirked. "I will always know where you are."

"Know. But not be?"

"Would you invite me to Sunday dinners if I stayed in LA?"

"Hmm. It might be worth it to watch my mother struggle to be polite."

A glint shone in his eyes. "I make better impressions on mothers than on fathers."

I coughed out a laugh. "Baba would take one look at you and skin you alive."

Neither of us mentioned how unlikely that prospect would be.

Tran had survived a Vietnam orphanage, Cambodian guerilla soldiers, street gangs, triads, ninja, and other enemies across the world. He could certainly diffuse the anger of an overprotective, North Dakota-born dad. That said, Baba would never approve of a former assassin for me.

Former? Or current?

"What will you do?" I asked.

"In life or today?"

"Either."

"Today, I fly to Cambodia to settle overdue affairs."

I thought of my unsettling dream as my plane had touched down in Shanghai. Had Tran really been that cold and composed as a child-soldier recruit? Would he have murdered my dear friend to prove himself and survive? He had killed twice as a child before joining that camp. I couldn't fathom how many lives he had ended since then.

"Retribution?" I asked.

His eyes turned cold. "No. Those men are long dead."

I contemplated the shiny tiles on the terminal floor. Did others need killing? Or was another woman waiting in one of his beds. I didn't know anything about Tran's present life other than the experiences we had shared.

He drew up my gaze as if reading my mind. "My life is filled with secrets I cannot share. Secrets that could get you killed, regardless of my efforts to keep you alive. One thing I can tell you is that you are not the same as me." He took my hand. "But I suspect I may have become a little more like you."

He kissed my palm and let it fall. "Last night was..."

"A singular event?" I said, hating the edge in my voice.

He raised a brow. "I was going to say inevitable, but if that's what you wish—"

"No." I blurted the word before my mind had thought it through. Could my heart afford another night with J Tran? My traitorous body didn't care.

"What I meant was..."

His sensual mouth curled into that infuriating smirk. "See you around, K."

I swallowed. "Back atcha, J."

As my three friends went their own directions, I pulled out my phone and shot a message to Ma.

At the airport now. My flight's on time. I'll meet you at the hospital as soon as traffic allows.

Ma: *I wish I could pick you up, but the doctors are performing two more evoked potentials in the morning. Each one takes several hours to perform. I want to be there in case there's anything they need.*

Me: *Stay with Baba. I have a friend I can call.*

Ma: *We'll talk when you're here. Rest on the plane if you can.* 😊 *Drink your chrysanthemum tea.*

Chapter Sixty-Two

Kansas gaped at my battered condition, then hoisted my luggage into her trunk. She waited until we were out of LAX and onto the side streets up the coast before grilling me about my trip.

"Dating Daniel Kwok must have been rough," she said with a smirk.

My rideshare friend had driven me to the airport for my flight to Hong Kong. Since Daniel would be there on business, the outspoken redhead had encouraged me to give him a chance. The emotional roller coaster had taken its toll.

"It kinda was, but I can't blame my appearance on him. My plans detoured in unexpected ways."

"Don't they always?"

"Yeah. I guess they do."

Kansas had picked me up from and dropped me off at several dicey situations in the last couple of months. She knew I worked for Aleisha's Refuge and the dangers my rescue and protection work entailed. She also knew where I lived – a location known only by my family, Uncle, and Tran. We were finding our way with the rest, but I considered her a friend.

She glanced at the sling securing my arm to my side. "Is that why we're going to Cedar Sinai?"

"No. My father's in the hospital."

"Is it serious?"

The question repeated in my mind for the rest of the ride, becoming more insistent as I rolled my suitcase up the hospital corridor. I could have dropped my luggage at the restaurant, but I wanted to go home with Ma at the end of the day. Whatever the doctors told us, we would need each other's comfort tonight.

She must have heard me ask a nurse for directions because she came out of Baba's room to intercept me before I came in. Her eyes roamed across my bruised and swollen face, the stitched gash on my cheek, and the arm strapped to my side. I was thankful she couldn't see the rest.

"I don't want to hurt you."

I held out my good arm. "It's okay, Ma. You won't break me."

She coughed out a cry and smothered me in a hug. "Only because someone already did."

I winced at the pain and refrained from telling her exactly how many *someones* had tried to kill her daughter in China and Japan.

"Is he awake?" I asked.

"Yes, but..." She rolled her eyes. "I didn't want you to be alarmed. Now, I'm worried about alarming him when he sees you."

"I can take off the sling."

"Are you kidding? Have you seen your face?"

"Um...got any makeup?"

"It would take a Hollywood professional to make you look right."

"So, how is he?"

"Resting. But the last four days have been hard."

"I know. They've been hard on you too."

She smoothed an errant hair toward her hasty bun. No stylish chignon today.

Baba called from his bed, sounding raspy and weak. "Is that Dumpling?"

I rolled my luggage into the room and perched it against the wall, staying sideways so he couldn't see the sling.

"Hey, Baba. I heard you were playing hooky from work."

"Lee got a vacation. I figured, why not me?"

I thought about everything Uncle and I had been through. Triads in Hong Kong. Gangs in Shanghai. Ninja and Yakuza in Japan. "Trust me. Uncle is as bad at vacationing as you."

He coughed. "I don't know, Dumpling. I think your old man has him beat."

I peeked at his appearance and turned away in shock. My father had lost a significant amount of weight since we video chatted ten days ago. His cornflower blue eyes had paled to an almost translucent gray, and his luxurious silver-blond hair had thinned. Only a few wisps covered the stitched-up gash from his first fall in the kitchen while Ma and I had been in Hong Kong.

I limped to his bed when he closed his eyes, then floundered at all the obstacles interfering with my hug. What if I pulled out his IV or disturbed one of the sensors that monitored his health? All those reassuring lights and numbers weren't reassuring me at all. They only reminded me how vulnerable my invincible father had become.

I leaned over the railing and draped my free arm lightly across his chest. The stubble on his face scratched my cheek.

"Disgraceful, right? Your mama brought me a razor. Hand it over, why dontcha." Baba never went a single morning without a shave.

I gave him the electric razor and watched as he ran the blades over his skin. I didn't comment on the patches of stubble he missed. This was the second time he had landed in the hospital during the three weeks I had been gone. How much of his frailty and weight loss had happened since then? Or had the last four days in the hospital stolen what was left of his youth?

Feeling presentable, he finally looked me in the eye. "For the love of Pete! What happened to you?"

I shrugged innocently. "Ran into a wall?"

"A wall of what? Rugby players? Honestly, Lily. This has to stop."

Lily, not Dumpling. Baba was pissed.

I plucked the shaver from his hand and dropped it on the tray. "Hey, what about you? Passing out in the kitchen. Two trips to the hospital. Sounds like the pot calling the kettle black, if you ask me."

He snorted at my slung arm and squeezed my free hand. The edges of the IV tape had peeled away from his parched skin. He caught me looking and sighed.

"Terrible, huh? All those kitchen scars, and farming before that." He flexed his fingers and turned over his calloused palm. "I'll never be a hand model, that's for sure."

"Your hands are fine, but you have to stop picking at the tape or the needle will come out."

"Damn thing's drive me nuts. These doctors treat me worse than a runaway cow, prodding me with needles, stuffing me into magnetic tubes, shocking me with electrodes. I'm done with it. I want to go home."

I glanced at Ma.

"The doctors should be here soon," she said. "They promised to come before his dinner arrived."

Baba snorted. "They haven't kept a single promise yet."

A woman in a white physician's coat knocked on the doorframe. "Hello, Mr. Knudsen. May I come in?" She looked more like someone's kindly mother than the bullying rancher Baba had described.

"Be nice," I whispered, then backed away to make room.

"This is our daughter Lily," Ma said. "She just flew in from Japan."

"It's nice to meet you, Lily. I'm Dr. Curtis." She crossed to the bed. "We have the results from your evoked potentials and blood work."

Baba nodded. "Let's have it, then."

Ma and I moved to the other side of the bed. She took Baba's hand and gave it a squeeze. Once we were settled, the doctor began.

"As you know, your MRI showed a lesion in your brain, only one, but worrisome in size. We followed up with the lumbar puncture. The elevated proteins suggested the possibility of an autoimmune disorder, inflammation, or infection. No cancer cells were found."

Baba exhaled a gust of air. "Well, that's a relief."

Dr. Curtis nodded. "We have also ruled out ALS, Parkinson's, Alzheimer's, or a stroke."

"Okay, then." He smiled at Ma, then turned back. "What does that leave us with?"

"The evoked potential tests we did this morning showed nerve damage that aligns with the brain lesion spotted in the MRI and the elevated proteins from the lumbar puncture. All of this, together, indicates multiple sclerosis."

Baba swallowed. Ma bit her lip to stifle a gasp.

"Are you certain?" I asked.

"We are."

"What does this mean?"

I had read varying reports about people living with MS. Some of them functioned well between relapses and maintained an active lifestyle. Others could barely walk or talk.

"There are four types of MS, two of which are progressive. It's too early to tell if your father has a progressive type of MS since we don't know if his current symptoms will ease into remission."

"But if they do?" Baba asked, doing his best to remain positive.

"Then you most likely have the relapsing-remitting type of multiple sclerosis known as RRMS. During remissions, your leg strength and vision should improve. You might still fatigue more easily than you have in the past, but your energy will be better. MS presents differently for everyone. There's no way for us to know. But there are disease-modifying therapies and medications your doctor can prescribe to stave off the relapses and treat the symptoms."

"What symptoms?" he asked.

"Fatigue, muscle spasms, cramping, numbness, pain. Trouble with your vision, confusion, memory, and cognitive issues. Depression, incontinence, irritability, loss of sexual drive."

Baba grunted. "Is that all?"

"Those are only possible symptoms you might face during a relapse, most of which you are suffering now. Many people diagnosed with RRMS enjoy long stretches of remission."

"What if it's progressive?" Ma asked.

The doctor smiled with encouragement. "As I said, the course of progression for MS is unique to each patient. If your husband does develop PPMS, then his doctors will focus on the symptoms. Occupational therapy will help."

"Speaking of which," I said, keeping the panic out of my voice. "My father owns a restaurant and cooks long hours every day. When he's not cooking, he manages the business. How is this going to affect his ability to work?"

Baba nodded at me as if I had voiced his next concern.

Dr. Curtis shook her head and addressed Baba directly. "I wish I could be more definitive, but you'll just have to wait and see. As things stand now, you need rest and care. I can recommend specialists for you to call, or you can ask your primary care physician for a referral. Stay positive. Eighty-five percent of people diagnosed with multiple sclerosis have RRMS. The odds are in your favor. You may be able to return to your restaurant at some point. In the meantime, I suggest you pass the business and cooking duties to someone else."

Baba contained his emotions behind a single curt nod. Then he stared at his knees in thought.

The doctor gave him a moment, then continued. "I'll visit you in the morning with a list of specialists in your area and literature on the latest disease-modifying therapies, drug treatments, and dietary recommendations. If all goes well, I'll discharge you after that."

Ma smiled and kissed Baba's head. "Did you hear that, Vern? You can finally come home."

Chapter Sixty-Three

A steam cloud scented with sizzling shrimp, garlic, and ginger billowed from the cooking station as Uncle poured sauce into the wok. He tossed the ingredients with a wire spatula and threw chopped scallions into the mix. After a few more ingredients, he slid his trademark sizzling shrimp onto a plate. He had prepared this same dish for Baba in a Shanghainese eatery the same year I was born.

Across the prep table, Bayani, our line chef from the Philippines who normally worked the deep fryer, steamer, and woks, cleaved a roasted duck down the spine while Ling, our dumpling and pastry chef, checked on the frying strips of meat for the crispy tangerine beef. Everyone's tasks had been augmented to cover what Uncle would normally have done now that he prepared all of the main dishes on his own.

The tone in the kitchen had changed with Uncle in charge – more triad enforcer and less North Dakota charm – but the kitchen staff adapted quickly since they had known him for years. They brushed off his gruff nature and followed his instructions as cheerfully as before.

I added serving spoons to the beef chow fun and shrimp and carried both platters through the swinging doors. One of our servers was out sick with the flu, and the dining room was packed for a weekday lunch. I dropped off the platters and continued to table nine, where two of my dearest friends wiggled their fingers and grinned.

I rested my hand on Stan's shoulder and kissed the top of his balding pink head. "When did you come in?"

"Just now. A table opened up. We stole it before anyone else had the chance. Hope you don't mind."

I pulled the rag from my belt and wiped down the surface. "Of course not." I passed the tip tray to a server. "This is for you. The couple on table six needs a refill on tea."

"On it," she said, and hurried into the back.

Aleisha stood up and wrapped me in her Earth Mama embrace. Those strong brown arms had consoled me and hundreds of other women and children at her refuge over the years. She never tired. And she never ran out of love.

She squeezed a final time, then held me out for inspection. "You're skinny as a stick. Don't they feed you in this place?"

Stan cupped the side of his mouth. "We know the manager if you want to complain."

I laughed. "Fat lot of good that would do. I hear she's a tyrant. Her partner is worse."

Aleisha's face glowed with pride as she gave me one more hug and sat.

Stan noted the customers waiting for takeout at the door. "Bustling business."

"Studio rush," I said. "We get a surge whenever a new production begins." I signaled to Naomi for menus. "I'll come back and check on you in a bit."

Aleisha waved me away. "Go, girl. Do what you gotta do. Stan and I had a craving for sweet and sour pork."

I laughed. "Well, next to Baba, Uncle makes the best. You want me to put in an order?"

Stan opened a menu and took Aleisha's hand. "No rush. My lady and I are on a date."

Aleisha giggled.

Giggled.

"Don't you listen to Stan," she said. "But he's right about the time. Everything's quiet at the refuge. We take our breaks while we can."

I missed them both and the work I used to do, but I couldn't be everywhere at once. If things ever slowed down at the restaurant, perhaps I could work a few cases in between.

Slowed down?

Who was I kidding? Managing Wong's Hong Kong Inn was a full-time job.

"I'm so glad you're here." I squeezed their shoulders. "I'll be back in a bit."

Seeing Stan and Aleisha put a bounce in my step far beyond my fully recuperated knee. I hadn't seen them since I had broken the news about Baba's health and my decision to run the restaurant on his behalf. Although it lifted my spirits to see them happy and hear that the women at Aleisha's Refuge were well, Aleisha was right about the weight loss, I barely had enough time to eat.

Days had passed before I returned to my apartment and unpacked. From then on, I devoted every waking moment to learning the restaurant business, organizing our staff to reopen, and helping Ma care for Baba. I even borrowed my father's car. No more biking, mass transit, or rideshares for me. I lived out of Baba's trunk and stuffed it with everything I needed to commute between my parents and Wong's Hong Kong Inn. Until I had things running smoothly and my father regained his strength, my former rescue and protection work was on hold. The only practices I maintained were my morning meditations and brief taijutsu or yoga movement at night.

I had brought Sensei's orchids to my apartment and found them happy places with diffused sunlight and a view of my home dojo and balcony lanai. Good thing they thrived on neglect. Sensei emailed me a week ago to say he would spend the rest of winter and spring in Japan.

I checked on the restrooms and unlocked the staff-only door in the back, which opened onto the stairs only Baba and I used. My ultralight racing bike hung on hooks from the wall. Although I still believed biking in Los Angeles was the healthiest, most expedient mode of transportation, I now had far too much to cart back and forth. On the rare occasions that I wasn't hauling my belongings or fetching supplies for the restaurant, I was too exhausted to pedal.

Living my father's life was kicking my butt.

But it also filled me with unexpected joy.

Our entire staff had pulled together and bonded closer than before in a united effort to make the restaurant succeed while I scrambled to learn and fill very big shoes. Overwhelmed by the tedious accounting and endless orders I needed to place, I finally allowed DeAndre into our inner sanctum upstairs. He took over the laundry, helped with checklists, placed smaller orders, and updated our social media and blog – an online presence I had created and had helped my father maintain. It benefited from DeAndre's enthusiasm and fresh young voice.

He skipped down the stairs, dreads bobbing and a huge smile on his face as he carried a fresh load of newly laundered and folded linens. Baba's high school intern would become a restaurateur, for sure.

"How's the lunch crowd, boss lady?"

"Busy. The studio orders are boxed for delivery. Did you order more duck?"

"Check."

"And the chicken feet on Uncle's list?"

"Double check."

"You're a wonder, DeAndre."

"Don't I know it."

He flashed a toothy smile, dashed down the back corridor to drop off the linen, and picked up the boxes on his way to the rear door. His brotherly banter had become a tad more professional now that I was in charge, but his wary respect for Uncle had markedly increased.

"Eh, lazy boy," Uncle yelled. "Hurry up with that delivery before you ruin my food."

"On it, Lee."

Uncle muttered angrily in Shanghainese and clanked his wok with his metal spatula to hurry DeAndre out the door. Then he looked at Bayani and Ling and laughed like hell.

I wagged my finger. "You're incorrigible."

"What?"

"You know what."

He ladled water onto the wok and cackled through the steam.

Uncle ran DeAndre like a Scorpion recruit, piling task upon task to prove his commitment and worth. I kept an eye on them both to make sure everything remained legal and safe. Truth be told, Lee Chang and I made a formidable team.

He swiped a cooking chopstick off the counter and sailed it across the kitchen at me. I plucked it from the air before it skewered me in the eye.

He cackled.

I grinned.

Some things never changed.

I turned in surprise as my parents entered through the rear door. This was Baba's first visit since he had closed the restaurant three months ago. Ma hadn't set foot in this kitchen in years.

Ling dropped a pork bun out of the steamer and apologized in Mandarin as it rolled onto the floor. Baba tried to stop it with his cane, lost his balance, and grabbed the storage shelf for support. Although he tried to laugh off the dizziness, Ma locked her arm in his as if he was gallantly escorting her.

Uncle glared at Ling. "There's more dim sum in the steamer if this one hasn't dropped them all on the floor. Someone get them a stool so they can sit down and eat."

Brett, a Desert Storm veteran, wiped the suds on his apron and set two stools at the end of the prep counter before Uncle had finished his request. As a former US Army staff sergeant, he always knew where everyone was. Baba had tried to promote him over the years, but he enjoyed the Zen-like quality of washing things clean. After the bloodshed I had inflicted and suffered in Osaka, I finally understood what he meant.

Baba patted Ma's beautifully manicured hand. "No need to fuss over us. We only came by to say hello. Isn't that right, Vi?"

Ma arched her brow. "If you meant did we come to check on your baby and make sure Lily and Lee haven't run her into the ground...then, yes, that's exactly why we came by."

"Balderdash. I said no such thing."

I snatched up the sweet and sour pork Uncle had just plated and wafted the fragrant steam toward my father's nose. "Whatever you say. I guess you won't want any of this."

"Hold on now. My name's on the storefront. I insist on quality control."

"*Your* name?" Ma asked. "Last I checked, this was *Wong's Hong Kong Inn*."

He grabbed a sticky chunk of deep-fried pork. "Since when do you care about cooking?"

"Since you went and got yourself sick. And I'll have you know I scramble a mean kimchee and eggs." She winked at me. "But I was referring to your daughter's name, not mine."

He ate the morsel and smacked his lips in approval. "Well, that's a horse of another color. If everything runs as smoothly as this kitchen, I'd say the restaurant is well named."

I blushed with pride at their praise, but I certainly hadn't done it alone. Everyone had stepped up to fill in for Baba's absence – Bayani, Ling, Brett, DeAndre, all of the servers – especially his number one cook. Uncle and I had collaborated on more than a well-run kitchen and sweet and sour pork.

"No one can replace you, Baba. We're thriving because you brought together an amazing team who have learned to work seamlessly and happily from you. I'm just following your lead and trying not to muck it all up."

Our staff returned to their tasks with bigger smiles than before.

Ma opened the top level of the steamer and chose har gao, turnip cakes, and tofu skin wraps for their plate. Then she removed that basket and released a new level of steam. She picked a new dim sum with her tongs and held it for my father to see. "Look, Vern. Your Dumpling has left dumplings for you."

He laughed with delight.

Then he looked sternly at me. "Don't discount your accomplishments. Your mother and I have seen how hard you work managing this restaurant and caring for me. Do you think I haven't noticed the light under your bedroom door in the wee hours when you spend the night? The YouTube videos and Ted Talks you listen to about the restaurant business? The accounting books you bring home and try to hide? You have applied yourself to business with the same discipline and dedication you applied with the martial arts. I am proud of the maturity and empathy you have shown."

His words struck home.

Discipline, dedication, and empathy.

Sensei's lessons had reached beyond the mat.

Uncle flipped a bite of sautéed tofu in the air and caught it in his mouth. Then he grinned and flipped one across the wok station to me. It flew with perfect aim – straight at my eye.

I rose to the toes on one foot and snatched it with my mouth.

Every moment presented an opportunity to train.

The course of my life had veered dramatically for a second time – first, with my sister's murder; now, with my father's hopefully temporary inability to work. During both transitions, the faster I had accepted the new conditions and motivated myself into action, the better I had felt. Bemoaning what I had lost would have kept me locked in the past.

Although most people believe ninja fight in the shadows alone, my parents, my teacher, and my friends would disagree. I was never alone with role models like them.

They fueled my spirit and picked me up when I fell. I did the same for them whenever I could. Their love and support gave me a new outlook on who I was and what I could be.

My father called me Dumpling.

My mother called me Lily.

J Tran called me K.

Whatever the name, I was ninja to the core, adapting to new realities and forging bravely ahead.

Acknowledgments

In order to properly thank the people who have helped me write this book, I feel a need to share some background on what Lily Wong and this series mean to me. From the moment she popped into my head, Lily has inspired me with her courage, her boundless athleticism (which far exceeds my own!), and her commitment to empower and protect women and children in need. Her self-questioning nature combined with the audacity of youth grounds me to the earth and lifts me to the stars. Sharing her Chinese and Norwegian heritage honors my parents and helps me keep their memory alive. I'm so grateful my mother knew of this project and that my father was able to read the first draft *of The Ninja Daughter* before they passed away.

Not only does Lily Wong connect me to my past and present through our shared ancestry, our current city, and our martial arts training, she connects me to the future through my darling granddaughter, Moana, who was born in Shanghai. When I created Lily Wong, I had no idea that my protagonist and my future granddaughter would share the same maternal Hong Kong roots. I often wonder...Did I welcome Moana into being in some unfathomable way? Or was she already waiting for me in my heart? Either way, *The Ninja's Oath* is dedicated to her.

I must also thank Moana's parents – our eldest son, Stopher, and our daughter-in-law, Joeye – for introducing me, Tony, and our youngest son, Austin, to the wonders of Shanghai and Hong Kong. That trip of a lifetime came shortly after I signed the two-book deal for *The Ninja Daughter* and *The Ninja's Blade*. Experiencing Hong Kong with Joeye and her family gave me a local perspective that enriched *The Ninja Betrayed*. And as soon as I saw Shanghai in person, I knew I had to send Lily there next. Experiencing that magical city in person and hearing insider perspectives from our son over six years added authenticity to the story that I hope readers could feel. Shanghai is amazing. I loved diving into its history for *The Ninja's Oath*.

Additional thanks go to Stopher for also bringing me to Japan, a country that has played an important part in my life since my parents met and married in Tokyo, where my two elder sisters were born. I often wonder if my family's history attracted me to the Japanese ninja martial arts.

From the inception of the Lily Wong series, I have strived to bust through the ninja myths and give my readers a peek into modern-day ninja training and practice. To accomplish this, I have relied heavily on my own journey as a 5th degree black belt in To-Shin Do ninja martial arts and my training experiences with skilled ninjutsu practitioners from a variety of schools. I wanted to share the comprehensive and pragmatic scope of our training as well as the little-known empowering and esoteric aspects that have meant so much to me.

For this particular book, I need to thank my primary teacher, Stephen K. Hayes – Black Belt Hall of Fame, co-founder of To-Shin Do, and ordained Tendai Buddhist priest – for allowing me to share his beautiful translations of the mantras and prayers Lily Wong recites. The esoteric and spiritual training I received from Anshu Hayes over the decades continues to enrich my life and daily meditation practice. The wisdom and lessons I share through Lily Wong reflect what is most important to me.

I also need to thank my ninja training buddy, Bryan Toutoshi Griffin, owner of Quest Martial Arts Raleigh, 6th-degree black belt in To-Shin Do, and United States Marine, during which he served two combat tours as a scout sniper in Iraq and Afghanistan. After my preliminary research for *The Ninja's Oath*, I consulted with him for hours before writing the sniper scene with J Tran. My deepest thanks to Bryan for his service, generosity, and friendship over the years. Any errors regarding that scene fall entirely on me.

I've been blessed with many skillful, dedicated, and empowering ninja friends. I truly could not have written any of these ninja adventures if I had not spent so many years training with them. Mahalo to the To-Shin Do co-founders, Rumiko Urata Hayes and Stephen K. Hayes, and all of the teachers, training partners, and students who have influenced my journey in the ninja martial arts. My deepest appreciation to everyone who continue to show up and support me long after I stepped off the mat.

When it comes to publishing, it takes a whole team. Huge thanks to Jason Pinter, my publisher and editor from Agora Books (Polis Books) for believing in Lily Wong and releasing her latest adventure in a phenomenal hardback release. Thanks as well to Kristie at 2Faced Design for the stunning book cover and the fabulous sales and marketing reps from PGW/Ingram: Christy Quinto, Joy Hucklesby, Sarah Rosenberg, and Adrienne Maynard. I'm so grateful to my literary agents, Nicole Resciniti, Lesley Sabga, and everyone at The Seymour

Agency for their caring and enthusiastic support for my career. I'm grateful as well for my incredible writing community from Crime Writers of Color, International Thriller Writers, Sisters in Crime, Capitol Crime, SinCLA, Mystery Writers of America, Horror Writers Association, HWALA, and all the wonderful local chapters and conference organizers who have invited me to present, teach, and share. And continued thanks to all the independent booksellers around the country that host my events and hand-sell my books. You have lifted my wings and helped me to soar.

And of course, my deepest mahalo to my patron saint of a husband, Tony Eldridge, and our youngest son, Austin, for their day-to-day encouragement, love and support. I would have imploded long ago if these men weren't in my life. And special thanks to my friends who keep me anchored and sane enough to write. Looking at you, Tracy Clark, Terry Shepherd, Dana Fredsti, Naomi Hirahara, Kim Stahl, Lisa Gardner, Don Bentley, Lee Murray, Jonathan Maberry, Jeff Ayers, J. Dianne Dotson, James L'Etoile, Sujata Massey, Cheryl Head, Alex Segura, and SO many more. Seriously, we could be here all day.

Writing is a rewarding yet arduous journey, made bearable on challenging days by the encouragement, support, and guidance from family, friends, colleagues, community – and readers like you. I can't begin to tell you how much it means to me that you read *The Ninja's Oath* and have found value and enjoyment from my work.

You can find book club extras, discussion topics, recipes, ninja videos, and more on my website: ToriEldridge.com. And please, join my reading 'ohana while you're there! You can also find me on Instagram (writer.tori), Twitter (ToriEldridge), Facebook and TikTok (ToriEldridgeAuthor).

Thank you all. Every kind word and review that you post brightens my day with a virtual hug.

Aloha nui loa,

Tori

About the Author

Tori Eldridge is the author of five novels; has performed as an actress, singer, dancer on Broadway, television, and film; and earned a 5th-degree black belt in To-Shin Do ninja martial arts. She was born and raised in Honolulu – of Hawaiian, Chinese, Norwegian descent – and has visited nine countries including China, Brazil, and Japan. She currently resides in Portland, Oregon after living in Los Angeles for over 35 years.

In addition to her Lily Wong series – which earned nominations for Anthony, Lefty, and Macavity Awards and won the 2021 Crimson Scribe for Best Book of the Year – Tori authored the Brazilian dark fantasy novel, *Dance Among the Flames*, and has short stories featured in numerous anthologies. Look for *Kaua'i Storm*, the first book in her new Ranger Makalani Pahukula Mystery Series, coming May 20, 2025.

Connect with Tori online at @ToriEldridge, @writer.tori, and ToriEldridge.com.